ROYAL SOULS

THE WITCH HEART

Ailan R McAndrews

Royal Souls
Copyright © 2022 by Ailan R McAndrews

All rights reserved. No part of this publication may be reproduced, distributed, or transmitted in any form or by any means, including photocopying, recording, or other electronic or mechanical methods, without the prior written permission of the author, except in the case of brief quotations embodied in critical reviews and certain other non-commercial uses permitted by copyright law.

Tellwell Talent
www.tellwell.ca

ISBN
978-0-2288-4985-8 (Hardcover)
978-0-2288-4984-1 (Paperback)
978-0-2288-4986-5 (eBook)

Keisha Ann Andrews
Born - August 5, 1978
Angel - December 6, 2019

At young, with friends, you play
Sister hand in hand, you stride each day
Your ship not fully nailed
Into life's rough water you naively sailed
Pirates quick to beauty and vibrant,
seeking treasure hidden deep
A port strong and safe was offered,
a promise none did keep
A captain new with pledge strong and rich
His ship, your broken boat you hitched
To land new, far and vast
A few coins are all you ask
Sails filled with young emotion
Warnings ached your captain's devotion
Soon the waters squall
Your captain's morals quickly fall
Safe port among new friends
Then a new captain to start again
Calm waters and anchor shared
A child born in your care
Soon another all seemed right
Then anew an internal fight
The enemy crept through organs weak
A surgeon's knife cutting deep
Fear not and courage you beamed from within
Important lessons taught two young men
A long battle fought hard and victory near
Premonition Faye woke sister with fear

On this day, your voice is lost
Raging emotion and man's machine the cost
Forty-one years your sail did fall
Four days after our final call
My funny name never heard again
at least until we meet at my end
Heart gentle and caring great
You earned your place at heaven's gate
I say a prayer and talk in lone
then wish a door would open and you were home.
Dad

This book is dedicated to my wife Annie, who only makes life better with every passing day, and my daughters Kenzie Marie, and Keisha Ann and her sons Noah and Evan.

To my wife Annie.
Thank you for your love and support
over the three years of writing the book
and the multiple times you read it.

To my wife's cousins.
Thank you, John and Anne O'Donnell of
Gourock, Scotland, for all your effort.

Thank you, Phil Burden, for your honesty
and friendship. No value can be placed on
either and both are rare these days.

To my brother-in-law Peter O'Donnell.
Thanks for breaking out of your genre and
taking the time to read it. I was elated to hear
that you liked Fantasy/Urban Fiction.

Thank you to my trusted readers, and a special thanks
to Tearsa Gurek for the extra effort and feedback.

The seed of royal blood, born under the sign of Nine, shall rise with power unmatched, to rule the world of magic.

BOSTON BLUES

Friday, August 29th — 0300 Eastern Time

"Here I am alone again, wandering streets in the dark of night that most sane people avoid during the day. Happy twenty-fourth birthday, Beth," she sighs.

Her twenty-fourth birthday marks fifteen years spent training. And what did she have to show for it?

"It's pathetic." The words make her stop in place, sadness rising. "I'm pathetic. I live in a condo, hidden by a magic shield that looks like a double stack of six rusty, abandoned shipping containers that haven't moved in twenty years."

The road, littered with recent repairs of deep holes, is as familiar as a sibling. She wanders the old district, spotted with the carcasses of half-broken warehouses, each scarred with boarded windows and absent roofs, and shipping containers stacked higher inside them. She weaves between the many streetlights burned out long ago and never repaired, and feels like she's visiting old friends who never change. Beth loves this section of Boston.

She continues walking, embracing a familiar list. "No relationships, no friends, no enemies, and… no family."

Her mind flashes back to the early hours of her ninth birthday, and the grief and self-loathing knots her stomach. The memory fills her ears with the sound of the roaring flames outside her bedroom window. She still feels the punch of the explosion that threw her into the neighbor's yard, where a firefighter later found her unconscious. A tear rolls over her cheek as a picture of her mom and dad flashes in her mind.

Mom, Dad. I'm sorry. It was a nightmare, and I didn't know how to control it then. I didn't mean to destroy the house.

"Please forgive me," Beth whispers. She always asks them to, even if she's never gotten an answer.

She pushes her hands deeper into her hoodie pockets and squeezes her arms against her body as she walks past eerie dark gaps between buildings and a slight movement across the road catches her eye.

Someone's in the shadows.

After fifteen years of wandering these streets, she recognizes subtle differences, like the faded outline of someone, across the road, trying to push their body back into the shadows of a deep doorway. She takes control of her emotions, and her lightweight hoodie shields the change of her eyes from green to the dull grayish glow of night vision.

Male. Slight build. Six feet or better, wearing a lightweight fog coat, slacks, leather shoes, leaning back against the wall. Is it a cop?

Her pace steady, she focuses on a familiar open gate leading into a container holding area near the end of the block. She lets her night vision fade before using only her eyes to glance back to the doorway as she steps from the sidewalk to cross the street.

Good, I'm almost there, and the creep in the shadows hasn't moved.

A burst of air, like a towel flicked in her face, flips her hood from her head, exposing her white undercut pixie hairstyle. As she reaches to recover it, she feels another burst of air and stops in the middle of the empty street. Still holding her hood, Beth cocks her head to listen above her and pauses.

"Did I hear horses?" she whispers.

She looks up while turning a full circle, then bringing her head level, she stands, still listening but hearing nothing. Not a single typical sound. She takes a step, and her chest tightens. Her breathing turns short and choppy, and her entire body tingles like a surge of electricity is flowing through her. Her heart pounds as a wave of blue light swims through the air, like an eel, getting closer to her. The light strikes her with the force of a bump, and she steadies herself.

I can feel the light passing through me. It's warm... and friendly.

Beth puts her hand to her chest and draws a full breath.

The sounds of the night return, and the fish market clock tower announces the time with three chimes.

"What the heck was that?"

Her heart racing, Beth snaps her head right, then left as she looks for the blue light but only sees the man from the shadows stepping out towards her.

She jolts back into motion, quickening her pace as she crosses the road to the old sandstone building at the main gate of the fenced holding area. Pushing her body back into the shadows of the deep entrance, she focuses on calming herself and waits.

He turns to enter the container yard and stops ten feet in front of Beth, sweeping his head left to right twice. The man, seeing only the shadows of the night and stacks of steel shipping containers waiting for their trucks, shouts out.

"Beth O'Corry. My name is Jack Sebastian. I need my life back and you're the only one who can give me that. Please, talk to me. I mean you no harm."

Beth stiffens.

How does this stranger know my name?

"Please. I mean no harm. I only need to talk to you."

Beth remains still. The man stands silent, anticipating, and she fights the urge to step out of the shadows to confront him. After a short time, his head hangs lightly and, giving it a quick shake of disappointment, he turns and walks away in the same direction from which he came.

Stepping from the shadows, she peers around the corner of the building as she fades back to a visible person, and watches Jack walk away with his hands in his coat pockets, his shoulders drooping a little.

"Who are you, Jack Sebastian, and why do you think I can give you your life back?" she asks herself.

Beth turns and walks into the fenced yard. Among the shadows are small shacks and large trucks hidden by containers stacked two or three high. She'd lived in this neighborhood for fifteen years, and no one had ever approached her.

"I've given no one my name," she mumbles.

An eerie feeling creeps over her.

"Has he been stalking me, and I've never noticed?" she whispers.

The thought hits a nerve, and she shrinks into herself, pulling her hands back so the hoodie sleeves cover them to the middle of her fingers, and crossing her arms around her midsection.

She continues walking to the exit across the container holding yard and when she turns the corner, the glowing neon 'Open' sign stops her.

"What the heck? When did that coffee shop open?"

Beth looks around, wondering if she's wandered into an unfamiliar area, but recognizes everything around her. There had never been a coffee shop in this area before, but if they make a decent chai latte, that would brighten up her depressing birthday?

A quick change of her eyes to night-vision and she scans the area.

No one in sight. No Jack.

Eyes turning green again, she reaches the front door and waves her glowing hand over the door handle.

"Vis meg magi," she whispers. (Show me magic.)

Nothing. It wasn't a trap. Beth grips the door handle and the heavy glass door squeaks as she pulls it open. The familiar aroma of freshly ground coffee charges her nostrils as she steps inside, and she draws a full breath through her nose. The aromatherapy relaxation starts, as she forgets Jack and the blue light for the moment.

The coffee shop is small, with only one table and two chairs. Beth assumes it lives off takeout clientele, like her. The elderly woman sitting behind the counter is braiding multicolored threads into a cloth, and glances at Beth with her eyes. Beth moves closer to the counter, and the spools of thread, hanging on the back wall, shimmer like a reflection of Sun off water. She watches as the Indian lady weaves the threads together and notices how they blend like streams of paint flowing against one another. The cloth looked like it was breathing because of the shimmer and Beth felt herself leaning towards it.

The woman stops weaving to stand, and Beth breaks her focus as she straightens to her full five-foot ten-inch height.

"That cloth is beautiful."

"You are very kind. How sweet would you like your chai, Beth?"

Beth steps back from the counter.

What the hell is going on? A second stranger knows my name tonight.

"How do you know my name?"

The woman goes on preparing the chai and says with a smile, "Many nights, you have a chai at the Jade Indian shop that is owned by my daughter. She has told me of you and the amulet you wear."

She points an aged finger at Beth's necklace.

Her soft tone and gentle smile help Beth calm herself as she moves her hand to her necklace.

Odd choice of word, Beth thinks and asks, "Why did you call it an amulet instead of a necklace?"

The woman places the chai on the counter and sets a takeout lid beside it. She circles the rim of the paper cup with her finger, whispering words Beth doesn't understand but recognizes from the shop she frequents.

Stepping forward to take the cup of chai, Beth says, "In the time I've been going to your daughter's shop, I've never asked what that means."

"A prayer that the tea may satisfy you."

The woman touches Beth's hand with one finger, gentle like her daughter does, and Beth smiles.

"Why did you call it..?"

The woman's eyes, wide open, fearful, focus behind Beth.

Beth releases the chai and spins, expecting to see a low-life with a gun. But she sees the explosion of light, followed by the faint crackling sound of electricity dancing across water.

I know that light and crackling sound.

Beth glances over her shoulder.

The woman is gone. So are her threads and cloth. She's a Witch.

Beth catches another flash of light in the mirror behind the counter. Turning her head back towards the entrance, she swings her arm in a circle, casting a swirling white mist from her glowing palm.

"This should be interesting," she says.

Abandoning her chai, she steps into the mist and disappears from the coffee shop.

***

"Come, Lochran! Come and face your fate! I will end you quick only because we played as children," taunts one of the six men mounted on horses.

"Well, what do you know, Rostovie Wolf-Horses? This is the strangest birthday ever," Beth mumbles.

Looking down from a familiar perch on the roof's ledge of a warehouse, she eyes the strange animals that she's only seen in images cast by her teachers during her lessons. Larger than Clydesdale-sized horses with faces like wolves, fangs sharp and visible, and thick, furred front paws different from their back legs, hoofed and hairy.

She turns her focus back to the men. Five of the six horsemen are laughing at the recent offer of a quick death, but the center horseman shows no emotion. The one talking spurs his mount forward a few steps toward a steel container where Beth can see a man on one knee, leaning against the container and holding his side.

The injured man, Lochran, she guesses, positions himself to peer around the corner of the container and replies with the same Scottish accent as the rider.

"Aye, and you've no changed since we were children, Galen. You're still grabbing at the kilt of power and vying for the affections of the stronger," he says. "When will you see you are nothing but a wretched outcast with your band of thugs and lack of honor? I'm sure the Captain of the Guard is so proud of his son. Or is it he be so disgusted he no takes notice of what you have become?"

Galen's mount lurches forward and snaps its teeth. He pulls back on the Hackamore style bridal, dismounts as he pulls out his wand, and his horse's ears lay flat as it growls, curling its upper lip, and baring teeth.

ROYAL SOULS

"Now, I'm going to kill you slow, Lochran. I will make you feel every limb tear from your body until you beg me to kill you!"

Beth narrows her eyes. "Yeah, you're tough when it's six to one against an injured person," Beth says. "Time for an intervention."

She steps down from the ledge and, turning, casts a swirling portal that lies an inch above the tar and gravel roof. With a sweep of her glowing hand over her body, she changes from her hoodie, sweatpants, and sneakers to a white halter top and pants, with white deck shoes and a gray hooded three-quarter length knitted shawl with protection runes around the hood, cuffs and hem. She hops into the air, dropping feet first through the portal as Galen prepares to launch his assault on Lochran. She reappears between the rider and the injured man, allowing the swirling white mist to conceal her for a moment.

Galen recoils, saying, "What's this?" and turns to look at the man on the largest horse, who remains calm, as the other riders bring their wands to the ready position. Lochran tries to stand but falls to his right side, no doubt weakened by his injuries.

She lingers in the front edge of the mist, stopping to look at Lochran, and it causes an angel like glow to form around her.

Handsome face, wavy black hair, and sapphire blue eyes. Very nice.

Lochran's eyes close then, his hair covers his face as his head falls forward, hard, to the asphalt.

Beth winces, "Ouch," and turns her attention to the six-kilted horsemen as her portal fades.

Her eyes scan right to left, and locking on the center horseman, she catches her breath.

What's happened? All I can hear is my heart pounding. I don't feel the breeze or smell the oily stink of the asphalt. His body. Thick and muscular. Are those battle-scars on his chest?

Her eyes shift.

Handsome face, shoulder-length, raven black hair, and glowing sapphire blue eyes. I've never felt like this before. Sweat is creeping down my spine.

The air horn in another yard forces her mind back to the moment, and she introduces herself with a cliché.

"You boys aren't from around here, are you?"

"We wish you no harm, lass, so please step aside and let us finish what we came to do," the center man says.

His voice is calm, deep, and melodic. He shares the same Scottish accent as the others, but there is something else about it. At that moment, Beth decides she could sit and listen to this man read a dictionary.

"Sorry, handsome," she replies, "but six against one is poor odds for anyone, and I'm sure the injured gentleman behind me wants no part of a losing fight. I think you and your posse could ride away, and we can all have a pleasant night."

Galen, who is short, stocky, and unwashed looking up close, drops his reins and stomps toward Beth, shouting, "Know your place, woman, or you'll feel the back of my hand."

Hearing Galen's ancient threat, Beth's hackles shoot up. "Oh, hell no."

Her shawl flutters from her body, and she pulls her arms back from her shoulders. She steps forward with her left leg, and arching her back, she swings her arms to the front, bringing her glowing palms together with a loud crack. A thick beam of white light shoots from her hands, hitting Galen in the chest, and he shouts in pain as he hurls backward. His body flails against a steel container thirty feet away, and his half-bald oily-haired head snaps back with a sound like a melon hitting steel, and he falls to the ground, unconscious.

Galen's Wolf-Horse paws the pavement, growling and snaps its teeth. Beth flicks her middle finger from her thumb, hitting the tender nose with a bullet fast bubble of ice, and it yelps, turning its face away.

Beth smiles mischievously, then looks back at Galen, lying unconscious, and says, "How's the back of my hand feel, tough guy?"

Seeing how easily Beth disposes of their companion unnerves the remaining riders, except for the center one. The rest sit higher in the saddle, pointing their wands at her.

Beth turns to the rider nearest her, saying, "Aw, isn't that cute? You have a little stick. What do you plan to do with that, cowboy? Start a campfire?"

The rider pulls his wand back high over his head, and throwing his arm forward, he casts a grapefruit-sized transparent ball at her. Beth throws her right palm forward, and a burst of light destroys the ball with the sound of a cracking whip. The six horses step back. Then, Beth makes a quick grabbing motion with her left hand, relieving the rider of his wand. Stepping forward with her left foot, she swings her right arm as if scooping her hand through a pond and throws it skyward, tearing the rider from his saddle. The screaming sounds of the tossed rider stop as he disappears into the foggy sky, and the remaining riders, except the center rider, are uneasy.

Beth turns toward the leader—she assumes from his calm he must be—as she rocks the captured wand back and forth between her fingers and thumb and places her right hand on her cocked hip.

"Well, handsome, are you sure you want to do this?"

"Your beauty has caused me to underestimate you, lass, but I have no quarrel with a Spirit Witch. May I ask your name?"

"Oh, you can ask, but I won't tell you... this time." Beth pauses. *Why did I say that?* "Maybe you should take your band of bullies and leave."

Beth, more expecting a fight, is surprised when he says, "As you wish, lass. Where is my other man?"

Beth reaches her arm above her head with an open hand, and closing her fist, she pulls down fast. The unmounted rider falls to the ground with a heavy thud directly in front of the leader's horse. Giving a slight bow, the leader circles his wand above his head, and the horse riders disappear with a flash of light and a slight sound of crackling electricity.

"Welcome to Boston, bitches," Beth says with a snicker.

Still smiling, Beth spins on her heel and walks to the steel container where Lochran lies, and kneeling on one knee, she pulls back his wavy black hair.

"Two black-haired, blue-eyed, handsome men in one day. This is definitely a day to remember," Beth says.

She raises his arm to see a gunshot-like wound to the side of his abdomen but also recognizes the telltale burn marks left by magic.

ROYAL SOULS

"Well, handsome, it's against my better judgment, but I know you won't survive if I don't do something. Besides, I want to know why magical people are in my neighborhood and if you, the band of thugs, the coffee lady, the blue light, and Jack are related."

Beth contemplates what she's said for a few moments before she stands, and giving her hand a quick flick, she jerks Lochran into the sitting position.

Pointing her finger skyward, she spins it in a circle beside her head and forms a swirling mist above, then walks behind Lochran and snaps her fingers. The portal drops to the ground, leaving no trace of either.

In the shadows, along the wall of an old warehouse across the yard, there's a slight outline of a figure with two slits of glowing green eyes. It turns and disappears into darkness.

WAKE UP CALL

August 29th — 0300 Pacific Time — Canada

Rhynan Doon snaps to sitting upright in his bed, his chest tight and his breathing short and choppy. Sweat beads on his forehead, he clutches his chest as though in pain, and his body tingles as if electricity is running through him. Through his open east window, he sees a wave of blue light coming toward him as he swings his legs from the bed. His feet touch the floor as the blue light slips through the glass sliding door of his, 'Design once, build many,' concrete building, striking him with the weight of a feather pillow.

"What's happening?"

The blue light wraps around his body.

It's warm... It feels... friendly.

The blue light rains to the floor like sparkling dust, and Rhynan draws a full breath as the pressure disappears from his chest.

"What the heck was that?"

He looks to his feet for remnants of blue dust, seeing none, then his alarm clock beeps three times, and he stares at it.

"I don't remember setting the alarm for three in the morning."

PAINFUL VISITOR

August 29th — 0300 Pacific Time — Canada

Rebekah Kheel, Director of TDF Logistics, looks out over the dark Pacific Ocean from her penthouse office window.

"Ahh!" She grips her stomach and drops to her knees.

"Oh!" She falls to her side and curls into the fetal position.

"Ahh!" she yells out, and her eyes snap full open as a blue light swims by her window, like a snake through the water. The light continues over the ocean, dropping toward the dark surface, and she rolls to her back and pushes the heel of her hands hard against her temples.

"Ahh! My brain is on fire!" she shouts.

She drifts toward unconsciousness, then the glow of the blue light disappears beneath the surface of the ocean, and the pain stops, so suddenly she retches. Sweat bursts through her skin, and the second wave of nausea brings her to the brink of vomiting, and she resists her body's urge by drawing a full breath.

Rebekah lay on the carpeted concrete floor, waiting for the flashes of nausea and sweating to stop before she lifts herself to her hands and knees. She pushes her palms out to her sides to stabilize her shaking body and tucks her head to her knees, waiting for the shaking to quit. Moments later, she lifts her head, drawing a breath deep into her stomach, and grips the cold metal frame of the floor-to-ceiling window. She lifts herself to her feet as her laptop beeps three times. She snaps her head toward her desk.

"I haven't turned that on since I arrived at the office," she breathes.

Rebekah turns back to look at the dark ocean through her reflection.

"The blue light faded from the skies the night they died and hasn't appeared since. I've never felt that kind of power before."

She pauses, drawing another full breath to help her body settle.

"In nine days, there will be a battle, and Sorcha will be out of her mind to find the prince first," she mumbles. She stops, setting her top teeth into her bottom lip, before glancing around her office.

You fool, she might have heard you.

With her hand still on the metal frame of the window to steady her weak legs, she turns back to the view of the ocean and feels cold air rush against her legs. Rebekah turns to the middle of her office, where a portal of black, swirling smoke forms, and her heart races, thinking about her comment.

Queen Sorcha stumbles out, her arms wrapped around her stomach, saying, "Rebekah, did you feel it? It was a power I haven't felt in over a thousand years."

Rebekah listens to the shortness of Queen Sorcha's breath and watches her stumble another few steps to the filing cabinets.

Rebekah makes a slight bow with her head saying, "Yes, My Queen."

Queen Sorcha places her hands on top of a filing cabinet and pulls herself to her five-foot-ten-inch height. She lets her stomach muscles stretch out before turning to Rebekah with a murderous glare.

"Rebekah, we have nine days to stop the reunion. It feels like they're closer than ever before, and I, for one, don't want to become a pile of dust on September 6th. We need to escalate our efforts if we are to survive. Do you understand?"

"Yes, My Queen."

Queen Sorcha turns back to her portal, and as she walks into the swirling black smoke, she gives Rebekah a quick glance and snaps, "Find the prince."

The portal disappears with the faint hissing sound of steam releasing.

I wonder if Sorcha heard the three beeps? I think they're a warning.

A Cold Morning

Friday, August 29th — 0630 Pacific Time — Canada

Rebekah stares at the ocean as the early morning sun floods the TDF Logistics office. She hears the faint 'ding' of the staff elevator and the doors opening and looks toward the sounds, but already knows who it is.

Rhynan Doon rounds the corner from the elevator to his office and gets startled.

"In early again, Rhynan?"

"Ah yes. Good morning, Miss Kheel. I'm having a tough time sleeping. You look fantastic, as usual."

Rebekah mounts both hands on her tiny waist and positions her five-foot eleven-inch athletic body like she's modeling her tight-fitting black midi dress. She lifts her chin while turning her head to complete the pose and the morning sunlight dances on the mid-back length raven black hair surrounding her face. Her skin is milky white, her features proportionate, and her eyes are like swirling blue pools of water.

"Rhynan, I never go out my door without looking fantastic." Rebekah turns her head back, making full eye contact. "Contrary to you. I can only hope some lovely young women caused your lack of sleep and ragged look? And if you don't stop calling me 'Miss Kheel,' as if I'm a fifty-year-old spinster, I'm going to tell Monica you asked about her."

Rebekah gives Rhynan a sinister grin as he stiffens from her threat, and she taunts him.

"I'm sure she will take every opportunity to bump into you. If you know what I mean."

"Oh-um, please don't do that, Miss Kheel. I mean Rebekah. Um, Monica is a nice lady, I'm certain, but a little too aggressive for my taste."

Rebekah cocks her eye toward Rhynan.

"Did you call Monica a lady? Well… we know different versions of Monica. Besides, my interest in your personal life is for business reasons."

Rhynan picks up the increasing tension in Rebekah's voice and, with a slight lean forward at the waist, she ensures his full attention.

"I have a logistics manager, 'you', with his head in the clouds, and I thought a night of one-on-one might bring you to work relaxed and clear-headed. Because, after the Asian shipping disaster, I'm almost ready to take one for the team myself. Fortunately, I've yet to convince 'me' that lowering my standards to fraternizing with the hired help would do any good. Do you understand?"

Rebekah's voice has near risen to the yelling point, and Rhynan looks up to lock eyes with her.

Oh, no. Is his lip quivering?

"Rebekah, why did I get this appointment? I graduated B+, and I've only been out of college for seven years. I've been in this position for two years and have come close to causing three major disasters, yet I keep this position. You have Michael, with ten years of experience and killer instincts, who could do a much better job, but you keep me in this position. I don't understand."

Rebekah, looking stern, examines Rhynan for a few seconds and the image of her older brother slips into her mind.

He has the same light-brown hair and brown eyes. He's handsome, in a boyish way, with a bit of extra weight, and he has the same name. This is not a coincidence.

"First, never raise your voice at me again," she snaps. "Second, Rhynan, do you doubt my ability to select the right people for positions in this company?"

Rhynan's face turns red, and Rebekah's lips form a sinister grin as she takes two quick steps, removing the space between them and increasing her height dominance. She places her right hand behind his neck with a gentle touch and leans forward, slow. She watches the fear build in his eyes as she nears his face.

Rhynan jerks sideways, dislodging Rebekah's hand, and scurries away like a scared puppy. He shoots through his office door, swinging it closed without stopping, sprinting to his desk and near diving on the automatic curtain button. Rebekah laughs and winks at him before the curtain breaks their eye contact.

Rebekah struts to her office, laughing. "Oh yes. What a spectacular start to the day."

Rebekah settles into the plush executive chair behind a dark oak desk, and rubbing her hands over the button tufted leather, she stares at Rhynan's door, thinking about how he responded to her physical contact.

Most men would have thought it opportune for either bragging points or a promotion, yet Rhynan disengaged instead of capitalizing. Something a prince might do? He has the same name as my older brother and looks like him. Why haven't I noticed the similarities until now?

"If he is the carrier, could it be that Prince O'Manus is manipulating Rhynan through his emotions and preventing his secret from being discovered?" Rebekah mumbles. "If he's not the carrier, I've wasted nine years of wet nursing that spineless worm, and there's no starting over if the blue light is a sign. If so, he will suffer the consequences before that day comes."

A clerical, walking in for work, opens Rebekah's office door, and Rebekah barely heard her timid voice saying, "I'm sorry. Were you talking to me, Miss Kheel?"

"No."

The curt reply scurries the young lady away as Rebekah reaches for the button to close her privacy curtains, but she feels cold air creeping up her legs. She draws her hand back, and turning her chair to the back corner of her office, the glass wall facing the employees blacks out as though liquid flows between two sheets of glass. Swirling black smoke forms into a circular portal, and Rebekah stands, anticipating Queen Sorcha's arrival.

Queen Sorcha walks out of the smoke, and Rebekah gives a slight bow with her head.

"My Queen."

Collar length black hair flutters as she exits the portal, momentarily covering her pale skin and red lips. Queen Sorcha's cold gray eyes lock on Rebekah's and her heart rate climbs thinking about her morning comment again.

"Rebekah, darling, you look smashing. I almost hate you for looking so good."

Both women laugh.

"Well, that's the second compliment I've received, so I'll take it that my morning efforts are a success."

"Well, Rebekah. An admirer?"

Rebekah laughs. "No. It was my burden."

Queen Sorcha walks close to Rebekah and, with a sinister grin, says, "Well, my pretty, your burden may soon be over."

Rebekah draws a sharp breath.

Queen Sorcha locks eyes with Rebekah. "Do you remember our brief discussion about the Crystals and the Stones?"

"Yes," Rebekah breathes.

"This news is worthy of your excitement, Rebekah, because presently twelve witches are on a mission to apprehend the 'Prince Stone.' And only hours ago, one of my spies stole a Crystal from one of the trusting Guardian Witches."

Rebekah's eyes are like saucers. "It's over. We win. You win. Sorcha, please, let me kill him. No, let me torture and then kill him."

Queen Sorcha's smile disappears.

"Given the weight of the news, I'll forgive the casualness. Despite that, you cannot kill him. If he is the carrier, a dead Rhynan means no prince."

Rebekah's smile fades fast, and Queen Sorcha places her finger on her chin as she turns away to contemplate while tapping her finger.

ROYAL SOULS

"Do nothing to him," Queen Sorcha says. "If the prince can sense danger or feel threatened, he may abandon his current host, and we'll be on the hunt again."

Queen Sorcha spins back to a stone-faced Rebekah.

"Make sure nothing happens to him before I get the Prince Stone."

Queen Sorcha doesn't wait for a response before disappearing through her portal.

Feeling the anger build, Rebekah returns to her chair as the black liquid retreats from her windows.

Casualness? Really? How dare she treat me like that after my years of loyalty?

Still thinking about his morning encounter with Rebekah, Rhynan mumbles, "I can't believe she was going to kiss me? I think she was going to kiss me? Why would she kiss me? I thought she was going to fire me, or at least a demotion. A demotion could be good."

Moments after Rebekah's windows black out, Rhynan opens his curtains to look at the office full of working people and then to Rebekah's office.

"Great. Black windows. Rebekah's in the monster meeting with the CEO. Perfect opportunity to get my morning latte."

Rhynan exits the front doors of his office building and walks across the concrete and paving stone courtyard to the lone coffee shop that supports two office buildings. He opens the coffee shop door and this morning's event with Rebekah disappears when Aaghnya looks at him and smiles. He always stops to enjoy her smile before continuing to the counter for the special chai latte that she makes him. Two customers move to the barista to pick up their order as Rhynan reaches the counter, and Aaghnya's smile turns to a frown as she places her hands on her hips.

"Rhynan Doon, I am not happy with you. You missed your morning chai, and you made me worried. Why did you do this to me?"

Rhynan enjoys Aaghnya's Tamil accent, but her demanding tone takes him aback. Still, her slight pout fuels Rhynan's attraction and, looking like a little boy using a made-up story to explain to his mother how a rock broke the window, he spews an explanation.

"Aaghnya, I'm sorry. My boss came in early, and she was upset with me. I thought I was being fired. Then I had to do some work until she went into a meeting. I'm sorry, Aaghnya, and you know I hate missing our mornings together."

A few moments pass, with Aaghnya saying nothing, before she turns away from him. Rhynan feels as if he's floating in outer space, so he looks at Aaghnya's sister Petia, working with the espresso machine. She smiles and shrugs her shoulders, so he glances at Aaghnya's other sister Dehlia, who giggles.

When Rhynan looks back, he can't tell what Aaghnya is doing, and he doesn't like that she hasn't responded.

He looks around to see if anyone is watching before leaning over the counter to get closer to her and half whispers, "Aaghnya, please don't be mad at me. It wasn't my fault, and you know I wouldn't do anything to upset you."

Rhynan shifts back to his heels, eyes wide in fearful anticipation as Aaghnya turns back to him, holding his chai latte and still pouting. She sets the hot drink on the counter. "Rhynan Doon. You will not do that again, or you get no more special chai."

Rhynan lets out a sigh of relief and smiles at Aaghnya, saying, "I promise."

She circles the rim of his paper cup with her finger while saying something in Tamil, then lightly touches Rhynan's hand with one finger. Relief rushes as if he's received a stay of execution when Aaghnya looks at him and smiles.

"Thank you, Aaghnya."

Still, with a sheepish look on his face, Rhynan takes his chai back to the office.

As always happens after he visits Aaghnya, Rhynan feels fantastic about the rest of the day, so he steps out of the elevator happy, and surveys the office.

"Rhynan, I need to see you in my office."

Rhynan, failing to notice Rebekah standing in the doorway of her office, snaps his head toward Rebekah's voice.

"First, I have to check my priority sheets and make sure things are moving, Miss Kheel... Ah, Rebekah."

"Fine. I'll see you in your office then."

Rebekah, confident, strides toward Rhynan's office, and he's slow to respond as he runs scenarios, reasons for the impromptu meeting through his mind. Rebekah stands at the closed door of Rhynan's office and watches the reflection of the main working office in the glass wall. Heads of staff pop up and down over the dividers like groundhogs in a field. Rhynan opens the door, and Rebekah walks to the front of his desk and waits, tapping her nails on her folded arms while he closes the heavy oak door. Arriving at his desk, he sets his drink to the side and presses the button to close the automatic curtain. A quick glance at the office, and he sees Michael using his tie to imitate a man hanging from a noose.

"Sit down, Rhynan."

He drops into the chair, relieved because he knows the desk between him and Rebekah ensures no repeat performance of this morning.

"Rhynan, this morning, I was trying to get you to understand something."

He moves to say something, but Rebekah puts up her finger and stops him, so he sits back in his chair.

"I get productivity by controlling people, and I control people because I find what motivates them or what they fear the most. I also find their weaknesses, which are my largest assets. Take Michael, for example. He's gay and doesn't want anyone to know it. I know this because one of the previous managers I promoted had a brief fling with him at a company retreat. Michael works like he does because I mentioned I knew the gentleman, but never mentioned that I knew he had the fling." Rebekah pauses. "Rhynan, do you understand what I did there?" she snaps.

"Ah yes, Miss Kheel… um, Rebekah. You threatened to expose him without ever making a threat. You pushed his fear button."

Rebekah smiles. "Yes Rhynan. Bravo. Now, take Monica as another example. I found out that she was having an affair with a married man. Well, two married men, to be exact, and both of their wives are in powerful positions. Now, were these women to find out what I know, Monica would have a tough life, so now she is my

'Whatever I need her to be' kind of gal. That is what I need you to do, so these curs," Rebekah points to the office behind the curtain, "understand that they will get the job done or else."

"That's cruel, Rebekah."

"Why, thank you, Rhynan. I like it when people appreciate my efforts."

He gives a slight shake of his head, acknowledging his wasted comment.

"Rhynan, I like you. You have excellent document skills and with any luck, soon your logistical and management skills will reach the same level. But if you think for even a second that I would kiss you or lower myself to the level of some lecherous, booty-grabbing employer who wants to get sued, you're dead wrong. Had you stood still, like most real men would have, I was going to whisper in your ear that you need to get a spine and take charge. I pay *you* to ensure productivity, and the company makes money."

Rebekah takes a breath to calm herself.

"That's what I wanted you to understand, Rhynan. Grow an enormous pair, show everyone you're in charge, man up. Pick a cliché, Rhynan, but I'm hoping you have caught on, so I don't have to turn Monica loose on you."

Rebekah clasps her hands in front of her and smiles.

"Now, get it done and forget about this morning. Because if I hear a single word about your false anticipation, I will make sure the next job you get has something to do with cleaning toilets. Do you understand me?"

"Yes, ma'am."

Rhynan pushes the button to open the curtain as Rebekah spins toward the door. She opens the door with force, stepping through as it hits the floor stopper, and it follows her to a close again. She marches toward her office, and with a quick glance at the working staff, Rebekah smiles because she doesn't see a single head above a divider.

Rebekah's office door closes, and heads pop over the dividers, so Rhynan pushes the button to close his curtain again, shutting out the questioning eyes and Michael smiling.

Rebekah monitors the office operations throughout the day, and to her satisfaction, everyone maintains a steady workflow, even though it's Friday. The staff work until the last minute, and Rebekah knows she's reinforced her command with her 'just loud enough' conversation with Rhynan.

Nearing the end of the day, Rebekah watches Rhynan when she hears the European-accented male voice.

"Why do you put up with him? There is no sign he is the one carrying the prince's soul, so let's kill him and if he is the carrier, the prince will die with him."

Rebekah turns her head to see Midas Pohl, her assistant director, standing in the doorway of the adjoining office. Rebekah rotates her chair and stands.

"Midas. Obviously, the lock on that door needs repair."

Her glare echoes her disgust for him.

"Again, there are three ways the prince can escape the body of the carrier. First, we touch the carrier of the prince with the Staff of Souls, which brings the prince out and gets him to his bride. The carrier dies, of course. No loss. Second, the carrier makes love to a powerful witch on the bed that the prince and princess never used, and both live.

ROYAL SOULS

Maybe. Last, the carrier dies, the prince moves to another body, and the search begins again. Which one would you prefer? Oh, I know. Why don't I tell Queen Sorcha that you want to kill him and get on with life? Now, which one would you prefer?"

Rebekah folds her arms across her healthy chest and, with an icy glare, waits for Midas' response.

"I am sick of this place, Rebekah. I want this done with. It's more than a thousand years of chasing the prince, and I am sick of it."

"We're all here because of you, Midas," Rebekah snarls. "If you had waited until the Queen arrived to make the first move instead of chasing your grand images of glory, we wouldn't be here. For that, every one of us is paying a debt. Foul this up, and I am sure the Queen will take great pleasure in killing you, slow and painful, over the next thousand years." She pauses. "Then again, maybe she'll have Le Glazier entomb you in glass and mount your statue in one of your favorite little playhouses. You can spend eternity listening to the frolicking of the young boys."

"Your Scottish is showing, you bitch." Midas turns to walk out the door.

Rebekah laughs, but her moment of cruel happiness ends as a smoke portal forms below the ceiling in the back corner of her office. Surprised, Midas stops short of his door and stares at the swirling smoke.

Fear in his eyes, he looks over his shoulder at Rebekah. "Did you know of this? Were you setting me up?"

"I would love to say your blood is on my hands, Midas, but I'm as much in the dark as you. Pun intended."

29

Midas, cautious, is ready to flee at any sign Rebekah is lying. An envelope drops from the swirling smoke before it disappears, and Midas pounces on it. Posing like a model again, Rebekah clears her throat and gives Midas a snarling grin as she flips her hand out, palm up.

"Midas, I never realized you were so eager to serve."

Tempted to tear the envelope open, Midas reasons with himself.

He walks to Rebekah, and as he gets closer, her stern look changes into a gloating smile. Midas slaps the envelope into her palm, and she says nothing to him for retrieving it. He turns away, mumbling, "Bitch."

She gives a little laugh as she breaks the red seal on the black envelope and unfolds it to read the red writing.

"Queen Sorcha commands your presence. Tomorrow at 1200."

Below the words is a snowflake with the letters "CR" in the middle.

Rebekah throws her hands to her sides, dropping the envelope. "Ah, I hate winter clothes."

Rhynan looks up from his computer, noticing the staff preparing to leave, and realizes it is past four-thirty on a Friday. He completes the new Asian shipping contract order and closes his computer. By the time he closes the door of his office, it's nearing five-thirty, so he stops by the coffee shop for another chai latte. He's disappointed to see Aaghnya isn't there, so he adds a bagel with cream cheese as a reward for making it to another Friday.

He collects his order, then exits to the busy street, and while walking, he thinks about the events of the day with Rebekah and mumbles to himself.

"What if she's not a mean person, and I've misjudged her? She is right. I'm too soft on the employees, and I know they take advantage of me."

He takes a sip of his latte.

"Oh, well. Monday will bring a better week, but for now, I'm going to enjoy my chai and bagel before treating myself to a Friday night movie. I'll stop in and see Aaghnya tomorrow morning, and she'll make everything feel good again."

Rhynan nears his condo and the elderly woman who comes around panhandling once a week is sitting on the concrete steps. Soon the manager will chase her off, which Rhynan thinks is cruel, so he always gives her a two-dollar coin, hoping it will help with her struggle. He approaches her and pulls the coin from his pocket, but notices the woman's fixation on the bag containing the bagel. Rhynan thinks about the soft midsection he's developing and hands the bagel and the coin to the woman. She grabs both, stuffing the coin in her glove, then opens the bag and tears a small piece of bagel. Placing it in her mouth like she's savoring the experience, she smiles at Rhynan and nods a thank you to him. Rhynan becomes sad, knowing that so little means so much, but happy about his decision to give her his unneeded snack. He nods back, smiling, then moves past the elderly woman and up the steps toward his condo entrance.

Rhynan notices the three men standing across the lawn looking at him and whispers, "That's odd. Why are they staring at me?"

One man turns to the other two, and then the three turn away from Rhynan as if discussing something. When the main entrance door closes behind him, he forgets about the day.

A NEW START

Friday, August 29th — 1400 — Eastern Time

Lochran blinks as his eyes focus on the ceiling. He lifts his head, and pain from the left side of his abdomen convinces him to lie back again. Placing his hand over the wound, he feels a thick bandage.

Someone has tended to my wound, which means they don't have the Crystal or the Stone, and why I'm still alive.

He moves his head to survey the room and sees he's at the farthest point from the opening.

Three walls and no bars. I'm not in a dungeon or torture chamber.

He rolls to his right side, controlling the pain as he pulls his legs out from under the sheet. He clenches his teeth as he pushes up with his right elbow and lowers his feet to the floor, then sits, letting the pain subside.

I'm naked and washed. How? A comfortable bed, my kilt and shirt hanging on a chair, and my boots underneath it. I don't understand.

He looks at the large opening at the end of the room with no guard, but a semi-naked female figure leans on a counter with her back to him. Lochran stands and, feeling the weakness in his legs, he places his hand on the wall for balance as he waits for his body to gain control before moving toward the chair.

He stops after a few steps because the female figure stands up, and he studies her.

Powerful leg muscles, firm buttocks, muscular back, and arms. Aye, this one is more than capable of running an enemy to the ground. That might explain why I'm still alive, or at least not in Queen Sorcha's dungeon.

Lochran takes another step toward the chair and stops again as the female figure stretches her arms above her head and then freezes. Beth sees Lochran's naked reflection in the large living room window, and she turns toward him while lowering her headphones to her neck.

Lochran recognizes the last person he saw before blacking out at the warehouse.

Beth points to the chair. "You should put your kilt on, and then we can talk."

Lochran gives a brief smile, nods in agreement, and moves to the chair, saying nothing. He dresses, except for his boots because of the pain from his wound, then turns to face Beth.

"Who are you, lass?"

"To save you any further unnecessary pain, you need to understand your boundaries," she says. "The first thing is the line on the floor." Beth points to the white line across the opening. "Cross it and you'll have a crap day."

Lochran looks at the white line on the floor, then back to Beth. "Are you daft? Do you think me so weak that I can no cross that line, lass?"

Lochran, despite his injury, launches himself into a run at Beth.

To Beth, it's slow motion as Lochran's body and face slam into the protection barrier, sending him flying backward.

Beth shakes her head and looks at Lochran's sprawled, unconscious body.

"Now, how did I know that was going to happen? It's a good thing I've seen it before, because when you wake up, you're going to peel that kilt off your face."

Beth turns to the refrigerator for a bottle of water, and as she walks back to the dining island, she reflects. "Lochran is the first person in my home in fifteen years of living here. Not even one of my school or magic tutors has entered my condo."

Fifteen minutes after slamming into the barrier, Lochran regains consciousness and learns he's added a massive headache to the pain of his wound, making his disposition worse. He pulls his kilt from his face and sees Beth, half sitting on the stool with her ankles crossed, sipping from a bottle.

"Did you enjoy your nap?"

"No," Lochran groans.

He rolls sideways and stands, thanks to the wall, and holding his hand against his bandage, Lochran limps up to the white line, giving Beth a sheepish grin.

"Aye, the white line."

"Aye, the white line," Beth repeats, nodding her head. She points the finger at him. "Stay there."

Standing, she sets her bottle on the dining island and walks to the corner opposite him. She kneels on one knee, putting both index fingers together on the invisible barrier, pulls her fingers apart, then down, creating a small opening. Beth casts a quick glance at Lochran before sliding a jug of lemon water and two pain tablets across the white line.

Beth closes the opening, then stands, saying, "Swallow the tabs to help with the pain and drink the water to re-hydrate."

Lochran says nothing as he limps his way across the room and, thanks to the wall again, lowers himself to one knee beside the pitcher. He pops the tabs into his mouth, consumes the entire jug of water, and eats the lemons. He stands, and Beth half sits on the stool again.

"Okay, blue eyes. I've lived here undisturbed for fifteen years, and until eleven hours ago, I didn't know there were other magical people around here. Now, I have an unwanted guest, and 'you' have a horse-mounted posse that wants you dead. Start talking."

"My name is Lochran," he replies. "Now, you need to tell me your name and why you were at the warehouse, lass."

"I'm Beth. I was getting a coffee at a nearby coffee shop when I saw light explosions from magic, so I popped in to see what the excitement was."

Lochran pauses. "How did you stop Galen and his band of cutthroats from killing me?"

Beth raises her brow in surprise. "Don't sound so displeased with me saving your life."

"Please, don't misunderstand, lass. I'm grateful for my life, and it's a debt I owe, but you were against the horsemen with no help. Aye, you look strong and battle-worthy, but it no make sense that you could defeat them alone."

"How do you think you got here, then? Did I wave a white flag, and everyone went home?"

Lochran studies Beth.

"I have met only three people who had the strength and magical skill to vanquish the horsemen, and you're no any of them. That makes me think you're allied with the horsemen and trying to get information from me, or you're using me as bait for the Guardians. I'll die before I tell you anything that helps that black-hearted witch Queen."

Beth stares at Lochran for a few moments, then shakes her head. She places her headphones back over her ears, and with a quick push off the stool, she turns and walks away from him, singing to the music.

He follows Beth with his eyes for a moment, and as she turns away from him at the top of her stairs, he asks, "Where are you going, lass?"

Beth throws her arms above her head, and with a couple of dance moves, she slips past the end of the dining island into her living room. She gives the armchair a sexy hip bump and spins to the side, shuffling between the leather couch and coffee table. Reaching the end of the coffee table, she spins, turns past the television towards the eight-foot-long picture window overlooking the East container yard that faces the harbor. She bumps into the matching armchair, moving the end-table and jiggling the lamp. Beth continues across the open floor, past the sliding door to her large sundeck, and toward the kitchen. She spins past the end of the counter and the back-to-back upper and lower cabinets, then drums her hands on the stainless steel fridge. Slipping sideways, she turns to drum her hands on the upper cabinet doors before dancing down the hallway. Beth passes two bedrooms to the laundry room that is backed against her twenty-foot by fifteen-foot bathroom with a large claw foot glass tub on a riser. As she spins to go back up the hallway, she slows to a saunter and contemplates the events of the last twelve hours.

The wizards mounted on the horses were going to kill Lochran. Why? What's he hiding?

She nears the kitchen and mumbles, "Lochran needs to tell me what's going on. Now."

She turns the corner from the hallway and sees Lochran sitting on the chair with his legs stretched out and crossed at the ankles. Then, Beth freezes. Her heart rate jumps and she stops breathing. Big yellow eyes, surrounded by the enormous head of a black predator cat, peer over the top step of her front entrance stairs. Lochran sees Beth go motionless, so he sits up straight, pulling his outstretched legs into position to move fast, and he watches Beth slide her headphones to her neck. The big black cat lets out a low guttural growl, and Lochran jumps up from the chair, moving as quick as possible to the barrier.

He stops as the big cat climbs the last stair and he shouts, "Abigail, my love!"

Beth's head snaps to Lochran to see him smiling. "Seriously?" she shouts.

Beth looks back at the cat.

Holy... crap. That thing has to be ten-foot-long. How did it get through my shield? He called her 'My love'? Shape-changer?

Abigail lifts her head toward Lochran, flicks her pink tongue up the side of her face, and winks as she draws her tongue back into her mouth. She looks at Beth, growls, and slaps its gigantic paw on the floor. Abigail turns away from Lochran, slipping along the side of the dining island into the open space between the kitchen and the living room. She turns back to Beth, and transforms into a tall, brown-skinned woman wearing bright colored beachcomber pants and a tattered half shirt. Her hair is Rastafarian style, braided with colored beads, and she wears jewelry made of bone and wood. Abigail has sharp facial features, and her body is muscular to her bare feet.

"You will set my man free, or you will die, witch."

Beth tears her wireless headphones from her neck, throwing them on the counter.

"Abigail, is it? So, you know, I've had more than enough of the life interference, the crazy magical people, and now break and enter by a shape-changer. What the hell are you doing in my home?"

"I say, release my man, or you will die, witch."

Beth looks at Lochran, then turns back to Abigail.

"You can have him as soon as he tells me why I saved him from the Horsemen."

Abigail, hands glowing, puts her arms out to her sides as if she's lifting a large tray with each. Both the coffee table and end table rise from the floor, and she swings her arms forward, launching the two tables at Beth.

A Natural Witch and shape-changer. Interesting and rare combination.

Beth swings her arm as though hammering a post into the ground with the side of her glowing fist. The flying tables slam to the floor, shattering into wood and glass pieces. Beth retaliates with a sweeping motion of her arm and open hand that fires shards of the coffee table and broken glass back at Abigail. Abigail flails backward, spinning in the air to avoid the flying debris, and Beth hears a shout of pain. Landing on her feet, Abigail grabs her right leg near a protruding piece of wood.

"That's it?" Beth shouts. "One minor wound from all that? Okay, I'm impressed."

"You will regret stealing my man, witch."

Abigail jerks the wood from her leg and moves her body sideways while sweeping her arm like a bowler launching a ball down the alley, and the shattered end table shoots from the ground at Beth.

Beth sweeps the flying debris aside as if swatting a bug while shouting, "Woman, you clearly have jealousy issues. And I didn't *steal* him, you dumb ass. I saved his life."

Beth knows she's stronger than Abigail, so she makes a grabbing motion with her hands and, swinging her arms toward Abigail, she slams the couch against the wall, pinning Abigail.

As fast as the couch hits Abigail, it explodes into pieces, and Beth reacts by crossing her arms in front of her face and casting a front body shield.

Abigail seizes the moment to throw an armchair, hitting Beth's shield and knocking her back into the kitchen.

"Ha! Give me my man, or you will suffer!"

Beth recovers her balance, saying, "I've had enough of your crap, little kitty."

Beth focuses her mind, and Abigail freezes with her hands in the ready position and twists her head left and right.

"Show yourself, Witch."

Beth runs straight at Abigail, jumping, landing a solid superman punch to the side of her face that puts Abigail flat on her back. Beth steps back and waits to see what damage she's inflicted, but Abigail recovers fast and props herself on her right forearm.

There's a sudden flash of emerald-green light off Abigail's face, and she cries out, throwing her left hand out as if she's yielding.

"Mehla, Mehla, is that you? Mehla, it's me, Abigail. Princess Mehla, can you hear me? Princess Mehla, please show yourself."

I think I must have hit her too hard.

Beth backs away from Abigail, cautious that it might be a trick, and Abigail smiles and cries at the same time while looking at her. Then, reaching for her, as if touching Beth's cheek, Abigail says, "Princess Mehla, it's me, Abigail."

"Guess that means I'm not invisible anymore," Beth says.

She holds her defensive stance until, from the corner of her eye, she sees Lochran take to one knee and bow his head.

"Princess, you are still wearing the amulet," Abigail says. Her voice is squeaky, and tears run full stream down her cheeks.

Beth stands, more relaxed, and reaches her hand to the pendant that has popped out from under her sports top during the fray.

Second time someone has called it an amulet.

"I… I never take it off. I was told to never take it off. How do I know you?"

"I was your best friend and bodyguard."

Abigail rolls her body to the left side and brings her right arm out from under her.

Beth snaps her glowing hands to the front of her body again. "Stop. What are you doing?"

Abigail raises her right wrist to show Beth a pulsing emerald embedded in gold.

"Your amulet glows because of danger, and it calls to my bracelet so that I will rush to you."

Beth lifts her amulet so she can see it and the bracelet together.

"Holy crap. The emerald is glowing and pulsing at the exact pace and intensity of your bracelet. My necklace has never done that."

Beth looks back at Abigail as she lets the amulet chain go, and she's drawn closer to Abigail.

I feel it. She's not here to hurt me. Something tells me I know her. How?

Beth doesn't realize that she has extended her hand to help Abigail stand until Abigail's arms swing over her shoulders and she says, "Princess Mehla. I have missed you so much."

Beth feels herself pulling Abigail into her, and it feels right.

"Hi, Abigail. I'm Beth."

Both laugh, shedding tears of joy, and after a long minute, Abigail releases her hug.

"I can't believe that I have found you," Abigail says.

"I don't understand how," Beth says, "but it feels like I know you, and I know we've never met."

"We are from long ago, and you have Princess Mehla inside of you."

"What…. What do you mean?" Beth says. "Are you talking about reincarnation? Are you saying that I look like Princess Mehla? This isn't making sense. What do you mean '*inside me*'?"

"I will explain, Princess."

Beth draws a deep breath, and her anxiety pushes deep into her stomach, where it disappears. Abigail shifts her eyes to the side, and Beth turns her head to see Lochran, still on one knee with his head bowed.

Beth covers her mouth, trying to muffle a slight snicker.

"I heard that, Abigail," Lochran says.

Abigail snaps back, "Lochran, you are mean to me. I never laugh at you."

Beth snickers again.

"Aye, and what is that then?" he says.

"It was me, Lochran."

"My apologies, Princess. I thought Abigail was sporting me. If I had been standing and could see who was talking or laughing, I would not have spoken out of turn. Please, forgive me, Princess."

Beth looks at Abigail, saying nothing, and then both women burst into full laughter.

Beth waves her hand and with a flash of light the barrier spell drops, and Beth says, "Lochran, get up."

Lochran lifts his head to see Beth and Abigail standing with their arms around each other's waists, smiling, and he smiles back.

"I cannot believe I'm looking at the two biggest troublemakers standing together again."

Lochran stands, still showing pain from his wound, and Abigail climbs into his arms like a python, wrapping itself around a tree. Putting her lips tight to Lochran's ear, she whispers, "I missed you, lover."

Beth snickers. "Now that's a cougar on a kill."

"That's a black jaguar on a kill, if you don't mind."

Abigail kisses Lochran like she hasn't seen him in a hundred years, and he returns the kiss in full.

Abigail releases Lochran with a peck on the cheek before walking to Beth and throwing her arms around her neck.

"I am so happy that I found you, Princess," she says, eyes shining. "This is wonderful."

Beth hugs her back. "It is, and overwhelming."

When Abigail releases her hug, Beth steps sideways, kicking the remnants of the earlier battle.

Abigail looks at the floor and snickers. "We should clean up this mess. Stand back and let me show you something Princess Mehla taught me."

Beth moves to the kitchen, and Lochran steps back into the room that was his cell, where he bumps into a hundred-pound punching bag. Startled, he looks over his shoulder and says, "Aye, what's this then?"

Beth looks at Lochran. "That's my workout bag, and, as you can see by the equipment, that room is my gym." Beth pauses. "Until I needed it as a cell. Then, as soon as I dropped the barrier and you stepped over the white line, the equipment went back to where it belongs."

Beth turns back to watch Abigail go to the center of the carnage, and Abigail calm herself, focusing, as she holds her hands in the air and moves them in a weaving motion as she closes her eyes. Abigail's lips move, but no sound comes out, and then she stops, bowing her head at the neck.

In seconds, the carnage returns to the original living space.

THE DREAM

Saturday, August 30th — 0500 Pacific Time — Canada

Rising near one-hundred feet, four ancient Stones mark the compass corners, north, east, south, and west, of the two-hundred-foot-wide natural amphitheater. The near-zero sunlight is ideal for the moss carpet under the feet of three-hundred Blood Witches, dressed in gray, with capes bearing a small, blood-red teardrop symbol on the collar tip.

From a rock ledge ten feet above them, Queen Sorcha scans the horde gathered from around the world, who all have gray eyes from a single drop of her blood on their tongue.

"Hear me, Blood Witches," Queen Sorcha says, and the murmuring crowd goes silent.

"Prince O'Manus and Princess Sadreen must not survive. Your fate depends on it. The spoils of victory or the pain and suffering from defeat both await you, but know better you die in battle than face me in defeat."

Queen Sorcha turns her head, giving a slight nod and two wizards move to seize a young witch, Kelly, standing close to them.

"What are you doing? Let me go! I've done nothing wrong!" Kelly shouts.

Kelly tries to kick and pull free as they drag her to the rock ledge that is now Queen Sorcha's stage. Queen Sorcha raises her hand, and the chattering horde goes silent again as she walks closer to Kelly, then stops as a swirling circle of black smoke appears a short distance away. A young witch, Caitriona, walks out of the portal, stopping a few feet from Queen Sorcha and bowing her head, says, "My Queen."

Still venomously eyeing Kelly, Queen Sorcha turns her attention to Caitriona, saying, "What have you discovered, Caitriona?"

"My Queen. The prince and princess requested the wedding held outside the castle gates for all the townsfolk to attend. Still, no one suspects your attack from the hidden Glen, and all the townsfolk of Brae's Garden have gathered to witness the union. The atmosphere is joyous and relaxed, and they have not fortified the guards as the Captain of the Guard feels relaxed and happy. At least he did when I left his chambers. There are many magical people in attendance, but of course, some await your arrival, My Queen."

Queen Sorcha touches her hand against Caitriona's cheek, saying, "Well done, my sweet. Your talents have proven most valuable."

"My Queen," Caitriona replies. She bows her head and, stepping back, she turns away to leave Queen Sorcha's stage.

Queen Sorcha returns her icy stare to Kelly, and gripping the young witch's jaw with one hand, Kelly announces her pain and struggles against the wizards holding her. The horde laughs as Queen Sorcha jerks her hand from Kelly's jaw and turns, shouting, "Blood Witches, hear me," and waits for silence. "This traitor has been delivering information to the Captain of the Guard, and my spy tells me the false information we have been feeding this little bird has worked. They are not ready for our attack, and in their arrogance, they have left us a greater opportunity for success."

The horde mumbles, and Queen Sorcha raises her hands to silence them.

"I am your Queen, and you must know your fate. Should you ever betray me or fail me today or in the future?"

Queen Sorcha turns to Kelly, speaking an incantation, then continues to repeat.

Mørke, slipp denne sjelen som jeg kan mate. (Darkness, release this soul that I may feed)

"What are you doing? Stop. Let me go. Please... Please don't kill me."

"Tearful begging won't save you," Queen Sorcha hisses.

Kelly screams as her body goes weightless and the two wizards holding her let go. Queen Sorcha increases the intensity of the chant while holding her glowing hands above her head, palms cupped toward Kelly, and casting a gray light. Kelly screams, now in agony, and the horde of Blood Witches witness a mist form around Kelly's floating body. Queen Sorcha levitates until she is face to face with her prisoner, increasing the intensity of her chant, and the beautiful young witch screams louder. The horde reacts as Kelly's soul floats away from her body, and she goes silent, hanging limp but still suspended by Queen Sorcha's power.

Rebekah Kheel walks to the front of the stone ledge and shouts to the horde.

"Witness your punishment for failure."

The horde shifts their eyes back to Queen Sorcha to witness the soul of the young witch turning to smoke, and opening her mouth, Queen Sorcha draws it in.

The vibrant young witch, her red hair and green eyes gone, is now a lifeless, gray, and wrinkled shell that drops to the stone ledge, making almost no sound.

With glowing black eyes, her long black hair dancing as if blowing in the non-existent wind, and robes shaped like black spiked butterfly wings, Queen Sorcha turns her floating body to her audience. Fear and disbelief cover the faces of the Blood Witches, and in a deep demonic voice, Queen Sorcha says, "Do not fail me."

She throws her arms out to her sides, like a rock star ending a concert, and in unison, the horde replies, "My Queen!" and kneels. She hovers for a few moments, then as her eyes return to their natural gray color, she descends until her feet touch the stone ledge again.

"It is time, my great horde of Blood Witches. Prepare for victory."

A portal opens at each cornerstone, and with wands at the ready, the horde splits into four groups, running into the smoke.

Queen Sorcha casts her portal, and when she appears at the Glen, sounds of battle nearby ring out. Hidden from the wedding by a hill and trees, it shocked Queen Sorcha to see half her force has already advanced.

"What happened? Who started the attack before I gave the command?"

Rebekah turns. "My Queen. We can find the treacherous leach after, but we must take this opportunity now."

Queen Sorcha turns to the two wizards, who grabbed Kelly. "You two are the strongest of the wizards, so I have chosen you to kill the prince. Succeed, and one of you will be my prince."

The men look at each other with contempt, turn back to Queen Sorcha, and bow their heads to acknowledge the offer. With a quick, circular wave of their wands, they each form a portal and step through the swirling smoke that disappears with them.

Queen Sorcha turns to her spy and says, "Caitriona, no matter how long it takes, you will stay close to your captain until I need you."

"My Queen."

Then, casting a portal, Queen Sorcha says, "Rebekah, come with me and we will destroy Princess Sadreen and ensure they do not fulfill the prophecy."

Queen Sorcha and Rebekah step out of her portal behind the cover of two large trees overlooking the wedding battlefield. They move around the trees to see the battle and the podium with the four throne chairs brought from the castle that looms in the distance.

"Rebekah, look. The Fire Kings lay dead on the podium," she laughs. "They only need to kill the two queens."

ROYAL SOULS

"My Queen, look. The prince and the princess, caught in the open, away from the podium and separated from each other."

Queen Sorcha leans forward to peer around the tree and, smiling, says, "Oh, Rebekah. This is going well."

Queen Sorcha looks back at the podium to see the two queens are now back to back, using their powers together to cast a shield.

Queen Sorcha steps out from between the two trees, shouting, "Fools! You let them join, and now you can't kill them. Focus on the prince and princess."

The Blood Witches abandon their attack on the queen's and, turning to the newlyweds, they break into a sprint toward them. Hearing Queen Sorcha's command, the Royal supporters and guards run to cut off the Blood Witches, clashing in a flurry of exploding curses.

Prince O'Manus, separated from the princess, faces Queen Sorcha's two wizards and eight witches surround Princess Sadreen.

Princess Sadreen shouts, "They have deceived you! I am more powerful than all of you together. Don't you see you are being sacrificed? I don't want to hurt anyone. That is not the way in Brae's Garden. We do not hurt anyone with our magic." Her words fall on deaf ears as the Wand Witches continue casting curses that bounce off her protection shield, and they force the princess to use the power she's locked deep within her.

Princess Sadreen raises her arms to her sides to shoulder height, and the eight witches move closer. Lifting her knee while swinging her arms to her front, she stomps her foot on the ground as she swings her arms together,

51

making a loud clap sound. Princess Sadreen's shield explodes outward, and the ground heaves, throwing the eight witches backward, smashing into boulders, trees, and the stone wall leading to the castle. The eight witches fall unconscious or dead and Princess Sadreen knows she had no choice, but still her heart is heavy and tears well in her eyes.

Sobbing, Princess Sadreen says, "I swore to the Witch of Loch Shin to never use my powers to harm another magical person."

A hundred feet away from Princess Sadreen, Prince O'Manus hears the crack of her attack, and without even a glance, he says, "Sadreen needs me."

The prince abandons his teachings of 'Care for life' and sweeps his hand across the surface of a water puddle at his feet, shooting ice darts at his enemy. One attacking wizard drops and the other, wounded, recovers and mounts another attack. A curse, cast from behind the prince, hits the wizard square in the chest, crushing him against a boulder, and Angus MacShannachan shouts, "O'Manus, the people are away safe!"

"Well done, old friend."

Princess Sadreen casts another shield before turning to see Prince O'Manus break free of his fight.

"I must wait for O'Manus," she tells herself until she looks toward the royal podium to see her younger sister, Princess Mehla, engaged in battle with four known, powerful witches.

Princess Sadreen draws a sharp breath, saying, "Mehla is in danger."

ROYAL SOULS

Prince O'Manus turns to see Princess Sadreen looking at the podium, and he knows she was in danger because of her love for her younger sister.

The Prince shouts, "Angus, with me."

Angus turns without thought, launching himself into a run, surveying the threats ahead, and he shouts, "O'Manus. Twenty enemies and only a few friends."

Two wizards secreted behind trees run out of hiding, and Andrew Craig casts a wooden shrapnel attack using a wagon destroyed earlier. Several pieces pierce Angus's body, and Prince O'Manus hears his friend's yell of pain and turns to see him hitting the ground like a sack of grain. The prince is quick to see where the attack came from, but not quick enough with his shield to avoid the curse cast by Midas Pohl. Prince O'Manus, struck with only a portion of the curses power that slipped past his shield, slams against the stone wall that leads to the castle, knocking him near unconscious. Stunned, the prince watches Andrew Craig walk toward his friend and knows Angus's fate if he does nothing. Midas Pohl descends upon him for the kill, so Prince O'Manus musters his remaining strength and casts protection over himself and Angus.

My injuries have weakened my magic. Those two warlocks might be strong enough to overcome it.

Prince O'Manus closes his eyes, whispering, "Your Prince needs you."

Midas, reaching the prince, laughs, saying, "Andrew. This was too easy. We will end the prophecy and collect glorious rewards."

"Do you want to call Queen Sorcha for the kill, or shall we give her the prince's head as a gift?" Andrew

53

laughs, glaring at Angus while raising his wand over his head.

"Sorcha?" Prince O'Manus shouts.

Andrew and Midas look at Prince O'Manus and Midas laughs, saying, "Ah, yes, your highness. The woman scorned."

The King's Guard's curse strikes Andrew Craig sideways, plowing him into a large boulder, ending any further taunts, forever. Midas Pohl, blocking a curse shot out of a King's Guard's portal, spins away from Prince O'Manus, and under fire, retreats to the trees to escape.

A King's Guard, pulling a vial of pure Faerie Pool water from his belt pouch, kneels beside Prince O'Manus, offering the Faerie Pool water to help heal his body, and saying, "We heard your call, King O'Manus."

"My father?"

The guard shakes his head and holds out his hand to help the future King to his feet.

The King's Guard is the Prince's only solace at the news of his father, and a moment of silence follows.

Prince O'Manus turns to one of the older and stronger guards, and in a softened tone, commands, "Roth. Guard Angus and call a healer, if any remain, and the rest follow me."

Prince O'Manus, capturing his emotions and energy renewed by the Faerie Water, turns to Princess Sadreen and Princess Mehla.

"Princess Sadreen's shield holds, but I can tell from her body that Princess Mehla's shield is getting weak. We must hurry."

ROYAL SOULS

Before Prince O'Manus can launch himself into a run, a guard grabs his arm and points. "My King, there, the trees."

"Sorcha! She will die for this treachery," Prince O'Manus says, and pulling his arm free from his guard, he pitches an explosive ball.

At the exact moment, Princess Sadreen looks over her shoulder to see her prince pointing, thinking it's at Mehla, and she abandons her full body shield for a warrior-style shield to run to her sister. She comes to the cold reality of her decision, realizing that Prince O'Manus wasn't pointing at Princess Mehla but throwing magic at Sorcha and Rebekah, who are running out from behind two large trees and casting curses.

Prince O'Manus had hurried his attack, and the exploding ball he cast falls short of its uphill target. Princess Sadreen, lifting her shield to guard her head from the flying chunks of earth, glances away from her attackers to Princess Mehla. Queen Sorcha's curse catches the bottom of Princess Sadreen's shield.

"Ahh," Princess Sadreen screams as a small amount of Queen Sorcha's curse slips past the bottom of the shield, striking Princess Sadreen in the abdomen, sending her flailing backward, and landing between two boulders that now shield her. Prince O'Manus witnesses his bride struck by Sorcha's curse, and reaching her seconds after she's struck down, he sees the gaping burn wound that covers half of her abdomen.

"Go, my love, before it is too late. I will find you," he says.

"Mehla?"

55

The Prince looks up to the podium and then back to Sadreen, smiling.

"Her black cat has changed the favor."

Princess Sadreen smiles, and a small circle of glowing mist rises from her chest and hovers above her.

"Rebekah, look. She's casting her soul to safety," Queen Sorcha says. "Now, I will end the prophecy and take her crown."

Shields on their fronts, Queen Sorcha and Rebekah pause, waiting for the moment of a clear shot at Princess Sadreen's vulnerable soul. Those moments allow the Samurai warriors of Japan and Mystical warriors of India, all long-time friends of both kings, to surround Queen Sorcha and Rebekah.

"Ahh..." Queen Sorcha spins sideways, struck by a flesh curse cast by an Indian warrior, and Rebekah blocks the same fate cast at her by a Samurai warrior. Rebekah casts a portal, grabs Sorcha, and pulls her from the clutches of certain death. Sorcha and Rebekah, still seventy-five feet away, cast killing curses at Princess Sadreen's floating soul, and a young Samurai Warrior, seeing the two curses, sacrifices himself by diving in front but blocks only one. Prince O'Manus steps between the remaining curse and Princess Sadreen's floating soul, knowing his body will die, and it will be enough for Queen Sorcha to think herself victorious. The portal engulfs Queen Sorcha and Rebekah before Prince O'Manus forces his soul out of his body, which dies a moment later, and those close to the Royals witness Prince O'Manus' soul fly west as Princess Sadreen's soul flies north.

***

ROYAL SOULS

Rhynan can feel the warmth of her hands on his shirtless back and smell the jasmine perfume she always wears at the coffee shop. Surrounded by light, swirling like the center of a hurricane, Aaghnya's face moves toward him, slowly, as she closes her eyes, and his heart races with anticipation.

Rhynan snaps awake at five-thirty in the morning, sweating, parched, and feeling nauseous.

"That was the most powerful dream I've ever had, and it's the first time Aaghnya's been in it. Why is she in the dream, and why did it change?"

He grabs a bottle of water from his nightstand and gulps it down.

"I swear I heard Rebekah's voice this time, but I couldn't see her face. The princess is beautiful and so friendly to people. I don't understand why they're trying to kill her."

He grabs another bottle of water from the nightstand and takes a gulp.

"Why did I protect the princess? Who am I in the dream?"

Rhynan feels a chill and touches his stomach, and feeling the sweat says, "I need a shower and some dry sheets."

He tries to stand, but his legs are too weak to lift him, so he lays back on his bed and, employing the many times used solution, he moves to the dry side.

"The dream had more people and more violence than ever before. What does it mean?"

He falls back to sleep and wakes again at eight-thirty. The changes in the dream rush through his mind as he strips his bed, then makes his way to the shower, but soon his thoughts change to his upcoming morning chai with Aaghnya.

"Good morning, Rhynan Doon," Aaghnya says, as he approaches the counter.

"Good morning, Aaghnya. How are you this fine morning?"

"I am feeling wonderful, Rhynan, and yes, it is a beautiful day. Would you like your chai, Rhynan?"

"Yes, Aaghnya, that would be great. Thank you. And can I have a breakfast sandwich with it?"

"Okay, no problem, Rhynan. Have a seat, and I will bring it to your table when it is ready."

"Thanks, Aaghnya."

To her sisters, this was the typical Saturday morning between Aaghnya and Rhynan. To an outsider, it's a rerun of a 1960s teenage high school movie where the awkward teenage boy doesn't have the nerve to ask the awkward teenage girl out on a movie date.

Rhynan likes the feel of the warm August sun beating on his back, so he sits at a table in a large bay window near the counter. Soon after, Aaghnya brings his breakfast and takes a seat beside him. She circles the rim of his cup, whispering in Tamil and then touches his hand lightly, as she always does, but as their skin meets, she stiffens. Her face goes blank of expression, and Rhynan sees the sudden change in Aaghnya's demeanor.

"Are you okay, Aaghnya?"

"Are you not sleeping well, Rhynan?"

"I've never seen you so serious. Are you okay?"

"You did not answer my question, Rhynan. Are you not sleeping well?"

He looks around, and the shop is empty except for an older couple on the far end of the other side and out of hearing range, so his verbal floodgate bursts open.

"I've been having this weird dream for quite some time," he says. "But last night it was different, and there were more people in it and more violence, and I don't understand what it means or why it's happening. It's like I'm a spectator walking around with a camera filming the carnage of this wedding, and these people with small sticks in their hands, which I think are wands, are causing chaos and destruction. It's like the war in those movies, but back a thousand years ago. Everyone is Scottish or Irish except near the end when Japanese and Indian warriors with cool swords appear and save the day using magic. Why did they need swords if they're magical? I don't understand the dream, and if the small sticks are wands, they're different from the *Harry Potter* ones. The dream keeps happening, but this time, near the end, I'm someone who throws himself in front of one of those things they are shooting." Looking gloomy, he says, "Aaghnya... I die. I thought if you died in a dream, you died in real life...."

He looks at her and takes a deep breath.

"Oh, wow. I'm talking like a lunatic, and I must sound like a lunatic. I'm sorry. Please don't think I'm a lunatic and stop talking to me, not that I would blame you, but I hope you still like me."

Aaghnya feels a rush of energy as she puts her hand on his and says, "Is that everything about the dream? Did you leave out any details? This is important, Rhynan."

"You're making me nervous. What's going on, Aaghnya?"

Aaghnya's tone is firmer. "You must tell me the dream, and you must not leave out any detail. Rhynan, this is important."

He's looking down at the table and blushes.

"Rhynan, I can tell that you are leaving something out. Please, tell me everything."

"Please don't be mad at me. I like you very much, and it would hurt if you're not my friend anymore, so please don't make me tell you everything."

She shoves her hand deeper into Rhynan's.

"I like you too, Rhynan, and you will always be my friend, so please don't be afraid to tell me."

"Aaghnya, the end of the dream. This is the first time it has ever happened, and you have to promise not to be mad at me. Please tell me you won't be mad. Please."

"I will only be mad at you because you didn't tell me everything. Do you understand?"

He gives a brief smile before telling her the new ending to the dream, and she smiles, leans forward, and kisses him on the cheek.

Aaghnya lingers before sitting back and looking at Rhynan in joyful disbelief of what she has discovered.

Turning to her sisters Aaghnya, in Tamil, says, "I have found the prince. We must tell our father and protect Rhynan until it is time."

"Okay. I sure didn't expect that, but I'm not complaining. What did I do, Aaghnya? And what did you say to them?"

Petia and Dehlia whisper to each other before Petia scurries to the back room. Then a flash of light, like someone has taken a picture, catches Rhynan's eye.

Aaghnya stands up to gather the cold items from the table saying, "I said I will get a fresh sandwich and chai for you, Rhynan."

Aaghnya's voice is like nothing he has heard before. She sounds relieved and her tone is near musical. Rhynan sits back, enjoying the warm sun on his neck, and languishes in the thought of Aaghnya's kiss and her sudden change. He looks toward Aaghnya and catches the same flash of light again before Petia returns from the backroom.

Huddled close together, Petia, Aaghnya, and Dehlia have a tense conversation in Tamil, and when Aaghnya brings him a fresh sandwich and chai, she joins him again.

"Petia sounds upset. Is everything alright?"

"Yes, Rhynan, everything will be good. We are short products, and I have to go get them before the end of the day."

"Can I help you in any way?"

Aaghnya pauses. "Do you like Indian food?"

"I love Indian food, Aaghnya."

"Good. You will come with me to get my product, and we will have Indian food at my grandmother's restaurant. Okay, this will be our first date."

Rhynan's head lowers, and he looks away from Aaghnya.

"Do you not want to go with me?"

"I want nothing more than to go with you, Aaghnya," Rhynan says, sounding frustrated, "but I have a bad habit of saying the wrong things on first dates and ruining them. I'm so excited about today that I'm afraid I might mess it up, and you won't like me afterwards."

"Rhynan Doon, I will remember that you sometimes say the wrong thing, and something bad that you say will not hurt me."

She gives him another peck on the cheek.

"Okay, ready when you are," Rhynan says.

HIDDEN WISP

Saturday, August 30th — 1700 Eastern Time — Boston

"Princess," Lochran says. "Excuse my forwardness, but do you have any food?"

"Of course. When was the last time you ate, Lochran?"

"I stole bread while watching the Blood Witches two days before you found me."

"Why did you have to steal it?"

"I was hiding under a shack where the Blood Witches had gathered and couldn't use magic, but I stole two slices from a loaf near a window."

"So that means you haven't eaten in three days? Yes, I have plenty of food."

Beth opens her refrigerator saying, "Help yourself," and Lochran's face glows.

Beth and Abigail watch as Lochran devours what should have been a three-day supply of food for Beth and then walk to the armchair and collapse into a food coma.

"Should we check if he left us something?" Beth says.

"There's plenty in the mess he left," Abigail says, and they both laugh.

Beth pulls a baby carrot from the bag as Abigail tears a piece of chicken breast away, and Beth asks, "Abigail, how did you find us?"

"Scent."

"Are you saying you can smell us?"

Abigail smiles and, pointing at the semi-sleeping Lochran, says, "He has been my mate for more than a thousand years. I know his scent and can find him anywhere."

"Now that's an enduring relationship. Nowadays, people run to divorce court after a thousand hours. Pathetic, when you think about it."

"Him." She points to Lochran. "He make me mad so many time but I will still claw through a steel wall to die at his side."

"Aye, and I for you, my love," Lochran says, his eyes fluttering open for a moment before he nods off again.

Abigail smiles at Lochran, and Beth nods her head.

"Okay then. You were walking by and caught Lochran's scent?"

"No, I was prowling through the containers and caught the faint scent of you, which I picked up at the warehouse where you found Lochran. Your protection barrier was masking Lochran's scent, but you have touched something outside, and I smell it. Then, I hear magic when something go through your protection barrier."

"What do you mean, you heard it?"

"When someone or something pass through a protection barrier, it makes a quiet sound like someone tearing plastic wrapping, and in my jaguar form, I hear it."

"Wow, that's cool, Abigail."

Abigail smiles with the praise before continuing, "I keep prowling, and your scent become stronger, and then I see a house cat disappear behind a container, and I hear that sound."

"The spell let you through as a cat? Why?"

"You must have brought a cat home with you, which told the spell cats are safe."

"I found a kitten, wandering and hungry, and being a good witch who likes cats, I brought it home and took care of it. It later took up residence with a mate in the gardens, and now the rodents aren't eating my plants. Win-win scenario," Beth snickers.

"Once I know I find you, I had to be careful of the man hiding in the shadows and watching the front gate."

"Six-one, skinny, with sandy blonde hair?"

Abigail nods, and Beth knows it's Jack Sebastian.

"Yeah, that's a problem for later. How did you come to know Mehla? You sound Jamaican."

"Yes, I am Jamaican, but I am also Irish," Abigail says before slipping a piece of orange into her mouth. "My mother was working as the housekeeper at the house that the Irish king keep in Jamaica. One day my father come to the house as part of the guard for the king, and my mother see him and fall in love. My father and mother don't meet for a few more days, but when they do, he fall in love. My father ask the king if he could stay in Jamaica, and for eight-year, he is Captain of the Guard. During that time, I am born."

"Any brothers or sisters?"

"My brother, he is dead…."

"Sorry, Abigail." Beth pauses before asking, "How did you meet Mehla?"

"The king calls my father back to Ireland when I am seven, and many think us strange because of our brown skin. When we go to the castle, Princess Mehla walk up to me, introduce herself, and give me a big hug." Abigail pauses, smiling. "Then she step back and look at her arms, give me a funny look, walk up to me again and try to rub the color from my skin onto her," Abigail laughs.

"Oh… my… what did you do?" Beth says, laughing.

"I smile and tell her the color won't come off. Then Mehla get this big smile on her face, and she tell me she love the way I talk and say I can be her friend. She take my hand, and I tell her I will be her friend, and the next day my father tell me I must always stay devoted to the princess and protect her."

"Wow, a bodyguard at seven. How old was Mehla?"

"Mehla turn ten one month later, and I will have you know, at seven, in my jaguar form, I could defeat a full-grown boar."

"Oh, I believe it because in your jaguar form now, you must be what… nine, ten feet from nose to tail and near four feet high, at the head? Abigail, nobody in their right mind messes with you."

"Yes, I am ten feet from nose to tail, forty-two inches at the shoulder and weighing four-hundred and seventy-five pounds of muscle."

"Ya, and a hundred and twenty pounds as a human. That's crazy," Beth says, laughing.

After a few moments, the mood quiets and Beth says, "How did your brother die if you don't mind me asking?"

Abigail's face turns sober, and her eyes drop to look at her hands. "Donley was only five and always changing in and out of his jaguar form like it was a toy." Abigail makes a slight sound in her throat.

"He must have changed into his jaguar form when he was in the striking range of the wolf scorpion hunting for food. My father found him in the forest behind the house, paralyzed in that form, which means he could not survive."

"Abigail, I've never heard of a wolf scorpion."

"The wolf scorpion come only from Jamaica, and only magic people can see it. The full grown scorpion can be two-feet long from claw to stinger, but it is invisible to the Ingen magi."

"Hey, I say *Ingen magi* too," Beth cuts in.

Abigail nods. "If the *Ingen magi* walk through its glow, the scorpion will sting them, like a mosquito bite but with a bigger red sore, and it goes away in a couple of days. The wolf scorpion can kill adult magic people and animals in less than five minutes with its sting if they don't know the spell to stop the poison. Even if they know the spell, the sting make your mind fuzzy, and it is hard for the person alone to cast the spell to stop the poison. Then, the scorpion leak acid from its wolf-like mouth, burning any type of flesh, and make it edible for the scorpion."

"Abigail, I am so sorry you lost your brother." Beth pauses. "But, so you know, I am never going to Jamaica." Beth waves her arms across her body like an umpire calling the runner safe.

Abigail laughs. "I will take you to my home, and you will be safe," she says, slapping her hand on the counter. "I promise you this, Princess."

"Yeah, we'll see."

Lochran opens his eyes again and says, "I hope my sleeping isn't bothering your hand smashing, Abigail?"

"Lochran, don't be mean, or I hide your wand."

"Oh, please do. At least someone will know where it is."

"You lost your wand?" Beth says.

"Oh, aye. Galen cursed me as I escaped through my portal, and I dropped it."

"Well, I took one from a Horseman."

Beth walks over to a kitchen drawer as Lochran drags himself out of the comfy chair and joins Abigail at the dinner island.

"Where do you get your wands? And don't tell me it's a secret alley," Beth says.

"The Faerie King makes them," Lochran says.

"Ya, right? Nice try," Beth says.

"And he is not a king," Abigail says.

"If she's the Queen, then he's the king," Lochran says.

"Lochran, this is not true."

Beth could tell this joust had endured many centuries.

"It's true, Princess," Lochran says. "The first wand-maker is Dumghill, the Faerie Queen's mate, and he built a shop for making wands and magical artifacts underneath their castle in the Faerie Glen. Then, Dumghill traveled around the world gathering disfigured magical children, taught them to be wand-builders and gave them a home away from those who wanted to destroy them. Afterwards, he gathered nine Cassubian silkworms that each produce a different colored silk thread, six burning oysters from the Lava Sea that spit out precious gems, and three ghost spiders that secrete a different precious metal. Then he built the Faerie gardens where they grew special healing herbs and trees used to make the wands."

"You say 'grew' as in the past tense," Beth says.

"Oh, aye, princess. They abandoned the Faerie Glen a long time ago. Blood Witches are determined to capture the wand-makers or garden Faeries and Undines. The wand-makers are Sorcha's priority and especially Dumghill or any of the Faerie Queen's children."

"That's terrible," Beth says. "Why is she after her children?"

"Sorcha will use the children for leverage to get Dumghill to make wands and the Faerie Queen to power them," Lochran says.

"I don't understand," Beth says.

"There's an order to making a wand," Lochran says. "First, you must go through the Trials, which tests you for the magic hidden inside you."

"I think I heard something about it during my training, but I never asked anymore."

Lochran smiles and says, "When you walk through the gate of the Trials, you can no leave until you reach the Faerie Queen, unless you never want a wand made for you. You can still use a common wand made by Dumghill, but your magic will be weak because you have no magic from the Queen."

"So, if you give up, you're done?"

"No, you can go back later when you feel ready, but the longer you wait, the harder it is. But know this. People have spent days in the Trials."

"How can they spend days in there?" Beth says. "That's insane."

"Aye, the Trials tests you for courage, justice, trust, honesty, greed, and your connection to the four elements of earth, water, fire, and air. The tests show how you manage each challenge and whether fear or greed rises. As you go through the Trials, the wand-builder assigned to watch how you meet the challenges picks the tree wood, herbs, colors of silk thread, and gems they will use to make your wand."

"For example, my wand has both ash wood and willow. The willow is to make the stubborn side more flexible, and the ash wood is for my strength and commitment. It has the yarrow herb to help me heal faster if I'm wounded. I have three of the four elements—water, fire, and air—so I have silks of blue, red, yellow, and orange silk because of my belief in justice. There is a thread of pure gold in the middle, because I am a man and a woman is silver, and three gems. Diamond for justice, green emerald for trust, and blue sapphire for honesty. Then, they wrap my handle in black silk because I'm a protector of life."

"Holy crap," Beth says.

"And then, princess, the wand-builder places the bits in a water grass wrap and gives it to Dumghill, the wand-maker, to hold. His magic weaves the parts together, except the water grass, to make the wand, and then he gives it to the Faerie Queen to power. Now, the Faerie Queen knows how you did on the trials, and she adds power to the wand to help your strengths and reduce your weakness. When she presents the wand to you for the first time, it learns who you are, becomes part of you, and grows stronger with you as you grow your magic."

"To see the wand made for someone is exciting," Abigail says.

"Abigail, have you seen a wand made?"

"Yes, Princess."

"The Faerie Glen sounds fantastic when it is full of life," Beth says and stops rummaging through the drawer.

"Ah-ha," she says, holding the wand by the small tip. "Little devil was hiding in my chopstick tray. It's quite pretty. It has blue, red, yellow, and orange strips, a black handle, and green, blue, and clear dots in the middle below the handle. Could it be a diamond? Sound familiar?"

"Aye, but the magic might not be the same as mine. And mine's not pretty."

Beth snickers as she walks to Lochran and sets the wand in front of him.

"No harm in trying, is there?"

Abigail raises her brow. "Not true for him, Princess, but for us, we are natural witches and can absorb any magic."

"Okay, good point."

As Lochran examines the wand, Beth asks, "So how do people get wands today if everyone's hiding?"

"The Underground," Abigail says.

"Oh? How's that work?" Beth says.

"No one can go through the Trials so the Faerie Queen secretly visits children when they first ripple with magic. She takes the form of a child the same age and plays games with the children to test them. Then she contacts Dumghill and tells him how the children did. Dumghill passes the information to a wand-builder who, from wherever they are hiding, selects the wood and all the other parts based on the information, and assembles the wand. Dumghill has a secret place where he keeps the wood, herbs, worms, oysters, and scorpions safe from the Blood Witches. The wand-builders hide there building the water grass packets, then Dumghill holds each packet to make the wands which he sends to the Faerie Queen. The Faerie Queen powers the wands and uses witches to deliver them, but the process is not as good as the trials."

"Hey, it sounds better than nothing," Beth says.

Abigail nods her head as Lochran looks at her with a furrowed brow and then turns to Beth.

"Princess. You say you got this wand from a Horseman?"

"Yes. Why?"

Lochran looks back at the wand. "Well, I'm pretty sure it's mine."

Abigail picks the wand up and spins it in her fingers. Looking at Beth, she says, "I think he's right."

"Why did the rider have your wand, Lochran?"

"I don't know, princess. He shouldn't have been able to pick up my wand and use it to attack you. Something's not right. I wish I knew who was with Galen."

"I can show you the man who attacked me after Galen mouthed off."

"Please, Princess, will you do that? It might help."

Beth waves her hand in front of them, and a swirling circle with the rider's face she took the wand from appears.

"I don't believe it," Lochran moans. "That's Bordan, my battle instructor from when I was a young soldier. He was like a father to me." Lochran pauses. "It's because of that training he can use my wand."

"I don't understand," Beth says.

"During my training, I gave him permission to use my wand, as did many others, so he could test the strength of our magic. I never thought he would turn on the Royals. Now, I understand so much more."

Lochran, deflated, finishes with a heavy sigh as he falls back into his chair.

"So then, it's your wand?"

"Aye," Lochran says in a defeated tone.

Abigail sees Lochran's mood changing to anger at the discovery of Bordan's betrayal, and before she can calm him, Lochran grabs for the wand. As his hand closes on it, a light explodes outward, and he catapults backward. The wand falls from his hand to the dining top, and a ghostly gray figure rises from it. The Wisp, secreted in a dark spell on Lochran's wand, turns to escape, and Abigail casts a holding spell that stops it from leaving the condo.

"They should put something in your wand for your fiery head, you fool!" Abigail barks.

Beth throws her arms out in front of her, like a clam slamming its shell closed, making a loud clap sound with her hands. Small rings of white light shoot from the tips of Beth's fingers, destroying both Abigail's spell and the ghostly wisp.

Beth walks toward Lochran, half hidden from Abigail behind the dining island, and kicks the bottom of his boot.

"Yo, girlfriend. Pull your skirt down. I don't need to see that."

Abigail slides in beside Lochran on her knees. She grabs the kilt hem on his chest and jams her fist with the hem into his groin. Lochran groans in pain as he curls into the fetal position.

Beth laughs. "Serves you right," she says and turns to walk away.

While slapping Lochran's shoulder hard three times, Abigail shouts, "You fool! That dark spell could have killed you, and the wisp could have given away our hiding place if I had not captured it."

Lochran looks up at Abigail, pain in his eyes. "Sorry, my love. I was mad seeing Bordan had betrayed us, and I didn't think."

"Stop swinging your fists and start using your head," Abigail says as she slaps Lochran's shoulder one more time.

"Aye, lass." He rolls himself sideways, then to his hands and knees. "Aye, you're right, love, but did you have to be so hard on me wee fellas?"

Lochran rights himself and limps his way to the armchair nearest the couch, where he lowers his body. Beth and Abigail snicker.

"Hey, Abigail, that's a good idea," Beth says, and they both move to the living room.

Abigail sits in the armchair across from Lochran, and Beth half lays with one leg stretched down on the couch and the other foot still on the floor. For a few moments, the three sit in silence, hearing only the sounds of the occasional truck moving past, a backup beeper, or the horn of a ship in the harbor.

Lochran closes his eyes and says, "Princess, why build your house here when you can go anywhere?"

Beth flops her head sideways, looking in Lochran's direction.

"I didn't build it. But it grew on me and I stayed."

Both Abigail and Lochran open their eyes, look at Beth, and wait for her to continue. Beth concedes to their stares a few moments later and starts the story.

"When I was nine, I woke one night to this roaring sound of a jet engine, and from my bed, I looked out my window to see giant flames. Then an explosion, that knocks me unconscious, launches me out of the house and into the neighbor's backyard. I remember waking in the hospital yelling, 'Mom! Dad!' An entourage of doctors, nurses, and police rushed into my room, and after three days of check-ups, child psychologists, and Child Services, of course, they left me to rest. That's when the mist appeared at the end of my bed." Beth pauses.

"When the mist cleared, a hooded, blonde-haired woman stood smiling at me. I wasn't afraid of her. Not even when she walked to the side of the bed, sat on the edge, and took my hand. When she spoke, her voice was melodic and soothing, but she had a strange accent, and she said, 'LysaBeth, I have a gift you must never remove.' She pulled this necklace from inside her sleeve." Beth puts her hand over the amulet around her neck. "When I saw it for the first time, it looked like a glowing, yellow egg inside a netted cage of gold. She put it around my neck, and a surge of energy goes through my body, like an electric shock, and then it felt as though my troubles had disappeared." Beth pauses again. "Then she said to me,

'LysaBeth, if you focus and believe that you are invisible, you will walk past everyone outside the door. Then, I will show you to a safe place of your own where you will be free of foster parents and government interference.'" Beth looks at Abigail. "And that was the first time I made myself invisible."

Abigail smiles and nods her head.

"The woman led me here."

"But how did you survive, Princess?"

"Everything I needed was here, Lochran. Food, clothes, money, everything. I even had study books, same as a school gives you, and I had to complete the lessons, or I couldn't access the other fun things or food," Beth laughs. "I tested the theory once, and after three days of no food, I understood I needed to complete my lessons."

Abigail and Lochran both laugh with Beth.

"Anyhow, the hunt for a missing nine-year-old girl, wearing only pajamas and slippers, was underway thanks to every media outlet and public service in greater Boston. No one believed I slipped past the guards, the cameras, or the staff without being seen, so they called it an abduction. A press release from hospital management and the police focused on a well-executed abduction along with a sacrificial rookie officer being suspended for dereliction of duty. I felt awful for the young police officer."

Her mind slips back to the first night she saw Jack Sebastian, and wonders.

"But I've lived here for fifteen years with no disturbance until you graced my life, and now hell is breaking loose. Thanks, Lochran, you jerk."

Lochran sits up, makes a bow from his waist, saying, "At your command, Princess," and the three of them burst into laughter.

The laughter dies off, and they sit back in their chairs again. The room goes quiet.

"Abigail, I know many witches have long lives but, you said that you have been looking for me for more than a thousand years. How is it possible for you to live that long?"

"Yes, Princess, I have been searching for you since the wedding."

"Okay, wait. The whole princess thing has to go away. I get it. You believe I'm Princess Mehla, but if you call out anything other than Beth to get my attention, chances are I won't answer. Please. Call me Beth."

"She's right, lass. If we're going back to the warehouse, we need to know that we can talk to each other."

"Okay, slow down, Lochran. Abigail hasn't explained how you have lived for over a thousand years. Then you mentioned a wedding, and now it sounds as if Lochran wants to go back to the warehouse to see if he can get his ass kicked again."

Lochran sits up to respond to the ass-kicking comment when Abigail puts her hand out to silence him.

"Lochran and I live, but we have also died."

Lochran's face goes expressionless as Abigail reaches across to take his hand.

"We are souls returned to this world to fight for Prince O'Manus and Princess Sadreen, so their souls can reunite, and the most powerful child of magic can be born." Abigail takes a breath and squeezes Lochran's hand. "In the year nine-sixty-three, the prince and princess married in the ninth month, on the sixth day, at the third hour. It was the union of the two most powerful magic families known."

"Matching numbers? Nine-six-three. Nine-six-three."

"Yes," Abigail says. "Nine is the infinity number and added together, the year 963, or month, day and hour, still make nine. This is the only time the nines will align, and it is how the prophecy begins."

"Who doesn't love a prophecy?" Beth says, but thinks, *More crap to think about.*

Abigail cocks an eyebrow at Beth's sarcasm before continuing.

"Sorcha and her followers, the Blood Witches, attack the wedding and kill King Aed of Ireland and King Aodh of Scotland. Sorcha fatally wound Princess Sadreen, forcing the princess to cast her soul from her body. An Indian warrior wound Sorcha during the attack, and her second in command, Rebekah Kheel, drag her through a portal to safety, but she cast a killing curse at the princess soul before the portal close. The prince see his bride's soul in danger and he throw himself in front of the killing curse, but before the curse hit him, he cast his soul out. Sorcha did not know that both souls survive the attack and fly away to safety, but soon she find out and has been trying to kill either soul since. Lochran was part of King Aodh's guard that was slaughtered in the first moments of the battle, along with King Aed's guard."

"What? Hold on, Abigail. They killed Lochran? And now he's here over a thousand years later?"

ROYAL SOULS

"Cut down from behind by a coward," Lochran says, choking back the emotion as tears well in his eyes.

Are they playing with me? This doesn't sound possible.

"Hundreds died that day trying to protect the Royals," Abigail says.

Beth hears the emotion building in Abigail's voice as she continues.

"I died with many magic arrows through my chest, trying to protect Princess Mehla. Queen Sorcha get wounded, and the Blood Witches abandoned the attack, so the Staff of Souls capture all the souls of those who died fighting for the Royals."

"What's the Staff of Souls?"

"The Staff of Souls is powerful. The Witch of Loch Shin, the Faerie Queen, and Dumghill crafted it from the wood of life, precious metal, and glass, with a large gem in the middle that is made from the magic of the Universe. They made the Staff, back when the kings agreed to the marriage between Prince O'Manus and Princess Sadreen."

Why is it that none of my teachers told me about the Staff?

Beth throws herself back against the couch, grunting.

"Abigail, the prophecy, and all the things attached to it keep piling up. I'm having a hard time believing it."

Abigail smiles. "Give it time. You will understand. Remember, King Aed of Ireland is Princess Mehla's father, which mean through Princess Mehla, you already know this. Let the princess guide you. Connect with the princess inside you."

"What? Like meditation?" Beth says.

"See, you are already becoming her when you talk like that," Abigail says. "Don't be a brat."

My life used to be walking to the beach, training, hover board racing, and training. My toughest decision was sushi in Japan or pasta in Italy, but now it's turned into a royal cluster and I don't like it.

Beth gives a brief smile. "Okay, sorry, Abigail. I'm a little frustrated by everything."

Beth relaxes.

It feels like I'm sinking into the couch. My body is tingling all over.

"This feels good," she says and relaxes deeper as the tingling increases.

GLASS PRISON

Saturday, August 30th — 1200 Pacific Time — Canada

The howling north wind drives the falling snow near horizontal through the air, reducing the visibility to near nothing. Rebekah and Midas, dressed in heavy coats, stand on a barren ledge near the front door of the Canadian Rockies' Glazier prison, holding their wands pointed into the roaring wind. Their shields ward off the blowing snow and cutting wind, but they still felt the -35 degree Celsius temperature. They approach a solid stone wall, and a small man-door appears, casting a faint light, beckoning Rebekah and Midas to step out of the torrent of weather.

Inside the foyer, carved into the rock formation of the mountain, six guards with wands stand at the ready, and Rebekah recognizes the team leader, Thomas, from his voice and strong French accent.

But before she can speak, he demands, "You will surrender your wands before entering the prison."

Rebekah's temper flares, and she flips her hood back, intending to spew threats, but Thomas cuts her short.

"Pardon moi, *Madame* Rebekah. I was not told that you were arriving."

"Yes, Thomas. Short notice for everyone," Rebekah snaps.

She opens her full-length coat, and no one steps forward to take it, so she drops it to the floor and walks through the guards toward two enormous doors.

Thomas blocks Rebekah's advance by positioning himself between her and the closed double doors.

"Pardon moi, *Madame* Rebekah, but you must surrender your wand."

Thomas places his hand out with his palm up, as Rebekah had done to Midas earlier.

"How dare you?"

She looks back over her shoulder to see a guard holding Midas's wand and the remaining five guards pointing their wands at her.

"I am sorry, *Madame* Rebekah, but I must follow my orders."

"From who?" Rebekah snaps.

"The Queen, *Madame*."

Rebekah hesitates, then slaps her wand into Thomas's palm.

"Please, *Madame*, be careful. The Queen is very unhappy," Thomas whispers.

Jaw muscles flexing and brow furrowed, she locks eyes with Thomas, thinking, *That makes two of us.*

Rebekah focuses on the heavy wood double doors, with wrought iron bracing and hinges, across the foyer, remembering that Midas watches her every move.

This morning she gets upset because I call her Sorcha, and now I get treated like a common witch. Something's not right and I intend to find out what.

Rebekah, marching forward, fuming, as the doors open to Queen Sorcha's temporary throne room, slows her pace as Queen Sorcha turns her head.

Oh, hell. Sorcha's eyes are glowing black. She's executed someone. Calm yourself, Rebekah.

She bows her head. "My Queen."

"My Queen," repeats Midas, making a much larger bow from the waist, failing miserably to camouflage his fear.

Queen Sorcha rises from her throne and floats toward Midas, landing only inches from his bowed head. She reaches under his chin with two fingers and lifts his head until his eyes look into two black pools.

"Irritate me for one second, Midas, and I will take great pleasure in feeding you to the pyre wolves."

A slight smile creeps out as Rebekah sees the fear growing in Midas's eyes.

Queen Sorcha turns to Rebekah, flicking her fingers from the soft skin under Midas' chin, drawing blood with her nails. Midas stifles a sound of pain, fearing he might provoke the queen.

Rebekah smiles, saying, "I so *love* visits with you, My Queen."

The heavy emphasis on the word 'love' brings a cruel smile to Queen Sorcha's face, and her eyes fade to the usual gray color.

Relax. Sorcha's in a reasonable state of mind again. If that's possible.

Midas moves away from the two women with his hand under his chin and a wounded look in his eyes, and Rebekah fights to not burst into full laughter. Still, she watches him with anticipation, wishing that he might do something foolish so she can destroy him in the name of protecting the queen.

Damn, no wand, she remembers.

"To what do I owe the 'pleasure', My Queen?" says Rebekah.

"Well, Rebekah. When I asked for you, it was because I had secured a Crystal and the Prince Stone, and I wanted to hear your thoughts of our future."

"That's very gracious, My Queen."

"Yes, I know. But things have changed."

I don't like where this is going. "How so, My Queen?"

Queen Sorcha places her hand inside the hook of Rebekah's elbow and leads her closer to the throne.

Rebekah catches her breath as the gray, wrinkled remains of six witches, still in glowing shackles, come into full view.

They're deflated human balloons. Six souls at once. She's gone mad.

Queen Sorcha stops walking.

"Until last night, I *had* one Crystal and the Prince's Stone, which meant that *I* had stopped any opportunity for the prophecy to be fulfilled. Now, because of six incompetent witches." Sorcha turns to Rebekah and points over her shoulder with one finger. "We have neither the Crystal nor the Stone. One wizard, Lochran MacIlraight, eluded the guard and absconded with both. Do you remember Lochran MacIlraight?"

"Of course, my Queen."

"Of course. We never forget our first love or lover, do we?"

Rebekah says nothing, knowing not to be provoked when the queen is in this state.

"Find him. Use your resources, and if there are any sightings, tell the Horsemen so they can capture him, and I can eat his soul for stealing from me."

Rebekah makes a slight bow with her head, accepting the task, saying, "Yes, My Queen. My Queen, why am *I* not able to portal into the prison instead of having to dress like a polar bear?"

Queen Sorcha turns to respond, but another voice rings out in answer.

"Because I decide who comes and goes from my prison, *Mon Cherie.*"

Both Rebekah and Queen Sorcha turn to see the voice owner walking toward them from a doorway across the room.

Rebekah doesn't recognize him, but she feels a rush through her body.

Tall, maybe six-three, handsome, powerful face, confident walk, great physical features.

"Rebekah, our host, Francois Le Glazier," Queen Sorcha says.

"*Bonjour, ma belle.*" Francois reaches for Rebekah's hand, and Rebekah pulls away, locking her stony stare on Francois. "Don't... ever... touch me."

Francois takes a step back. "Ahh, *oui*. As you wish, *Belle.*"

You won't be so cocky if I claw the smirk off your incredibly handsome face, you little twerp.

Rebekah gives him a cat-fight smile.

I can't believe how much I want him.

Queen Sorcha steps between them.

"Rebekah. Could you go find that thief now?"

"Yes, My Queen." Rebekah doesn't take her eyes from Francois until she bows her head to Queen Sorcha and spins on her heel to leave, with Midas scurrying ahead of her.

Queen Sorcha looks at Francois as he watches Rebekah walk away, and he whispers, *"Elle este magnifique."* (She is magnificent)

"Don't even think about it. She'll kill you if I don't."

Queen Sorcha returns to her throne.

Francois gives Queen Sorcha a smirk and walks toward the door from where he entered. He pauses near the large doors to the foyer, where Rebekah stands, waiting for her coat.

"Excuse moi, Rebekah?" he says in a low tone.

Rebekah turns back to Francois, saying nothing.

"Might I tempt you with a tour of the dungeons?"

Rebekah catches his low tone and responds in kind. "Is that a pathetic effort to get me alone? I don't see the thrill of walking around in empty dungeons."

"Au contraire. We have many guests from many countries that need daily discipline." Francois delivers a perfect smile.

Rebekah saunters toward Francois, studying him.

His smile has my heart racing. "Are you lying to me?"

ROYAL SOULS

"*Cherie*, I know who you are and what you are capable of, so why lie to you?"

He is not lying, I can feel it, and I'm sweating. I haven't been so attracted to anyone since my teens.

As she gets closer, her walk becomes more relaxed.

"Yes. Relax, *Cherie*. On my tour, if you don't kill anyone, especially me, you can bring your wand for the… greatest satisfaction experience."

"If we play and you tear my heart out, I will skin you alive over the next five hundred years and then drop your bleeding, festered body into shark-infested waters."

Francois steps close enough to smell the faint scent of rosewater. "If we play, and you turn unfaithful or distrustful, you will spend the next five hundred years in the dungeons as my unhappy guest. Then I will kill you."

Rebekah's and Francois' eyes lock in silence until she says, "Let me get this prophecy thing laid to rest, and we should talk." Rebekah gives Francois a mischievous smile.

"It would be exciting to have a steady playmate, such as you, *Cherie*."

Rebekah can see the want in his eyes.

A kindred spirit, maybe. Interesting.

She turns toward the door again but stops as Francois whispers.

"*Cherie*, wait."

Rebekah looks at him, and he looks toward the throne.

Rebekah glances at the throne in time to see Caitriona appear through a portal.

"Well, well. Someone has privileges. Don't they, Francois?"

Francois steps closer to Rebekah and whispers, "*Oui*, but this is not my decision."

Rebekah turns her head back to Francois and scans his eyes. *I can feel his honesty.*

"Use caution, Rebekah. I would very much like to see you again."

Francois walks away, and Rebekah turns to the foyer with a quick glance back to the throne.

"They're cozy," Rebekah whispers.

Rebekah's mind rushes back to the early morning of August Twenty-ninth and her foolish comment about how Sorcha would be out of her mind to find the prince. Her survival instincts kick into overdrive.

If I'm no longer the favorite of the Queen, should I fear for my life?

Rebekah marches past Thomas, snatching her wand from his hand, and ignores the guard at the door, holding her coat. She steps into the harsh, minus thirty-five cold ripping wind and snow only long enough to cast a portal for herself, leaving Midas standing alone to watch her and the man-door disappear.

"You bitch!" Midas shouts and casts a portal back to the office.

***

Rebekah's portal opens outside a small shack in the Louisiana bayou, and as she steps out, her heels sink into the soft earth. She looks toward a quiet splash sound and sees a large tail flick.

"Hmm. I could use a bite to eat myself," she says.

She turns her head back to the shack as a small black man, clothed in tattered pants and shirt, emerges from the hidden side. He stops at the corner of the porch, keeping himself partly hidden.

"You know I don't like surprise visits, Rebekah."

The man is soft-spoken with a Louisiana accent.

"I'm sorry, Obadiah, but it was necessary."

He doesn't respond for a few seconds.

"What do you want?"

"I'm worried. I may be on the outs with Queen Sorcha."

"With what you know about her, that is very dangerous for you, Rebekah. What did you do?"

"The morning of the blue light, as I was recovering, I made a comment to myself that she may have heard, but I'm uncertain. The comment was not malicious, but I fear she may have taken it that way."

Obadiah steps away from the corner of the porch. "If you're not sure, then why do you think she no longer holds you her favorite?"

"She's showing favoritism to a younger witch named Caitriona."

"I know this witch. Sorcha's little spy."

Rebekah's heart rate jumps, but she holds her composure.

"How... How do you know her?"

"Sorcha captured a young witch under my protection, claiming that she tried to steal from her and sent Caitriona to find me. I met with her in the city, then I met with Sorcha, who tried to recruit me for her cause. I refused because Sorcha only wants the two-thousand witches I protect as meat for her killing machine."

"Obadiah, did you check yourself for one of Queen Sorcha's spy spiders?"

"I have not survived for over two-thousand years by being foolish, Rebekah." He stomps up the steps of the porch and into the small shack.

Rebekah pursues Obadiah and, as she passes through the door, she says, "Obadiah, I'm sorry. I didn't mean to offend you."

Obadiah spins back to Rebekah with a furrowed brow.

"Rebekah, I have never seen you like this. Calm yourself."

"What do you mean?"

"I know fear when I see it in someone's eyes and hear it in their voice."

Rebekah takes a long pause.

"Obadiah, you are the one witch on this planet that Sorcha will not challenge."

"Are you asking for protection, Rebekah?"

"I don't know, Obadiah." Rebekah sighs. "I have given everything to Sorcha, but as of late, she prefers other company, and she's using other people to do things she trusted only to me."

"What did you say that worries you?"

"The night of the blue light, I made the comment that she would be out of her mind to find the prince before September sixth. I only meant that she would drive everyone as hard as she could to find the carrier, and she is using every means on all the potentials, but so far Rhynan is the most promising. I meant nothing malicious."

"That's it? That's what you said?"

"Yes."

"Rebekah, you have taken this too far. There is nothing there to offend her."

Rebekah folds her arms across her chest, saying nothing for a few moments.

"Okay. Maybe you're right. I want this over. I guess everyone else does, too."

"Yes. We do, Rebekah."

"Alright. I have to go find someone."

"Who?"

Rebekah is silent for a few seconds.

"Lochran."

"Ouch."

"Yeah. The idiot stole from Sorcha, and now she wants to suck his soul out."

"What did he steal?"

"A Crystal and a Stone that Sorcha stole from the Guardians."

"One of the nine Crystals, and either the Prince or Princess Stone. Am I right?"

"What do you know?"

"I hear the Horsemen were after him in Boston, but they had an unfortunate meeting with a Spirit Witch who showed significant power, and... I hear the witch's charm captivated the lead horseman."

Rebekah taps her finger against her bottom lip as she paces.

"One Spirit Witch bested the six Horsemen?"

"You know of this?"

"No, Obadiah. Queen Sorcha didn't tell me about it."

"Maybe you have something to worry about."

"Maybe it's a test."

"You should go to the old waterfront district of Boston and find out."

"I should. Instead, I'm going to follow someone there."

"The lead horseman?"

"Oh, yeah." Rebekah gives Obadiah a devilish smile.

"Now that's the Rebekah I know." Obadiah gives a full crooked tooth smile.

"Thanks, Obadiah. Ta, Ta!"

Rebekah casts a portal and disappears.

PRINCESS MEHLA

Saturday, August 30th — 1800 Eastern Time — Boston

To Beth, it's like a movie plays in her mind.

She can see four adults sitting at a table, talking and laughing. As she approaches, one man says, "King Aed, we are very pleased that you and Queen Draya took this private meeting to discuss the future alliance between our two kingdoms."

King Aed nods. "Ireland feels the backlash of the problems you are battling in Scotland, King Aodh. It only makes sense it should unite us through marriage, and I propose to you we should hold no secrets, only to avoid stressing our agreement."

King Aodh is silent as though to measure King Aed, and then King Aodh moves his hand across the top of a nearby candle and lights the wick. "A leap of faith in our Irish allies, King Aed."

"Only a real ally exposes themselves," says King Aed, waving his hand over a candle and the wick lights.

It surprises King Aodh, who then bursts into laughter. "How long have you been able to control fire?"

King Aed sits back in his chair before starting the story of his dream.

"Six-years-old, I entered a cave and at the first turn, to my surprise, I see a light glowing where there should be dark. I was holding my wooden sword in the ready position, and when I turned the next corner, I saw a cloaked figure waving their hands over a table." King Aed makes sweeping hand motions back and forth, imitating the mysterious figure. "There was a flash from a bowl on the table, so I asked, 'Who are you?' A soft, womanly voice said, 'Welcome, Prince Aed.' The woman said she had come to me with a gift. She turned toward me, slipping the hood from her head, and her beauty struck me."

The king puts his hand over his heart, and everyone laughs.

"And what of me, Aed?" Queen Draya says.

"There are no words for what you did to my heart, my love," he says, taking Queen Draya's hand in his and raising it to his lips.

"I hope you are as quick with a sword as you are with your lies, Aed," she replies, and everyone laughs.

King Aed continues. "I remember lowering my wooden sword until I felt the tip touch the ground, and the words, 'You are lovely, my lady,' slipped past my lips."

"Ha, trying to manage a woman's heart at six," King Aodh barks in a praising tone, and everyone laughs.

Queen Isabelle chimes in, "Pay no attention to this one, King Aed. I know of the sordid affairs he had in his youth."

King Aodh's face goes serious. "Only to gain the skills needed to keep such a magnificent queen satisfied."

Queen Isabelle looks at Queen Draya. "The quickest sword in the kingdom," she says, and everyone laughs.

King Aed continues his story as the laughter slows.

"She told me I was kind because I complimented her, and when she bowed her head, the colored candlelight shimmered off her blond-white hair like Sun off the water. She lifted her head, and her eyes glowed like blue pools of light. But I still had no fear of this woman. Then, she asked me if I would accept a gift, and I asked, 'What is this gift?' She told me that her gift allowed me to control fire and air and protect me from my enemies, but I must never use it for personal gain. So, I asked, 'When should I use the gift?' She said I should only use it to protect the people from our enemies. Then she said, 'If I could keep the gift a secret from non-magical people, I could become a great king in the realm of magic and my children powerful with magic.' I held out my hand to receive the gift, and I woke in my bed with a bump on my head."

"I thought it a dream until I turned nine and made a fire in front of my father and mother. They demanded I keep my abilities hidden for fear of an uprising. But unknown to them, I would sneak away and practice in secret until one day when Draya saw me practicing and approached me. I panicked until she showed me she could control water and earth and make potions from herbs."

King Aodh reaches across to Queen Isabelle, taking her hand, and then looks at King Aed. "Isabelle and I had a similar dream at the same age. My first fire, at nine, was not in front of my father and mother but my best friend, who kept my secret."

King Aed nods. "A loyal friend, indeed."

"I met Isabelle one night when I found myself separated from my father's army. The raining weather blew in fast, forcing me to seek shelter and use my magic to start a fire," King Aodh says. "Isabelle, hidden behind some rocks, had been gathering herbs and saw me make fire by waving my hand. She realized the sudden change in the weather had caught her, and knowing the area well, she knew I was in the only cave for miles. When Isabelle approached the cave, she drew back her hood, and I was so stunned by her beauty that I forgot everything around me."

King Aodh smiles and winks at Queen Isabelle. "It felt an eternity before Isabelle asked if she could share my fire. Then, I apologized for my manners and declared that my mother and father might have beaten me for being so rude to a lady."

Everyone laughs.

"In the cave, Isabelle said she saw me make fire with the wave of my hand. I did not know what to do. My secret was out, and I feared everyone else finding out. Not even my mother and father knew of my magic because I feared being locked in the dungeon or, worse, losing my head. I put my hand on my sword as though I was going to strike Isabelle, and fearing my intentions, she made a flicking motion with her hand. A small stone struck me above my eye." He points to the scar. "It knocked me backward, and when I recovered my balance, to my surprise, Isabelle stood with both palms facing up and two large stones floating in the air. She yelled at me not to move or she would crush me with the stones," King Aed laughs as he clinches his fist, praising her anger.

"I took my hand from my sword and raised my palms to my waist with an upward pushing motion, and both my palms burst into flames. I looked Isabelle in the eyes and told her if she missed me, I could burn her alive."

King Aodh, sounding ashamed, looks at Queen Isabelle. "Tears rolled over her cheeks, and I realized the thought of harming someone with her magic, or worse, being burned alive, was causing her great anguish. I closed my hands, extinguishing the flames, and I stood looking at Isabelle until, in a calm voice, I asked if I might know her name. She answered with a shaky voice, and then I apologized for acting a coward."

King Aed and Queen Draya give a quick nod of approval and smile.

King Aodh places his hand on top of Queen Isabelle's.

"My first reaction was an act of fear. I should have never made such a cowardly threat to a lady, and I asked her forgiveness."

Queen Isabelle smiles at King Aodh and places her other hand on his, giving it a squeeze.

Listening to King Aodh tell his story, King Aed and Queen Draya both realize their daughter will marry into a family that understands love and kindness.

King Aodh takes his hand from Queen Isabelle's and sits back in his chair. He smiles at the Irish Royals, who are beaming with happiness from the story and the king's outward display of affection for his Queen.

"I explained to Isabelle that my magic is secret, and I feared incarceration if anyone were to find out. I suggested I should have taken the time to explain and asked that she not reveal my secret... or drop the large stones on me."

"Queen Isabelle, were you holding those stones in the air the entire time?" Queen Draya asks.

"Yes."

"You are powerful."

King Aodh explains they talked most of the night, and he realized how powerful Isabelle was at fourteen. When he woke in the morning, to the callings of his father's guard, Isabelle had left, and he didn't see her again for two years when their parents announced their arranged marriage.

Queen Isabelle adds, "When I went back to my village, I told my father, the Chief, that I had met Prince Aodh, and he had seen to my well-being during the night. I told my mother how honorable the prince had acted and that he would make a great king and husband. Of course, I was right."

The queens laugh, and the kings shake hands, signifying a pact and arranged marriage.

The laughter stops, and the four turn to look in Beth's direction, but past her.

Beth turns her head to see two cloaked figures standing in front of an open field and a Staff with a large gem in the middle floating between them. The tall blonde figure reaches both her hands out toward Beth while the shorter, three feet high, holds a small vial, shining of a blue liquid, and has a wooden barrel sitting beside her.

Beth looks back at the four Royals in time for them to disappear from her dream as if they're melting, and she turns toward the cloaked figures. As Beth approaches, the tall woman slips her hood from her head, and Beth feels as though she recognizes her.

"Do I know you?"

"Yes. Since you were nine," the woman says. "I gave you that." She points to Beth's amulet.

"Are you the one who comes to me in my dreams to talk and teach me?"

"Yes, and I led you to safety and your home."

"You were the one leaving me food and supplies, and you built my home. You're Freya, the Witch of Loch Shin."

"Calm yourself, LysaBeth," Freya says. "You are right. The reason you don't remember me is that you are walking in Mehla's dream, not yours." She offers her hands to Beth, saying, "LysaBeth, you are safe here."

Beth hasn't heard her full name since her mother called her for dinner on the night of the house fire. She knows to trust this woman, so she reaches for her hands, and as she takes hold, a mild electric shock jumps between them. Beth draws a deep breath, then closes her eyes. Freya lets a whisper of mist from her mouth, and it floats across to Beth, slipping between her open lips. Beth stiffens, arches her back for a few moments, then relaxes and opens her eyes.

"What happened? I feel fantastic."

"Princess Mehla's soul has hindered your magic from within," Freya says. "I have broken the chain that was holding you back from your full potential. LysaBeth, you are the key." The seriousness of Freya's tone spikes Beth's heart rate, then Freya lets go of Beth's hands and, stepping back, she places her hood on her head.

"LysaBeth, remember," Freya says. "You cannot fight the Glazier alone."

"I'll be careful," Beth says, but the seriousness of Freya's tone chills her.

The witch gives Beth a slight smile, and breaking eye contact with her, Beth turns her head to the shorter person. The person lifts their arm, and her cloak slides back, revealing a deformed hand with crooked fingers holding a vial containing something blue.

"Drink this, Child."

"What is it?"

"Are you still scared of me, Child?"

"I recognize your voice. You came to me in my nightmares, teaching me how to control them and how to walk in my dreams. No, I'm not scared, but I am curious."

The woman reaches her disfigured hands up to her hood and slips it back.

Beth doesn't flinch.

Misshaped skull, patchy hair, enlarged forehead, bulged eyes, bent nose, thin lips, crooked teeth, wrinkled skin with warts.

Beth handles the visual of birth disfigurement like a seasoned medical professional as she crouches on one knee.

"I'm sorry this happened to you. It must have been challenging."

"Oh, this is nothing," she laughs. "You should see my husband. Now he's an ugly Faerie."

Both the woman and Freya laugh, and it brings a gentle smile to Beth's lips.

"So, you're a Faerie?"

"Not any Faerie, LysaBeth. I am Egret, the Faerie Queen."

"I'm sorry if I offended you. It wasn't my intention."

Egret giggles and waves her hand.

"I'm playing, Child."

Both Freya and Egret think it was funny, so Beth smiles.

"How did you become the Faerie Queen?" Beth says after a pause.

"I was born a disfigured child in southern Ireland near Cork," Egret starts. "The holy man and the Chief banished me and my parents, Gareth and Anne, from our village because they thought I had a disease or was evil. My parents went north, but the story of an 'evil spawned' baby ran ahead of us, and every village demanded to see new babies before allowing them to stay. Village Chiefs saw me and drove us away, so my parents went to Scotland, hoping to outrun the untrue, diseased, evil child story that plagued us."

Beth snickers at the pun.

"When we reached the shore near where Belfast sits today, no one would take us across until a fisher took pity on me. He sailed us across from Ireland to Scotland and suggested that we could be safe if we went to the Isle of Skye. My father tried to pay the man for helping us, but he refused, even though he had fallen on hard times with fishing. I remember holding my hand up toward the man, and his hand, with dried, cracked flesh and twisted fingers from hard work, covered mine. I was the only one that saw the images of gold coins and jumping fish

101

glow inside his hand, and later his purse was full, and he flourished as a fisher again."

"Karma," Beth says.

"Or magic prophecy?" Egret says, raising her brow and letting Beth contemplate.

"When we finally neared the boat crossing to the Isle of Skye, my father made camp for the night in the woods. We met another family, Donnell and Caitlin from the Orkney Islands, with a disfigured male child, Dumghill. Our fathers agreed to travel together but, reaching the boat crossing, they couldn't find a captain willing to take Dumghill and me on board. Again, a desperate local fisher agreed to make the journey. When our families reached the shores of Skye, our fathers paid the fisher twice his price for telling no one where we landed, and he agreed. My father bought a horse and cart filled with straw from a farmer to carry us, and we journeyed to the Cuillin Mountains."

"Donnell, Dumghill's father, had lived in the foothills for eight years as a boy before being abducted by Vikings and taken to the Orkney Islands, sold as slave labor, then freed by King Aodh five years later when they defeated the Norse. When they reached the bottom of the mountains, they found pools of blue water and plenty of wild game to hunt, so they made a camp and shelters. Early one morning, my mother startled awake to find me missing, so she woke everyone else only to find Dumghill also missing, and a panicked search began."

"I can't imagine the fear going through your parents," Beth says.

Egret nods, continuing, "After a short time of searching, my mother notices a gentle glow of blue light at the bottom of a waterfall with stairs cut into the rock. Dumghill's father led the way down the stairs to the base of the waterfall. They crossed behind the curtain of water to the side where the blue light glowed, and it shocked our parents when they entered the cave. They found Dumghill and me, at five months old, grown to a height of three feet overnight."

"What? How?"

"And we spoke full Gaelic while talking about the drawings on the cave's walls."

"Holy crap!"

"Our mothers called to us, and to this day, I remember the joyful tears in their eyes as we ran into their arms."

"That's awesome, Egret," Beth says, as Egret's eyes brighten and glass over and Beth's memory flashes how it felt when her mother hugged her.

Egret forces a soft smile before continuing. "Dumghill and I told our parents of the ghostly mist that carried us into the cave, and a voice that we understood told us we were gifted and offered each of us a gold chalice of blue water. We drank, and it changed us into adults, and our magical powers grew while the voice explained the drawings on the walls and our importance in a prophecy. I told our parents how the drawings depict the magical birth and rising of the most powerful witch born of royalty. Then, I explained how the drawings depicted a great battle for control of the hidden world of magic that rages until the murdered royal couple's souls reunite. I showed them how the seed of the couple's child, meant for their wedding night, rises to the sky when the reunited couple kiss and seeks a pregnant woman from the princess's lineage. Then Dumghill walked to a wall drawing of a full-grown witch, reached into a hole at her feet, pulled out a wand made of grass, twigs, herbs, and colored ribbons, and told how the voice had instructed him in the art of wand making. The voice said, 'I was to be the Faerie Queen, over the Faerie Pools and the Faerie Glen, and Dumghill is my mate, and maker of wands and magical artifacts'."

Egret sighs, saying, "We could see the disbelief on our parents' faces, so we hugged them, for the last time, and stepping back, I waved my hand over my head, and the cave came to life with light, fruit trees, vegetable gardens, and a cask of wine. Then Dumghill waved his arm above his head, and fire without wood lit in the middle of the cave, drying the air and filling it with warmth, and beds of straw with sheepskins appeared."

"Our parents knew we no longer needed their protection or help to survive, so we thanked them for their sacrifice and love, joined hands and disappeared, but didn't leave. We stayed in the cave, hidden behind the Veil separating magic and the non-magic world, and watched our fathers console our mothers. We laughed when our fathers noticed the two piles of gold coins appear on a ledge, along with the two gold chalices that held the blue liquid we drank. Dumghill had spelled the gold coins to replenish until they were no longer needed, but when our fathers placed their hands over them, the light in the cave went dim, and the fire grew smaller. We laughed harder as they tried different ways to take the coins and Chalices without losing the fire and light, but soon they realized the choice we had given them. Live in the cave, on the Isle of Skye, or use the gold elsewhere."

"LysaBeth, we listened and laughed with them as they ate and drank wine that night, discussing the choice laid in front of them, and then they slept on the straw beds covered with sheep skins until morning. They said many beautiful and loving things about us. Heartfelt words."

"In the morning, our parents left the cave with their gold, and when they reached the bottom of the steps, we made the cave disappear. Our mothers wept with the finality of their decision, but they climbed the stairs, then stood there looking at the waterfall. The stairs faded, and we said goodbye as our parents turned away to start their journey to a new life."

Beth feels a tear roll over her cheek before saying, "Egret, that's beautiful."

"Like our children."

"You and Dumghill have children?"

Egret waves her hand, showing a beautiful Faerie with long white hair, features like a master-crafted porcelain doll, semi-transparent wings shimmering with light, and holding a bow.

"Egret, she's beautiful. Is that your daughter?"

"Yes. That is our first daughter, Seraphina. Protector of the Woodlands. We have not seen her for years because she hides from Queen Sorcha and her filth."

Beth is silent, thinking of her parents, then asks, "Egret, did you see your parents again?"

"We were told to stay away from them, but we gave them dreams of us doing well. We also watched our brothers and sisters, from behind the Veil, and occasionally," Egret snickers, "we could influence events in their favor."

"Brothers and sisters. Egret, that's great."

Egret's smile disappears. "Until we watched our parents, their children and grandchildren pass away. We out-lived our bloodlines, so we stopped watching them and tended to our own and the war."

The flattening of Egret's voice keeps Beth from saying anything more about Egret's family, and Egret places her hood back on her head before holding the vial out again.

"LysaBeth, in here is one drop of Faerie Water in pure water from the Faerie Pools. This vial of water will strengthen your body and your bond with Princess Mehla's soul, allowing you to use her power. You need to drink this to succeed."

"That sounds serious."

"Drink, Child. We will talk more."

Beth takes the vial, removes the stopper, tilts her head back to pour the contents into her mouth, and swallows.

"Wow, that was…. Hey, what's happening? My skin. It's burning. What did you do to me?"

Beth grabs her head with both hands.

"Ahh, my head! It's going to explode!"

Moments later, it stops.

Beth opens her eyes.

"Ouch. I'm glad I was kneeling. What the heck happened?"

Beth switches her gaze between the two women, and they smile, satisfied.

"LysaBeth." Beth looks at Egret, and she says, "This barrel holds the Faerie Water and Faerie Pool water you will need for the battle, and it will hide in your favorite place. Only give one drop of Faerie Water to anyone, no matter the circumstances."

Beth takes a quick glance at the barrel, and both women disappear.

"Hey, come back," Beth says, standing up, looking around at the empty field. She looks back to the barrel. It's gone.

***

Beth feels the punch of an explosion, like the one when she was nine, and sudden stabbing pain in her right leg, and she cries out, echoing the sound of a woman behind her. Turning, she sees a woman with a small stick in her right leg.

Multiple cracks of wand magic pull Beth's attention away from the woman. Beth glances over at the once empty field. A body flies backward from being struck with a curse as four wizards wearing blue and white capes cast curses and run forward. Then, another dressed in gray casts a fire curse at a witch who screams as she bursts into flames. A wooden cart, between a group of witches in gray and another group with green and white cloaks, explodes, and the wooden shrapnel tears through the green and white cloaks.

Beth looks to her right again and the injured young woman, now hiding behind a boulder, has four Wand Witches bearing down on her. Abigail shoots out from behind a rock and her jaws lock around the skull of an attacking witch and the others scramble. To Beth's left, the two kings and queens from earlier fight off an attack together. Then Beth sees Lochran, wand in hand, running to the aid of the four Royals until a magic arrow shoots out the middle of his chest, and he hits the ground hard.

"This must be the wedding battle that Abigail was talking about earlier," Beth says. "The young woman behind me must be Princess Mehla because I felt her pain."

Movement at the corner of a big rock catches Beth's eye.

"Is that the coward that killed Lochran?"

Beth points her glowing palm at the big rock and focuses on flipping it. As the boulder flips onto the cowardly assassin, she hears Mehla grunt.

She turns and looks at Mehla, asking, "Did I do that, or did she?"

Beth hears a female voice call out to Mehla and Beth looks up from Mehla to see a woman carrying a half-body protection shield running toward Mehla.

"Long, red curly hair, a flowing dress, and a tiara with an emerald jewel hanging against her forehead, like Mehla's. That must be the bride, Princess Sadreen," Beth says.

Beth feels Mehla's heart rate climb as she jumps up from behind her protection and points at the trees to the right of Princess Sadreen. A woman dressed in black casts a curse at Princess Sadreen, hitting her magic shield, and Princess Sadreen flails backward, letting out a scream and slamming into a rock.

Beth sees a man with a royal purple cloak and a crown running to Princess Sadreen and says, "That must be Prince O'Manus."

To her left, Beth sees the remaining three of the four witches that were attacking Princess Mehla recover after Abigail's attack and they move forward, cautious as Abigail's cat form slips behind a boulder.

A short distance from Princess Mehla, Abigail changes to human form, saying, "Mehla, you're hurt."

Mehla, still focused on her sister, Sadreen, says, "It is minor."

From the corner of her eye, Abigail sees the three witches drawing their arms back and shouts, "Mehla, look out!"

Abigail dives across the front of Mehla, blocking magical arrows cast by the attacking three witches.

"Ahh..." Beth cries.

She grabs her abdomen and doubles over in pain. One arrow has pierced both Abigail and Mehla, and as Abigail's flying body continues past Mehla, the arrow, through both, pulls sideways and rips its way out of Mehla's abdomen, leaving a gaping wound. The pain drops Beth to her knees, and she cries out, echoing Mehla again. Abigail hits the ground, and two wooden sticks shoot into the throats of two of the attacking witches. Seeing her friends drop, the third witch stumbles in shock, and then a flash of light burns its way through her chest. She falls to the ground where her downed friends wait for her, and the last thing she sees is Princess Mehla grinning in victory.

Mehla looks back to her sister in time to see Prince O'Manus throwing his body in front of a curse, and the souls of the prince and princess fly away.

"I will see you again, Sadreen," Mehla whispers as she clutches at her stomach, staggers, and falls to her knees next to Abigail.

Mehla lifts Abigail's head. "Abigail, thank you."

"Princess, save yourself now, and I will find you. Remember, always wear the amulet."

Mehla sets Abigail's head on the ground. She looks around, seeing her father, King Aed, lying dead near King Aodh and her mother, Queen Draya, sheltered behind a shield of ice with Queen Isabelle. To her right, the mystical Samurai and Indian warriors have appeared in great numbers, and the Blood Witches are retreating.

Beth feels Mehla getting weak from blood loss, and Mehla closes her eyes, drawing the last of her strength to the center of her body. Mehla's body collapses toward Abigail's, and an orb of pure white light rises from Mehla's solar plexus before her body hits the ground beside Abigail. The Orb floats sideways, hovers in front of Beth, and then shoots away.

Abigail smiles, then her eyes go empty.

***

Beth snaps upright and covers her eyes because the sunlight, through her living room window, hits her in the face.

Disoriented, Beth asks, "Wow. Did I fall asleep?"

"You were glowing as bright as a night fly, wee lass. I couldn't believe my eyes."

ROYAL SOULS

"Your entire body glowed with green light, and you were floating. You connected with Princess Mehla, didn't you?"

"Yes, Abigail. I sure did."

Beth takes her hands away from her face to look at Abigail and Lochran, and they stop moving. Beth can tell from the sudden change in their excitement that something's wrong, but she ignores it and jumps up from the couch, sprinting to Lochran. She throws her arms around his neck and hugs him as though he's a long-lost brother found.

"Lochran, I saw you die trying to help the Royals, and I want you to know that Mehla dropped a giant rock on the coward who killed you."

"Aye, she was always good to me," he says, hugging Beth back. "Thank you, lass."

Beth and Lochran separate, and she can see the emotion as Lochran tries to smile through the tears welling in his eyes.

Beth turns and shouts, "Abigail, you are unbelievable! The way you threw your body across Mehla's, stopping those arrows, hitting the ground wounded, and you still stopped two witches and set the third one up for Mehla."

Beth takes a deep breath before saying, "Abigail, that was amazing."

Abigail walks to Beth and puts her arms around her neck.

"And I will do it again to protect Mehla from harm."

Beth and Abigail step away from each other, smiling.

"Hey, do either of you drink Scotch whiskey?" Beth asks.

111

Abigail and Lochran smile.

Beth turns to a small cabinet in the kitchen and returns with three glasses and a bottle of Scotch. She pours a drink for each of them.

Lochran waves the glass under his nose, giving a big smile, saying, "Now, you are a princess."

They laugh as they reach forward with their glasses, clinking them together, and Lochran says, "*Slainte mhath*."

They sit at the island, and Beth tells them about her dream, while Abigail and Lochran name people she describes, then describe what they saw happening to Beth. The conversation slows, and Beth thinks of the out-of-body experience with Mehla and her meeting with the Witch of Loch Shin.

"Freya, the Witch of Loch Shin, is from Norway. Right?"

"Aye, she is," Lochran replies.

"Egret told me her story, but how did Freya get to Scotland?"

"Legend goes, she's a Seer from a Viking village in Norway and ran away to Scotland to escape death," Lochran starts. "She was nine when she dreamed an assassin would sneak into the village and the Chief's hut on the full moon. In secret, she warned the Chief, and he set a trap to capture the assassin. Using torture, he discovered it was his brother who hired the assassin so he could take the Chief's place. His brother didn't know of the trap and, seeing his plans thwarted as he watched the assassin from a distance, he escaped the village before the Chief discovered the treachery. The Chief sentenced his brother to death and put a bounty on his head."

"The Chief confided in Freya many times in the future, and his wife became jealous of the attention he was giving Freya and her family so the wife planned to rid the village of Freya. Freya saw this in a dream and sent her family away but assassins caught them, and fearing for her life, she ran. Her gifts helped her to elude the assassins until a voice instructed her to go to a hidden cave at Loch Shin in Scotland."

"The voice led her to a trustworthy boatman, who ferried her from Norway to the Orkney Islands, and then guided her to a blind old man. The old man gave her a staff of wood, carved with runes, and told her to protect the Staff with her life as she needed it at the end of her journey. He gave her money and the name of a boatman, to take her to Scotland, then ordered his apprentice to escort her to the boat. As they rode away with the old man's horse and cart, his hut caught fire, but the apprentice never turned to look."

"Freya reached Scotland as a storm moved in, so she took refuge at an inn, but she could sense she was in danger from the sailors stranded by the storm."

"Lochran, that's brutal. She was only... TEN... ELEVEN?"

"Aye, but the voice came to her as she ate hot food and directed her to a farm where an old woman gave her refuge and supplies."

"Freya left the farm early in the morning, and for five days, magical signs guided her through rough terrain, avoiding any unwanted encounters on the traveled paths. On the fifth day, strength near gone, the Staff pulled her arm toward the jagged rock at the mountain base, where a blue light seeped out through a crack into the dark cover of night. She mustered the last of her strength, then the rain fell heavy, except on her and on a path she hadn't noticed before. She climbed through rock and shrub, one-hundred feet, to the blue light, but saw no way to reach it. Exhausted, Freya collapsed to her knees, and the end of the Staff struck the mountain, and a cave appeared. Near collapse, she pulled herself to her feet and staggered into the cave, and the voice told her to drink the blue water from the chalice."

"Laying on a straw bed and covered in sheepskins, Freya woke. A fire that had no wood or smoke warmed the cave, trees of fruit flourished, vegetables grew in fertile soil, and smoked fish lay on a rack."

"The walls, painted with pictures, told a story of a royal baby born in the cradle of war and guarded by a burning wolf. The drawings depicted the baby will grow to be the most powerful witch born. Then Freya noticed one drawing, separate from the rest, that showed an old woman holding the glowing hand of a young girl. Asking what it meant, the voice only said, 'In time.'"

"Many scrolls of parchment stacked in the cave's corner showed her how to practice magic, to manipulate the elements of water, air, earth, and fire. Freya learned the secrets of herbs and how to conjure, so she could trick the mind. She learned of secret caves around the world that allowed her to travel undetected while learning the magic of other countries. She learned that many seek the power of the caves to rule with force over lands and people, and she understood greed."

"Freya dedicated herself to magic, and she didn't notice time passing by until the day she was in a cave in Ireland. It shouldn't have happened, but a young girl wandered in while Freya performed magic. It was young Princess Sadreen and, smiling at Freya, she asked if Freya could teach her to do magic. Freya took Sadreen's hand and saw how the years were slipping by, then Sadreen's hand began glowing inside hers."

"Freya thought of the drawings in her cave at Loch Shin and remembered the one drawing depicting an older woman holding a child's glowing hand. She knew this child was part of the prophecy, so Freya agreed to tutor Sadreen."

"Wow, that's so cool, Lochran."

"Now Mehla will help you prepare for the last battle," Abigail says.

"Well... I hope I'm up for the task."

Beth takes a sip of her drink and says, "Did Freya's staff become the Staff of Souls?"

"Aye, much later."

"You say the Staff collected the souls of the dead at the wedding. How did the Staff know which souls to take?"

Abigail doesn't respond right away. "Beth, what is the same with Lochran and me?"

"You both have blue eyes?" Beth says and shrugs her shoulders.

"You need to look in the mirror."

Beth, feeling anxiety build, keeps her eyes locked on Abigail as she sets her drink on the island top. She lifts herself from her chair, hesitates, then runs to the bathroom.

"What the what! How the hell did this happen?"

Lochran and Abigail laugh when Beth stomps back to the dining island and stops at the end.

Placing a fist on her hip and pointing the finger at her now blue eyes, she says, "This isn't happening."

Through the laughter, Abigail makes a playful swat at Beth, saying, "Let me tell you." She gets her laughter under control before saying, "Before the wedding, every Scottish and Irish sworn protector of the Royals drinks one drop of Faerie Water mixed with pure Faerie Pool water. This marks their souls forever and turns their eyes bright blue."

Abigail laughs saying, "Same as yours." Abigail and Lochran burst into laughter as Beth puts a 'Not impressed' look on her face, so Abigail forces herself to stop laughing and says, "But remember. Anymore than one drop of Faerie Water, and you could die or turn into a Faerie."

That's why Egret said, 'Only one drop'.

"Oh… crap," Beth says. "I had a drink of blue water in the vision, and now I'm a blue-eyed defender of the Royals. Great…. Not."

She reaches for her drink and takes it in a single gulp.

Leaning forward on the counter, Beth hangs her head. "You know. Before the last three days, if anyone had mentioned Faerie Water, I might have dropped them in the ocean." Then Beth pops up her head. "Hey, wait. Colored contacts. Problem solved." and they laugh.

The laughter settles, and Beth looks at Abigail, asking, "So, any witch, with bright blue eyes like 'ours' is a good guy? Right?"

ROYAL SOULS

"Yes. When Sorcha make a Blood Witch, she put a drop of her blood on their tongue, and it turn their eye gray and mark their soul, so she can find them. Putting her blood on a person's tongue marked by Faerie Water will only dull the blue eyes. But, if she does it many times to the blue-eyed witch, it turns the eyes gray, or it kills them."

Furrowing her brow, Beth thinks about the other black-haired, blue-eyed handsome man she met on the same day she rescued Lochran.

He still had bright blue eyes, but he worked for Sorcha.

"What bothers you, lass?"

Beth snaps back to reality. "Yeah, I'm good. I was thinking. The leader of the Horsemen. His eyes are as blue as yours and his hair is as black. Why is he working for Sorcha?"

"What are you on about, lass? I no remember any man with blue eyes and this color of black hair is only in our lands. The only men chasing me were Galen and his four Blood Witch cutthroats."

"No. When I put myself between you and the *six*, not five, men, the leader was a handsome blue-eyed man on a wolf-faced steed. You must have hit your head hard before I got there."

"A wolf-faced steed? This sounds familiar. Did you ask his name, lass?"

"No, but he asked mine," Beth says with a chipper smile.

"Well, you can ask him tonight if he's there," Lochran says as he reaches for the bottle of Scotch.

117

Abigail stops Lochran's hand short of the bottle. "If there is trouble, lover, you need a clear head."

"Tonight? Says who? And why will there be any trouble? Where are we going?" Beth asks.

"To the warehouse, lass," says Lochran with a half-smile.

"Wait, what? You were serious? Why are we going back there?"

Lochran leans forward like he's about to tell a secret. "The Crystal and the Stone," he says and sits back in his chair with a boyish grin.

BAD MEMORIES

Sunday, August 31ˢᵗ — 0830 Pacific Time — Canada

The middle of the black portal in the corner of Rebekah's office bulges out as Queen Sorcha's body pushes through the swirling surface.

"Rebekah. I am told that we have seen the Witch of Loch Shin and the Faerie Queen, and the other night a Spirit Witch protected Lochran and defeated the six Horsemen. Perhaps someone has found the prince or thinks they know who the carrier is?"

Rebekah holds her composer, not letting on that she knows this already because of Obadiah.

"My Queen. How's that possible? You are the only one powerful enough to defeat the Horsemen. Who told you this, My Queen? I will find the truth."

"Calm, Rebekah. Calm yourself. I trust the information."

Rebekah takes a deep breath.

"Much better, my lovely," Queen Sorcha says, placing her hand against Rebekah's cheek before returning to her walk around the office. "The young witch who fought with the Horsemen used white light magic to toss one of them over thirty feet, smashing him into a steel container and rendering him unconscious. She then destroyed a curse, cast at her, relieved the wizard of his wand, and made him disappear into the night sky. When Karse demanded the return of his missing rider, she pulled the rider out of the fog and he landed at the feet of Karse's mount. She kept the rider's wand as a souvenir."

Queen Sorcha stops walking to look at Rebekah.

"A true Natural Witch, who we don't know. A threat, maybe?" Rebekah says in a contemplative tone.

Rebekah looks at Midas as he joins the meeting.

"My Queen," Midas says. "We only knew one witch with such power, and we found her dead body after the wedding attack."

"There were three witches that had the power to control such magic, and you let them get away by attacking too soon," Queen Sorcha growls.

Midas feels nauseous as Queen Sorcha pushes her palm of glowing gray light toward him, like she's setting her grip on a glass jar. He feels the tightness in his lungs, his breathing becomes choppy, and his heart slows. The burning sensation in his chest tells him her death grip is tearing the life out of him. He falls to the carpeted concrete floor as Queen Sorcha releases her grip on his life and she bends toward him.

"Know this, you Cassubian worm. If you weren't as strong a warlock as you are, I would destroy you now. But, because you're stronger than most of the Guardians, you will do as I say, or you will be dog meat. Do you understand me?"

Midas doesn't know why he's happy the Queen's spell for blacking out the office prevents any sound from escaping the room, other than no one else can hear her shouting at him.

He nods his head and groans, saying, "Yes, My Queen."

The image of Rebekah frowning at his failed destruction fades as he passes out.

Queen Sorcha stands to her full height, takes a long breath, and turns to Rebekah.

"Rebekah, darling."

The Queen's call escapes Rebekah because of her fixation on Midas.

"Rebekah!"

Rebekah's focus snaps, saying, "My Queen."

"Darling. We still need to know if Princess Mehla's soul survived and if she has returned to help her sister. Do you know yet if Rhynan Doon is the carrier?"

"I've seen no sign of the prince, but this morning he said he was having a hard time sleeping, so I've offered a young woman to ease his mind."

"Excellent, Rebekah. He is the most promising of all the candidates, and someone beside him could see signs of the prince. Is this young woman someone you trust?"

"I'm not confident that I can trust her, and if she were to fail, killing her might be tricky."

"Rebekah. A spy in his bed would be the most opportune. We have searched for more than a thousand years for the prince's soul, and I am tired of stealing life from young witches. I want to be whole again."

"Yes, My Queen."

Queen Sorcha turns, casts a portal in the corner, and disappears with a slight crackle as she walks through it.

Rebekah looks down as Midas stirs and she kicks his foot, saying, "Get out of my office, you drooling worm."

Midas pulls himself from the floor and, stumbling on weak legs, he pushes through the door connecting his office to Rebekah's. She reaches behind her back, pulls her wand out, and with a quick flick, locks the door.

She sits in her office chair, contemplating, and her mind drifts back to her childhood in Scotland.

I knew Prince O'Manus as a young boy.

The story of the events leading to her meeting Prince O'Manus rushes through her mind.

His father, King Aodh, along with the king's guard, killed a Viking raiding party, and when the sounds of the battle faded, they heard the crying of a child. It came from behind the blacksmith's hearth, where the blacksmith sat, holding his raped and murdered wife and eldest son. His other son lay unconscious with a cracked skull, and his one-year-old daughter stood by her father, crying.

Before the king arrived, the Vikings had cut the blacksmith's fingers from the dominant hand, so the king kneels beside the blacksmith and sealed the bleeding fingers with his power of fire. Placing his hand on the little girl's head to comfort her, the king, taking it away, saw a small circle glowing in his palm and knew the little girl had magic in her. The King ordered the family taken back to Brae's Garden, where he gave Paulrig Kheel land to farm and animals to care for. Now, he could help his impaired son, Rhynan, and his daughter, Rebekah, grow to adults.

ROYAL SOULS

Rebekah snaps back from her trip through memory lane, and after a few moments of silence, she wonders. "If it's not Mehla, could it be Angus or Lauranna?"

Then Rhynan walks by with a file folder, and she watches him as he files the documents.

"Rhynan, Rhynan, Rhynan," she mumbles. "Is the prince hiding inside you thinking no one will suspect he is there because you're mentally diminished, like my big brother? I did him a favor when I put him out of his misery. If I have to keep cleaning up your messes, you might as well be my big brother... or do you want to be my house pet? That's it. I could think of you as one of those tiny dogs that does everything to please its master."

Rebekah stares as he walks away and remembers how she found Rhynan.

A young witch, Billie, was dating him at university when she learned of the hunt for the prince and the story of the wedding massacre. One night, Rhynan, in a fitful dream, called out for Angus, so Billie, hungry for power and recognition, sought Rebekah and shared the information. Rebekah repaid Billie by taking her to Queen Sorcha, who turned her into an empty shell by sucking out her soul.

"And since then, I've been watching over him," she mumbles.

"Oh hell, I'm losing my mind," she snaps.

Rebekah watches Rhynan's door close, then spins her chair until she's looking out toward the ocean and contemplates solutions.

BITTER COFFEE

Sunday, August 31ˢᵗ — 1000 Pacific Time — Canada

Rhynan rolls onto his back and stretches.

"What a great sleep. I haven't slept like that in years."

He rubs his hand on his sheet and then on himself.

"No sweating last night. I feel great. What a fantastic night with Aaghnya and her family at the restaurant and the delicious Indian food, wow."

Rhynan rolls to his side and bunches his pillow.

"Unbelievable. I didn't even say anything insulting or regrettable."

His face brightens as he lay reminiscing of the successful evening with Aaghnya until, with a burst of energy renewed, he swings his feet from the bed, and sitting up, he looks at the clock.

"Holy wow. I slept almost twelve hours, and I feel… fantastic."

Rhynan springs from his bed, ready for anything the world, or Rebekah, can throw at him, and as he passes his full-length mirror, he stops to assess his thirty-two-year-old body. His full head of light-brown hair, which he only combs it with his fingers because of the natural waves, has

124

the occasional strand of silver. Unlike many of the guys Rhynan works with, his facial skin is pristine, so he has a smooth, unblemished complexion that adds to his boyish features. He has square shoulders and a hairy chest that are both in need of more muscle. Rhynan glances toward his workout machine and decides he should clean all the accumulated clothes and books from the abandoned piece of equipment.

"I'm sure Aaghnya would prefer a buff boyfriend rather than a soft body," Rhynan tells his mirrored image.

He slaps the side of his tummy and smiles as he turns toward the shower.

Later, with his hands stuffed in his front pockets and a spring in his step, Rhynan walks toward the coffee shop feeling the warmth of the British Columbia, August, morning sun. He reaches the top of the steps that lead down to the coffee shop courtyard and stops.

"The shop is busy, considering it's Sunday," he mumbles.

Then he sees Aaghnya, and he watches as she floats between the tables, gathering dirty dishware and wiping the tabletops clean. She smiles and talks to customers, fills their requests for utensils or condiments, but always moves with the grace of a dancer. He notices how she picks up the chairs and places them under the tables so as not to disturb the peaceful ambiance. Rhynan sees, for the first time, that Petia and Dehlia are moving with a similar rhythm and grace as Aaghnya.

"I don't think I've ever realized how good it makes me feel when I see Aaghnya," he says.

"Rhynan Doon."

He snaps back to reality to see Aaghnya standing with the coffee shop door open, smiling and waving. He yanks his hand from his right pocket, giving her a full-wave. "Aaghnya!" he shouts and starts down the five steps in front of him.

As the toe of his shoe touches the second step, Rhynan's mind wanders.

If I was in a musical, I could dance down the next three steps and flick my hand from the railing in perfect time with the drumbeat. I could shuffle over to the nearest flower planter with a quick jump, touching my shoe to the corner and spinning in the air to a perfectly timed landing. Then, I would shuffle and turn on the next two planters with three quick steps into the arms of the beautiful lady waiting for me.

Rhynan smiles as he approaches Aaghnya, knowing he isn't ready for his dance musical debut.

He's a few steps away from her when panic sets in.

What do I do? We've only started dating last night. I could take her hand and say good morning, or do I put one arm around her and give her a quick peck on the cheek? Maybe I hug her and hope she doesn't get offended?

Aaghnya solves his dilemma by letting the door go and wrapping both her arms around his neck. Her slim, athletic body presses hard against him, and her arms tighten. Her hand slides up his neck, into his hair, and he feels the warm touch of her lips against his neck and then the side of his face. Rhynan realizes he's wrapped his arms so far around her slim body that he's sure he can feel his own shirt.

Rhynan has always found Aaghnya's Tamil accent sexy, but with her body pressed against him, his mind rages as she whispers, "I am happy to see you, Rhynan." His emotions explode. The knot in his stomach tightens, his skin covered in goosebumps, and he feels himself squeezing her even tighter.

"I'm happy to see you too, Aaghnya," he breathes.

Aaghnya's body relaxes, so he releases his arms, and when their eyes meet, her deep brown eyes look like two shimmering vats of swirling dark chocolate. Her perfect smile, proportionate, sharp features, black hair, and flawless brown skin, burn the ideal picture into his memory. He's frozen in Aaghnya's beauty until she slips her soft, warm hand into his and reaches for the door. As she pulls the door open, she gives him a sexy sideways glance, and Rhynan knows he will do anything for her.

Rebekah watches the closing scene of Rhynan's musical play out from behind the sun-shaded glass of the office building lobby. Seeing Aaghnya give Rhynan her sultry look drives Rebekah to scold herself as though she's listening to Queen Sorcha.

"Oh, Rebekah darling, how you have underestimated Rhynan Doon. That lady-killer played you like a teenage girl on her first party night."

Rebekah simmers in silence until feeling a chill at her back. She spins, expecting to see Queen Sorcha, but she's the only person in the empty tile and glass lobby. After a momentary pause, she turns back toward the coffee shop where Rhynan sits at an alcove table by the counter.

Rebekah's eyes go cold as she snarls, "Time to teach you the real meaning of a woman scorned, Mr. Doon. Shall we find out what other little secrets you're hiding deep inside?"

Rebekah turns her left-hand palm up as she pulls her wand out of the cloaked sheath on the small of her back. She spins the tip of the wand above her palm, casting a ball of smoke, and moments after, a male face appears in the smoke.

"I want you in that coffee shop, and don't let him out of your sight, or I will tear your heart out," Rebekah snarls.

She clinches her hand into a fist, crushing the smoky globe, and she spins her wand arm, casting a portal.

"Why is it so busy, Aaghnya?"

"There is a boat show at the marina, so we get many customers today."

Rhynan surveys the shop, noticing two teen girls, three people from another department who live in the area, and the same elderly couple as yesterday. A group of eight people gets up to leave, and five young men, casually dressed in windbreakers, khakis, and soft deck shoes, walk in the door. They chatter away as they move to the corner table vacated by the group of eight, and Dehlia slips in front of the men to clean the table. They stop talking as they wait for her and look in Rhynan's direction, making him feel uneasy. Aaghnya notices their interest in Rhynan, so she quickly cleans his table.

"Rhynan, you will sit here, and I will bring you chai tea and Indian breakfast food, yes?"

"Thanks, Aaghnya, but you're busy. Are you sure you have the time? If you're too busy, I can come to the counter and get it from Petia or Dehlia. "

"Rhynan Doon, I am the only one who will bring you food, and you will only take food from me. Rhynan, do you understand?"

"Ah yes, got it," he says.

Dehlia walks behind Aaghnya, and she and Petia giggle, so he returns a sheepish smile to them.

His eyes follow Aaghnya behind the counter, and he notices how she talks with Petia and Dehlia in a near whisper as she makes his breakfast.

"I wonder if they're talking about those five men who keep looking at me?" Rhynan mumbles.

Aaghnya brings Rhynan his breakfast and sits beside him.

"Aaghnya, is everything alright? You seem to be upset about the five men in the corner."

"Everything is wonderful, Rhynan, so eat your breakfast while it is warm, but first, you must drink this."

Aaghnya hands him a blue liquid in a glass vial and he holds it at eye level, looking through the vial with the light shining on it.

Aaghnya doesn't see the reaction of the one man at the corner table when he sees the vial in Rhynan's hand, nor does she see him make a magic call to Rebekah Kheel.

Rhynan lowers the vial, pulling the stopper and waving it under his nose.

"Is this the same drink your grandmother gave me last night? She is such a wonderful lady. It's not alcohol made from a secret family recipe, is it? It made me feel a little loopy last night."

"Rhynan, we do not drink alcohol because it poisons the body and weakens the mind."

129

"Oh, okay. So, what's in the drink?"

Aaghnya says, "The blue liquid is an ancient recipe good for what is inside you. I would do nothing to harm you, Rhynan Doon."

She takes his hand, and he pours the drink into his mouth.

"Rhynan, I need to tell you something that you may not believe, but it is very true."

The seriousness of her tone and her facial expression make Rhynan nervous.

"You're going to break up with me, aren't you?" He looks away from Aaghnya.

"Rhynan Doon, you will listen to me. I will be with you for the rest of your life."

She reaches across the table, placing her hand on Rhynan's cheek to pull his face back toward hers.

"It is what I have to tell you that will make you understand the dream you were having and why I must be with you forever."

Rhynan dons a blank stare and is about to ask Aaghnya if she's proposing to him when the two teen girls and the elderly couple get up to leave. Aaghnya hears the noise of the heavy chairs sliding on the ceramic tile flooring and glances around at the movement in the shop. Suddenly, she stops, eyes wide.

"What's wrong, Aaghnya?" Rhynan says.

She turns her head, and in Tamil, tells both Petia and Dehlia, "The men in the corner have gray eyes." Petia and Dehlia hurry into the back room, closing the curtain, and Rhynan notices a flash of light. He's about to ask Aaghnya what the flash was when he feels the blue drink having the same euphoric effect on him as it did last night.

Am I hallucinating? Why is Dehlia dressed in Indian dance clothing?

The chime for the cafe's main door breaks Rhynan's focus on Dehlia, and he looks to the door to see Rebekah walk in.

"That's odd. I've never seen Rebekah in the coffee shop before or at work on the weekend," he mumbles.

Aaghnya watches the five men sitting in the corner nod toward the woman who just entered. Then, like a synchronized team, each put a hand inside their windbreaker. The woman returns the slight nod.

Momentarily oblivious to Rhynan, Aaghnya whispers in Tamil, "One man is holding a wand down by his leg, and they all have gray eyes. The men are Blood Witches, which means this woman is a witch."

Aaghnya stays calm until Rhynan leans forward, and she feels his warm breath touch her ear.

"Aaghnya. I don't speak Tamil but, the woman who walked in is my boss, Rebekah Kheel," he whispers.

The name hits her with a slap, and Aaghnya's head snaps to Rhynan as he moves away.

Still in Tamil, she says, "She is here for my Rhynan Doon."

She grabs his head between both hands and kisses him hard on the lips. Then, Aaghnya jumps up, and swinging her arm in a full circle, she casts a protection spell around Rhynan.

"Aaghnya, what's wrong? What are you doing?"

"Rhynan, your boss is one of the most ruthless witches alive, and she is here to take you to her Queen. If she takes you, it means you will die, so this will not happen. You must stay where you are because I have cast a protection spell to keep you safe."

"Aaghnya, are... are you telling me you're a witch?"

"Yes, Rhynan. I am a powerful witch, and I will do everything I can to protect you."

Rhynan struggles to believe what Aaghnya says until she jumps in the air, spins, landing bare foot, and he's taken aback by Aaghnya's new look. Shiny copper and green Indian dance clothing, open at the mid-riff revealing the fine lines of her tight abdominal muscles, covers her body. The halter-top like bodice, clipped in the middle with a hanging gem, and her arms, covered in a puffed sheer fabric attached to the halter shoulder, is almost as revealing as Rhynan's imagination. The pant shaped bottoms with a fan like center are snug to her toned, muscular legs. Aaghnya's eyes are bright and her skin has a copper glow. Her straight black hair is now full and moving around her shoulders, medusa like. Her eyes are outlined and shadowed with a subtle copper and green, and her lips have a glossy copper hue.

She locks eyes with Rhynan and, with a sultry tone, asks, "Do you like me as a witch, Rhynan Doon?"

"Oh, ya," he breathes. "Aaghnya, you.... you are the most beautiful witch ever."

"But, I am the first witch you have met?"

"Ya, maybe not," he says, looking toward Rebekah.

Dehlia, dressed similar to Aaghnya but in red and cream tones, says something that turns Aaghnya towards

Rebekah and there's another flash of light from the backroom. Petia appears from behind the curtain, dressed similar to Dehlia but in blue and yellow tones, and both jump over the counter, taking stances as if they're starting an Indian dance.

Rhynan looks toward Rebekah, seeing the five men from the corner table, wands in hand, on one side and the three people from the other department, with wands in hand, on the other side.

"Well, well, well. Mr. Rhynan Doon, you little ladies' man. Or should I say Prince O'Manus? The girls always did swoon whenever you walked through the village, so why not here?"

Rebekah's mischievous smile reminds Rhynan of the previous morning.

"I see you've found yourself a gorgeous Indian witch to play with, and, of course, she has friends to help her guard the precious soul of Prince O'Manus."

Rebekah's cruel laugh scratches Rhynan's nerves as she turns her attention to Aaghnya and moves a few steps to her left like a gunfighter squaring off.

"Does he know about the Prince? Have you told him it's not true love?" Rebekah says and tauntingly pouts. "I'm assuming, of course, you're the powerful witch he makes love to? Have you told him it's only duty? That you're taking one for the team, sort of thing? Let me guess… you don't want to break his tender heart?"

"Rebekah, are you out of your mind?" Rhynan shouts, stepping out from behind the table, only to bump into the protection barrier. Rebekah laughs, then her face contorts into a tooth-bearing snarl as she returns her full attention to Aaghnya.

"Now that I know Rhynan is the carrier, because my man saw you give him Faerie Pool Water, I'm going to take your little prince to Queen Sorcha, even if I have to level this entire city to get him."

Casting her wand arm at Aaghnya, Rebekah fires a bullet like blue light from the tip of her wand. Aaghnya sweeps her arm across her body, and the blue light explodes only a foot in front of her face, shocking Rhynan. He can't believe what he's witnessing because he's always thought there was no such thing as magic.

The five young men, and three other employees from TDF, join Rebekah in attacking Aaghnya and her sisters and the decor of the coffee shop quickly changes from modern relaxed to rubble. They dance in different rhythms, defending and retaliating with occasional snapping hand gestures that cast light and energy of Subdue Magic. The display cooler and the front counter are fast being reduced to pieces of pressed wood and plastic shards. Petia groans and Rhynan looks around Aaghnya to see a small fragment of plastic sticking out of Petia's calf muscle.

Outnumbered by nine to three, they still smile and only fight using Subdue Magic because of their teaching to respect life. Even through the escalating and explosive carnage of destructive light, fire, ice darts, shrapnel of wood, metal, and stone, Rhynan witnesses the calm, dancing grace of Aaghnya and her sisters. But he still fears for their survival.

Then a section of the wall near Rhynan explodes open, knocking him backward, and as the dust clears, Rhynan picks himself up, hearing Rebekah shout.

"You fool, we need to capture him, not kill him."

A young warlock across the room, distracted by Rebekah's scolding, flails backward because he let his guard down long enough for Petia to knock him unconscious.

Behind the area where the front counter used to be, four circles of colored light appear, and four wizards from Aaghnya's family walk out to join the fray, putting the odds at eight against seven.

Rhynan breathes easier, saying, "Now I know what the flash of light was for."

He can see people outside the coffee shop, scattering for safety from the flying debris as the large window next to Petia explodes outward. Rhynan's hope of victory is short-lived when six black swirls of smoke form in the far corner of the shop, and Rebekah laughs out loud. Aaghnya looks at Rhynan, and even though she's still fighting, she winks at him.

Another explosive sound and the floor-to-ceiling glass at the end of the shop turns to sand, and Rhynan sees Monica standing there with her wand at the ready.

"You're a witch?" Rebekah snaps. "Well, not for long, you little tart."

Rebekah snaps her wand at Monica, and a blue ring appears around her. Monica feverishly waves and pokes her wand at the blue ring with no effect, and it snaps to her body shape, cocooning her. Her scream curdles Rhynan's blood as she bursts into a figure of hot blue flame and disappears.

Six more witches step out from the swirling smoke portals, and Rhynan shoots Aaghnya a look of despair after witnessing Monica's demise. Aaghnya keeps smiling while she dances, and again she gives Rhynan a little wink that makes him smile until an explosion tears the smile from his face. He jumps back as half of the cinderblock wall and entrance door explode inward, tossing four of the six new Blood Witches into an unconscious pile covered in shattered blocks. Eight witches of the Irish Guardians launch themselves into the fight, and the odds now favor the prince.

Sorcha will be furious about losing the prince. Why isn't she here yet?

Rebekah surveys the battle, and seeing an opportunity, she snaps her wand like a whip, bouncing a curse off Rhynan's protection shield.

"Retreat!" Rebekah shouts as she dives into a black smoke portal.

Rebekah's curse strikes Aaghnya, and she explodes backward. Her flailing body tears down the remains of the curtain covering the backroom and she crashes hard into the supplies stacked against the back wall. Dehlia loses focus and looks toward Aaghnya. The wizard Petia had only knocked out earlier, seizes the opportunity and launches a piece of sharp plastic into Dehlia's back before diving into his portal.

Rhynan freezes, seeing Aaghnya struck down by Rebekah, and he convulses. His legs shake as they weaken, and he falls sideways. He reaches out, grabs at a table

ROYAL SOULS

for balance, missing, and crashing into a chair-back he bounces off, twisting and striking his head on the corner of the mounted bench seat. Blood spurts from the cut eyebrow, and he vomits as he hits the floor hard.

Rhynan's mind, overrun with the sound of screaming and seeing Aaghnya smashing against the back wall, crumples inward to painful, deep memories.

His mind runs back to his childhood, remembering how his father destroyed everything good in his life.

Rhynan spent his youth with an abusive father who took pleasure in seeing him suffer, and as a young child, he had no toys or anything that nurtured his creativity. He had no friends because his father acted cruelly to anyone who visited, so he developed no social skills. He made sports teams at school, and his father would ground him for no reason, making him unreliable to the coaches, so they removed him from the roster.

His mother left when he was nine, so Rhynan suffered daily sessions of physical and verbal abuse, which drove him to the streets of downtown Vancouver. Four years later, his father died from over-consumption, and Rhynan found himself in the care of Child Services after being caught stealing food from a street vendor. The court recognized Rhynan's act of theft was survival, as he couldn't, earlier, have used any of the outreach programs or missions without the risk of being sent back to his now deceased father. Then, at thirteen years old, Rhynan found a new lease on life through adoption, but his father's mental and emotional damage would linger.

"He's messed himself bad, Colin. I'll not touch that."

Rhynan, lying in a puddle of vomit and blood, hears the words but doesn't understand until he opens his eyes. His memory kicks him back to reality, and he snaps to a sitting position, screaming, "Aaghnya!"

He sees several men standing around him, then looks across the room where Petia, sobbing and surrounded by other Indian witches, cradles Dehlia.

Rhynan turns back to the faces of the men close to him.

"Aaghnya? Is Aaghnya alright? Where is she? I have to go to her. She needs me." He tries to stand but stumbles, legs weak, and stays on the floor.

"Colin, what do we do?"

Rhynan recognizes the Irish accent of the man standing in front of him, and he whimpers, "Do you know where Aaghnya is?"

The man leans forward. "They took her body away."

The emotionless words strike Rhynan like someone kicked him in the stomach, and he retches before passing out.

CRYSTAL AND STONE

Sunday, August 31st — 2200 Eastern Time — Boston

"Crystal? Stone? What the heck, Lochran?" Beth snaps.

Lochran smiles, leaning forward, and says, "To reunite Prince O'Manus and Princess Sadreen, the Guardian witches must perform the Circle Ritual to release the princess from the Orb that protects her."

"This is getting so confusing," Beth says, and she lets out an audible puff of frustration. "Okay, I'll bite. What's a Circle Ritual?"

Lochran continues. "Nine Guardian Witches stand in a magical circle of exact dimensions, holding the Crystals and surrounding the Orb. The circle is fifty-four feet in diameter, and they hold their crystals, with the royal symbols aimed at the Orb. Six Chiefs from around the world, holding artifacts from both Fire Kings, stand on a circle twenty-seven feet in diameter. Then, three witches, holding the two Stones and the Chalice of Oaths, full of Faerie Pool water from the original wedding, stand in the circle, thirteen and a half feet in diameter, and closest to the Orb. When the clock strikes three on the morning of September 6th, the Crystals shine on the Princess's

Orb, and the six Chiefs cast a light from their wands, transferring the magic of the artifacts back to the Princess. It will release the princess from the Orb, so she can join with the Prince after the Staff of Souls brings him out of the carrier."

"Sounds simple," Beth says, rolling her eyes. She sits back with a blank look on her face, and Abigail breaks in.

"When Princess Sadreen cast her soul from her mortal shell, it fly to the Witch of Loch Shin, who cast an indestructible orb around the soul. The witch waited to hear the prince was safe, but he came under attack. The Witch of Loch Shin know someone betray her, so she send the Orb to a secret place and pick thirty-six Guardian witches to guard it. Then she cast a spell on the Guardians, so they could never betray the location."

Beth jolts upright like someone poked her with a sharp stick. She draws a quick breath, and both Abigail and Lochran smile, giving a nod of their heads.

"Oh, that is so cool. The Princess, she's been hiding here in Boston since the wedding? That's why the magical lunatics are showing up here."

"And that is why there are so many witches in this State," Abigail says. "The Princess send out occasional magic pulses for the Prince to find, and it has ignited the magic in those capable of receiving it."

Beth lets out a chirp of excitement, and Abigail puts her index finger against her lips as she playfully swings her hand at Beth's head.

"Quiet, before you tell everyone."

"So, where's the prince?"

"We don't know yet," Lochran says.

ROYAL SOULS

Beth stops bouncing around in her chair.

"Lochran. What do you mean you don't know yet?"

"The Prince uses mortals to carry his soul, and every time the mortal's body dies, he has to find a new one. So, he has had many hosts while trying to find the princess. We must find the mortal with the prince's soul in him and guide him here, so he can reunite with the princess."

"Lochran, you make it sound so simple. How's that going?"

"Aye, not as well as we hoped. We had the nine Crystals, but we still needed *Clach a' Phrionnsa*, the Prince Stone, and *Clach a' Bhana-phrionnsa*, the Princess stone. The stone's glow blue for the prince and green for the princess to show they're alive. To track the prince or princess, you use the light in the middle of each Stone that moves to the side of the Stone that you must travel to find the prince or princess."

"Similar to a modern compass," Beth says.

"Aye. King Aed of Ireland asked the Witch of Loch Shin to make the stone for Princess Sadreen after she wandered into a cave and got lost for two days. The witch thought it such a good idea that she made one for the prince and gifted it to King Aodh."

Beth asks, "Lochran, do the stones work the same on the souls without the body?"

"Yes. Now, the trick to using the stone to find the prince is the pulse. The closer you get to the prince, the faster the stone will pulse until it matches the prince's very heartbeat. Sorcha stole the Prince's Stone to help her find the mortal, so she could draw the Prince's soul out, capture it, and kill it with a curse. Then Sorcha had one of

141

her filth infiltrate the Guardians and grab one of the nine crystals to stop the princess' resurrection. Sorcha had the upper hand until *I* stole both from Sorcha on the same day she stole them, and I hid them in the warehouse."

"That's why they were after you," Beth says. "Why didn't you say that instead of letting Abigail and me destroy my condo?"

"I didn't want to spoil her fun."

"Ya. Sure. You wanted to watch a cat fight, didn't you? I'll remember that," Beth says, and shakes her finger at him.

Abigail snickers.

"Hold on," Beth says. "Galen said he was going to kill you."

"Ah, Galen. He don't have enough brain to fill a chicken egg," Abigail says.

Beth smiles.

"Why you smile? It is not funny."

"Your Jamaican accent. When you're mad, it comes out strong."

Lochran laughs out loud, and Abigail squints her eyes at him.

"If he kill Lochran, he never find the Stone or Crystal, and Sorcha skin him alive." Abigail leans forward. "If I don't eat him alive first."

Everyone laughs.

"Sorcha knows we need the nine crystals to make the Circle of Nine Witches," Abigail says. "As long as she has either, we cannot reunite the Prince and Princess. I bet she sucked the souls out of the witches who lost them to Lochran."

ROYAL SOULS

"She can do what?"

Abigail takes a deep breath to calm herself. "Remember when you join with Mehla, and you see the battle?"

"Yep."

"You remember seeing the witch in black being dragged through the portal?"

"Uh, huh…"

"Sorcha get struck with a flesh curse, and her second in command, Rebekah, drag her to safety. But Sorcha's wound threaten her life, and she must use a parasite spell to steal the life of another witch to stay alive. I hear she has perfected the spell and can now steal the soul of a witch in less than a minute. But she must keep using the parasite spell whenever her wound reappears, or she dies."

"Holy crap. That bitch must die."

Both Lochran and Abigail smile.

"Aye, that's the spirit."

"What?" Beth says.

"What you said." Lochran leans forward. "That bitch must die."

Beth glances at Abigail with a furrowed brow and then back to Lochran.

"I never said that," and she turns back to Abigail. "Did I?"

"Mehla."

"Excuse me? Abigail, what do you mean, Mehla?"

"Beth, Mehla is telling us what we do."

"Are you telling me that Mehla is taking over my body and talking through me?"

"No, no, no," Abigail says, grabbing Beth's hand. "Your bond with Mehla. It is becoming so strong that she

143

share what she think with you, and you speak it. Nothing more."

"That's a lot, Abigail."

"Listen to me," Abigail says. "This is good because the more your bond grow with Mehla, the more protected you are and the more powerful you become."

"And she's not taking over my body. Right?"

"No. But you can take Mehla's power into you when you need it."

"And why would I want to do that if she's talking through me without my knowing it?"

"Beth, Mehla has been inside you since you were a baby. She has done you no harm and never will. The amulet, you say the witch give it to you in the hospital, and right away you felt better, as if a surge of energy go through you, right?"

"Yep."

"The amulet is not only to call me for protection, but to help Mehla control her power. Mehla could not hide her power from those trying to kill her without the amulet. Beth, know this. Mehla, she is stronger than Princess Sadreen, and you can use that power."

Beth sits back in her chair and absorbs what Abigail has said.

I'm way too deep into this crap, and I don't want to be here. I need to slow this down.

"Princess, you look worried?"

"Abigail, I'm not sure about going from a carefree witch to being in the middle of a war that is over a thousand years before my time. Everything is moving way too fast. I'm not sure of anything right now."

"You are doing fine."

"I don't know about that."

The room goes silent for a few moments.

"Abigail, what's the Glazier?"

"Who told you this name?"

"When I was in the dream with Mehla, Freya told me not to fight the Glazier alone."

Beth glances at Lochran and sees the worry in his eyes.

Lochran leans forward.

"Princess, that is a serious warning from the witch. With the Glazier supporting Sorcha, she will have the advantage in battle."

"Okay, what's a Glazier?" she asks again, leaning in toward Lochran.

"Naise Lagrandeur, the Grand Witch of France," Lochran says, "invented a spell to entomb a living plant in glass and then restore it to its natural state. He later developed the spell to do the same to a person, and then he figured out how to keep someone alive for decades while frozen in glass. After that, he built a prison to hold the evilest and dark criminals from the magical world, and then he started selling his services to the world. Naise taught the secrets of glassing to his five sons and one daughter, and they flew around the world entombing criminals before bringing them to the prison. People started calling them the Glazier until someone coined the name of Le Glazier, and this became the name they're called by when they apply their services. Naise disagreed with the name of Le Glazier, but he couldn't risk his new business to demand they use Lagrandeur Glazier."

"All was good until the daughter, Maria, and the two youngest sons, Robert and Francois, made plans for a hostile takeover of the prison and the business. Naise found out, so he tried to entomb the three first, but he missed, and they ran. Five years went by with no further attempts, so they thought their father had given up trying to imprison them. Robert, Francois, and Maria dropped Lagrandeur and changed their names to Le Glazier to start a prison and capture service."

"But before they could start the business, the three older brothers, Esian, Noah, and Evan, found Maria in a tavern and captured her with the Glass curse. Ready to return to their father with their catch, Robert and Francois used identity spells, masking their true appearance, and captured the three older brothers."

"Robert and Francois now had their siblings in glass and control of Esian's prison hidden somewhere in the Canadian Rockies. They hid their siblings in the lowest dungeon of the prison and made plans to overthrow their father and take over the prison in the French mountains."

"They say Francois has his father's talent with magic, so Francois created a spell to protect them from anyone they trained, from using the glassing spell against them. Without his father knowing it, Francois made his way into his father's prison in France and cast the rebound spell on him. Francois then walked to the front door of the French prison and demanded to see his father, who, without hesitation, tried to entomb him. The spell backfired, entombing Naise and now Robert and Francois each had control of a prison, and they moved their siblings back to the French prison with their father."

Beth shakes her head in disbelief.

"Robert kept the prison in the mountains of France, and Francois kept the one in the Canadian Rockies," Lochran finishes.

"Then Francois developed a very close, personal relationship with his best client. Queen Sorcha," Abigail adds.

"Why is she the best client? I thought she embraced evil?"

"Storage of the witches bound to her," Lochran says. "That means over two-thousand witches waiting for the call to battle."

"Why store two-thousand witches? It makes little sense."

"It does if those witches die and you want to be sure you have an instant army of Blood Witches," Lochran replies.

"Okay, Sorcha has an army of over two-thousand witches in a deep freeze, but it sounds to me as if the Royals have more friends than that."

"Oh, aye, they have more friends, Princess, but we don't know how many witches Sorcha has recruited from around the world or how many are in France."

"Oh, wonderful. The Olympics of witch fighting," Beth huffs as she drops herself against the back of her chair again. After a minute of silence, she sits up straight.

"Alright, let's do this. I'll check out the warehouse, and if it's clear, I'll make that light flash." She points at the light on the office shack across the way. "Then, you come and get the Crystal and Stone, and we get out of dodge before anyone knows we were there."

"No!" Abigail snaps.

"Why not?"

"It is too dangerous for you to go alone."

"What? Abigail, I'm a Spirit Witch."

"What if Sorcha is there with Rebekah and many Wand Witches?"

"Aye. But maybe she wants to go alone to find that handsome man on the horse?" Lochran snickers and winks at Abigail.

A mist forms above Lochran, and Beth leans forward.

"Lochran, have you ever tried to swim in shark-infested waters?"

Both Abigail and Lochran go silent.

"I... I meant no disrespect, Princess. I was only teasing and I swear I'll no do it again."

Beth stands up, turns toward Abigail, and gives her a quick smile and a wink.

"I'll get dressed," she says, walking away.

Abigail laughs, and Lochran lets out a massive sigh of relief as the mist disappears.

Beth dresses in stretch pants, sport top, zip-front hoodie, and cross-trainer shoes before returning to the dining island. She casts a portal that takes the trio to the roof of the same warehouse where she first saw the Horsemen and Lochran.

***

Lochran pokes his head out from behind the rooftop mechanical shack to search the night-cloaked holding yard. He pulls his head back and turns to Beth.

"It's too dark to see between those containers," Lochran whispers to Beth.

"Stand still." She taps Lochran on the temple, and his eyes change to the same glassy gray color as her own.

"That's brilliant," he says. "It's like the day."

Beth turns to do the same to Abigail.

"Oh... My... Cat eyes?"

"Shh. Yes. I can use my jaguar night vision without changing my body."

"Oh, that's super cool, Abigail."

Abigail smiles, and the three turn to look over the warehouse yard.

Abigail looks at Beth. "The figure across the yard, standing in the shadows against the warehouse wall, looks familiar."

"Ya. I got this," Beth says.

Beth slips into a portal, and seconds later, reappears a few feet behind the unsuspecting figure.

She waves her hand behind his head and then helps him to the ground as he collapses. She props Jack against the wall in a semi-sitting position, and with her index finger pointed at him, she circles her hand over his body, casting protection, then returns to the roof.

"Well, that was motherly of you," Lochran says.

Beth squints. "Think sharks before you talk."

Lochran stiffens, looking like a child who lost their video game privileges for a month, and Abigail stifles a snicker.

Beth turns to Abigail. "I'm going to see if it's safe."

Beth steps out of her portal at the same spot as when she intervened between Lochran and the Horsemen.

Cautiously, she walks toward the open door of the warehouse, turning her head left and right, until a figure to her left steps from behind a container across the yard. Beth can see the kilted male figure with her night vision as he walks toward her and stops at the halfway point.

"I had hope that you might come back here again, lass."

Beth's eyes change to the new blue as she says, "I thought I might take the chance you would be around here, alone."

Beth walks closer to him while still glancing around the containers.

"Aye, calm yourself, lass. I came alone. No one hides to attack you."

"Nice to know." She watches as he walks under the only yard light and says, "Well, don't you look handsome."

"Do you approve?" He holds his hands out, as if inviting opinion. "It's been a while since I last wore my clan kilt and shirt."

"Well, if you went to that trouble for me, I most definitely approve."

He places his palm against his solar plexus, making a slight bow. "I could go through more trouble than this for the opportunity to meet with you, lass."

"Might I know your name?"

Smiling, he gives another slight bow at the waist.

"I am called Karse, and may I know your name... this time?"

Beth feels something drawing her closer to Karse until she can reach him with her outstretched hand. She places her palm in the middle of his chest as though holding him back from a romantic advance, and she catches her breath as a tingling wave rushes from her hand through her body.

"Beth."

"Beth, a name as beautiful as the woman."

Beth's heart is pounding so hard she doesn't connect the voice with any potential danger until Karse's head snaps sideways. Beth turns her head to look in the same direction as a woman and a dozen others walk out of the shadows.

"Hello, Karse," she says.

Karse looks back at Beth. "I promise you, lass. I know nothing of her being here."

"And who is she? The wife?"

"Nay, lass. Rebekah leads this rabble of Blood Witches."

Rebekah Kheel, Beth hears. She feels a surge through her body. *I've got this, Mehla.*

Beth gives Karse a flash smile and, dragging her hand over his thick chest, she steps away from him.

"Well, well, well, Karse," Rebekah says. "I don't blame you for sneaking off to this secret rendezvous. And to think, everyone else suggested you had lost faith in our Queen. Maybe they were jealous? I know I'm feeling a touch of jealousy at the moment."

Rebekah gives Beth a mischievous smile.

Beth smiles back at Rebekah.

"I must admit," Beth says. "I'm feeling under-dressed seeing you in that cocktail dress and heels. Dressed to kill, and here you are in the old warehouse district. You should get out more often."

Rebekah gives a sinister laugh, saying, "After seeing you, my little sweet, I must admit, killing is not the first thing on my mind."

Beth casually moves a few more steps away from Karse and hears in her mind.

Beth, beware.

"Well, I hate to disappoint the best-dressed lady at the party, but I came here hoping to find that handsome hunk of man," Beth says, flicking her finger in Karse's direction.

Rebekah pouts. "That is very disappointing. It's been a long time since I've felt my heart flutter."

Beth notices half of Rebekah's entourage has edged closer to the open warehouse door during their verbal fencing competition.

"So, what brings you and the minions to the warehouse district?"

"It's a two-part visit, and the first part you already know." Rebekah glances at Karse. "Loyalty is such a fickle thing, and one can never be too careful. But, it's fortunate, we arrived in time to see the reason Karse slipped away, and there were no lies. Queen Sorcha might have been disappointed to find out I had to kill such a fine specimen."

Responding to her threat, Karse moves closer to Rebekah, and she gives him a fake smile.

"Relax, dear Karse. All's forgiven."

"That's great," Beth says. "If it's all good, then maybe you and the litter of pups can go home, and we can continue our impromptu date in peace?"

"Oh, that was good," Rebekah breathes. "No one has ever called me a bitch in such a lovely manner." She

ROYAL SOULS

straightens her posture and locks eyes with Beth. "You don't know who I am, do you?"

Beth shakes her head as she gives a quick lift of her brow. "Not a clue."

Okay. Let's keep this going, and we might get out of here without... Beth's thought disappears as Lochran's voice interrupts.

"Looks like we've arrived in time."

Beth and Rebekah turn toward the voice as Abigail and Lochran walk out from behind a steel container with wands at the ready, and Rebekah turns her icy stare back to Beth.

Beth shrugs. "Perfect timing, as usual."

Rebekah looks back to Lochran.

"Lochran MacIlraight, you thief," she snarls. "Give me the Crystal and Stone, and your playmates will live."

"I think there's a serious lack of incentive in your offer," Beth says.

"Queen Sorcha killed the six witches that allowed Lochran to steal the Crystal and Stone," Rebekah hisses before turning back to Beth. "You could say she's big on punishment."

Rebekah gives a quick lift of her eyebrows and a sultry smile before saying, "But, if ever you're in need, I could argue leniency and perhaps incarceration in my private dungeon?"

"Yes, I've heard about Queen Psycho and her soul-sucking trick," Beth says.

Rebekah returns a surprising look to Beth. "Oh?"

Beth places her fist on a cocked hip. "And the private dungeon sounds like an offer a girl shouldn't refuse, but I'll pass."

"If you know who Queen Sorcha is, then you know who I am?" Rebekah pauses, then in a sultry tone says, "Oh, you little gamer. I want you even more now," Rebekah laughs.

"Yep. Psycho number two. Second in command. I've heard one of your killing sprees makes the plague less than the common cold."

"Well, thank you," Rebekah says. "You certainly know how to play with a girl's heart."

Without breaking eye contact with Beth, Rebekah shouts, "Last chance to save your friends, Lochran."

"Karse, what are you doing here?" Abigail shouts.

Rebekah, surprised, spins on her heel to look at Karse.

"Karse, fraternizing with the enemy, are we? Maybe I'm not so sure of your intentions this evening."

Rebekah shoots Beth an evil look.

With a fake smile and a shrug of her shoulders, Beth says, "Who knew?"

Rebekah changes her body position, and slipping her hand behind her back, she draws her wand from the invisible holder in the small of her back. She casts a curse that slams Karse against the wall of a building across the yard, and he drops like a sack of flour.

Rebekah spins her body saying, "*Schut-para-sit.*" and as though cracking a whip, she casts the curse at Lochran knocking him back, spinning sideways and crashing into the warehouse.

Abigail screams Lochran's name and runs to his side.

ROYAL SOULS

"Find the Crystal and Prince Stone," Rebekah barks, and half the Blood Witches start toward the warehouse opening.

Seeing both Karse and Lochran fall, Beth feels anger welling in the pit of her stomach and she becomes disoriented.

"Enough, you evil cur," Beth shouts.

Her skin warms, then glows as she rises from the ground.

Rebekah moves away from Beth, casting a fire attack that engulfs Beth in hot blue flame. The twelve Blood Witches band together to join Rebekah with an assault of curses aimed at the heart of the floating ball of fire. A loud crack and Rebekah's attack disintegrate into a cloud of smoke that disappears with the slight breeze of the night.

Rebekah freezes in disbelief. Beth, wearing the same dress and crown with the hanging emerald stone, has transformed into a reflection of Princess Mehla from the wedding night.

"Princess Mehla?" Rebekah whispers.

One of the Blood Witches casts a curse at Princess Mehla, who swats it away, and without hesitation, casts a curse, entombing him with ice.

Knowing she's not powerful enough to fight Princess Mehla, Rebekah seizes the opportunity to jump through a portal before the princess can turn on her. The remaining eleven witches follow Rebekah's lead.

Transforming into her black jaguar body, Abigail walks into the open below Princess Mehla and, looking around, gives a low growl. The princess sinks toward

155

Abigail, and as she nears the ground, her glowing stops, and Beth falls to her knees and hands.

"What the heck happened? Where is everyone?"

Abigail pads over to Beth, slipping her enormous head under Beth's arm, lifting her upper body onto her muscular cat shoulders, and Beth's face lay against her neck.

"Abigail. You're so soft and warm," she says and reaches her other arm around to hug Abigail.

Moments later, Beth giggles, saying, "Abigail, you're purring."

Beth hugs her tighter, then releases Abigail and rubs her hand along her back. "I don't understand what happened, but thanks for being there, Abigail."

Abigail shoots Beth a quick look, winking, before running back to Lochran, so Beth turns her attention toward Karse.

"Where is he?" she says, shifting her head left and right. "Did Rebekah grab him during her escape? Or was he a setup? I felt something when I touched his chest. Did he? Maybe he recovered and moved to safety? No, he would have jumped into the fight against Rebekah, I'm sure. I think?"

She walks toward the warehouse he slammed into and glances around the yard for him.

"He's gone, and so is Jack Sebastian," she says.

Beth turns back to see Abigail holding Lochran. His limp form makes her ill-feeling. "Oh, please don't be dead."

She sprints toward them and the pale gray color of his face scares her. She kneels beside him, and the tears slipping over Abigail's cheeks tell the story, so Beth lifts Lochran's shirt to examine the wound and sees a nest of worms.

"Abigail, that's a parasite spell."

"Yes. Those worms will keep eating at his flesh until they kill him."

"That sick bitch," Beth says. "If I get the chance, I promise I will make sure she never does this to anyone again."

"BETH, BEHIND YOU!"

Beth shoots straight up and spins in the air. Suspended above Lochran and Abigail, Beth, surrounded in a ghostly glow, faces three witches from earlier who have returned. The three slip to one knee with their heads bowed and wands on the ground, and the witch in the middle puts her hand out with the palm facing Beth.

"Hold, Princess. We only want our friend back," she says, gesturing to the wizard shrouded in ice, "and to deliver a message."

Beth floats back to the ground.

"Tell me your message."

"Queen Sorcha says she will save your man friend for the Crystal and Stone, or the spell will kill him within three days."

"Tell your Queen if my friend dies, I will spend eternity hunting her and Rebekah only to destroy them. I will keep your friend, who will be the first to suffer the consequences of Rebekah's treachery."

The witch's eyes soften. "Please, Princess," the woman begs. "He is my husband, and I begged Queen Sorcha to let me return and try to gain his freedom because they will not."

Beth, silent, holds her stare at the witch, sensing her honesty, and knows the witch is right.

"Your queen cares nothing about you. Take your man and leave."

"Thank you, Princess."

The trio slowly reach for their wands, then stand and hesitate before running to the ice statue. Beth waves her hand to thaw the wizard as the lead witch casts a gray smoke portal over them. The portal drops to the ground, leaving emptiness for Beth to stare at in contemplation.

"If I get out of this alive, I'm giving up chai lattes," she mutters.

Beth turns and kneels beside Lochran.

"You used Princess Mehla's power today," Abigail says.

"Let's talk later. We need to get Lochran to my place."

"No, not your house. It is too dangerous. I know where we must go, but first, you must use Mehla to find the Crystal and Stone."

"Okay, but I'm putting a shield over this place."

Beth stands and touches the building before throwing her arms in the air and swinging them in a big arc, casts the spell.

"Okay, now for the Crystal," Beth says.

"I will help you contact Mehla."

"Abigail. Did you see the floating and glowing? The princess and I are tight."

Abigail smiles, saying, "This is good."

Beth walks into the warehouse, packed full of boxes, crates, and small steel containers, and stops only a few feet inside the opening. She looks for any sign of the hidden Crystal, seeing nothing but something is drawing her to the middle of the warehouse.

Beth walks to the middle of the warehouse, turns a circle, seeing no sign of the Crystal.

A voice in her head surprises her.

Use my light, Beth.

"Mehla? How?"

Come to me, and I will help you.

Beth hesitates, wondering how much control Mehla is gaining over her mind and body?

She takes a relaxing breath and focuses on bringing Mehla's power to her core. As the energy builds, Beth can see the glow of white light reflecting off the stacks of cargo, and she rises to the ceiling. As Beth settles three feet below the steel rafters, her light becomes translucent, emerald green. The green light acts as an x-ray, and she sees through every box and container in the building. Beth turns a slow circle until, from over her shoulder, she sees a blue light glowing. It shines from under a double stack of steel containers near the back corner of the building.

Before Beth can lower herself to the floor, strings of light, identical to the thread the old woman in the coffee shop was weaving, float toward her, shaping into the same piece of cloth. The cloth hovers in front of her, reflecting a different light from the middle, and Beth reaches out to touch it. An electric shock jumps to her finger, and the cloth swims toward the wall, turning back into strings, and Beth's floating body follows. Her feet touch the concrete floor a short distance from where the colored threads disappear into a large steel grate mounted on the wall. Beth walks to the grate, finding a single blue thread hanging, and she takes it between her fingers. Another shock and the grate disappears, revealing a multi-cut Crystal with a blue and green symbol on the largest surface. Beth looks around for any signs of Rebekah or her minions before she kneels to reach for the Crystal.

"Ah!" A battle flashes in her mind as her fingers touch the Crystal.

Beth watches six witches lose their lives trying to protect the Crystal. Then, a woman wearing a crown like Princess Sadreen's stands over the bodies, laughing. Anger wells in her stomach, and she pulls the Crystal to her body before standing.

That bitch has to die.

Beth recognizes the angry voice of Mehla and whispers, "Agreed."

She turns to the four containers in the corner and sweeps them aside with a throw of her arm. Beth levitates the heavy steel floor grate and finds the Prince Stone wrapped in a rag, hidden in a pipe.

As Beth exits the warehouse, Abigail sees both the Stone and the Crystal in Beth's hands, and she smiles until Beth looks right at her with glowing green eyes.

Abigail sets Lochran's head on the asphalt, jumps up, and marches until her face is only inches from Beth's.

"Beth, release Mehla. You do not need her power. Release her. NOW."

"What is your problem, Abigail?"

Abigail watches as Beth's eyes turn blue again with each blink.

"Beth, you must not keep Mehla's power in you for longer than you need." She turns back to Lochran. "We must leave in case more Blood Witches are hiding."

"I'll drop the barrier."

"Beth, get close, so I don't have to make a large portal."

Abigail sits Lochran up as Beth walks beside her and places the Crystal and Stone in Lochran's lap to free her hands.

Beth waves her arms in a long arc saying, "GO."

Abigail casts a portal over the trio as Beth looks across the yard to see Jack Sebastian standing where Karse landed earlier.

The portal drops over them, and Jack watches the flash of light and hears the slight electrical sound as the trio disappears. He nods his head, smiles, then turns away from the warehouse to disappear into the shadows of the night.

LADY LAURANNA

Monday, September 1st — 0500 Eastern Time — Boston

Beth looks around as the portal climbs and changes to smoke.

"Great, Abigail," Beth says. "A circular room with a wall of swirling, black smoke and a single lit candle floating in the corner. A trapping spell. The candle must be for the ambiance," Beth says, waving her hand while using a French accent. "What more could a girl ask?"

She gives Abigail a 'Not impressed,' look, saying, "We're in trouble again, aren't we?"

Abigail glances around as she lowers Lochran to the floor, then looks back at Beth, winks, and takes her jaguar form.

"I take it that means 'Yes'?"

Beth's body tingles.

Easy, Mehla.

Beth switches to night vision and searches for signs of weak spots on the wall. Abigail walks the entire circle with her nose near the floor, and Beth changes her eyes to normal in time to see Abigail's tail flick before she launches herself into the blackness.

A woman screams, and the curtain of black evaporates like heavy smoke swirling in the wind.

Beth looks around the giant empty warehouse before she walks to where Abigail stands, poised to bite the throat of a young woman.

"Please don't kill me. I beg you."

Beth looks at her.

Same black hair, blue eyes, milky skin and Scottish accent. Familiar?

Beth kneels close as Abigail's teeth touch the skin of the young woman's throat, and she squeals.

"And who might you be?" Beth asks.

"She is my daughter, and you will release her unharmed, Abigail." The commanding Scottish voice comes from behind them.

Beth looks at Abigail with eyebrows raised. "Someone who knows you in your kitty form."

Looking over her shoulder at the voice, Beth sees two women walking out of a shield mist that wavers as it disappears. Beth stands while Abigail changes into her human form.

"Not a friendly welcome, Lauranna," Abigail says.

Beth hears the young woman on the floor scurry to her feet to walk around them to her mother's side.

"Breena cast the trapping spell because she thought it would protect the rest of the Guardians," Lauranna says. "Now she has learned it doesn't work on a shape-changer and will make changes." She turns to Beth. "Abigail, you have brought someone new."

"My name is Beth."

With authoritative posture, Lauranna says, "I assume you are a witch and a friend of Abigail's?"

"Yes, to both questions."

Abigail notices Beth's blunt answers to Lauranna's questions, but says nothing.

Lauranna and the other witch, Fiona, are only a few feet from her when Fiona shouts, "My Crystal."

Fiona makes a fast dash for the Crystal lying between Lochran's legs, and Beth casts a shield over Lochran. Fiona bounces off the shield, like a stone skipping across the surface of the water, and recovers, assuming a fight stance.

"Give me my Crystal now, or you will regret it."

Abigail sees the grin on Beth's face and knows she's not surrendering the Crystal.

"Beth. Why are you doing this?" Abigail says.

"Fiona, wait," Lauranna says. She walks closer to Beth. "Yes, why are you doing this?"

Without taking her eyes off Fiona, Beth says, "She claims the Crystal is hers. Why?"

"Fiona has been protecting that Crystal, as a mother, would protect a child, for nearly four-hundred years. She has earned the right to call it hers."

"A mother would die protecting a child, so how did she lose the Crystal and survive?"

"Fiona is a respected Guardian witch. How dare you ask that?" Lauranna snaps.

"Fiona, tell me how you survived the battle when so many others died?" Beth says.

"Wounded, I fell unconscious behind the rocks."

"You're lying," Beth says. "I saw the battle and the six witches who died trying to protect the Crystal, and I didn't see you in the fray."

Beth feels her body tingling, and she knows Mehla wants to jump into action, so she calms herself.

"What do you mean, you saw the battle?" Lauranna says.

Still, with her eyes locked on Fiona's, Beth says, "When I touched the Crystal, it showed me the fight." Beth raises her arm and points at Fiona. "She wasn't in the picture."

Lauranna, Breena, Abigail, and Beth are all looking at Fiona.

Lauranna asks, "Fiona. How is that possible?"

Beth notices Fiona slipping her hands behind her back and then sees the edge of a black glow around Fiona's right wrist.

Is she a Dark Spirit Witch?

Fiona's eyes change to glowing black pools.

"I'm taking that Crystal back to my Queen and your dead bodies with it."

Fiona twists her body right, throwing her glowing left hand at Lauranna and Breena. Lauranna throws her arm across her front, but the curse still knocks them to the ground. Abigail steps forward, casting a curse, but Fiona side-steps it, swinging her left arm wide like a roundhouse slap, and sends Abigail flying backward, crashing into a support column for the roof. Fiona spins and her glowing right hand snaps toward Beth, casting a beach ball-sized ring filled with razor-sharp blades and steel spikes. Beth leaps into the air and opens her arms as if welcoming the ring into her body. She brings her hands together in a large arc, and Fiona, stunned by how easily Beth captures her magic, watches the ring shrink to the size of a baseball. Fiona moves sideways to launch a second attack when Beth changes to the glowing image of Princess Mehla, and Fiona stops.

"In Ireland," Mehla shouts, "treason against my sister, Princess Sadreen, carries the penalty of death!"

Mehla's hands go to the prayer position. Lifting her elbows, she rolls her fingertips back until they touch her chest. Her hands form a V, with her palms facing Fiona, and she snaps her fingertips toward Fiona. The compressed ball shoots back at Fiona, striking her mid-chest and leaving a hole.

Fiona drops like a dress slipping from a clothes hanger, making a small sound as she hits the floor.

A few moments later, Princess Mehla hears Abigail's throaty growl and slips back to the ground, where Beth finds Abigail sitting.

She puts her arms around the powerful black cat, saying, "Abigail. I love the way you purr."

She tries to tighten her arms around her, but Abigail pulls away hard, and Beth's hand slaps the concrete as she catches herself from falling. Abigail returns to her human form, saying, "Beth, why did you kill her?"

"What are you talking about, Abigail? Kill who?"

Beth catches movement to her right. She turns her head and sees hundreds of Guardians have appeared during the fray, and they have dropped to one knee with their heads bowed. Lauranna and Breena are only a few feet away, and they scramble to recover from Fiona's attack, stopping in the bowing position.

"Abigail, what happened? Who did I kill?"

"Beth, do you not remember? You killed Fiona instead of capturing her for questioning." Abigail draws a sharp breath. "Beth, where is your amulet?"

Beth's hand slaps against her chest, and she feels nothing. She thinks back through the battle at the warehouse.

The chain is unbreakable, so no one could have grabbed it.

Her mind shifts to the condo.

"It must have slipped off when I was changing clothes, and I never noticed."

Beth realizes everyone is still kneeling.

"Lauranna, please stand."

Lauranna and the remaining Guardians stand.

"Princess, please accept my apologies for both my daughter and me. The way we treated you wouldn't have happened had we known it was you from the start."

Beth can hear the worry in Lauranna's voice.

"There is nothing to apologize for, Lauranna, because I wanted to keep Princess Mehla a secret until I knew what was happening."

"Princess, I promise the Guardians will keep your secret."

Beth looks at Lauranna with a cocked brow while throwing her arms and hands toward Fiona, saying, "I think the enemy is inside the gate."

"Yes, Princess. Of course."

Abigail steps up to Beth's side.

"We need to get your amulet before Princess Mehla takes over your body again."

"*You* need to get Lochran healthy, and *I* need to get my amulet."

Beth turns to Lauranna. "Is there anyone here who can help Lochran?"

"What happened to him?"

"Rebekah cursed him with a parasite curse," Abigail says.

"Do you remember hearing the curse?"

Abigail shakes her head with a disappointed look on her face.

"She used, '*Schut-para-sit*'," Beth says.

"Thank you, Princess."

Lauranna turns to the five witches who came up behind her, telling them what she needs, and they move toward Lochran.

"Princess, you need to remove your shield?"

Beth waves her glowing hand.

"The Prince Stone," one of the five witches says as she points at Lochran's lap.

Lauranna and the witches look at Abigail and Beth in surprise. Beth turns to Abigail.

"You tell the story, and I'll go find my amulet."

Beth casts a portal and walks through it while Abigail spurs everyone into saving Lochran.

***

The smell of the salty ocean air and rotting ocean flora rushes her senses as Beth slips out of her portal onto a magic hover board under the pier beside her condo. She slips between the pilings and through the protection shield, to the hidden section of pier her condo is on. She reaches her hands, with glowing palms, over her head, saying, *Vis meg* (Show me), forming a looking portal and checks the herb and vegetable gardens for unwanted magical people.

"All clear," she whispers.

She casts an opening through the pier deck and jumps up from her hover board into her garden area, circles her hands to levitate an inch above the deck, and darts under her raised condo. She enters through a shielded secret entrance in the bathroom cupboard and, touching the wall, she whispers a spell to paralyze anyone in her condo. "*Paralyzer fiender.*" (Paralyze enemies)

Beth steps out of the cupboard and walks to her bedroom, where she finds the clothes she wore before the warehouse battle. As she lifts the shirt from the floor, the amulet drops to the carpet, and Beth kneels to pick it up but hesitates as she takes the chain in her hand and Mehla's voice rings in her mind.

Beth, you don't need the amulet anymore. You have control of my spirit, and it will be easier to use my powers if you're not wearing the amulet. Trust in your power. Remember, Freya says you are my equal in the last battle. You are as powerful as me. Trust yourself.

Beth lets the chain slide from her hand, leaving the glowing amulet on the carpet, and goes to the kitchen to get a bottle of water from the fridge. She holds the bottle to her lips, and as the cold water trickles into her mouth, a green laser light zips across the wall toward her. The water bottle hangs, unsupported, for a moment as Beth spins toward the front stairs with both hands glowing and ready to cast. The bottle hits the floor and water splashes on her, but her gaze stays fixed.

"Show yourself," she shouts.

The light sweeps across the room again in the same pattern.

It's coming through the living room window. No way SWAT is getting through my protection spell.

Beth drops her hands, stands, and waits for the sound of an attempted breach.

The green laser light passes through the room in the exact pattern again, and as Beth walks toward the window, her eyes glow green like the glow in her palms and she shouts, "You want to fight me! Death welcomes you mortals!"

Beth spins away from the window and runs to her bedroom, dropping to her knees hard as she scoops the amulet and slides the chain over her head. The chain touches her neck; her body shakes, her stomach cramps, and she throws her arms around her midsection as she falls sideways into the fetal position, blacking out.

"LysaBeth, do you hear me?"

Her mind's eye clears, and she sees the face of Freya.

"I hear you, Freya."

"Well, it's not good to hear something and not pay attention," Freya, now in the room with her, says. "You let Mehla have control, and the pain you're feeling is the amulet pulling her from your body. I told you not to remove the amulet."

"I'm sorry, but I didn't realize the amulet had slipped off while I was changing clothes."

The Witch of Loch Shin kneels beside Beth.

"Child, you are our only hope of getting the prince and princess together, and if you let anything interfere, the entire magical world will suffer for it. LysaBeth, you are the only person in both worlds who has the power to save the future of magic, and we may never get another chance. Egret and I have taught you spell's that should take a hundred years for someone to master, but you have succeeded in fifteen years."

Freya takes a quick breath.

"LysaBeth, the spirit of Princess Mehla is the only thing that can hurt you. The amulet doesn't hurt her. It heals her and stops her power-lust and disregard for life, and that is why you killed that witch tonight. It wasn't you who did it, but Mehla using your body to vent the anger she has built since her death at the wedding."

Beth opens her eyes. She's lying on her bedroom floor, and the sun is slipping under the horizon.

"I understand, Freya." But Freya has faded away with the dream.

Beth puts herself on her knees.

"Thanks for the beat-down, Mehla. You suck."

She lifts herself to her feet, stretches her body to loosen her muscles, and, moving to the door, she stops and speaks into the emptiness of her condo.

"Sorry if I caused you any grief, Freya. It won't happen again."

Beth draws a full breath, and a surge of energy takes away the muscle pain, signaling her apology accepted.

She makes her way to the fridge to get another bottle of water, grabs a towel, and throws it on the floor to soak up the first one. The towel hits the floor as the green laser light flashes across her wall again.

"What the heck. Who's the idiot with the laser?"

Beth walks to the side of her living room window, where she peeks around the corner and sees Jack Sebastian. He's standing against the warehouse wall, across the lot, sweeping the laser light as if he's auditioning to be a lighthouse.

"Thanks, Jack. You idiot," Beth says, and she casts a portal.

"What the hell do you think you're doing, you dumb ass?"

Jack jumps away from the building and spins one-eighty to face Beth.

"Don't do that."

Beth grabs the laser light from Jack and turns it to dust in her hand.

"Why don't you hang a freaking neon sign that says, 'Hey, a witch lives here!' and save yourself the lost time, you *dumb ass*."

Beth's eyes change to smoky glass, and she scans the surrounding yard.

"That's cool. The eye thing," Jack says.

"You're lucky no one else saw that stupid laser trick. Do that again, and I'll dip you in fish guts and drop you in the ocean off the coast of Australia. Got it?"

Jack steps back, putting his hands in the surrender position, saying, "Yes, Ma'am."

After a few seconds of silence, Jack smiles.

"So that's how you did it, then?"

"Did what?"

"You conjured up one of those circle things and disappeared right out of the hospital. No wonder there was no trace of you, and I never saw you sneak out."

"So, you're the rookie cop?"

"Yep, top of my class with a college degree and all the right recommendations. I should have made captain in ten years, maybe Chief in twenty, but your little trick has me chasing cheating wives and husbands, finding run-away kids, or bail jumpers. Thanks for the crappy life."

"I'm sorry it screwed your life up, but it wasn't intentional, and by the way... I was nine. What do you think I'm going to do to change that?"

"I need you to prove to the new Chief of Police that the abduction never happened, and I didn't screw up. He wrote one of my letters of recommendation, and I'm positive he'll still give me a chance at a career."

The look on Beth's face tells Jack that it's a hard sell.

"While you take a day or two to think how to do it, as an incentive, I might have something you lost."

Beth cocks her eyebrow. "Lost? You're crazy."

"Oh? Six-foot-two, Scottish accent, and built like a tank?"

Beth never had the desire to know someone until she met Karse at the warehouse for the first time, and then again when Rebekah disturbed the impromptu meeting. Her heart races from the thought of finding him again, and she steps closer to Jack.

"You know where he is?"

"I might," Jack responds, cocky, and Beth steps nearer still.

Her finger an inch from his face and eyes steeled, she says, "You need to focus your idiotic brain on the place that Karse is at, or I swear you're going swimming."

Jack closes his eyes so fast that his forehead burns with pain until nausea and vertigo, from traveling through a magic portal for the first time, take over.

Jack knows he's falling sideways and opens his eyes in time to see his living room lamp shade slam into his face. He falls on the end table beside his broken easy chair, crushing it, and hits the floor. Then he hears Beth's familiar, demanding tone.

"What happened to you last night? I came to find you by the warehouse, and you were gone."

Karse, lounging on the couch, waits a moment, then points at Jack as he pulls himself from the rubble created by his crash landing.

Beth looks at Jack as he steadies himself.

"Thanks for saving him."

"Told ya," Jack says.

Beth turns back to Karse. "Why haven't you left?"

"Lost my wand. I convinced Jack to find you, so I could ask for help to find it."

Beth stares at Karse.

My heart is pounding so hard, I can't tell if I can trust this man. Strange how he does that to me.

Karse looks past Beth at Jack.

"She's still trying to decide if she can trust me."

"True," Beth snaps.

"How come you don't need a wand, but he does, and why is he called a witch or wizard instead of a warlock?" Jack asks.

Beth lets out a gentle sigh as she turns to Jack.

"Everyone's a witch," she says. "Wizards are male witches, if you want to be specific. So, Karse, technically, is a wizard. Warlocks, again male, practice evil or dark magic."

"The down and dirty—Everyone has magic in them, and a few, enough magic that they can learn how to use it through spells and a wand. When needed, the Universe sees fit to create a witch with abilities way beyond the average, like me. Most witches control or manipulate the four elements of earth, water, fire, and air. They can't use the fifth element, the Spirit of the Universe. We, the natural or spirit witches, don't need wands because we draw power from the Spirit by focusing our minds on the result. In most cases, by the time an ordinary witch casts a spell or curse with a wand, we've defeated them by seeing what we want. There are wand witches near the edge of being a Natural or Spirit witch who can do damage to a real Spirit witch."

"So, you're immortal and bulletproof," Jack says.

"No," Beth says. "The Universe creates balance. There are groups of witches, called a Coven of Nine, that can bind themselves together and overpower a Natural Witch, but they can't kill the Natural Witch. The grouping happens when a Spirit Witch goes out of control or turns dark and tries to rule the world. When the grouping is not possible, because the Natural Witch kills them, the

Universe steps in. It creates another Natural Witch who fights to create balance again."

Beth pauses as she turns her head to Karse.

"Like me."

Karse can see by the sober look on Beth's face she has realized her purpose, and he nods.

"So, I take it that little skirmish at the warehouse was with the Natural Witch that's gone out of control?" Jack says.

Beth shakes her head. "Not even close. That was her second in command and the minions. They were there looking for someone," Beth says and glances toward Karse, "and something. We need to go."

Beth turns her head back to Jack with her finger pointed at him. "You better stay away from my place, or I will...."

"Yeah, yeah. I know. Swimming with the sharks. Got it."

Beth steps up to Jack, still holding his hands in the surrender position.

"Hold out your right hand, palm up, and lift the left side of your shirt."

Jack doesn't move until Beth locks eyes with him and cocks her eyebrow.

"Yep," Jack says, following her orders.

Beth hears Karse snicker at Jack's reaction as she touches her left index finger to Jack's palm and the right index finger against his bottom rib on the left side of his body.

"If anything happens to you that involves witches, place your palm over this spot and hold it there. I'll find you as quick as possible but tell no one. You must hold it there for a few seconds to activate it because you don't want it to go off in the shower."

Beth takes her hands away from Jack. She turns, pushing her palm toward an empty spot in the kitchen, casting a swirling circle of white mist. She stretches her other hand toward Karse, and he jumps up from the couch to take it, happy knowing that she's trusting him.

Jack stares at the glowing dot in his palm as it fades away, and as she steps through the portal, Beth looks back at Jack, saying, "Oh yeah. About that shower."

Jack looks toward the portal as it closes with the slight sound of electricity, and he stares at the empty spot. He thinks about everything that's happened and his new understanding of a world he never believed existed.

Jack hears two solid thumps behind him and jumps, turning to see two packets on his kitchen table. As he gets closer and reads each label, his stomach and legs go weak. 'United States Bearer Bond. One-hundred thousand dollars.'

Jack feels warm tears run down his cheeks, and before his legs give out, he sits on his only remaining broken-down kitchen chair that is built from two broken chairs. He looks around at the broken and tattered furniture, rust-stained sink and leaky faucet mounted on a broken cabinet, cracked windows, and the peeling paint of his dive apartment.

"I can't take a shower," he whispers. "It doesn't work, and the scum-lord won't fix it."

He folds his arms across the packets and places his forehead on them.

"Thank you, Beth."

No one hears the quiet sob of Jack Sebastian as hope sheds the chain of wrongful dismissal from fifteen years ago.

FROZEN PROPHECY

Monday, September 1st — 1000 Pacific Time — Delta

Rhynan hears voices, smells of vomit, and remembers the battle at the coffee shop before opening his eyes.

How did I get into my bedroom?

Sitting up, he listens to the voices in the other room before calling out, "Aaghnya?"

Silence follows until Rhynan hears the footsteps before his bedroom door opens.

"You should get yourself cleaned up," says the red-bearded, husky man with a brush cut, piercing green eyes, and an Irish accent.

"Who are you? What are you doing in my apartment?"

Colin stares, stone-faced, at Rhynan for a moment.

"I'm Colin. Captain of the Irish Guardians that saved your life. You're a mess. Clean yourself up, and then we'll talk."

Colin leaves Rhynan to sort himself out, and as he stands at his dresser, he remembers the battle. Tears roll down his cheeks and fall onto the neatly folded clean clothes in the drawer. He gathers what he needs, and stepping into the hallway, Rhynan ignores the man walking past him who says, "The pain goes away. You'll be fine."

Rhynan doesn't respond to the man's advice and continues to the washroom for his shower. He finishes his shower and throws his dirty clothes in the hamper by the back door of his apartment. He walks to the end of the hallway, where it opens into the main living area, to see Colin standing in the kitchen while four more men and one woman sit in his living room. They go silent as Rhynan walks in.

"Why are you in my apartment?"

Colleen, second in command of the Irish Guardians, stands up from the big lounge chair, where Rhynan sits to watch weekend sports.

"Rhynan, it's crucial that you hear what I have to say. Please, sit."

Rhynan stands there for a moment, then tears run down his face and he chokes on the words, "Aaghnya's dead. Isn't she?"

Colleen looks around the room, and everyone shrugs their shoulders or shakes their heads.

"Who's Aaghnya?"

"Aaghnya is my girlfriend, and she was fighting Rebekah to save me. I don't understand why she had to do that."

Rhynan breaks into a full sob, and the men in the room look away.

"Rhynan, listen to me," Colleen says. "During the battle, a girl died, and another injured, but I don't know the names or who died. Rhynan, we have more important things to discuss."

Colleen's words sink in, and Rhynan lifts his head as he remembers seeing Petia holding Dehlia's body and crying.

"Dehlia. Dehlia died in the fight, so that means Aaghnya is still alive. I have to go to her," he says, as he brightens. Rhynan wheels his body toward the front door, and Colleen grabs his arm saying, "No, you don't."

"Ow, that hurts."

"Rhynan, you are being hunted and you need to listen to me," Colleen says.

"No. I'm going to Aaghnya. She needs me."

A giant of a man slips from behind Colleen and grabs Rhynan, forcing him into the easy chair and lowers his head close to Rhynan's, saying, "You need to listen to her, laddie."

Through a flood of tears, Rhynan squeaks out, "Why won't you let me see Aaghnya?"

"Rhynan, you need to listen to me," Colleen says again.

"And get a backbone," interjects another Guardian.

Colleen grabs a footstool and sits on it in front of Rhynan.

"Rhynan, listen to me."

Colleen spends twenty minutes telling him of the prince's soul, what the dream meant, and why Aaghnya had to defend him against Rebekah. Rhynan, with a vacant look, nods his head.

Why are they trying to keep me from Aaghnya? I need to go to her.

"Rhynan, are you alright?" Colleen says.

"Uh-huh." Rhynan nods. "Witches, royal spirits, Irish Guardians, end of time. Holy smokes."

"So, you understand. You don't leave this place without us? Yes?"

"Absolutely."

Colleen stands up and walks over to Colin.

"All right, lads," Colin says. "Watch him, and we'll return soon."

The rest of the Irish Guardians nod as Colin casts a portal in the kitchen. The two Guardians step through it, disappearing with the slight sound of electricity, and Rhynan pushes himself away from the sound. He stares for a short time, then scanning the room, he sees the Guardians smirking at him.

"That's how you got here from the battle this morning," Darrin says.

Rhynan recognizes the reddish-blond hair, piercing green eyes, and stern tone from the coffee shop this morning, and he feels nauseous. Looking for a distraction, he grabs the television remote control, turns the television on, and the viewing menu opens. Rhynan finds a rugby match in full swing, grabbing the others' attention, so he kicks his lounge chair back and puts his feet up.

After several minutes, the picture changes, and the game pauses. "Halftime break," Rhynan says. "Is it okay to do my laundry?"

"Rhynan, do nothing foolish, or you'll be sitting in that chair with chains," Darrin says.

Putting his hands up, Rhynan surrenders, saying, "I wouldn't think of it."

Rhynan gets up to gather his wash, and Darrin signals the other Guardians to watch him. Michael, a muscular, freckle-skinned redhead, places himself at the end of the kitchen counter, where he can see both the hallway and the television.

Rhynan collects his laundry and turns to Michael.

"I'm going down the hall to load the machine."

"Aye, remember what Darrin said. Don't be foolish."

Rhynan nods his head and moves to the closet at his back door. He props the closet door open, blocking Michael's view to the back door, then slips out and hustles down the stairs to his secure locker. Rhynan changes into the riding gear he stuffed inside the dirty laundry and retrieves the mountain bike hanging from the wall. He moves to the end of the lockers and surveys the main entrance of the underground parking. Rhynan gets a break when another owner opens the gate to enter the parking garage, then across the lot, he glimpses the man who came out of his bathroom.

They're outside, guarding the building. I need to wait until the gate is closing.

Rhynan rides through the closing gate and waves to the groundskeeper out in front of the building, who waves back. He turns onto the road and looks in his side mirror.

They don't know it's me leaving.

He pedals faster.

Ten minutes after Rhynan leaves the apartment, Darrin turns to Michael. "Where is he?"

"There, doing the laundry."

"Have a look."

Michael jumps up and walks down the hall to find the back door unlatched.

"He's gone," Michael shouts.

Darrin exits a portal in the back corner of the building and calls a Guardian out of hiding.

"What have you seen?" Darrin says.

"Nothing but three cars in and a bicycle rider out."

"Damn. The bicycle rider. He's the one with the prince in him."

The other Guardians from the apartment appear behind Darrin, who turns to Michael.

"Get Colin."

Michael disappears, and soon after, Colin steps out of a portal with Michael and Colleen in tow. "How the bloody hell did this happen?"

"He needed to get the stink out of his clothes, so he asked to do his wash," Darrin says. "Michael was watching him, but this Rhynan is slippery. How is it we weren't told that he had a bicycle in the back hall? Whose fault is that?"

Colin doesn't respond right away as he thinks through the first security check. "There was no bicycle in the hall. Michael, check the parking."

Micheal returns minutes later. "I found a locker open with his laundry in it. It must have been where he had the bicycle."

Colin nods his head before giving Michael a quick pat on the shoulder.

"Alright, lads. Darrin's right. He's a slippery one. Now we need to find him fast before that blood-thirsty bitch Rebekah does. Any ideas?"

ROYAL SOULS

Across the street from Rhynan's apartment building, three Blood Witches peer over the grocery store roof's raised edge. They watch the Irish Guardians until one witch takes her wand, points it toward the garbage dumpster behind the Guardians, and none notices the little puff of smoke.

The spy spider makes its way from behind the garbage dumpster into a stack of rubble next to Gareth, a Guardian, standing guard. Gareth turns, his kilt brushing the rubble, and the spy spider latches on to the inside of the material.

"Look," Colleen says, pointing to the roof of the grocery store. The rest of the Guardians turn to see the gray smoke of a portal before it disappears from the rooftop.

"She knows now," Colleen says.

"It's a race to the death, lads," Colin says.

"Wait," Michael says. "The restaurant? The one we tracked him to with the brown witch."

Colin points to a Junior Guardian. "Do you remember where to find it?"

The young man nods his head.

"Get reinforcements," Colin says.

The young Guardian jumps through his portal, and Colin looks at everyone.

"Make no mistake. We're in a fight for our existence."

Michael casts a portal to the restaurant and stands aside as the rest jump through.

***

The Guardian portal opens into a parking lot across from the waterfront restaurant owned by Aaghnya's family. The Irish Guardians take cover behind a car and Colin looks through the door glass of the car to see Rhynan pull his bike from the trunk of a taxicab. Rhynan calls out to Aaghnya's sister Petia, as she greets customers coming to the restaurant. Petia, fear in her eyes, runs toward Rhynan, meeting him in the center of the parking lot.

"Why are you here, Rhynan? It is Dehlia's wake and not safe for you to be here. We are being watched."

The air shifts as three large portals take shape, each near one-hundred feet away from the front door of the waterfront restaurant, at the north, east, and west points.

"Rhynan, they have found you," Petia says, before leaping into the air, spinning and landing dressed in the same style of battle clothes as she wore during the coffee shop battle.

"Save the prince at any cost," Colin says, leaping out from their hiding spot and charging across the street with the rest of the Guardians close behind.

Blood Witches pour out of the three portals, and Rhynan freezes, dropping his bicycle in the center of the parking lot. A curse cast at Petia misses both of them but is still close enough to Rhynan that it causes him nausea and disorients him. Rhynan staggers, tries to steady himself, then stumbles again at the sight of Japanese wizards jumping out of a pruned brush in front of the Japanese temple across the street. They engage the Blood Witches on the east side as they run toward the restaurant, and the Irish cut into the fight with the Blood Witches from the north portal. The restaurant's front door explodes open, and Indian warriors rush out to battle the witches coming from the west portal.

Rhynan staggers toward the garden as an errant curse hits the ground, and the explosion sprays him with earth and foliage. He turns away from the explosion, misses an airborne Blood Witch, struck by a curse, flailing past him, but a swinging arm catches him in the shoulder. He spins from the strike, and staggers back toward the center of the parking lot. Then Rhynan glances around, disoriented in disbelief as the carnage ignites his memories of Aaghnya at the coffee shop, and he freezes in the middle of the parking lot.

Petia sees Rhynan, still and blank, staring into the carnage. She runs to him and pulls him to a statue of Aiyanar, guarding the pathway to the restaurant, saying, "Rhynan, don't move."

She sweeps her hand from head to toe, casting protection over him before returning to the fight.

Rhynan looks around at the battle and slides down the pillar as desperation crushes his mind. He wraps his arms around his legs and pulls his knees tight to his chest as his mind folds inward like an induced dream overtaking him.

Aaghnya jumps over his bike, spins in the air, and Rhynan witnesses her magical change to her witch look.

Aaghnya? She's so beautiful. She's coming to save me?

Her body slams against him, and he shocks back to reality, throwing his arms around her.

"Rhynan, we need to get to the restaurant."

"Aaghnya, it's you. You're alive."

"Yes, Rhynan. We must get you to the restaurant. NOW."

Rhynan never thought Aaghnya a physical person, so it surprises him when she breaks his hug, taps his head and foot, and lifts him to his feet.

"Wow, Aaghnya. You're strong."

Aaghnya jerks him sideways, out of the line of fire, as she blocks a curse and starts dancing toward the four witches advancing on them.

"Rhynan, go to the restaurant!" she yells.

The Blood Witches have the restaurant surrounded, and the prince's defenders are being pushed back toward the center of the parking lot. Rhynan, launching himself toward the restaurant door, sees a wizard, wearing a blue cloak with a silver snowflake emblem on it, slide out from behind the other statue of Aiyanar, opposite him. The wizard raises his wand over his head, and Rhynan follows his stony stare.

"Aaghnya. He's going to attack Aaghnya," he mumbles.

Rhynan Doon, as a child, had courage beat out of him by his father, so in his lifetime, he's done nothing risky or heroic, but something deep inside turns him toward Aaghnya. He stumbles, falls, and the gripping hot pavement tears into the flesh on his hands and bare knees. He rolls, then spins to his feet and, with a few steps, throws his body against Aaghnya's, blocking the curse cast by the wizard. Rhynan's body hits the ground, then the curse snaps him to a standing position, and his eerie cry pierces the ears of everyone on the battlefield. The fighting stops, and all bear witness to the first mortal suffering the excruciating glassing curse.

ROYAL SOULS

Hoarfrost-like crystals form on the surface of Rhynan's biking shoes and climb up his body. More layers of the crystals form on top of the first, forming a thick glass, and as the crystals climb his bare legs, his skin turns grayish-blue.

"Rhynan, no!" Aaghnya screams.

Aaghnya's eyes burst with copper light that surrounds her body, and she unleashes an attack that forces the Guardians to drop to the ground and the Blood Witches to retreat.

Rhynan lets out another banshee scream as the glass reaches his midsection, and Aaghnya ceases her attack to run to him. Tears rolling down her cheeks, she touches Rhynan's face. "Why did you do this, Rhynan Doon?"

The curse reaches the middle of Rhynan's chest, and he screams again as his heart feels the touch of the glassing curse.

Pain shoots up his spine to his brain, and through the agony, he whispers to her with his last breath, "Aaghnya, I love you."

The glass covers his throat, silencing him, and as it creeps over his face to the top of his head, Aaghnya cries out.

The Guardians were back on their feet, stunned, as they watched the last moments of Rhynan's suffering.

Darrin looks around. "They're gone."

Everyone looks around to see the Blood Witches have retreated in victory.

"Didn't know he had it in him," Colleen says. "But like a real man, he gave it all to the women he loves."

189

Aaghnya looks at Colleen, brow furrowed, eyes squinting, and face tight. "I will get my Rhynan Doon back."

"Where's Colin?" Michael says.

The Irish Guardians spread out to look for their captain. Michael shouts, "Over here."

The Irish Guardians gather at the corner of the building where their captain lay, lifeless and burned. They stand silent, stunned by the loss.

"We're losing too many good people," Colleen says.

Petia's agonizing cry shocks the Guardians to draw wands and rush to see its cause. When Aaghnya pushes through the crowd, she cries out also, because their father lay lifeless on the pavement.

The Indian warriors gather to recover their fallen elder, and Darrin takes to one knee as a symbol of sharing their grief. Once the Indian leader is through the restaurant's door, Darrin stands and turns toward the Irish.

"I know where we have to take Rhynan," Colleen says.

Michael points to the back of Gareth's kilt, where the leg of the spy spider hangs below the hem. "What's that?"

Gareth looks around his hip and grabs his kilt, so he's holding the spider in his grip, and as he brings it around to the front, it explodes into smoke.

"Now we know how they're tracking us," Colleen says. She pauses, then points to Rhynan. "But how did they know where he was? Because he was here before us."

"Check each other for more," Darrin says.

"Aaghnya, tend to your father, then join us," Colleen says.

"Where will I find you?"

ROYAL SOULS

Colleen steps up to Aaghnya and whispers in her ear. "Okay, I will be there."

Shattered emotions, Aaghnya walks away and passes through the restaurant door. The Guardians pick up Colin's lifeless body, gather around Rhynan's glassed form, and Colleen circles her wand above her, casting a portal that drops over them.

***

Queen Sorcha jumps out of her throne, stopping only inches away from Francois.

"Rhynan Doon is the carrier, and you have him in glass?"

"Ahh, *oui*."

Queen Sorcha's face lights up, and she spins back to her throne, mounting it in a regal form.

"Queen Sorcha." Francois pauses as Sorcha cocks her head and poses. "With no one knowing, I sent one of my best to the fight, and he glassed the carrier. Now, they cannot get the prince out of the glass, so they cannot reunite him with his bride. It is done. No?"

"Yes, Francois," Queen Sorcha shouts, laughing, then breathes, "I win,"

Caitriona steps out of her portal and bows her head.

"My Queen. Such radiance."

"Yes. It is a victorious day."

Queen Sorcha lowers her head to look at Caitriona.

"Where... is it?"

Caitriona bows again. "My Queen, I bring you a greater gift."

191

Queen Sorcha's face turns sober as she stands. She pauses, and with an icy glare, walks to Caitriona, putting her index finger under her chin and lifting until their eyes meet.

"Did... you... fail me?"

"No, My Queen. I promise I have done something even better than retrieving the Crystal or Stone."

"Explain."

"My Queen. I heard them say they are taking Rhynan to a secret place, so I put a glass spider on the glassed statue that may lead us to the princess."

Queen Sorcha contemplates Caitriona's actions, and her face changes to an evil grin as she lets her hand slip from Caitriona's chin to her cheek.

"You never cease to amaze me, Caitriona. Well done, my little spy."

"My Queen."

FIRST BLOOD

Monday September 1st — 1200 Eastern Time — Boston

Beth's portal opens on the same warehouse roof as the night before and, stepping out, she releases her grip with Karse, but he doesn't. She looks over her shoulder to see his head and thick shoulders slip through the mist, and her heart races again. Karse walks out of the portal and, keeping his eyes locked on Beth's, he raises the back of her hand to his lips and places a gentle kiss. Beth swings her body into Karse and throws her arms around his neck, kissing him as he wraps his muscular arms around her. A few moments later, she puts her hand on the side of Karse's face and, lifting her head away from his, she says, "To be continued."

"Aye, lass," Karse says with a long sigh, and he releases his bear hug on her.

She turns away from him, gives her head a slight shake as if to clear her mind, and she peers around the roof-mounted mechanical shed to survey the yard.

"I don't see anyone," she says, turning back to him. "I'll take us between the containers on the other side, across from the spot where you hit the wall."

"Beth, be careful. The enemy could be close."

I can sense it. He cares.

She touches the side of his face before casting a portal above them. It drops, and they disappear.

Knowing a wand witch can cause her surface injuries, Beth, cocky, walks out of the portal between the containers and surveys for threats.

"Karse, it's good."

They slip their way through the containers until they can see where Karse crash-landed after Rebekah sucker-punched him. Kneeling close to each other, they scan for Karse's wand.

"Got it," Beth whispers.

Beth points to the spot where the wand lies, and Karse leans into her as though siting a rifle.

His musky smell is driving me crazy. I think it's sandalwood. I love sandalwood.

"I don't see it."

"Six feet right of the steps, laying in the pile of rubble."

"Aye, I see it."

He turns to Beth, looking into her eyes, and she can't hold herself back.

She releases her passionate kiss, and he winks, saying, "Sharp eye, lass."

He bolts away without thought or plan, and Beth shakes her head.

"Wow, who does that remind me of? It must be a Scottish male thing."

Beth looks left then right for threats but sees none until a shadowy figure, cast from the top of the containers, grows longer on the ground as the person gets closer to the edge.

The figure raises its arm above its head with a wand in hand.

"Karse!"

The shadow on the ground changes position as the surprised witch reacts to Beth's shout.

Beth throws herself into the air between the figure and Karse, spinning like a figure skater and swinging her arm out like a prizefighter throwing a roundhouse punch. A quick flash from Beth's glowing right hand as she casts a curse, and the assassin launches sideways, falling from the container to the pavement. Karse reaches the rubble and, with a quick stab of his hand into the pile, he recovers his wand, and spins back to Beth in time to block a curse from a Blood Witch attacking from between two buildings. He flips his wand into the air and catching it in his fist, he retaliates with a motion like a hammer blow to the head of his attacker, and she grunts, folding into a pile. Beth touches down from her aerial defense, and as she turns to Karse, several smokey gray and black portals open near the warehouse where Lochran hid the Crystal and Stone.

"Beth, it's a trap. They left my wand here, knowing I will come for it."

She saunters toward him as he points toward the opposite end of the yard, where more gray and black portals are opening. Beth surveys the battlefield and drops her arm on his shoulder as if she's leaning on a car roof.

"Hmm, Blood Witches at both ends. Yep, it's a trap. But I didn't imagine catching this many dumb-ass witches in it."

Karse breaks into a barrel-chested laugh, and after, he looks at Beth, says, "I think I'm in love with you, lass."

Without breaking eye contact, Beth takes a couple of sultry steps backward with a touch of exotic in her smile, and says, "Delighted to hear that."

She spins toward the warehouse, where she first found Lochran, and her desire for Karse shatters in disbelief.

A forty-foot rolling ocean wave of smoke crashes to the pavement and explodes skyward. The smoke drifts away with the gentle breeze of the day to show the enemy.

"Oh crap," she whispers. "Hey, Karse? I think it's a tad bigger than a few witches," she says.

The smoke finishes clearing, and Beth shakes her head. In front of her must be a fifty-foot line of witches and wizards, and at the center, several witches clad in glistening red and black robes.

"Of course, Rebekah's leading the pack," Beth mumbles.

Dressed in heels and a red, three-quarter dress, Rebekah stands next to a woman clad in black robes, with a pattern of gray runes on them.

Okay, the woman in black robes is new. Wait, I recognize that crown. Princess Sadreen was wearing it when I saw the wedding battle.

"That must be the self-ordained Queen Sorcha," she says.

She surveys the entourage of witches that surround the queen and says, "They must be the Queen's royal guard and most trusted or best zealots."

Karse steps up behind Beth and touches her shoulder.

"That's Queen Sorcha with her royal guard and most trusted followers."

Beth curls her lips inward to stop her from bursting into laughter.

"Beth," Karse says. "I'll stand with you to the end, but even with your magic, I don't think we can win this battle. Queen Sorcha is a Spirit Witch like you."

Beth turns sideways to see both ends of the enemy's force and Karse.

"I can survive, but you might not. Time to get you out of here."

At that moment, Rebekah raises her hand, and the witches on the outer perimeter of the warehouse yard point their wands skyward, casting a shield that prevents Karse from leaving.

Beth looks at Karse. "Well, then. I guess it's a cage fight."

"Aye. We have to make sure the enemy regrets getting in the cage."

Karse gives Beth a quick glance and a mischievous smile that makes her giggle.

The light of the moment slips away as two snow-white cats, half a size larger than a full-grown male lion, make their way from behind Queen Sorcha and take a position in front.

"Holy crap. Those cats are magnificent," Beth says.

"I can think of better ways to die, lass."

One makes a turn sideways, and Beth notices how the flowing mane reaches to its tail in a thick line down its back. The feathering hair, hanging from the elbow of the foreleg, sweeps the surface of the ground around the paws. Their eyes are a glassy red, and they each sport two long fangs, on the top and bottom jaws, with a slight curve and they glisten like polished white granite.

"Ouch," Beth says.

"What is it, lass?"

"Those fangs will hurt if those kitties get the chance to bury them into your flesh."

"Aye, like I said. I can think of better ways to die."

The big cats let out a mighty roar, and Beth feels the vibrations rolling through the air.

"Okay. I've had enough of the posturing."

"Aye," Karse agrees.

"Rebekah," Beth shouts. "I see you're dressed to kill, as usual."

"Yes. How unfortunate for you, my little beauty," Rebekah says with a sinister laugh.

"That woman's laugh irritates the hell out of me," Beth says to Karse and then to Rebekah shouts, "I must admit, Rebekah. I'm disappointed."

"Oh, and why is that?"

Beth waves her hand across her body as though she's presenting the entourage.

"Well, all this and you without someone in black leather and holding their leash. A missed opportunity, don't you think?"

"Oh, please tell me you're volunteering, my little sweet?"

"Ya, that backfired," Beth breathes.

"Enough playing, Rebekah," Queen Sorcha snaps. "I am Queen Sorcha. Where are the Crystal and Prince Stone, Princess?"

Karse looks over at Beth.

"Princess, is it?"

"Later."

"Oh, aye. If we live through this, I'll be getting an answer... Princess."

The absolution in Karse's voice touches an emotion never felt, and her heart races. His commitment to die beside her sinks Cupid's arrow deep, and her breathing rate spikes.

She looks at him and thinks, *What a feeble effort at looking stern.*

She lets a sultry smile form and winks, crushing his faux toughness, and he breaks. Laughing.

"Oh, aye, absolutely later."

Beth turns her attention back to Queen Sorcha and company.

I need to snap her mind and force her to make a mistake.

"Wow, psycho one and two at the same party. You know, Sorcha, you might take a few fashion tips from Rebekah. It could improve your chances on the dating scene."

Rebekah's face turns stone cold, and her glare tells Beth she's started a popularity contest between Rebekah and Sorcha.

Rebekah sees Queen Sorcha looking toward her from the corner of her eye.

"How dare you insult our queen, you little bitch!" Rebekah shouts before turning and bowing head to Queen Sorcha.

Queen Sorcha floats upward until she's three feet above Rebekah and shouts, "You will call me Queen Sorcha, and I will have the Crystal and Stone, now."

"Rattling the birdcage was easier than I expected. Two for the price of one," Beth says to Karse. "Let's crank it up a notch."

"Of course," he replies.

Beth laughs out loud.

"Uh, huh? The whole queen thing ain't happening, Sister, and as for Princess Sadreen's crown, well, that's nothing less than pathetic jealousy."

A surge shoots through Beth's body, and she knows that Princess Mehla approves of Beth's verbal attack.

Queen Sorcha floats higher, eyes glowing black and skin fading to gray, with her robes fanned into spiked wings, and Beth throws her arms in the air and shouts, "Yes!"

The Blood Witches move away from Queen Sorcha because they've witnessed her kill a half dozen witches for not bowing in her presence during her current mental state.

Then Beth cranks disrespect over the top.

"Oh, by the way. Princess Mehla wants that crown back, so when I'm finished kicking your ass, I will take it."

Karse looks over his shoulder at Beth.

"Oh, aye, that should light the fires."

Beth giggles. "Stay very close to me."

She feels Karse's back touch against hers, and she smiles.

"Take them," Sorcha shouts.

"Wow. What a lovely male, demonic voice you have. How many cats have you got in that bag?" Beth shouts.

Beth knows nothing can stop her from leaving, but she isn't sure if trying to pull Karse through the shield will kill him. She turns and casts an armor spell over him.

Karse tries to turn to her, but the spell holds him like a cocoon.

"What are you doing? Let me fight with you!"

Beth walks to the front of Karse.

"Sorry, handsome. I want you to survive this with me, so we can have that talk later. The best have tested that armor shield spell, so I know you'll survive."

She winks at Karse as the first curse cast from Rebekah's side hits the back of his shield.

Beth spins, both hands glowing, and she launches a curse that spreads like shrapnel from a grenade. Eight witches, running toward her from the cover of a warehouse, drop. She spins again to the other side, throwing the same curse, downing an equal number of witches on the container side of the battlefield.

"This might still be a quick victory," Beth snickers.

"Ahh! What the hell?"

Beth looks at a burned and bloody hole in the right side of her shirt and, looking right, she sees a witch standing in the open with the glow of a shield around her. She's giving Beth a 'Come and get me' look before she disappears.

"How did she do that? There's no way she should have been able to cast that spell."

"Ahh!" Beth cries out.

She turns to see one of the big cats has slipped around her and tore through her shield with its paw, ripping her pants and inflicting a burning flesh wound to her left thigh.

She throws her arm sideways, shouting, "*Drepe!*" A light flashes from her palm as she casts a curse, but instead of a pile of dust, the cat tumbles backward twenty feet, unconscious. Beth notices a faint rippling in the air around the unconscious cat's body, so she changes her eyes to night vision and sees black lines of energy flowing from Queen Sorcha to the cat.

"What the what? Is she casting a shield or sharing her power?"

She changes her eyes back, then whispers, "Time for the big gun. Mehla, I need your help."

Beth waits.

Nothing.

What the hell, Mehla?

Beth, release me. Remove the amulet and we can destroy Sorcha together.

After the last beat down you gave me, it's not happening, Mehla.

A blinding streak of black-blue light rips across the landscape, on Beth's right side, with four quick bursts of light, and then the left, with four more bursts of light, and the shield over the battlefield quivers and fails. Beth looks over her left shoulder at Karse and, from the corner of her eye, she sees the second Snow Lion leap into the air toward him. She twists her body right to cast a curse when something brushes the side of her head and shoulder. Beth ducks away from the unknown streak of black that hits the Snow Lion broadside, spinning it sideways and slamming it into a steel container.

202

"Abigail!" Beth shouts.

The first snow-cat, recovered from Beth's curse, responds to its downed mate with a loud roar. Abigail spins, ears pinned and teeth bared, to the snow-cat and responds to the challenge with as loud a roar. Beth is stunned at how ferocious Abigail looks as she pins her ears again and takes two quick steps forward to meet the attacking white lion.

The display of raw power awes Beth as the two opponents each unleash a flurry of clawed paws that sounds like sledgehammers slapping a hanging side of beef. After exchanging flesh tearing rights and lefts, the white lion launches its large body upward, trying to gain the top advantage. Abigail catches it in midair, pulling the Snow Lion into her, and the two cats grapple for the dominant position while trying to sink their teeth. Beth recoils, catching her breath, as the lion rips its claw along Abigail's ribs and the torn flesh oozes blood.

"Oh no. Abigail," Beth cries out, as she remembers the pain she felt when the lion clawed at her.

Abigail pushes her haunches deep under the lion and, heaving straight up, she pulls the lion off its rear legs, breaking its strength giving stance, and twists it in the air. She thrusts upward with her rear legs, pushing the lion higher into the air and twisting her hips over the back of the lion as she lays her weight on its back. As the lion falls to the ground, Abigail lets go long enough for the white cat to shift its weight to land on its feet and expose its back. As her weight drives down on the lion's back, she digs her claws into the lion's flesh for grip, and opens her powerful jaw wide. Abigail plunges her teeth deep into the neck and skull of the lion, sinking her long fang teeth into its brain before delivering a neck-breaking twist of her head, ending the fight.

"Yes! Abigail, you did it," Beth shouts.

Beth doesn't notice the second lion, only feet behind her, but as it shoots forward, Beth steps toward Abigail, unwittingly blocking the attacking lion.

"Ahh!" Beth yells as her body bounces off the Snow Lion.

As the Snow Lion stumbles from the collision, Abigail releases her jaw lock on the first lion and spins toward Beth. Abigail launches herself into the air, twisting to avoid the open jaws reaching up to tear her throat, and her opponent slides underneath her. Abigail's body crashes onto the back of the white lion, and she sinks her claws deep into the cat's shoulder and chest muscles, delivering her powerful bite into the back of the lion's skull and neck.

Beth hears the snap of the snow-lion's neck as Abigail rides the lion to the ground, ending the fight in a single blow. Beth tries to stand on her wounded leg and falters. The muscular arms surprise her, lifting her, and her body turns sideways, until she's face to face with Karse. She throws her free arm around his neck and pulls his face to hers.

Abigail growls, and Beth lets Karse go.

"What's wrong? Oh, Abigail, you're bleeding. We need to get you back to the Guardian healers."

Beth's eye catches the movement behind Abigail, and she looks around at her first battlefield. The number of injured or dead witches left lying on the ground in the short time the battle lasted shocks her.

"Karse, turn a full circle, please. Slow."

Her quiet tone catches Karse's ear, so he watches her face as he turns.

Beth realizes how heavily focused on Abigail she was, so she hadn't noticed the Guardians arriving, Sorcha's retreat, or the property and physical damage caused during the battle. The Guardians have driven the enemy back and captured witches that Sorcha abandoned. Beth sees Guardians repairing property damage and clearing minds of the few who witnessed the battle to reduce exposure of the magic community.

"Guardian witches sacrificed themselves to help me. I didn't want anybody hurt because of me. No... no.... this isn't good," Beth says.

Karse watches as Beth's eyes pool, and she brings her hand to her face.

Abigail growls again.

"Sorry, Abigail," Beth says in a cracked voice and she casts a portal that Abigail limps into, and Karse carries her through moments later.

***

As they exit the swirling white mist at the Guardian warehouse, one healer notices Beth's injuries and rushes over, but Beth stops her.

"Abigail and the others first."

"As you wish, Princess."

The healer witch makes a small bowing gesture with her head and turns back to Abigail.

"You need care for yourself, Princess. Royals first," Karse says.

Beth leans her head into Karse's chest, saying, "Uh, huh. Royals first."

"What bothers you, lass?"

"Abigail. The others." She looks around the room. "They're hurt because I got my ass kicked by being a cocky little twerp instead of heeding my training."

"Beth, how many battles like today have you fought?"

Beth leans her head back on Karse's chest.

"First one. And I got my butt handed to me."

"Please, listen to me, lass," Karse says. "The kings and queens or chiefs of old grew up learning battle strategy from a young age. You've no seen this before, and I can say, you did well against a very seasoned opponent."

"That's not helping."

"Sorcha and Rebekah have won many campaigns over more experienced opponents than you, and that made you an easy challenge."

"Karse, you're not scoring any points in the positive feedback column."

"Next time, you'll be ready for them and more aware of the tactics they use. And remember, no one likes it, but soldiers die in war and, like yourself or Abigail, they suffer injuries."

"If Abigail dies, I will never forgive myself."

"And if she didn't defend you, she would feel the same, but fear not, lass."

He turns his body, so Beth can see Abigail's tail swishing across the ground. The end of it curls upward, and Beth giggles through tears of joy.

ROYAL SOULS

Beth feels a rush through her body and says, "I love you, Abigail, and I'm so sorry."

I'll make sure Abigail knows it was you who said that, Mehla. She'll appreciate it.

Beth waits for Mehla to respond but gets nothing.

Still not talking to me? Fine, but I'm not setting you free.

Beth feels a ripple in her chest and she draws a breath. As she lets it out, Karse asks, "Are you good, lass?"

"I don't know."

Beth and Karse are silent for a few moments as she looks around at the many wounded.

"Karse. Look at the casualties from such a quick fight, and we have a war ahead of us. I can't live with the deaths of so many people on my mind."

"You're experiencing the shock of the first battle. We go through it as leaders."

"Why am I a leader? I didn't ask for this. There's got to be a way to reunite the Royal souls without the bloodshed."

Karse thinks of how much bloodshed he has seen during his time with Queen Sorcha and understands Beth's heart.

"You need to see the healers now, and then we'll talk again."

He turns to a witch near him and stops as two witches walk out of blue smoke. Beth feels his arms tighten, so she lifts her head from his chest to see Lauranna and Breena.

"Karse, what's wrong?"

Karse doesn't answer, but when Beth looks back at Lauranna and Breena again, they both have their mouths covered with their hands, and tears trickle down their faces.

"I don't believe my eyes," Karse says.

Karse releases Beth's legs, and they swing under her to stand on her own.

Hurting, Beth takes a step away from him, and Lauranna takes her hands away from her face.

"Karse. My son. My handsome son. I was told you died in battle after they released you from the Staff."

"Mother, I was told the same of you, father, and Breena."

Karse shifts his eyes to his sister Breena.

Lauranna runs the last few steps into Karse's arms, and Breena hesitates as though she still doesn't believe her eyes. Karse kisses the top of his mother's head, and he pulls her tight to his body.

Beth sees the emotion that washes over Karse's face and whispers, "Now that's a man that can love."

Karse hugs his mother for a full minute, then lets her go and opens his arms to Breena, who leaps the last few feet.

Throwing her arms over his shoulders, she breaks into a sob, burying her face in the side of his neck.

"Karse, I have missed you so much."

"And I've not gone a day without thinking of you, Sister."

He pulls her tight to him and looks at his mother, who is smiling, seeing her children together again.

"Mother, how did you survive this long if you didn't die in battle?"

"We cast our souls into the Staff to use its longevity power, hid our bodies with a cloaking spell, and protected them with a hibernation spell. Our souls only need to return to our bodies to wake them, but I fear we have nothing remaining in our lives because this war has been too long."

Lauranna turns to Beth.

"Princess, if I may? Where did you find my son?"

With Breena still in his arms, Karse turns, and their eyes meet.

Beth's eyes grow soft. "We found each other."

"The Clan MacShannachan is forever indebted to you, Princess, for returning the son of the Chief."

"Chief? Well?" Beth lifts an eyebrow and cocks her head at Karse.

"Later."

"Oh, you got that right, Mister."

"Karse. Have you offended the princess?"

"No, Mother. She no told me she is a princess, so I no told her I'm the son of the clan Chief."

"Oh." Lauranna notices the wounds on Beth's leg and hip. "Princess, you're hurt."

Breena's head pops off Karse's shoulder. She pecks him on the cheek as he lets her down, and wiping her tears while walking to Beth, she looks at the wounds.

"I know who to get," she says.

Breena breaks into an easy run toward the healer's room at the back of the building as Karse steps closer to Beth and sweeps her up into his arms.

"Karse!" Lauranna blurts. "You can no grab a princess like that. Princess, I'm so sorry. Please forgive my son."

Beth realizes that earlier, Lauranna, shocked to see Karse, forgot Beth was in his arms, so she kisses Karse on the lips and turns to Lauranna.

"He's forgiven."

Beth lays her head against his chest and neck, and Lauranna smiles.

"As you wish, Princess," Lauranna says with a slight bow and with a chipper, continues, "Karse, follow me."

The Grand Healer, Tonique, dressed in colorful robes, with skin as black as coal and scarification in intricate patterns, examines Beth's wounds. Beth, distracted by Tonique's scarification, isn't listening when Tonique asks, "Did you see if she cast this with a wand or by her hand?"

Lauranna's face pops into Beth's line of sight. "Princess?"

Beth snaps back to reality. "Sorry, what was the question?"

Tonique repeats it.

"I never saw a wand."

Tonique applies a paste and casts a healing spell as she moves her hand in a small circle over the wound.

Beth recognizes the spell from her training but doesn't let on that she knows it, and soon after the paste dries, her wounds disappear, leaving only a light discoloration on the skin.

Tonique turns to Beth. "You must find this young witch. If she is a Natural Witch, she is being turned evil by Sorcha. You don't want to fight two natural witches at the same time."

Tonique turns and walks away, leaving Beth to think about the young witch's part in today's battle and how short it was.

Was it a distraction for the cat to get behind me? Why didn't she try to finish me? Why the taunting smile and keeping her distance?

Beth looks to Karse and notices how Breena is bubbling with excitement, having her big brother back after more than a thousand years, and Lauranna sits poised like a proud mother watching her two children play together. Beth watches for a few more minutes as both Lauranna and Breena talk and joke at Karse, and she misses her mom and dad. Then it stops, and Karse stands and walks away, but after a few steps, he turns back to his mother and sister.

"Father lives? I was told that Prince O'Manus left him wounded on the battlefield and ran off. That's why I joined Sorcha, to get even for letting my father, and both of you, die like cattle."

A baritone voice booms through the room as if from above.

"Karse. It's true, then. My son is alive."

Karse turns to the floating apparition that resembles his father and half-smiles.

"Father, what am I seeing?"

"Sorcha did this to me," Angus MacShannachan says.

"She has much to answer for, Father."

"Aye, Son, she does, but remember you are the Chief now, and you need to keep your head about you."

"I will, father, but you're not dead, so I can no be Chief."

"I can lead no more with what Sorcha has done to me, so I pass the responsibilities to you. Karse, I'm as good as dead."

Karse sees his father's feeling of defeat as Angus slumps his head.

"She will pay for this, Father, once we have victory."

"Remember, Karse. We don't know who will survive to be victorious."

Beth hears Angus' comment and walks toward Karse, but the apparition turns to her before she can ask what he means.

"You have a wench with you. Are you a daft boy?"

Beth freezes. "What? What did you call me?"

Lauranna runs up beside Karse.

"Angus, don't be angry. This is Princess Mehla."

"How do you know this?"

"Because I have seen the princess, and Beth also wears the amulet."

"I'm tired," Angus says and disappears.

Karse turns to Beth, saying, "Will you forgive him for barking at you like a mad dog?"

Beth knows Karse is going through a lot with discovering his family alive after a thousand years, so she steps close to him.

"Only if you kiss me."

"I will kiss you anytime you wish, lass,"

Sliding his arm around her waist, he pulls her tight to him. The passionate kiss reminds Lauranna of how it felt when Angus used to take her in his arms, and she smiles as she walks away.

Karse pulls his lips away from Beth's and watches as her eyes open to show swirling green pools.

"Do you always change your eye color when you kiss?"

"Well, considering you're my first kiss, I'm not sure what you mean?"

Karse leans back and furrows his brow. "Oh, now you're blue again. Nice trick."

"Wait. Tell me what you saw."

"When you opened your eyes after our kiss, they were green, and now they're blue."

Lauranna, intrigued by the conversation, walks back to Karse.

"I saw the wedding battle in a dream. During that dream, the Faerie Queen gave me Faerie Water while I was talking to her and Freya, the Witch of Loch Shin."

Beth sees the surprise on all their faces, and Lauranna challenges Beth.

"You.... have talked with Freya and Egret?"

"Ah, yes. Many times over the last fifteen years. My parents died in a house fire and Freya came to me in the hospital and helped me sneak out."

Lauranna steps closer to Beth and whispers.

"What is your true name, Princess?"

The tension in Lauranna's voice bumps Beth's heart rate and she says, "LysaBeth Macha O'Corry."

Lauranna steps back, silent, eyes wide and her hand on her chest.

"What is it?" Beth says.

Lauranna turns her head to Breena. "Quick, bring Tonique."

Breena dashes away and soon after Beth hears feet running back to them. Lauranna grabs Tonique by the shoulders, and leaning close to her ear, whispers. Kneeling on one knee, Tonique removes her colorful head-wrap, and it surprises Beth to see a living tattoo on Tonique's hairless head, twisting and heaving as if trying to break free of the skin.

"Princess, may I hold your hand?" Tonique says.

Beth looks at Karse first, and then Lauranna before looking back at the tattoo.

"What are you doing?"

"Please, Princess. I promise no harm," Lauranna says. "We think you may be from a lineage we thought lost, and Tonique can tell if you are the missing link."

After a pause, Beth reaches her hand toward Tonique and she feels the rough skin of Tonique's hand slide into hers. Tonique places the back of Beth's hand against her forehead. The tattoo stops moving. Beth feels the same burst of energy as when Freya grabbed her hands during the dream.

Beth's sight blurs, and she falls sideways saying, "Karse…".

Karse's powerful arms catch Beth before she reaches the floor, and as her head lands against his chest, her eyes close, and she collapses into exhaustion hearing, "I've got you, my love."

214

THE RAZIIAIR

Tuesday, September 2nd — 0700 Eastern Time — Boston

Musky sandalwood. Karse. Who are the voices?

Beth's eyelids flutter as they open, and she raises her hand to her forehead. Karse's face slips into focus above her.

"LysaBeth, are you well, lass?"

"What happened?"

"You ignored your training," Freya snaps. "When you use large amounts of magic, as you did to battle Sorcha, you must eat and rest."

Beth closes her eyes and puts both her hands over her face.

"I'm sorry, Freya, with so much happening, I didn't think of it."

"Drink this, child."

"Egret?"

Beth drops her hands from her face and looks to her side. Egret is standing with her arm out and a glass bottle containing something red hanging from her crooked fingers.

"What is it?"

Beth wraps her hand around the bottle, and stern-looking Egret turns to walk back to Freya.

Karse helps Beth to the sitting position, and she takes a small sip, then two drinks of the liquid.

"Egret, it's fantastic! What is it?"

Egret looks back with a scowl. "Pure nourishment for foolish children who ignore their training and responsibilities."

Beth lets her head fall against Karse's shoulder as she lets out a grunt of frustration, then shouts, "Enough!" Her head pops up. "I'm still learning this crap and none of my training prepared me for this overload of a thousand-year-old war."

The healing room goes silent, and Karse places his hand under Beth's chin to lift her head until he's looking into her wet eyes.

"They love you and are trying to help you, lass."

Beth places her hand on Karse's cheek before sliding it around the back of his neck to pull his face to hers. Pressing her lips to his, a surge of calm flows through her body, along with her desire to make love to him.

Smiles appear on the faces witnessing the passionate kiss.

Beth pulls her face back from Karse's, and he can see the calm in her green to blue eye change.

"Do you still think you're falling in love with me?" Beth whispers.

"No, lass. I'm very much in love with you. I will die for you."

"As the princess, I order that you cannot die for me for at least five thousand years," Beth says, giving him a quick peck.

"As you command... Lysa."

"Ya, sorry. Left that out too."

Freya and Egret turn to Lauranna, each giving her a slight nod, and Freya says, "Your son might be the one. She only has to say it."

"Drink all of it!" Egret's bark shatters the tender moment between the two, so Beth drinks the remaining liquid, and Karse takes the empty glass bottle, placing it on a table at the end of the cot.

Tonique, Lauranna, Freya, and Egret walk to Beth's side.

"LysaBeth, what did you see in the vision?" Tonique says.

Beth looks at Tonique, who's dressed in bright-colored robes and now has a full head of hair woven in small braids with colorful beads and threads intertwined.

"Tonique, you look fantastic."

"My hair has returned because the magic of the tattoo is no longer. It feels good to have my hair again." She smiles, showing her perfect white teeth that glow against her black skin.

"LysaBeth, we must know what you saw," Freya demands.

"Wow. Okay." Beth turns her body to put her feet on the floor. "I was standing in a throne room with a woman. She had black, wavy hair and bright green eyes, dressed in a soft green gown and cape with symbols on them. She had an emerald crystal hanging on her forehead from gold thread woven through her hair."

"Did she speak?" Tonique says.

"Yes." Beth nods her head, and after a long pause, she says, "She called me by name and said I have great strength and must use it to bring the balance back."

Beth pauses again while searching the eyes of the foursome looking at her.

"Then she said," Beth pauses. "She said, 'I am with you, my daughter, find me. Hurry.' The image turned into a puff of smoke that flew into the middle of my chest, and it's the last thing I remember."

Beth waits for a response but gets nothing.

"Freya. You and Egret know what it means." Beth pauses and her eyes tighten. "Don't you?"

"It is me you should ask, LysaBeth. I have been your mother's best friend for her entire life," Tonique says.

"My.... My mother? What do you mean 'her entire life'? My parents died on the morning of my ninth birthday in a fire that I caused while having a nightmare."

"LysaBeth, you did not," Tonique says. "The parents you knew were Irish Guardians assigned to protect and train you. The Blood Witches who attacked your house started the fire to force the guardians out in the open because they were told the Guardians knew of something that could win the war."

"What are you saying? Are you saying my mother is still alive? My birth mother? My father? Where is he?"

"Calm yourself, LysaBeth," Tonique says. "We don't know where either of your parents is, but if your mother is reaching out to you, she must be alive."

"If you're her best friend, why don't you know?" Beth shoots up from her cot with fists clenched. "Or is this something else to pile on top of the other crap I'm dealing with?"

Beth feels lightheaded, and her legs weaken, but before she can fall, Karse's powerful arms wrap around her, and she lets herself fold into his body as he guides her back to the cot.

"I don't think you're ready for battle yet, lass."

"Tonique, I'm sorry," Beth says. "I'm so confused."

Beth hears a low growling sound and rotates her head against Karse's chest to see a big, black jaguar head only inches away from her face.

"Abigail." Beth throws her arms around Abigail's neck, near slipping from the cot, but Abigail moves her body to keep Beth steady.

"Oh, Abigail. You always know when I need you."

Beth hugs her tighter. Abigail purrs, and Beth giggles.

"Well, Princess. You know how to pick your bodyguards," says another voice.

Beth looks up from the back of Abigail's neck without lifting her head to see Lochran standing at the end of the cot and smiles at him.

"Lochran, old friend," Karse shouts.

Karse walks by, and Beth watches him and Lochran as they grab each other's arm near the elbow and continue walking until half their bodies collide. Smacking each other on their backs and breaking into a banter of Scots Gaelic, they step apart and let their arms loose. Beth smiles at the reunion before she turns her head, sliding her face against Abigail's warm, soft coat until she's looking back at Tonique. Sliding her hand against Abigail's neck, she kisses her on the head.

"It was Mehla who earlier said 'I love you, Abigail' and I promised her I would tell you, but I'm sorry I couldn't kill those cats before they hurt you." Abigail pushes back against her.

"LysaBeth, what do you mean?" Freya says.

"I cast a killing curse on the snow lion that slashed my leg, and it only knocked it back twenty feet when it should have turned it to dust."

"That should *not* have been possible," Freya says.

Beth nods in agreement. "Freya, I changed my eyes, and I could see a ribbon of black energy flowing from Sorcha to both cats. I couldn't tell if she was shielding the lions or transferring her power?"

Freya looks at Egret, then back to Beth.

"Sorcha's practice of stealing the life from young witches has blackened her Spirit magic. She's possessed by evil magic now. Beth, you must focus on the problems at hand, and we will focus on Sorcha."

"Oh, great. Not only is Sorcha unstable, but she's also drawing black magic from hell. Sure, let's crank it up a notch. Why not?"

Beth lays her cheek against the top of Abigail's head as she strokes her neck, and neither Freya nor Egret say anything to Beth's sarcasm. Beth lifts her head again, takes a deep breath, exhales, then sits up straight.

"Tonique, how did you know my mother?"

"Abigail is your protector, and she will give her life to save yours, right?" Tonique replies.

Beth pets the back of Abigail's neck, realizing the size of her massive head that's covering her lap from her stomach to kneecaps.

"Yes, because I have Princess Mehla inside me."

Abigail lets a low growl slip out as she lifts her head to look Beth in the eye. Then she slides her tongue up the side of Beth's face.

"Blah, gross Abigail. No kitty kisses. I saw you bite those other cats, and I'll bet you haven't brushed your teeth or... or even had a kitty cookie."

Beth wipes her hoodie sleeve on the side of her face as Abigail puts her head back on Beth's lap and starts purring again. Beth smiles and gives Abigail a quick kiss on her head.

Tonique laughs. "Abigail is here for you, not only Mehla, as I am for your mother. Until she disappeared without a trace of magic or a sign of her location."

Tonique throws her arms out to her sides, and swirling, thick, black smoke engulfs her, forming a wall ten feet high and near double in width. Beth sees the outline of a figure inside the smoke before it explodes outward, exposing a nine-foot-high black-feathered bird shimmering in the sun's light.

Abigail lifts her head from Beth's lap, and as Beth stands, she lips the word, *Wow*.

"Tonique, you're... magnificent."

Beth sweeps her eyes over Tonique, catching ripples of blue-black as Tonique makes slight moves in the afternoon sun seeping through the windows. Small colored tips peek out from under a thick ridge of feathers along her side. As

Tonique turns, a multicolored breastplate flickers in the sunlight.

Beth looks back to Tonique's side, saying, "The colored tips match the colors in that," and points to the breastplate.

Karse walks beside Beth saying, "Her breastplate."

"What is she?" Beth says.

"She... is a black Raziiair War-bird," Karse says.

"War-bird?" Beth looks at Karse with surprise.

Karse nods his head once. "My father told me of his first battle when he was only fourteen," Karse says.

"Fourteen? That's crazy."

"He rode with his father's army of five-hundred soldiers and witches, thinking the enemy was only a small force hiding in the mountains of the highlands. The enemy hid its army with a cloaking spell cast by a powerful witch, and when they rode out of the portal in the middle of the open valley below the mountains, soldiers and witches poured out from behind cloaking shields, surrounding my grand-sire's army. Outnumbered ten to one, the witches in my grand-sire's army cast a shield, but it was no match for the number of surrounding witches."

"A young witch hid inside a supply wagon when they left the castle because she wanted to go with her father, who was captain of the Witch Guard. When she saw the battle rising, she became afraid and tried to run to her father, who was helping to cast the shield. The young witch reached her father only in time to see him struck down. Then, the young girl started screaming, and it became so loud that it hurt the ears of everyone in the valley, stopping the battle. Her scream reached such a high pitch, soldiers were falling unconscious. Then they could no longer hear her scream, but the young witch still stood over her father's body, back arched as though she screamed at the sun, and a bright white light formed around her. As the shield protecting my grand-sire's army collapsed, the girl's white light replaced it, and one of the enemy soldiers pointed between the mountains at a small, bright white light in the sky. The rest turned to see what the soldier was pointing at, and a witch screamed, 'Raziiair!'"

"My father said the Raziiair dived over the mountain top and split into three lights, with one going down each side of the battlefield and the third, the brightest, through the middle. He said the light was so bright that they dropped to their knees and covered their heads. But, he looked to the side, through his fingers, to see the colored cords hanging from the Raziiair's body, and a man exploded into dust as one touched him. The light passed over him, and a loud sound, like someone ripping heavy cloth, followed. My father lifted his head, turned to watch the lights fly down the valley and into the sky until they were high above the ground. He took a quick glance around the battlefield to see half the enemy destroyed or wounded. He looked back to the three white lights as they hung, like stars in the sky, for a few heartbeats and he could see the outline of three birds through the white light before they pivoted and plunged back to earth for a second pass on the enemy."

"They made no sound coming up the valley, but the sky grew brighter as they got closer, and my father's army covered their heads again. He said you could see your arm hair standing up with little sparks flashing at the ends as the Raziiair laid waste to most of the enemy, and the ones who remained sought only to escape sure death. He said the following sound was as if a hundred whips cracked in three heartbeats. My father said that the Raziiair went up the valley toward the mountain with such speed they scraped the mountain and burned every living plant so fast that nothing has ever grown there again."

Karse pauses for a second. "The Raziiair left behind three burn marks, now called the Three Lashes."

"Holy crap," Beth says. "But they never saw the Raziiair to know their colors? Only the light they make?"

"Ah nay, lass. The Raziiair looped over as the young girl's shield faded," Karse uses his hands and body to imitate the Raziiair looping in the sky, "and came back into the valley, landing on the rocks above the battle. There were three birds with riders. One bird had feathers so blue they shimmered with black edges, another snow-white and yellow edges, and the third was black with blue edges."

"The same as Tonique," Beth says.

"Aye, it was the biggest of the three, and the rider of the black one spoke to my grand-sire and named the young witch a Raziiair Siren. He ordered that my grand-sire make sure they care for the young witch if he ever wanted the Raziiair to help him again."

Beth stares at Karse with a blank look.

"LysaBeth, do you not believe me?"

"What happened to the young girl?"

"The Raziiair Siren?"

Beth nods. "I take it she's as rare as the Raziiair?"

"Oh, aye. With her secret guarded, she grew into a beautiful woman." Karse pauses as he leans sideways to look behind Tonique. "And my father married her."

"What?" Beth spins to Lauranna, who wears a shy look. Beth feels it necessary to give her a slight bow, which brings a gentle smile to Lauranna's lips before she returns a single nod of her head.

"That's unbelievable," Beth says as she looks up at Tonique.

"Aye, lass," Karse continues. "The Raziiair has a body shape like the peregrine falcon. She can fly at speeds over three-hundred miles per hour with her rider in the saddle or even faster with no rider."

Beth looks at Karse and cocks her eyebrow.

"Yeah, right? As if someone can sit on the back of something flying that fast."

Karse points at the base of Tonique's neck and above the start of the wing.

"Look closer, lass."

Beth steps closer as the feathers over the base of the neck open, revealing a sunken saddle coated in black feather Down. Then two bones, each covered with the black feather Down, pop out of Tonique's side. One is shaped to catch the rider's knee and the other to catch the rider's heel.

"Tonique, that is so cool," Beth says.

Tonique opens her beak and lets out a guttural tapping sound that makes Beth laugh.

"So the rushing wind couldn't pull the rider out of the saddle?" Beth says.

Tonique pulls the shield feathers together, forming an air dam over the rider.

"A cockpit? Unbelievable," Beth says.

Beth reaches to touch the feathers, and Karse jumps forward, grabbing her hand.

"Don't do that, lass. Raziiair takes heavy offense at being touched by anyone but their rider."

Tonique swings her head, knocks Karse to the floor, then nods like a horse at Beth, giving permission.

Karse regains his feet and makes a slight bow to Tonique.

"My apologies. I was only following my lessons."

Beth looks over her shoulder at him with a mischievous smile.

"Girl to girl privileges, big boy."

Tonique nods her head again, which makes Beth laugh.

"Aye, Princess," Karse says.

Beth strokes the feathers. "They're soft as silk," and the colored cords under the feathers extend out more.

"Are those the colored cords you mentioned in the story?"

"Aye, lass."

"How do they work?"

Karse holds his hand out. "Let me show you."

Karse takes Beth's hand, leading her to the front of Tonique, where he points to the breastplate.

"Nothing can pierce that breastplate, and when she flies, it gathers energy from the flow of the wind against it. Under her skin, the cords connect to the breastplate, and when she dives into an attack, they hang out as poisonous

ROYAL SOULS

vines from a tree, waiting to touch prey. It's as if you're struck by lightning. The power from the breastplate likewise creates the bright light shield around her and the rider when they are attacking the enemy. It blinds the enemy so they can't see her body, which leaves no target to hit. The light for Tonique will either be blackish-blue during flight alone or blueish-white during an attack with her rider."

Beth looks up at Tonique. "You rock, girlfriend."

Tonique nods her head.

"And that's not the best of it, Princess."

Karse points. "Look at her beak, but don't touch it."

Tonique lowers her head toward Beth, stopping above her.

"No way. Your beak. It's razor-sharp."

Karse points to the razor-sharp tips of her claws.

"And she can tear through any metal armor. She is formidable in battle."

Beth pauses for a few moments.

"Why did my mother need such a deadly protector?" Beth spins. "Hey, wait. Karse, did you say a blackish-blue light?"

"Aye, lass. Why do you ask?"

"When we fought Sorcha, a blackish-blue light shot over the sides of the shield, taking out the witches that were casting it. Tonique. That was you?"

Tonique squawks and nods her head.

Freya emerges from behind Tonique and points to the breastplate.

"LysaBeth, you must put your hand against her breastplate."

227

Many years ago, Beth learned the hard way that it's wise to listen to Freya, so she walks to Tonique and, putting her hand along her neck, she slides it down the feathers until she's kneeling on one knee. The thick, protruding breastplate covers wing to wing, starting at the bottom of the throat and ends before her legs except for a small dart that extends between and past her legs. Beth examines the markings on the breastplate before putting her palm against the middle, and it turns transparent.

"I can see a box."

"Take it out, child."

She looks over her shoulder at Freya.

Beth turns back to the breastplate, places her hand in the middle again, hesitates, then pushes. She feels the pressure against her palm releasing, and her hand slips through the outer layer, sinking deeper until she touches the box. She hooks her fingers around it and, thinking not to hurt Tonique, she picks it up enough to remove it from Tonique's chest.

Beth looks up at Tonique. "I hope my arm's not covered in weird, gooey stuff when I pull the box out."

Tonique stomps her foot and lets out a guttural noise.

"I hope that was a laugh?" Beth says.

Lochran tries to break the tense moment and says, "Gives new meaning to a storage chest. Got any whisky in there, Princess?"

Karse smiles, but Abigail spins with her ears pinned, baring teeth, roaring at Lochran before slapping the floor with her enormous paw.

Karse looks over his shoulder, smiling, and Lochran shrugs his shoulders. "Was it something I said?"

Abigail lets out a low guttural growl that lasts for a few seconds, so Lochran walks over and sits on a chair near another cot.

Beth stands, holding a box near the size of a computer mouse, and the breastplate returns to its rigid form as she turns to walk back to the cot. She stops and spins back to Tonique, shouting, "Wait!"

Black smoke swirls around Tonique, but Beth's shout stops the transformation.

Freya says, "What is it, LysaBeth?"

Beth walks in front of Tonique and kneels again to run her hand over the breastplate.

"The markings on the box and Tonique's breastplate are the same as the markings on my mother's gown and cape."

"Yes. The symbols of your bloodline," Freya says.

Beth looks up at Tonique and then back to Freya.

"Then why did Sorcha have the same symbols on her robes?"

The room goes silent for a long time as Beth stands.

"That's impossible, Princess," Lauranna says as she joins Freya. "The symbols will cripple her if she tries to harness their power."

Beth looks from the box to Lauranna, saying, "I swear they are identical."

Egret joins as Tonique finishes her transformation back to her human form.

"I think we know who attacked LysaSearin, forcing her to vanish and sending your father into hiding if he's alive," Egret says.

"LysaSearin…" Beth chokes. "Is… Is that my mother's name?"

Tonique steps out of her black smoke to Beth's side and slides her arm across her shoulders to comfort her.

"Don't be sad, child. Your mother is LysaSearin Macha O'Corry, and your father's name is Killian O'Hannon."

"Freya, Egret. You knew the whole time and didn't tell me?"

"Only to protect you from charging off on a rescue mission you weren't ready for," Freya says.

Tonique puts her other hand on Beth's bicep as she pulls her close to console her.

"Why did other witches attack my parents?"

Tonique's smile washes away, and she looks across the room at the others.

"We didn't know why until you told us of the symbols on Sorcha's robes. Come sit, and I will explain."

Beth turns to walk back to the cot only to see Abigail stretched out on the mat in front of the bed, exposing her unhealed wounds. Claw marks to her belly and side, along with two large puncture holes, in the chest muscle below her neck. Beth knows they're holes from the upper fangs of the snow lion, and as she turns to sit on the cot, she reaches over and slides her hand along Abigail's shoulder.

"I'm so sorry, Abigail."

Abigail lifts her enormous head and shakes it as if to say 'No.'

"I have carried that box since the last time I flew with your mother, and now the rest of my powers should return."

"What do you mean, Tonique?"

"I had to sacrifice powers to keep whatever object hides in that box from those who could use it for the wrong reasons."

"You mean you didn't even know what my mother put in here?"

"No. Your mother trusted me to protect it, and that's enough."

Beth puts her thumbs against the front edge of the box, with firm pressure upward, and the lid pops. She pauses before lifting the top to see a roll of cloth, and reaching in with the tips of her fingers, Beth feels something wrapped inside. She hooks her fingers around the roll of fabric, and the object inside rolls against her palm as she raises it for everyone to see. Beth sets the box on the floor and, taking hold of the loose end of the cloth roll, she lifts, unraveling it. In Beth's palm lay the emerald crystal her mother was wearing on her forehead in Beth's vision, and she takes a long pause before looking around the room. Lauranna, Egret, Freya, and Tonique have their heads bowed.

"She's dead, isn't she?"

"If she isn't, she is in grave danger without her crystal," Freya says.

"When was the last time anyone saw her?" Beth says, looking at Tonique.

"Midnight, December 31st, twenty-three years ago," Tonique says. "Four months after you were born, she placed you in the care of the Guardians for protection while she went to find a rogue Natural Witch who was killing Wand Witches and stealing magical artifacts."

"Was it Sorcha?" Beth snaps.

"Calm, LysaBeth. What do you know about Sorcha?"

"She's a soul-sucking psycho killer. Why?"

"Sorcha arrived with her mother, Lillian, at a magical village called Brae's Garden, when she was eight years old," Lauranna says. "It was a time of witch hunts and brutal executions, but they didn't understand how Sorcha and Lillian passed through the barrier of the entrance cave. When tested for their magical abilities, neither showed any real magical skill, except Lillian displayed the potential for potion-making. Queen Isabelle felt the need to have such a person on the castle staff, so she gave Lillian and Sorcha a small hut beside the herb and vegetable gardens, and Lillian worked with the healers, making potions and healing salves."

"Not long after, Sorcha goes to the castle with her mother and meets Prince O'Manus. The prince and Sorcha became companions, spending much of their free time together, and as they grew older, the queen saw Sorcha had become infatuated with the prince. She gave Lillian and Sorcha a bigger hut, closer to the village, and away from the castle. She ordered the guards to restrict access to the prince, so Sorcha's visits became rare, chance meetings when the prince wandered through the village. Over time, the queen became satisfied she had thwarted any relationship between the prince and Sorcha, so she relaxed the restrictions on the prince."

"Around thirteen years of age, the prince became known for his curiosity about trade skills. He frequented the village to learn or practice such skills as blacksmith and woodworking, or to hear the needs of the people. On one such occasion, the prince was learning the art of throwing a fishing net when he saw Sorcha collecting water from the nearby falls, so he visited her. Prince O'Manus and Sorcha spent until dinner sitting by the waterfall talking, and once more, the prince grew fond of her company and the delicious fruit drink she always carried. They agreed to meet more often, in secret, but before parting that day, Sorcha placed her hand on the prince's cheek, moved her body against his, and gave the prince a long, full kiss on the lips. As the prince walked back to the castle, he felt his stomach flutter, and he longed for Sorcha's company and another kiss."

"Over the next few weeks, the two met every day, and the prince became infatuated with Sorcha until one day, when Sorcha led the prince to a secret cave where they became lovers for the first time. The queen noticed a change in the prince and approached the king, so they asked the prince what had put the bounce in his step. When he avoided answering, the king ordered the prince followed, and they discovered the romantic relationship with Sorcha. They brought the prince to the throne room to remind him of his duties, which meant he could not marry Sorcha. Enraged, the prince turned red with his power of fire, and the queen doused him with an ice spell before calling Freya."

Lauranna looks at Freya.

"The drink that Sorcha carried with her was a love potion," Freya says. "When I used magic to see the prince's inner spirit, I saw a flash of magenta around his heart, which meant the love potion was to intoxicate him slow, so as not to show a drastic change. The king ordered Sorcha and her mother captured, but their hut was empty when the guards went to arrest them. When the prince, cured of the love potion, heard of what happened because of Sorcha, he became furious, but Sorcha and Lillian had disappeared. Until years later, on the morning of September 6th, when Sorcha and her Blood Witches attacked Prince O'Manus' and Princess Sadreen's wedding. As you know, it was a brutal massacre."

"Your mother, LysaSearin, is not the first LysaSearin in your bloodline," Egret says. "The first LysaSearin married by arrangement at sixteen and had a daughter who inherited the magic of your bloodline. Soon after the child was born, the first LysaSearin met her true love, a wizard, and LysaSearin's husband caught her doing magic and tried to kill her. She ran to her true love to escape, but it forced her to abandon her daughter, who we now think was Lillian, and had the name of LysaLillian Macha O'Corry."

"Shut the front door. Are you saying that Sorcha is my cousin?"

"Distant Cousins, and it's a good thing no one can hear you yelling, or we may need to defend ourselves from the Guardians," Freya snips. "We think so, knowing her robes have your bloodline symbols."

"The first LysaSearin left a diary," Egret says, "and in it, she tells of an attack against her by a powerful young witch thirty years after her first husband, and we think it was her first daughter, LysaLillian."

"She had another daughter?"

"Yes. LysaSearin and her second husband had another daughter, LysaDechtire Macha O'Corry, who continued the Lysa line."

"In the diary," Egret continues. "LysaSearin tells how the young witch tried to use another witch to channel her power, so she could attack from two sides at once. The witch that she channeled through wasn't strong enough to handle the power of a Lysa witch and died as soon as the attack began. LysaSearin defeated the young witch, but she escaped before your mother could find out who she was. Suspecting LysaLillian, LysaSearin called upon the Lysa mother and cast a spell, preventing anyone of the bloodline from killing another of the bloodline and forever preventing the loss of the lineage. She then created a spell preventing arranged marriages and stopping the female witches of your bloodline from any want of a relationship until they discover their true love."

Beth contemplates before she glances at Karse and then back at Egret.

"Do you think Sorcha knows this and is testing us and her spell? What if she's figured out a way to use the body of someone else with her power, and what if she used the young witch to attack me as a test to see if it might work? What if she hasn't perfected the technique yet, and she could only wound instead of destroying me? Maybe they attacked my mother and father that way?"

Egret's eyes shift to Tonique, then Lauranna before turning to Freya.

"Freya, do you think LysaLillian could have created a possession spell and taught it to Sorcha?" Egret says.

"It is against the laws," Freya says, "for a Natural Witch to possess another person, magical or otherwise, even if that person consents to the possession. The powers of the Natural Witch will condemn the host to a brief life and a horrible death." Freya pauses, then sighs. "But, yes. It is possible, and that may be a way around the protection spell that LysaSearin cast over fifteen-hundred years ago."

Feeling overwhelmed and lost, Beth rolls the crystal back into the cloth and reaches to pick up the box.

"Beth, what are you doing?" Tonique says.

"I can't do this."

"LysaBeth, you are the only one who can do this."

"Why? Why can't the four of you find Sorcha, imprison her, and end it? I don't want to fight a thousand-year-old battle. Look… Look what I've done to Abigail, Karse, and not to mention my mom and dad! Real or not."

"Anger clouds your thinking, LysaBeth. Calm yourself," Freya says. "You know the Universe forbids Egret and me from interfering. You are the one who has the strength to bring the balance back to the magical world."

Beth drops the wrapped emerald into her lap before she puts her face into the palms of her hands. She rests her elbows on her thighs and cries.

Even knowing her wounds will cause her great pain, Abigail changes to human form. She kneels in front of Beth.

"Beth, you did not hurt me or anyone else."

Beth pulls her face from her hands to see Abigail's face only two feet from hers. She throws her arms around Abigail's neck, breaking into tears.

"I'm so sorry for getting you hurt, Abigail. I was foolish and arrogant, and I promise I will never do that again."

Abigail pulls back from Beth with a stern look on her face.

"You did not hurt me, I said. I am a warrior cat that lives to protect you. We are fighting to reunite the prince and princess, and we will suffer pain and have scars to show like you do now," Abigail says, pointing to Beth's injured hip.

"But Abigail, if I hadn't been so arrogant thinking that I couldn't get hurt, it wouldn't have happened."

"Your thinking is wrong," Abigail snaps.

Beth sits back in surprise at Abigail's loud response.

"Think of everything you have learned from one battle. You are not someone who grew up learning battle strategy from a young child, yet you stood your ground when outnumbered and learned who your enemy is. Beth, that is a gift many never get."

Beth hears the echo of the words that Karse spoke after the battle, and she looks at him as he poses an 'I told you so' look.

"I hate you," she tells him.

Karse smiles and winks, bringing a soft smile to Beth's lips as she looks back at Abigail.

"Well, I won't put anyone in that position again."

"You have no control over this. Soldiers fight and die, and we remember them in victory. You do your job, and they do theirs. Try to save everyone, and you will lose everything."

Beth's face goes emotionless as the weight of what Abigail has said hits like a hammer blow. Karse steps to her side, and going to one knee, he takes her hand.

"LysaBeth."

"Yes. I do. I want to spend forever with you!"

Karse smiles. "I was going to say that you have generals to make battle strategies, and the weight of victory is not yours alone to carry, but I am more than pleased to change that to a proposal of marriage if you wish?"

Beth scans the faces in the room, and Abigail smiles at her as she gives a wink. Beth turns back to Karse, grabbing his right hand with both of hers.

"Karse, you are my first kiss, and since then, I have wanted nothing more than to have you as my man forever. Maybe it's the family curse telling me you're the one. I don't know. But what I know is…. I want you, forever."

Karse slides his left hand into Beth's left hand, and a band of white light forms around Beth's wrist while a band of blue light forms around Karse's wrist. The two bands pass through each other, switching places, and continue to travel up their arms as tattoos, mixed with the runes from Beth's bloodline and images and signet lines from Karse's bloodline. An intricate pattern takes shape on their left hands as the bands of light climb toward their left shoulders. Burning Beth's sleeve away, the light ring climbs, and the tattoos take shape around their arms, stopping below the left shoulders. The white band disappears, and Karse's tattoo ends with a crown that wraps around the top of his bicep. The blue band disappears, leaving a Tiara wrapped around the top of Beth's bicep.

Karse looks at the crown on his arm and follows the tattoo back to the tiara on Beth's arm, then to her eyes.

"It looks as though you have your wish, lass, and I could no be more pleased."

Beth smiles at Karse through tears, and she slips her right hand around Karse's neck as she slides from the cot into his arms. Crushing her body against him, her lips press to his, and swirling blue and white light surrounds them, sealing the magical union forever.

After the long sensual kiss, Beth pulls her face away from Karse's and brings her forearm up between them.

"I've always wanted ink," she says, leaning forward for another kiss, and then, "Ow. That hurt."

"What is it, lass?"

Beth reaches under her knee, finding the emerald crystal that had fallen from her lap. As she brings it up, the cloth falls open, and her tear falls, landing on the emerald, and it glows.

"Ahh!" Beth cries, falling forward into Karse's arms.

"LysaBeth, what's wrong?"

Karse lays Beth back, cradling her body in his arms, and after a few seconds, she opens her eyes.

"How long was I out?"

"Only a few heartbeats, lass. What happened?"

Karse sits Beth up as Freya and the others gather to listen.

"I had another vision."

"Your tears brought the emerald back to life," Freya says.

"Yeah, go figure? My tears on a magical object of my mother's," Beth says.

"What was your dream, child?" Egret asks, ignoring the sarcasm again.

"I was in the same throne room as last time, but my mother wasn't there. I went through a secret passageway, into a corridor, and down some stairs as torches lit by themselves. Then, I reached a room that had no doors or windows. She called my name, and when I called out for her, she said, 'I am weak. Help me, LysaBeth'. Then I woke up."

Freya, Egret, Lauranna, and Tonique turn away from Beth and whisper.

"Hey. No more secret talks," Beth barks.

The foursome looks back at Beth to see her stern look, and Freya says, "You're right, LysaBeth. We think you have to go home and find your mother."

"Yeah, I don't remember seeing a throne room or any secret passages in my condo."

"No, LysaBeth. You must go home to where you were born." Tonique pauses. "Your castle in Ireland."

"I… I was born in a castle? In Ireland? Are you saying that I really am a princess?"

"Yes, LysaBeth. Your mother is the Witch Queen of Ireland. The throne room you keep seeing is in your birthplace and the last room you were in before you came to America for safe hiding," Egret says. "They hid the castle deep inside the highest mountains of Ireland, with many spells protecting it, and if your mother is hiding there, it's because she knows the magic around the castle will protect her. She is reaching out to you because the magic is getting weak, and you must help her. Put the emerald to your forehead and focus on your mother."

"Wait. What happens when I put the emerald to my head?" Beth asks as she and Karse stand.

240

"You will take your mother's bloodline power into you, making it so you can pass through the magic barriers to locate her," Egret says.

"How many cats can you put in one bag?" Beth asks. "I have Mehla roaming around in here, even though she was a bitch and didn't help battle Sorcha, plus whatever other things you two have poured into me over the years." She points at Egret and Freya. "Now, you want me to add more power?"

"What do you mean, Princess Mehla didn't help?" Freya says.

"I tried to get her to help battle Sorcha, and she demanded to be released first. I said 'No way,' so she opted out of the cage fight and hasn't spoken to me since."

Freya and Egret smile.

"Show me the amulet," Freya says.

Beth grabs the chain at the front of her neck and pulls.

"What happened? The amulet... it's turned green."

"You have succeeded, child," Egret says. "Mehla is in the amulet and not in your body. She is ready for the last battle."

"How did that happen?" Beth says.

"You didn't give in to fear during the battle, and Mehla needs that negative energy. When she didn't get it, she became weaker than the amulet's power, so it drew her into the amulet," Freya says.

"Okay. How does that help with the last battle?" Beth says.

"The power of the amulet will calm her, and when you release her, she will be your ally," Egret says.

"I will keep it safe," Freya says as she reaches her hand out to Beth.

"Are you saying that I don't have to wear this anymore? What if I need to call Abigail?"

"Your mother's crystal will call her if you choose to use it," Freya says.

Beth becomes stone-faced like an old card player trying to read the table.

"This better not send me off the deep end."

She slips the amulet over her head and places it in Freya's hand. Beth raises the emerald to her forehead, and Karse touches her arm before it touches her skin.

"Are you sure, lass?"

Beth stops long enough to give Karse a quick peck before pressing the emerald rune against her forehead.

Her body tingles, and she takes a deep breath.

"Are you alright, lass?"

Beth's hand falls away from her forehead, leaving the emerald rune floating as fine strands of pure gold weave themselves through her hair.

"Your hair," Karse says. "It changed to black."

She feels a rub at her ankles and looks to see two strands of ribbon weaving themselves around her ankles. Beth tries to touch her head, but she's frozen with her arms straight out to her sides.

"Is someone pulling my hair?"

"No, lass. It's growing fast," Karse says.

The two ribbons circle her body as they climb, and then, separating, they circle her arms like serpents until they reach her hands, where they turn into puffs of smoke and float together. The smoke lingers, then grows to

ROYAL SOULS

cover her body, and Beth feels as if she's climbed out of a hot shower into a cool room. As the smoke clears, like someone blowing out a candle with a gentle breath, she feels exhilarated, as if the worry of the magical war has disappeared, and she looks at Karse, who, with a look of shock, has backed a short distance away.

"Karse, are you okay?"

"I thought you were the most beautiful woman I had ever seen, and I had wanted nothing so much, but now, LysaBeth, my heart is going to explode with desire."

Beth revels in Karse's words for a moment before taking a step and raising her arms out to hug him.

She stops saying, "What the..."

The raven black, skin-tight sleeves covering her arms shimmer like Tonique's feathers and Beth looks at her body to see she's wearing a black tactical suit. As she bends backward at the waist and swings her head to look behind her, a sheet of thick, black curly hair drops from her shoulder into her face, and she snaps up straight.

"What the what happened?"

Beth makes eye contact with Tonique first, who is smiling the biggest smile Beth has ever seen, and throwing her arms over her head, Tonique laughs, "LysaBeth, now you are ready to learn how to fly the Raziiair."

Beth sees a mirror to her left and walks in front of it. She's dressed in a full flight suit that looks like Tonique's feathers, and her pixie-cut hair has changed to a thick, curly, blue-black mane hanging two feet from her head. The glowing emerald on her forehead has fine gold strands woven through her hair as it did her mother's in the dream. Beth pauses, realizing how much she looks like her mother, and pride fills her until the fear of losing her before she gets the chance to meet her takes hold.

"The suit you wear now is yours forever," Tonique says. "When you need to fly with the Raziiair, it will cover your body as soon as you sit in the saddle. The suit protects you in any weather or temperature, and it helps that Raziiair can generate the heat needed to survive in sub-zero temperatures during flight."

"Sub-zero? Great. Remind me to keep a hat and gloves in my pocket."

"LysaBeth... don't talk like that. The suit will give you those things."

"Really?" Beth says, looking at Tonique, who nods.

Looking back at her reflection, Beth mumbles, "Hell, I was joking."

Beth looks over her shoulder at Karse and his frozen stare. Locking her eyes with his, she marches across the room and throws her arms around his neck. She lifts her body up his and hooks her leg behind him as his arms pull her in so tight it's hard to breathe. Beth wants the intense kiss to last forever but pulls her lips away and slides her face along the side of his until her lips press against his ear.

"We need to have that talk when I get back."

"LysaBeth, I've wanted nothing as much as I want you, but you need to save your mother."

Beth slides down Karse's chest, and as her feet touch the floor, she turns to Tonique.

"Why do I have to fly the Raziiair?"

Tonique says, "We have to fly to your castle because you cannot use a portal through the barriers yet, and if they're broken, you may walk into an ambush. It is safer to fly and slip into the castle under dark."

"Oh, okay. Good points. So, when are you planning to leave?" Beth says.

"Now," Tonique says.

"In full daylight?"

"I understand you have an ability that will solve that problem?"

Beth turns back to Karse and touches his face.

"We'll have that talk."

"Come back to me, LysaBeth."

As the last of the transition smoke clears, Tonique lowers herself so Beth can place her foot on the bottom bone and lift herself into the sunken saddle. She slides into place and sets her other foot in position. Air pouches in the saddle fit her body as she slips her head under the flared feathers. Her knees settle on the soft padding of the knee bones, and as the long shield feathers lay over her body, her hands find two handlebar bones. She looks around, and the feathers lay in such a way that she can see through them.

"I'm only missing a heads-up display," she mumbles.

When we fly, you will see what I see.

"Tonique, I can hear you."

Yes, LysaBeth. The crystal is your mothers, so you and I can communicate the same way she and I can.

Beth's heart races as she looks through the feathers at Karse, looking as though he was told his new puppy ran away.

Breena walks to the back of the storeroom and waves her hand over a trapdoor on the floor. The split door drops open, revealing the ocean waters thirty feet below and gentle waves breaking against the pilings that hold the building above them.

Breena steps back as Tonique walks toward the opening.

Focus your invisible power on me, LysaBeth.

Tonique leaps forward, and her giant wings snap open as they fall through the opening in the floor.

Beth's invisibility shield flows through her hands, into the grips, and around Tonique as her wings pull them forward.

Relax into the saddle and let your body lay against me.

Beth let her weight spread over Tonique's back like a track racer on a motorcycle and she feels the air sacs under Tonique's skin adjusting to her shape.

PYRE WOLF

Tuesday, September 2nd — 1200 Pacific Time — Delta

"Where are we?" Michael asks.

"This is an abandoned warehouse for the old fish cannery, one street over," Colleen says. "We set this place up last year when we heard rumblings of Blood Witches in the area. It's old and unsafe for the cannery to use, so the lads came in and shored it up so we could use it as a hideaway for large numbers. Open water on the south side, public docks on the east side, public parking lot on the west, and the village to the north. Easy to defend."

"Leaving the mess was a good idea," Michael snickers.

"Keeps the locals in the dark when you try to gather three-hundred Guardians," Colleen laughs.

"Fooling them is a simple task," Michael replies.

Aaghnya walks out of a portal near Rhynan's glassed shape, and walking to the statue, she presses her forehead against the glassed head.

"Rhynan Doon. I know you can hear me. Why did you do it? Why did you jump in front of that curse? I am supposed to save you. It was my duty to save you. I have saved myself for you, and my duty has changed to love."

247

The Irish Guardians near her hear the emotion building in Aaghnya and drift away.

"Can he hear her?" Michael whispers.

"Aye, that's part of the curse," Colleen says. "You can hear everything around you. They can punish you by letting you hear what you miss or want the most, or they can make your sentence less painful with music or stories."

Michael shakes his head. "I'd prefer death."

"Aye, me as well."

"Please be strong," Aaghnya says. "I will free you. I promise."

Colleen spins away from Michael and walks back to Aaghnya.

She places her hand on Aaghnya's shoulder, saying, "Let's get to work on making that promise come true."

The rest of the Guardians gather close.

"What do you have in mind?" Darrin says.

"The prince is in this glass, and we need a Glazier to break it, so we're going to kidnap one."

"Before I tell you how mad you are," everyone laughs, "I'll ask if you have a plan?" Michael says.

"Yes, I have a plan, but I need to wait until someone gets here before we can discuss it."

"Who else is coming?" Darrin says.

"You'll see when he gets here."

"He?" Darrin says.

The air shifts and thickens, and the occasional flame licks the air as it reaches through the swirling red smoke, and embers float out to die an icy death for leaving the burning portal.

A five-foot-tall male Pyre Wolf, Gaisras, steps through the gateway with a slight gush of heat that reaches out and brushes Michael's body, so he raises his arm to shield his face as he steps back. The flame-covered red wolf stops as his burning tail clears the swirling smoke and looks around, with eyes like flowing lava, then snaps his jaws together as if to warn everyone. Gaisras shakes his body, putting the flames out, and tiny embers from the glowing, hot mane fall to the concrete. Gaisras turns his head to the portal, growls, and snaps his jaws together again, and an open-cloaked man, muscular with grayed skin and shiny silver eyes, steps out of the smoldering portal. He carries a staff of carved wood with precious metals woven around it and a large gem embedded in the middle, above his hand.

"That's Angus MacShannachan," Darrin says. "He's the prince's best friend and carries the Staff of Souls."

Many Guardians catch their breath as the heads of two more snarling Pyre Wolf, Teine and Lasair, push through the portal and take their places opposite Gaisras. The Guardians move back from the heat cast by the Pyre Wolf, and a fourth head pops through the portal.

"Mother Mary," Michael says.

Pyreus, the largest wolf, with its face, mane, and shoulders mottled with black patches, steps out of the portal. A claw mark down the right side of his face has left his eye split in half, dead as black coal, and the flesh on the side of the nose and through the lip hangs ripped open, leaving the eye fang and gum exposed. The claw marks carry through the jaw muscle until they tear their way out of the flesh at the bottom, and the tip of the right ear hangs bent and lifeless, with a large hole through it.

Pyreus' muscular body slips out of the burning portal and walks to the side of Angus.

"Will you look at that?" Michael says. "The last one is over a foot taller and two feet longer than the others."

"Look at the battle scars across his body," Darrin says.

Pyreus stops, sniffs the air, and growls. The intensity of the flames and heat from his body push the Guardians farther back, and the other three growl as Pyreus moves toward the glassed figure. As if chanting, their growling turns rhythmic, deeper, and their bodies glow brighter, and with every step they leave burned paw prints in the dust covering the concrete floor.

"They're going to start the building on fire," Michael says. "It's a good thing that's it forty feet to the rafters."

The Guardians move back from Rhynan's glass-cased body, but Aaghnya stands her ground.

She makes a graceful sweeping bow before dancing, and as she moves, the pyre wolves stop, their growl and glow softening, and Angus walks to the front of the four wolves. Angus watches Aaghnya's dance until she circles behind Rhynan and stops. Then he continues to the glassed figure, followed by Pyreus.

Placing his hand on Rhynan's chest, Angus, in Scots Gaelic, says, "*Goirid bidh thu saor, seann charaid.*" (Soon you will be free, old friend).

The four wolves turn a charcoal color and lay down in front of the glassed prince.

"Where's your captain?" Angus demands.

"Chief Angus. Our appointed captain died in battle, and I am next in command. My name is Colleen. I sent for you."

ROYAL SOULS

Angus looks over his right shoulder at Colleen as she walks past the wolves.

"We can only hope for such a death," Angus sighs. "How secret is this place from the Blood Witches?"

"The Irish Guardians in this building have been putting their lives on the line since the beginning," Colleen says. "There are no spineless traitors here."

Angus looks around at the faces of the Irish men and women, which show their determination for justice and fulfilling the prophecy.

Angus looks back at Colleen. "Your command then."

Colleen nods her head.

"Man your posts," Colleen says, and the Irish move to their positions.

Aaghnya walks around Rhynan and kneels in front of Pyreus. She rolls her hands like rubbing a ball, forming a block of ice between his front paws, then slides it under his throat. He lays his big, scarred head on the block, and a burst of steam rises.

Angus looks over his shoulder. "Pyreus is content."

Aaghnya moves to the wolf lying next to Pyreus and again forms a block of ice and slides it under her throat.

Angus says, "She is Teine, Pyreus' mate."

Aaghnya smiles at her, then moves to Gaisras' mate, Lasair, who lifts herself into a low crouch and growls. The other wolves look at Aaghnya and raise themselves from the ground, and Lasair moves toward the glassed statue.

Aaghnya stands, and as Angus reaches the growling wolf, he says, "What is it, Lasair?"

251

The wolf moves closer to Rhynan, growling and sniffing, and Aaghnya sees the spy spider move away from the wolf.

Casting a spell in Tamil, she cups her hands together with a loud pop, and the spider floats away from the glassed figure in a bubble. She turns away from Rhynan, holding her cupped hands out from her chest.

"It looks like the one we found earlier. Those bloody spiders are everywhere," Michael says.

"You have seen these before now?" Angus says.

"Aye," Michael says. "We killed one that was on Darrin, and then we checked everyone for more before we came here. We didn't check the glass statue because it had happened only minutes before, and we left straight away. Someone put it there after the curse."

Angus turns to Pyreus and commands in Scottish.

"*Dion do phrionnsa.*" (Protect your prince)

The four wolves glow red and build heat, forcing everyone to back away.

Colleen shouts in Irish.

"*Cosain an prionsa ar aon chostas.*" (Defend the prince at any cost)

Colleen says, "We have another place to take the prince that's fortified with many more Guardians."

"Aaghnya, can the spider still hear us?" Colleen says.

"No. None of the magic on the spider works now."

"Good. Michael, you're in charge of guarding the prince if it comes to a fight. Select your team of six now."

Michael says, "Aye."

"Darrin, you command the west and the south."

Michael and Darrin turn to walk away when a section of the south wall, far from the discussion, explodes inward. High-speed wooden shrapnel tears into the bodies of the unsuspecting Guardians closest to the blast, and witches scream and flail away from the disintegrating wall as they're struck by the flying debris.

"Blood Witches!" Colleen says.

"TO BATTLE!" Angus shouts.

Aaghnya flattens her hands together, and the spy spider explodes into smoke, then she walks to the other side of Rhynan, putting herself between him and the attacking witches. Aaghnya jumps and spins, landing in battle dress, and takes her stance, calming herself, as the heads of Pyreus and Teine slide into her peripheral vision. She turns her head to Pyreus' healthy eye.

"No one will take my Rhynan Doon," she says.

Pyreus turns his head toward Aaghnya and snaps his jaws together with a deep snarl. He looks back to the attacking witches, growls, and snaps his jaws again as Gaisras and Lasair shoot past and plow into the fray.

Aaghnya holds her stance as the fight takes shape and more gray and black portals form along the walls. The bulk of the Irish Guardians rush forward on the heels of the pyre wolves as Angus and Colleen bark orders.

Lasair turns a hard left into a group of Blood Witches casting curses at her, and Angus shouts, "*Rolla Teine, Lasair.*" (Fire roll, Lasair)

She snarls, and with a loud crack, bursts into a fireball, like someone striking a wooden match head. Lasair drops to her side and rolls across the group of witches, leaving five deep scorch marks on the concrete from the witches caught under her tumbling body. As Teine regains her feet, the flames die, and she returns to a glowing fiery red.

Four Blood Witches appear, as though they catapulted over the abandoned cargo container to Aaghnya's left, and she starts her dance to defend Rhynan. Teine snarls and leaps, turning her body sideways as she bursts into a fireball, catching the four witches against her side. The scream is momentary, and Aaghnya sees four quick puffs of smoke rise above Teine's back.

Teine lands in the rubble and turns back toward Aaghnya, making a clicking sound by tapping her jaws together, and Pyreus joins in, making the same sound.

Aaghnya stops her dance. "Are you laughing?" she asks Pyreus, and he nods. "You are being a bad wolf," she says, shaking her finger at him.

"PYRE WOLF! RETREAT! RETREAT!" calls a voice from somewhere in the foray.

The attack ends as fast as it began, and the Irish Guardians go about the gruesome task of collecting their wounded and dead from the battlefield. Colleen surveys the carnage and notices several boats in the harbor with onlookers standing on the decks, pointing at them.

"Angus, those people on the boats. I'll wager they're calling the authorities. We need to abandon the warehouse," she says.

"We have a prisoner here," a voice calls out.

Colleen rushes to the voice in time to see a spider climb from under the Blood Witch's shirt and shoot a dart into the witch's throat.

"Sorcha takes no chances," Colleen says.

Colleen looks at Michael and Darrin as Angus joins them.

"It's time to take the prince to his bride," Angus says. "The locals are gathering to the noise of the explosions, so we need to clean this up and leave."

"Have a healer cast the Mind Weavers to those boats," Colleen says. "And make sure they destroy those bloody mobile phones."

Colleen turns to Aaghnya, saying, "We need to check everyone for these spiders before we go because we can't afford to take any with us this time," Colleen says.

"I can stop the spider from following us," Aaghnya says.

"How?" Angus says.

"When I captured the spider earlier, I felt the source of its magic. I can block it by making one portal that everyone will use, and the spider will not pass."

"Are you certain?" Colleen says.

Aaghnya nods her head, and Colleen turns to Michael.

"Repair the damage and leave no trace. We leave now."

Michael leads a team of witches to the end of the half-destroyed warehouse, and, like a synchronized force, they wave their wands, and the walls stitch themselves back together, cutting off the prying eyes of the people who saw the fight. Michael glimpses wavering air behind a large group of on watchers and whispers, "Mind Weaver."

"I'll take the prince with me," Angus says, "Pyreus will guard him until we get the glass removed."

Aaghnya casts a portal.

"Angus, walk through this first."

A spider falls to the ground as Angus disappears, and Aaghnya captures it.

Angus reappears on the other side of the portal as it closes, and he looks back to see the spider floating in the air.

"I don't believe it," he says.

"I'll wager you didn't know that one's been riding on your kilt," Michael says.

Angus looks at Michael. "Fair wager, lad, if not for the fire portal."

"That means it climbed on you here?" Colleen says.

"Aye. Nothing survives the fire portal unless I shield it with Staff magic."

Angus looks back to Aaghnya.

"Your magic is powerful. We'll need that strength to win this battle."

Aaghnya flattens her hands together, and the spider turns to smoke.

Angus looks to the Pyre Wolf. "*Dhòmhsa.*" (To me)

Angus lays his hand on the shoulder of the glass statue, and the Staff blinks a bright blue light, then he lifts the staff overhead to form a large, fiery portal above the prince and the pyre wolves gather around the glassed statue.

Teine stops to look at Aaghnya.

"Thank you. I will see you at the next place," Aaghnya says. Then, forming a ball of ice twice the size of a grapefruit, she tosses it to Teine, who playfully tosses it in her mouth as she walks toward the others.

The portal drops over Angus, Rhynan's glassed figure, and the four pyre wolves and Aaghnya's stomach tighten as she stares at the emptiness.

ROYAL SOULS

Colleen places her hand on Aaghnya's shoulder, saying, "Don't worry yourself. I think nothing gets past the wolf."

Aaghnya looks at her and smiles.

"Time to go. I hear sirens. I'll focus on the place we're going," Colleen says.

Aaghnya places her hand along the side of Colleen's face for a few moments before casting a new portal.

"*Déan deifir anois*," (Hurry now) Colleen says.

The Irish Guardians run into the portal until only Aaghnya and Colleen remain, and Colleen takes a last glance around, noticing a partial human shadow on the ground.

Colleen grabs Aaghnya's hand and points at the shadow. Aaghnya lets the portal close, and they hide behind a couple of barrels. Soon after, a young girl walks out, and after a few moments of looking around, she makes a quick spin of her wand and a mirror portal forms in front of her face.

"My Queen. They've figured out a way to stop my spiders."

"Did the other spy succeed?"

"Yes, My Queen. They still don't know."

"Perfect. Return to New Orleans and wait for further instructions."

"Yes, My Queen."

With a wave of her wand, the mirror portal changes to full size, and the young witch steps through, disappearing.

Colleen and Aaghnya stand.

"I don't believe it. We have a traitor." Colleen says.

257

Aaghnya can hear the disappointment and disbelief in Colleen's voice, but before she can say anything, a door bangs open.

"Police. You're surrounded!"

Colleen snaps back to the moment as Aaghnya forms the portal again, and they disappear.

"Stop! Police!"

The lone officer stands with a vacant look and lets his gun arm drop to his side.

"Impossible," he says.

DESPAIR

Tuesday, September 2nd — 2300 Eastern Time — Boston

LysaBeth. We are near Ireland. LysaBeth. Wake up, child. Remember where you are.

"Tonique?" Beth lifts her head. "Tonique. Did I fall asleep?"

Slowly, LysaBeth. You slept deep. Let your body and mind wake.

"Tonique. You're puffed up like a bed."

Your mother used to say, 'Best sleep ever'.

"Tonique, how do you do that?"

Raziiair have air pockets under the skin that we can fill to support your body and let you stretch out like you are in your bed.

"I have to say, my bed never felt this good."

Both laugh.

I am going to let the air out. Let your body change back to a rider.

Beth's legs slip along the sides of the great black Raziiair as the cushioning covering the saddle deflates, and she sinks into the rider's position again. She feels the more rigid surface of the bone against her knees and feet as the air sacs supporting her chest slip away and the handle bones reappear. Beth takes hold of the handle bones as the shield feathers crack open, letting a gentle flow of fresh air leak in.

"The fresh air feels good, Tonique."

Tonique laughs. *It wakes the senses.*

Beth's eyes change to Tonique's view, and she can see the faint outline of land far below them.

Do you want to practice LysaBeth?

"What do you mean, Tonique?"

When our eyes are the same, see where you want to go or the maneuver you want to make, and we will do it.

"Seriously?"

Beth focuses, and after a quick barrel roll, Tonique's wings fold back into the dive position, and her tail feathers and head bend downward, putting her into a power dive.

Beth's heart rate jumps as her body goes light in the saddle, and she pulls on the handles, tightening her body against Tonique. The shield feathers draw down against her, and pressure around her ankles and knees from swelling air pockets locks her legs into place. The shield feathers tighten more, sealing the cockpit, pushing her tighter against Tonique, and she feels the slight rippling of the shield feathers against her back as they gain speed. As they get closer to the rough waters of the Atlantic Ocean, Tonique feels Beth tighten.

Calm, LysaBeth. Wait... Wait... Now.

Beth sees them in level flight above the whitecaps, in her mind's eye, and the spray from two waves crashing together shoots across Tonique's face.

ROYAL SOULS

"Tonique. Is that your white light shining on the water?"

Yes, child.

"It's bright as daylight."

Tonique laughs as they rip across the surface until they snap skyward at the shore's rock bluff and barrel roll through the climb until they level to a calm soar in the night sky, and Tonique's light fades.

"Woo-who!" Beth shouts as she pops out from under the shield feathers.

LysaBeth. I needed that, Tonique says, laughing. *It's as if I were flying with your mother again. Thank you.*

"No, thank you, Tonique. You're amazing."

They soar for a few moments, and Tonique says, *Let's get you home, child.*

Tonique makes a slow roll as Beth tucks in beneath the shield feathers again, and they start a slow spiral downward toward MacGillycuddy's Reeks and Beth's home.

Tonique bounces as the crosswinds at the southern end of the mountain range push against her, and pockets of cool and warm air lift and drop her body. Beth squeezes her knees and hands tighter, triggering Tonique's air sacks to tighten around her legs as they descend deeper into the valley, and Tonique changes her eyes to night vision.

How do you like that, child?

"That's cool, Tonique, but I've had night vision since I was twelve years old."

What? Who taught you this?

"One of my trainers taught it to me as a birthday gift that year."

LysaBeth, night vision is not a human gift. Who was the trainer?

"I don't know her name. Ask Egret."

Tonique doesn't reply to Beth's answer.

We are here.

Tonique flares her giant wings and settles on an outcrop of rock above the middle of the mountain. Beth slides out from under the shield feathers and waits for Tonique's transformation to finish.

"Where's the front door?"

Tonique points to a large crevasse behind the corner of the rock face. Beth moves to the opening but stops a few feet short as the emerald rune on her forehead glows.

"Your home knows you are here, child. The magic barriers still hold."

Beth draws a deep breath, holds, and releases slowly to calm herself. She can't tell if she's tense because of potential danger or if it is the anticipation of finding her mother in time to save her. Beth steps into the crevasse, and the emerald light glistens on the wet rock. She passes through the last layer of magic protection and the crack of sunrise fills her eyes, and she catches her breath at the site of a large stone castle two hundred yards away. She walks an unkempt path toward the Castle, and despair builds as she gets closer to see decaying vines, broken garden frames, and trellis' that serve only to increase the failing image.

"Do not despair, child. There is still life." Tonique points to a small plant with a single blue flower, sitting in a window near the corner of the Castle.

ROYAL SOULS

Beth and Tonique climb four stone stairs to a large wood and iron front door, with carvings in the frame matching the box's symbols. On the right side of the door, there's a slot cut into the wooden frame, and Tonique walks to Beth's side, pointing. "Place the box in the hole."

Beth reaches her hand to her lower back, pulls the box from a pouch under her long black hair, and places it in the slot. A glow of white light surrounds the box as it sinks into the wall, and Beth steps back. The light flows liquid, outlining the front door until suspended, then the door changes from wood and iron to a swirling portal of soft green light.

Tonique lifts her hand toward the door. "Go, child. Your home is welcoming you."

Beth walks through the portal into a lifeless foyer of cut stone and large wooden beams with an empty water fountain in the middle. The curved stone stairs with carved wooden banisters and cut and chiseled stone risers lay coated in heavy dust. The large crystal chandelier with unlit candles hangs from a massive wooden beam above the lifeless fountain. To Beth's left is a curved wall of stained-glass, faded and bleak, and to her right, a carved archway.

"Where is that green light coming from?" Beth whispers.

Beth turns toward the light, and as she passes through the archway, the light becomes brighter and begins pulsing. The emerald crystal on her forehead pulses, reminding her of Abigail's bracelet and the amulet.

"The light is coming from behind that stone."

263

Beth climbs two stone stairs to a six-foot-high and two-foot-wide rune stone of emerald crystal, surrounded by carved wooden blocks, with a leather pad at the base. A plaque of copper, with writing tooled into it, lay angled in front of the pad.

Beth stops and looks back at Tonique, standing outside the archway and asks, "What is this?"

"You must bring the life back to the castle," says Tonique. "Kneel on the pad, read the inscription, and then place your forehead against the emerald crystal."

Beth turns and looks at the copper plaque, then back to Tonique.

"How am I supposed to read something that's in a language I don't know?"

"You will."

Beth pauses for a few moments before turning back to the emerald stone, and she feels energy reach out, pulling her.

Beth kneels on the leather pad, draws a deep breath, exhales slowly, and focuses on the copper plaque. A few moments pass, and she whispers, in Irish Gaelic:

"Lysa, máthair Spirit Witches,"

"éist le d'iníonacha LysaSearin agus LysaBeth."

"Breathe draíocht isteach sa teampall mar sin,"

"b'fhéidir go dtroidfimid i d'ainm agus cothromaíocht a thabhairt."

> Lysa, mother of Spirit Witches,
> hear your daughters LysaSearin and LysaBeth.
> Breathe magic into this temple, so
> we may fight in your name and bring balance.

Beth leans forward, and the small crystal strikes the rune-stone as her forehead touches it. She lingers against the cold, refreshing surface, then realizes the sound of the crystal striking is echoing and building in intensity.

Beth sits back on her haunches. "Tonique, the light from the stone is pulsing faster and getting brighter."

Beth hears the 'splat' of a water drop, then a second, and a third. She looks over her shoulder at a steady drip of water from the fountain spout, then it turns to water running, and the fountain takes on colors.

Beth looks around, and the color is seeping into every surface, from every direction. The plants show life with shining greenery and flowers, and pictures etch their way into the stained glass.

The fountain runs with a full shower, shooting out the top and the candles mounted on the chandelier light. Pop, pop, pop...

Beth laughs. "Tonique, the Castle. It's coming back to life!" and she scrambles to her feet.

Tonique is in the foyer dancing with her arms and hands stretched above her head, and she laughs.

"LysaBeth, help me."

Beth and Tonique stop moving as the voice echoes through the room.

Beth runs to Tonique. "Where is she?"

"Where was she in your dream, LysaBeth?"

Beth closes her eyes and thinks of the vision. Looking around the room, she moves until she's standing in the same spot as the dream, and she points to the wall.

"The hanging curtains underneath the stairs. Behind there."

Beth and Tonique run to the hanging curtains and pull them open, finding a solid stone wall.

"Ahh." In desperation, Beth throws the curtain back at the wall. She spins, stomps back to the fountain, and looking around the room, she relives the dream in her mind's eye.

"There. How's that possible? The chandelier candles are in a reflection at the end of that wall across the room."

Beth sprints to the end of the wall and reaches forward to touch her reflection. Her hand passes through into nothingness. She steps through her image, exiting the spell tunnel at the top of a staircase. Torches, ahead of her, light with a pop, as in her vision, and she runs down the stairs. She hears Tonique's sandals slapping against the stone stairs as she nears the room at the bottom and slows to a crawl.

"The room from the dream," she whispers.

Tonique joins Beth at the center of the stone room, with no doors or windows.

"Tonique, what do I do?"

"Look at the wall stones for a clue, LysaBeth."

They separate, and after several minutes Beth shouts, "Look, a symbol from the box!"

"Touch it, child."

Beth covers the symbol with her palm and waits.

"Nothing."

"Here, another one."

Beth runs to Tonique.

"There must be one on each wall. I'll check this one, and you look there."

After a time, she says, "Here, another one, LysaBeth."

"I've got nothing."

Beth and Tonique stare at each other for a few moments.

"I've got it," Beth says. "It's the three symbols on the front of the box. I have to touch them in order."

Beth walks to the wall with the first symbol, then the second, then across the room to the third, and waits.

"Nothing… Why?"

"LysaBeth," Tonique says, pointing to the floor.

Beth looks. "That's the symbol from the top of the box." Beth touches it first, then the other three in their order, and waits.

"Nothing."

Tonique points to the floor saying, "Maybe that one is the last."

Beth touches the three symbols in order, and kneeling on one knee, she places her hand over the rune symbol and hears the voice.

"Say the words."

Beth presses her palm to the symbol.

"*Lysa, máthair Spirit Witches,*"

"*éist le d'iníonacha LysaSearin agus LysaBeth,*"

"*Breathe draíocht isteach sa teampall mar sin,*"

"*b'fhéidir go dtroidfimid i d'ainm agus cothromaíocht a thabhairt.*"

Beth jumps up from a loud crunching noise as the wall in front of her splits and opens outward, letting torchlight into the hidden vault. She draws a sharp breath as the first rays of light strike a body lying on a thick cushion supported by a stone platform. Beth recognizes the green dress from her dream.

Tonique dashes through the opening wall, and reaching LysaSearin, she puts her hand on the unconscious woman's chest and waits.

Beth, shaking, looks at her hands, which are colorless from clenching them so tightly, and she looks back to her mother as Tonique turns her head toward Beth.

Tonique smiles. "She lives! There is life in your mother. We need Faerie Pool water."

Beth throws her arms across her chest, tears flow down her face, and laughing, she says, "I have some."

"Get it."

Beth spins her hand in the air, and a small vial falls into the other palm. She walks to her mother's side, and looking at her, she sees the resemblance.

"I have no memory of you," she whispers.

Tonique reaches her hand across, but Beth doesn't see it.

My mother... My birth mother. I didn't know you were alive, or I would have found you sooner. I'm sorry.

"LysaBeth."

"What? Oh, sorry. Here."

Beth looks back at her mother and whispers, "Please live."

Tonique removes the stopper from the vial and lets three drops fall onto the corner of LysaSearin's mouth, and they watch as it creeps into the slight gap and disappears. They wait in silence until LysaSearin's mouth opens enough that Beth and Tonique see the movement, and Beth catches her breath. Tears roll down her cheeks again, and she smiles as Tonique kisses LysaSearin's forehead.

ROYAL SOULS

"Come back to us. Your child waits for you," Tonique breathes.

Tonique looks up at Beth. "She will live, but she needs nutrition." Tonique waves her hand.

A glass jar containing a red fluid shows up on a shelf behind LysaSearin's head.

"Is that the same liquid Egret gave me?"

"Yes, it will help your mother recover faster, but she can only have a few drops at a time."

"How long before she wakes?"

"I do not know, child. We must assume she has been asleep for over twenty years. This could take days."

Beth looks around the stone room at runes carved into the walls, ceiling, and floor and recognizes the runes carved on the platform supporting her mother are the same as the box. An emerald rune-stone stands on the back wall, smaller but mirroring the one upstairs, only pale and lifeless.

Tonique reaches for the bottle of red liquid and drips a few drops into the corner of LysaSearin's mouth, and her lips close. Beth feels butterflies in her stomach in anticipation of meeting her birth mother.

"We will leave her to absorb the water and nutrition. We have other things to do."

"What! I'm not leaving her here unprotected."

"Calm, LysaBeth. This is your home. You command it. You know how to shield your mother, so I can care for her, and she will be safe."

"I'm sorry, Tonique, but as overwhelming as all this is... again. I don't see how anything could be so important that I should walk away from my mother, whom I've just found?"

"LysaBeth! You will not shout at me!"

Beth is silent for a few moments. "I'm sorry, Tonique."

"You will see your mother and talk with her, but we have other lives in the castle that we must save."

Beth catches Tonique's tone of urgency, so she places her hand on her mother's and reaches her other hand out to Tonique. Tonique takes it and puts her empty hand on LysaSearin's, closing the circle.

Beth closes her eyes, saying, "*Skjerm dette livet.*" (Shield this life.) Her hands glow, and a wall of light surrounds all three of them for a few moments, then fades to nothing.

A few moments later, Tonique and Beth release their grip, but Beth keeps her mother's hand and leans to the side of her face, saying, "Mom, please come back to me."

Beth places her mother's hand back on the cushion, then turns and walks to the vault entrance. She puts her hand on the wall and reaches out to Tonique with the other, then pauses, saying, "Tonique, the walls. They're getting warm."

"Yes, child. I felt the warmth growing in the air. The magic returns to the Castle, and it's caring for your mother."

Beth looks over her shoulder at her mother and sees a slight shimmer of light in the pale emerald rune stone on the wall behind her and realizes it's showing the life returning to her mother.

She turns back to Tonique, asking, "Why didn't you know of this room?"

"We will both ask your mother that question."

Beth nods her head and says, "Take my hand and put your other one on the door."

Tonique reaches out to Beth, grasping her hand, and Beth closes her eyes, saying, "*Skjold fra alle.*" (Shield from all.) Her hands glow, and a flash of light fills the room.

The light fades and Beth opens her eyes, saying, "Only you and I can open this room or touch my mother."

"Fear not, child. I will be with her until she wakes, and then we will fly again."

Tonique laughs and throws her arms in the air.

Beth smiles, giving a quick glance back to her mother. "What do we need to do?"

"Wake the Raziiair from healing hibernation."

"Say what?"

Tonique walks toward the stairs, and Beth follows as the doors to the vault close.

Stepping out of the secret entrance, Beth squints as the first light of the morning sun, slipping into the foyer, fills her eyes, and she catches her breath.

"The gardens are alive. Look at the flowers. Oh my, that's a stag with a deer and rabbits. Yep, I could call this home."

"It is your home. Now come with me, and we will wake the Raziiair."

Beth walks toward Tonique as she places her hand on a large column near the stairs and spins around it to disappear with a slight pop.

Beth giggles. "Nice one, Tonique."

Beth walks around the column, expecting to follow Tonique, but nothing happens. She pauses, then places her hand on the column, copying Tonique's spin, and disappears with a slight pop sound. Beth exits the spell tunnel at the top of a staircase carved into a rock wall. As she descends, the cool, damp air reaches up to her, and by the time she touches the bottom, she can see her breath floating away. She stops and throws her arm as if tossing a ball to a child and says, *"Belyse"* (Illuminate). A light floats toward the ceiling, becoming brighter until it fills the enormous cavern.

"Carved stone columns, runes carved into the stone walls like they're chiseled on pages from a stone book." Captivated by the carvings, Beth whispers, "What language is that?"

Halfway around the cavern, a small stream of water flows down the wall, from ceiling to floor, into a shallow pool, but the depth stays the same.

"That must drain through the ground. I don't think I'll ever swim there," Beth mutters.

She turns toward a light on the other side of the cave.

"The light is coming through that small opening with a ring of frost around it."

Beth raises her hand and clenches her fist, extinguishing the floating light.

The temperature drops as she gets closer to the opening, and she ducks to a semi-crouch to walk through the frosted, short tunnel. She stops at the exit.

"Come, child," Tonique says.

Beth stands tall and takes a quick glance around at the ice and frost-coated room before she looks up at the shape of an egg, covered in ice, mounted thirty feet high on a column of clear crystal. The base of the column, five feet in diameter, tapers to three feet at the top with a fluted base holding the egg.

"Oh, look. An egg cup," Beth whispers.

She walks past Tonique to the column and looks at the carvings that reach halfway up to the icy surface.

"Wow. I've never seen symbols like that."

"That is the language of the Raziiair, and those are the names of the families we have flown with."

Beth notices the symbols on the first line nearest the bottom match the box her mother's crystal was in, so she kneels and places her hand on them.

"The first LysaSearin was the first rider of my ancestor, and it was then that my family swore to always be the Raziiair of the O'Corry Lysa," Tonique says.

Beth looks over her shoulder to see Tonique has changed from her colorful one piece dress into a loose fitting flight suit and boots.

"Why the change of clothes?"

"The suit will protect us during the wakening of the Raziiair. You must change into yours."

"That sounds ominous," Beth says as she stands and waves her hand over her body from head to knees, changing to her flight suit.

"Come." Tonique walks to the other side of the column.

Beth walks around the column to find Tonique standing in front of a pedestal with a black crystal, shaped like a feather laying on it. The box Beth took from Tonique's chest is sitting beside it.

"Hey. How did that get there?"

"That box is from your family's magic and used for many things, like protecting the Raziiair by locking a protection spell inside. This crystal feather is only one key. You or your mother are the other. When you hold the box in your hands and I place this feather crystal inside, it will drop the protection spell and wake the sleeping Raziiair."

Beth drops to one knee, placing her hand on the ground.

"Finn min fiende." (Find my enemy).

Beth looks up at Tonique. "Sorry, Tonique, but it sounded odd that I should be the one to unlock the Raziiair. I lost sight of you, so I had to check that the enemy hadn't been hiding in the cavern, captured you, and used an identity spell."

"Your mother, always tested for the truth," Tonique says, laughing as Beth stands. "LysaBeth. This is the last Raziiair rookery left, so your mother protected it by locking it with blood magic, knowing someday you will find your way home."

"Good thing Sorcha didn't find it first."

"Even if she knew where the Castle is, she could not get here because she does not have the key. When you entered the crevasse, the shield magic sensed both your mother's crystal and the box you had hidden."

"Okay, let's do this."

Beth takes the box in hand, opens the lid, and Tonique places the crystal feather inside. It melts down to nothing before Beth closes the top, and Tonique turns to look at the wall across a pond of ice.

"Uh, Tonique? Nothing's happening."

Beth looks closer, surprised to see Tonique's eyes are white.

"Great. The rest of the instructions might have been useful before you checked out."

A voice echoes in her mind again. *LysaBeth, trust in your family.*

"What does that even mean?"

Beth looks around for a clue.

"Wait. Trust in your family. The family symbols at the bottom of the column."

She walks to the other side of the column, kneeling to the bottom row of symbols, and the box in her hand glows. Beth touches the box to the column, and with a hissing sound, it slides into the family symbols. When it disappears, she stands and walks back to Tonique to find the surrounding ground clear of snow and ice, and the box has reappeared on the stand. Beth takes the box and places it in the pouch at the small of her back and it shrinks to become unnoticeable.

"I knew you could find the answer," Tonique says as she wakens from the spell and laughs. "Look. Water builds on top of the ice pond," she says, pointing to the ground.

"Ice pond? Hey, the air is warming, fast," Beth says.

"It must reach forty degrees Celsius in less than two minutes for the sleeping spell to break, or the Raziiair could die."

Pointing again, Tonique says, "The pond turns orange."

"Oh, that ice pond, on the other side of the cave. And it turning orange is a good thing?" Beth says.

"Okay.... now it's red," Beth says, looking at Tonique.

"Whoa," Beth says as her and Tonique's flight suits add head and hand coverings in time for a loud *whoosh,* and the surface of the ice pond catches fire.

A burst of hot air hits, pushing them back, and Beth shouts over the sounds of the roaring flames, "Is this supposed to happen?".

Tonique shouts back, "Yes, that is why we changed into the suit. Watch." Tonique points at the wall on the other side of the burning pond as the flames climb until the entire surface is burning and Beth feels herself sweating. Water and ice splash down beside her as the icy surface of the egg and column melts, revealing the chiseled crystal. Suddenly, the surface of the burning wall slips into the roaring flames, dousing them and filling the cave with steam. Tonique waves her hand, clearing the mist, revealing a honeycomb shape with twenty transparent eggs containing human figures curled in the fetal position.

"Tonique, they're moving."

"Yes, the flames did their job."

Tonique waves her hand over her body, changing back to her full-length colorful dress so Beth changes back to her pixie-cut look.

Beth follows Tonique around the column as the first three eggs float forward from the honeycomb to where the ground is now dry. Touching the ground, the eggs burst, releasing the life supporting fluid that evaporates, and dropping the human figures to unfold. One figure, a young black woman, dressed in aerobic shorts and top, with sharp features, an athletic body, and hair in long, colorful braids, stands and looks at Tonique.

"Taelene, I feared we were not in time."

"I had faith, Mamma."

Beth looks at Tonique. "Mamma?"

"LysaBeth, meet my daughter, Taelene."

Taelene looks at Beth and says, "LysaSearin's daughter?"

"Yes. Nice to meet you, Taelene."

"Yeah, well. You can find yourself another ride because I ain't going to be nobody's pet."

"Taelene! How dare you talk to a Lysa like that? LysaBeth, I am so sorry for my daughter's manners."

"What's this about, Tonique?" Beth says.

"Oh, I'll tell you, Princess," Taelene says. "It's about the little princess thinking she's going to ride my back and take control of my mind. That ain't happening. I make my life and my own decisions, and I don't care about no history or pact, so you can carry your own damn bags. Got it? Princess?"

"Taelene! You are born to be LysaBeth's Raziiair and protector, as I am her mother's. This has been a great honor for our family since the beginning."

"Mamma, I don't care who Miss Lilly thinks she is. There is no way I'm putting my life on the line for that spoiled little brat."

"LysaBeth," Tonique starts, but Beth raises her hand to stop her from saying anything else as she walks toward Taelene.

"Oh, careful, Princess. You get up in my face, and you're going to find yourself with a fat lip."

Taelene feels the cold of the stone floor against her face and opens her eyes. Lifting her head, she looks around, seeing only Beth, half sitting on a stool with her ankles crossed, sipping a bottle of water. Taelene sits up, and after a second or two of gathering her thoughts, she turns seething mad and jumps to her feet.

"The little princess had to use magic to get her way, huh? Got no spine, Silver Spoon?"

"Mirror's right there, mouth, or you can touch that big lump on the side of your cheek." Beth points to Taelene's right cheek. "Care for another?"

Taelene touches her sore left cheek between her eye and ear. "Nice sucker punch."

"Oh, no, honey. I walked right up to you and rang your bell."

Taelene paces back and forth like a caged cat but doesn't see Tonique step back into the shadows.

"It's just you and me," Beth says. "This is your chance to beat the little princess black and blue."

Beth stands up, throwing her bottle of water to the side.

"Yeah, right? Then I get hunted for the rest of my life."

"Nope. You broke the pact. The reality of it is, you won't be leaving this cave alive either way, so you might as well give it a shot, tough girl. Go out swinging for the fence, bad-ass."

Taelene stops pacing as Beth's words of finality sink in, and Beth can see the emotion rising, so she takes her well-practiced kick-boxing stance.

"Come on, dead girl. Show me how tough you could have been with the right attitude."

Taelene's eyes pool, and as the first tear rolls over her bottom lash, Taelene says, "I didn't ask to be born into servitude."

Beth relaxes. "What do you mean, servitude?"

"I'm supposed to be the little pony Mommy and Daddy didn't buy you, right?"

"You are an idiot. Who filled your head with that crap because your mother and mine are the best of friends? They have fought together on the ground and in the air. They eat at the same table and share the same wine. My mother demanded that Tonique be present when I was born, and my mother trusted Tonique to carry a secret message that she knew could save her life, and it did. If we had grown up together, we could have been formidable in our teens, and neither my mother nor father would have gone into hiding. And I might not have spent the last fifteen years of my life, up to yesterday, thinking that I killed my parents in a fire."

Beth has reached a volume that has Taelene frozen with surprise. Tears stream down Taelene's cheeks as Beth continues.

"Do you know that until last Friday, I had lived my life alone since I was nine? In the last six days, I have saved a man's life, met the love of my life, fought the wicked witch Queen, married the love of my life, and left him ten minutes later to save my mother. And now I have to execute my mother's best friend's daughter because she's got bubble gum for brains."

Taelene's crying slows. "Why have you done this?"

"Because the soul-sucking wicked witch, Queen Sorcha, is trying to take control of the magic world by killing the souls of Prince O'Manus and Princess Sadreen, and I'm the Spirit Witch born to stop her. And you, you dumb ass, were supposed to be my ride into battle and through to victory."

"My mother told me of the calling, and I ignored it."

"How long ago?"

"Fifteen years ago. I kept having a dream where I was flying with a girl on me in Boston."

"That's where I live."

Taelene covers her face with her hands to hide her crying, but her shaking shoulders give it away. She slides her hands down her face, looking at Beth.

"I am so sorry, LysaBeth. I never wanted to understand what it meant, and now I have shamed my mother and my family bloodline forever." Taelene drops to her knees.

Beth shakes her head and says, "Do you know how many times I've screwed up and made Freya and Egret so mad they've wanted to turn me into something edible?"

Beth takes a deep breath and exhales.

"Taelene, get up."

Taelene stands.

"Before you kill me, can I ask that you tell my mother how sorry I am?"

"No." Beth points behind Taelene. "Tell her yourself."

Taelene spins and runs into her mother's arms and buries her face deep into her neck, sobbing.

"Mamma. I'm so sorry I didn't listen to why I was to be her Raziiair or what it meant. I was foolish, and I've shamed our family for it."

Tonique comforts her daughter for a few moments, and then Taelene stands tall.

"Mamma, I love you."

Taelene walks back to Beth, taking a deep breath and blowing it out hard, says, "Okay, I'm ready."

"Yeah, I'm hungry, too, so stop being a dumb ass."

Beth walks past Taelene, and her head follows Beth in surprise.

"Tonique. How's my mom doing?"

"She moved a finger."

"Awesome."

Tonique stops and turns back to Taelene as Beth walks away.

"Well, come on, girl. You need to eat, too, or you won't have the energy to train."

A tearful Taelene runs to her mother, hugs her, and they walk arm in arm to the stairs.

After a visit to her mother, Beth joins Tonique and Taelene at a table covered in fresh fruits and vegetables from the blossoming orchard and gardens. They joke and laugh in the noon sunlight as they plan their training.

Then, silence takes over as an envelope falls from a blue smoke portal in the foyer.

"I've got it," Taelene says.

She walks to the white envelope lying on the floor, examines it for a few moments before asking, "LysaBeth, do you want me to open the envelope over here?"

"No, Taelene. I can contain spells while opening it, and besides, I can't afford to lose you."

Taelene smiles at Beth's response, then circles her hand over the envelope, floating it over to Beth.

Beth moves her hand as though wiping the mist from a window, forming a bubble around the envelope, and it peels itself open.

"We have the prince. We need Naise Lagrandeur from France. Meet the Guardians at Château La Grouse," Beth reads out loud.

Beth looks at Taelene. "I guess we train under fire."

"I'm game if you are."

"Do you know where in France the Château La Grouse is?"

"Yep. I've located it in my mind."

"Wow. Built-in GPS and maps. Looks like my new ride has all the upgrades."

"LysaBeth," snaps Tonique. "That was cruel. I am going to tell your mother that you are being a brat."

"Oh, Tonique. I'm only playing."

Beth runs around the table and throws her arms around Tonique's neck, and she laughs.

"So am I," Tonique says, and they both laugh.

"Oh, okay. I get it," says Taelene. "My mother calls you a brat, and she gets a hug. I call you a brat, and I get knocked out. Nope, I got it. Uh-huh."

Beth walks to Taelene and throws her arms around her neck. "That will never happen again. I promise."

Taelene hugs Beth back. "Same here."

MAIDEN VOYAGE

Wednesday, September 3rd — 0900
Eastern Time — Boston

"Taelene, you've never had a rider?"

"No."

"Taelene, Beth has flown with me, so she can teach you."

"Tell you what, Taelene. Let's you and I start from the beginning. Two rookies. Let's start with the transformation and go from there."

"Sounds good to me. Thanks, LysaBeth."

Tonique steps forward to say something, and Beth interrupts.

"Hey, it's you and me together, so let's figure out what works for us."

Tonique steps back and says, "Taelene, the first time the bones come out, will hurt because you have never used them. Your body will suffer for not using it, so try to use all your abilities as soon as possible."

"Yes, Mamma."

"Take it at a speed that you're comfortable with," Beth says. "No rush. I need you healthy."

"LysaBeth, I did this. I made poor choices, and now I have to fix them."

"Okay, your call. Oh, by the way. Since you and I are going to be best of friends for the rest of our lives, it's Beth."

Raised gardens, now full of life and stunning in the sunshine, surround the large deck at the back of the castle, and to one side, a large wooden ramp extends past the cliff's edge. Beth, Taelene, and Tonique walk onto the back end of the ramp, where Taelene transforms.

"Tonique. Taelene is as black as you in her bird form, so how come her feathers show edges of red instead of blue like yours? And why is her transformation smoke red?"

"Her father, Tefari, was a Royal Crimson, the rarest of the Raziiair. He was longer than me, with a bigger wingspan, so not as maneuverable. It cost him his life in a battle when he tried to outmaneuver a smaller enemy who got above him and struck through the rider, tearing his spine."

"That's horrible."

Beth reaches out, and as her hand nears Taelene's neck, her vision suddenly changes to Taelene's. She snaps her arm back and breaks contact.

"Holy crap. Taelene, did you get that?"

Taelene nods her head.

"What happened?" Tonique says.

"My vision changed to hers, but I hadn't even touched her."

Tonique smiles, placing her hand against Taelene's neck.

"Your mother and I shared the vision as soon as she touched me, but you two are more powerful together than we were."

Tonique places her hand on Beth's arm.

"LysaBeth, I must warn you. Be careful what you ask Taelene to do so soon. As a young Raziiair, she was stronger, faster, and more maneuverable than I had ever been, and I have not seen her fly for many years, so I do not know what happens to her flight dynamics when she reaches her peak speed. If she slides instead of turning, you could slam into the earth or a building or a mountain, ending her life and maybe yours. LysaBeth, the last of the Royal Crimson blood, is in Taelene, and she is the only hope that one may be born again."

"We're going to take it slow. I promise you, Tonique."

Beth touches Taelene's neck.

"No pressure there, Taelene."

Welcome to the Tonique and Taelene saga.

Beth snickers.

Tonique nods at Taelene and steps back.

"Are you ready to try the saddle?"

Taelene's shield feathers open as the bones for the heel and knee pop out, and Taelene squawks.

"Taelene, take it slow," Beth says. "I need you to fly without pain."

Taelene turns her head toward Beth and nods.

Beth smiles saying, "Tough girl."

Taelene opens her wings as she lowers herself. Beth puts her foot into the heel bone, hand on the knee bone and saddle, to pull herself up when her clothes change into the flight suit. Beth steps back and looks around her body.

"Taelene, this suit. It looks and feels different from the other, and the coloring matches your black and red shimmer now."

Beth slides her hand down the sleeve. "Oh, that's cool. The material feels like it's moving on my skin. I think it's compensating for the external pressure."

She presses her hand against her stomach.

"Taelene, the suit is acting like something a jet pilot wears to compensate for G-Force."

Taelene squawks and nods her head.

Beth stretches her arms upward, lifts her knee than the other, feeling her new suit move with her body then, feels a gentle pull at the back of her head. She reaches back over her shoulder to find her long black hair braided flat and loosely tethered to the back of the suit.

"Taelene, the suit is awesome. Talk about an upgrade. Wow."

"LysaBeth," Tonique growls.

Beth looks at her. "No. I'm not being mean, Tonique. Taelene is knocking it out of the park with all the upgrades."

Beth pauses, and her mood flattens.

"Tonique, I'm a Spirit Witch. Why do I need a G-suit? If Taelene can fly like you say, we should be able to rip it up in any fight."

"Did you think maybe the suit can take the impact of a curse from a Wand Witch and keep it from harming your body?"

"Ahh, ya. Never thought of that."

"LysaBeth, your mother never went into battle without thinking about my survival. Never forget that Taelene is my daughter."

A few seconds later, Beth says, "Taelene, I'm sorry. That will never happen again."

Taelene nods and slips her wing behind Beth, pulling her toward the saddle.

Beth climbs into the saddle and sits still for a few moments before using her mind.

Taelene, can you hear me?

Yes, LysaBeth.

Cool. I'm going to turn off the connection to your eyesight until we're flying.

You can do that?

Yup.

Nice.

How do you feel, Taelene?

I don't even know you're there.

Awesome. What's this 'T' shaped bone for?

I didn't know it was there.

"Tonique, what's the 'T' shaped bone for?"

"What? Taelene, I didn't know you had it," Tonique says.

Taelene shakes her head, but Beth can hear her.

Neither did I.

"She didn't know either, Tonique. What's it for?"

Tonique remains silent.

"Tonique… what's it for?"

Silence.

"Tonique. What's wrong?"

Beth's hand falls to the "T" bone, and a pouch appears on her stomach.

"Hey, where did that come from?"

"I will tell you about the 'T' bone, but you must promise not to try it until you have training. You must promise me."

"Easy, Tonique. I promise."

"Only Royalty can fly the Royal Crimson," Tonique says. "The rider can hook their tether," she points at Beth's belly, "to the 'T' bone and stands on the saddle to use their wand magic while the Raziiair uses the cords, beak, and talons. When the rider is standing, there is a protection shield around them they can cast through, giving them advantage over any saddle witch."

Beth puts her hand against her belly, and lifting the flap of the pouch, she sees two gold rings joined by a red cord. She lifts the rings out and hooks them over the 'T' of the bone. The bone tips extend and curl back to the shaft to make seamless loops, anchoring Beth to Taelene.

LysaBeth, I can feel you. I feel your heartbeat and your breathing.

"She says she can feel my heartbeat and breathing."

"Yes, you're connected to her and your bond is the strongest it will ever be. The witch shares their power and the Crimson becomes invincible until physical combat. If you die while connected, so does she."

"That's how your husband died. Isn't it?"

"Yes, his rider was an arrogant young prince who had won many battles on my husband's back and would listen to no one. He used the lifeline too much, and the enemy learned his weakness, so he became an easy kill. He took the last of the Royal Crimson with him."

"Okay. We... are waiting for the training. How do I take it off the bone?"

"Take a ring in each hand and hold it, so it does not touch the bone, and wait for the bone to let go."

Beth followed the instructions and put the rings back in the pouch.

"Taelene, can you give me some padding in the saddle? Your spine is a little sharp."

Beth feels Taelene tense up.

Hey. Only if you're ready, Taelene.

LysaBeth, I don't care how much it hurts. I will use all my air sacks at once and get it over with.

Taelene, don't.

Taelene, already puffing up, lets out a shrilling squawk and falls to her side.

Beth rolls out of the saddle and over her shoulder to a standing position facing Taelene.

"Abigail!" Beth shouts.

Tonique glances at her but says nothing.

Beth rushes to Taelene as soon as she can see her through the red smoke and kneels beside her.

"Taelene, why did you do that? I need you."

Tonique kneels, and Beth looks at her to see a calm smile.

"Okay, what did I miss?" Beth says.

"Damn, that hurt."

"Taelene, you're okay?"

Taelene and Tonique can hear the genuine concern in Beth's voice.

"That was very brave, Taelene, and now you never have to feel that pain again," Tonique says.

Taelene looks at Beth. "Yeah, and maybe someday I'll meet a bird-man. But I hope I don't marry the guy and leave ten minutes later."

Beth lifts Taelene to her feet. "And when I get back, I'm going to have a nice long talk with him. In private."

Taelene snickers. "Yeah, I'm still waiting to find my bird-man."

"Really? I guess we're more alike than we thought."

"I like that. Means you got a head for what you want."

"Actually, it's a spell my first ancestor put on the family to prevent us from marrying the wrong man."

"Okay, now that's what I call control issues."

Both laugh.

"What do you say we try this again, and then we'll go find your bird-man?"

"Damn straight, girlfriend, but first, who's Abigail?"

"What?"

"When I fell, I heard you shout 'Abigail.'"

"Really?" Beth's shoulders sag, and her head droops forward. "Oh, man. That's bad."

Beth takes a deep breath and, looking at Taelene, she explains the relationship between her and Abigail and how badly wounded Abigail was in the fight with Sorcha and the snow lions.

Tears well in Taelene's eyes, and she steps forward, throwing her arms around Beth's neck.

"Thank you for including me with Abigail. No one other than my Mamma has ever shown that kind of concern for me. I so want to be your Raziiair, LysaBeth."

"I promise not to get you hurt, Taelene."

Taelene steps back. "Sorry, but that's a promise you can't make or keep."

"I'm going to try. And I wish everyone would stop telling me, 'I can't say that'."

"We're going to take risks, and we are going to get hurt. Beth, I've been told you can't make solid decisions when you let fear cloud your mind."

Taelene glances at her mother.

"LysaBeth, your mother and I have won many fights, but we have also suffered wounds," Tonique says.

Beth nods.

"Let's do this," Taelene says.

Beth steps back as red smoke builds around Taelene, but she doesn't notice Tonique walking away until Taelene squawks.

"Tonique, where are you going?" Beth says.

Tonique turns around, smiling.

"You two don't need anyone to help you. Now, I will take care of my best friend."

Taelene's wing touches the back of Beth's neck, and she hears Taelene.

Tell her I love her.

"I love you too, daughter," Tonique says, without waiting for Beth to relay the message.

Taelene gives a loud squawk.

"What the what? How did you do that?" Beth shouts.

Tonique waves over her shoulder without turning around and disappears through the door.

Beth and Taelene spend the next hour talking and discovering the talents they have together.

"Well, what do you think? Ready to try flying together?" Beth asks.

"It's gotta happen," Taelene replies.

"When you're ready, and remember, at your speed."

"Okay, Beth, but can you do me a favor?"

"Absolutely."

"Can you let me keep control until I'm certain that I can fly the way I feel is right?"

"You're the pilot in command, Taelene."

"Thanks, Beth."

Taelene transforms, and as Beth settles into the saddle, she dives off the ramp, and Beth laughs.

"Thanks for the take-off warning, Captain."

She tucks in under the shield feathers and changes her eyes to Taelene's.

Taelene puts herself through a grueling course of twists and turns, rollovers and dives, barrel rolls, and climbs until she settles into a soaring flight.

Okay, Beth. Let's see what we can do together.

Beth pulls her body tight to Taelene, imaging a sharp turn and done.

Wow. That was easy. Let's get fast, Beth.

Okay, Taelene, relax. You've already done all these maneuvers today.

Beth feels Taelene relax and imagines the same maneuver that she and Tonique did, minus the ocean.

Beth, this is easy. We've got this. It's nothing like what I imagined it would be.

I have to say; you scare me with how quick you are, Taelene. Your mother was right. You are the fastest Aston Martin in the garage.

ROYAL SOULS

Taelene laughs. *Thanks, LysaBeth.*

"Hey, what happened to Beth?"

After a compliment like that, no way.

Beth laughs. "Let's go say our goodbyes. You're driving."

Beth walks into the vault, sees the rune stone on the wall that now looks half-filled with soft light, and walking to her mother's side, she takes LysaSearin's hand in both of hers, lifting it to her chest, and sighs.

"Mom, I wanted to be here when you woke, but, I'm sorry, this war is taking Taelene and me to France," she says to her mother's pale form. "The Guardians have the prince, but he's frozen in glass, so we're going to get the wizard who invented the spell and set the prince free. Tonique is staying here to care for you, and I'm going to reinforce the protection spell on the entrance and the castle. All the gardens have come back to life, and the orchard is bursting with fresh fruit. Mom... Mom, please come back to me."

Beth feels a slight twitch of her mother's finger against the back of her hand.

"Yes, that's it. Fight for life, Mom, and we can find my father together. I'll come back as soon as I get this guy, Naise Lagrandeur, delivered to the Guardians."

Beth squeezes her hand before putting it down, then leans over and kisses her mother's forehead.

"I understand why you sent me away. There's nothing to forgive. You made the right decision."

Beth passes her glowing hand over her body, changing into her flight suit, and lifts the emerald crystal from her

293

forehead, and the threads of gold through her hair slip back into the crystal. She changes back to her street look and places the crystal on her mother's forehead, and the gold threads weave their way through LysaSearin's hair.

"You need it more than I do."

Beth straightens herself, pauses, then turns to leave the vault. Climbing the stairs, she looks down at the closing doors, waiting for the seam between doors to disappear, and thinks about not leaving the mother she's never met and only just found.

Tonique and Taelene wait for her at the top of the stairs and Tonique throws an arm over the shoulders of each as they walk to the castle entrance. Tonique says, "Remember to let the magic flow between you and your bond will grow fast and you will be stronger."

"We will, Mamma. Thanks for your help today."

"That's what mothers do."

They stop at the entrance and Beth says, "Tonique. What do I do here?"

"Walk through, you will see. I will stay inside, and the magic will know me."

Beth and Taelene walk through the swirling green smoke and, with a hiss of air, the family box appears in the slot. Beth takes the box from the slot outside and slips it into the hidden pouch at the small of her back. The heavy wood frame with the wood and iron doors opened inward reappears as the green smoke fades. Taelene and Beth place a hand on the outside frame and join their other hands together.

Beth closes her eyes, whispering, "*Skjold fra alle*." (Shield from all)

ROYAL SOULS

A flash of light covers the castle. Beth opens her eyes and waits until her hands stop glowing before she lets Taelene's hand go.

"Now, only the three of us can get in."

Beth and Taelene turn to walk away from the castle, and Taelene waves to her mother, saying, "See you soon," and the doors close.

Neither speaks as they walk to the crevasse and the non-magical world. Beth and Taelene cast the protection spell again, and then Beth looks back at the castle.

"We've done everything possible, except for the outer face. Ready for a new world?"

"All mapped in and ready to go."

Beth and Taelene cast the protection spell one more time on the inside of the crevasse, and stepping through the shield, they get slammed against the rocks by pounding wind and rain.

Taelene looks at Beth. "Perfect day for a maiden voyage, don't you think?"

Beth bursts into laughter as red smoke swirls around the two of them, and she climbs into the saddle.

"Whoa, bad hair day."

Beth feels the air sacs fill to clamp her legs in place.

This is going to be a bumpy ride. I hope you don't get airsick.

Honestly, I never thought about it until now. Thanks, Taelene.

Hang on. Here we go.

Taelene launches from the rock ledge, getting slammed by a crushing wind that drives her back hard, and her breastplate strikes a sharp rock face. She twists her wings

295

into the wind to catch airflow lift that pulls her clear, and slipping sideways, they gain speed, aiming for an opening between two mountain peaks. Taelene bounces through air pockets and, missing the mountain on the right, she changes her angle of attack, slipping to the southeast. They break out of the mountain winds, catch an updraft, and climb to the clouds.

That was intense, Taelene. How did you know to do that?

I went hurricane surfing one year when I ran away from home, so you could say I'm a bit of an expert at ripping the winds.

Noted for future reference.

I've aimed us for France, so you can take a nap, and I'll wake you when we're close.

That's not fair.

Actually, it's part of our bond. As you sleep and rejuvenate, my body heals, and my strength rebuilds, so we both get something from you sleeping.

Okay, cool. Does this rain affect you?

Change your eyes, Beth.

Beth connects with Taelene to see a red glow that cuts through the rain and clouds like infrared light.

That's so cool.

Yeah, I can see through any weather. It's a Royal Crimson gift that came from my father.

So, no other Raziiair has this gift?

Not that I know of.

Handy upgrade, Rudolph.

Taelene pops the shield feathers open, and the rain pelts Beth.

"Okay, okay. No reindeer jokes."

The shield feathers close.

"Taelene, that was mean girl stuff."

Uh-huh.

Both laugh.

Beth, rest. It will help me heal.

"Don't have to ask me twice. I'm tired."

Beth lays forward as her legs stretch out on the soft cushioning of Taelene's air sacs, and she lays her face on the soft feathers.

LysaBeth, wake up. You are in danger.

"Taelene, are you okay?"

Yeah, Beth. What's wrong?

"I heard the Lysa Mother. She says we're in danger. Taelene, how long have I been asleep?"

Not long. We're near England's east coast.

Beth changes her eyes to Taelene's as she scans the surrounding skies to see nothing.

"Taelene, sit my back up and open the shield feathers. I need to look up."

Beth returns to the rider's position and looks up through the rider's shield to see the faint outline of wings.

"Taelene, how far can you see through the clouds?"

Two-hundred, two-hundred-and-fifty yards, depending on cloud density. Why?

"We've got company above us."

Beth feels Taelene tense up.

"Easy, Taelene. We don't know if it's a friend or foe."

Foe. Definitely foe.

"Why do you say that?"

The rookery under your castle is the last one, and those Raziiair are resting while their bodies heal. Any Raziiair out in this weather is not friendly.

Beth looks up again.

"Okay, things are getting worse. I can barely see the outline, but there are now four Raziiair above us."

LysaBeth, what do we do?

"Calm, Taelene. I'm a Spirit Witch. I can shield us, and we can rip these guys apart."

No can do. You cast a shield, and we drop like a rock. You shield yourself and not me, and you break our connection and knock me out. Again, drop like a rock.

"Alright, we stay in the cloud cover... Oh crap, clear skies ahead. "

Beth looks up.

"I count six above us now."

Yeah, how about the other four below us?

"They're diving from above!"

LYSABETH, WHAT DO I DO?

"TAELENE, BATTLE FLIGHT."

Beth locks herself into position, and as she bonds with Taelene, a calmness that Taelene has never felt before takes over.

Taelene snaps a hard right into a one-eighty turn, and the six Raziiair from above overshoot.

Nice move, Beth.

It gives us a bit of time to get it together, Taelene. How's the cord power?

All good.

Are you ready to turn that Raziiair bad girl on full blast?

Let's do this.

Beth sees Taelene in a downward twist for the first attack and Taelene's wings snap back into a dive position, and the four targets below scramble, but her speed increases so fast that they rip across the top of the lead Raziiair and Taelene's cords drag across the rider. The sky lights up with a lightning flash, and the Raziiair squawks as its wings wrap around itself, and it plummets toward the cold of the Atlantic Ocean.

Taelene surveys the enemy like a veteran aerial combat pilot.

Beth, they're trying to box us in, and two more are hiding in that gigantic cloud.

Beth lets go of the handle bones saying, "Open shield feathers."

Taelene's shield feathers open, and her royal crimson glow surrounds them. A windless cockpit forms around Beth, and with glowing hands Beth casts dart like arrows at a Raziiair rider trying to loop into a top position. She hits her target, and Taelene tightens her air sacks on Beth's legs as she snaps left and up with a quick roll left that puts her right behind another enemy bird.

"Sweet move, Taelene."

Beth fires once from each hand, injuring the Raziiair but missing the rider, and the enemy breaks away. Taelene rolls right and dives as the cords from another Raziiair pass over Beth, missing deadly contact. Taelene's air sacs tighten harder around Beth's legs as she twists out of the dive, having reached a speed of over two hundred miles per hour, and she turns, head to head, with two enemy birds. Her bright red light blinds the enemy as she rips between them, rolls, and Beth fires sideways through the cockpit shield as she spins past the targets.

"Damn. Only got one."

Plenty of targets ahead, Beth.

Taelene is still gaining speed when another red Raziiair glow streaks across the top of two enemy Raziiair and the riders explode into nothing. Taelene turns to attack two more enemies, but they retreat as the new, unknown Raziiair turns back toward them.

Taelene slows, and her light fades.

"Taelene, anybody you know?"

No. You?

"Not a clue."

Look, it's slowing and spiraling toward the ground.

"Shield feathers, survey the area."

Beth tucks in as Taelene makes a turn and rolls.

Nothing. Only the other Crimson. Even the two rats that were hiding in the cloud have gone.

"Are you sure he's a Crimson? I thought your mom said you were the last of the Crimson."

Only the Crimson have a red glow in a fight.

"Okay. The Raziiair is on the ground. Let's see what they want. You drive," Beth says firmly.

Thanks, Beth.

"By the way... You rock, baby."

Both laugh as Taelene circles the unknown Raziiair, then flairs to land, facing the other War-bird.

The rider stands in the saddle with her wand at the ready position, so Beth stands in the saddle.

"WHO ARE YOU?"

"I AM PRINCESS RETELLA OF THE AFRICAN TRIBE. I DEMAND YOU IDENTIFY YOURSELF."

"Wonderful. Just what I need today."

Taelene snickers. *I like her. She reminds me of the... 'old' me.*

"Exactly," Beth mumbles.

"I AM LYSABETH OF IRELAND."

"YOU LIE. THE LYSA OF IRELAND IS DEAD."

She casts an energy ball with her wand, and Beth catches the curse and crushes it between her hands.

"I AM VERY MUCH ALIVE, AND MY MOTHER, LYSASEARIN, LIVES. DON'T DO THAT AGAIN, OR YOU'LL NEED A NEW WAND."

Princess Retella, seeing Beth is a Spirit Witch, slips her wand into her sleeve before bowing, so Beth floats to the ground.

The princess climbs down from her Pearl Canary Raziiair and kneels on one knee.

"I apologize for attacking you, LysaBeth, but I was told there were no Lysa alive."

"My mother and I were both in hiding, but now we're going to make things right. Please, stand up. How is it you have a Royal Crimson? I didn't know there were any other Royal Crimson alive."

"He was a gift when I was a little girl. I have kept him hidden from everyone because I thought he was the last. I see your Crimson is female. Why is a Spirit Witch using a Raziiair?"

"We're traveling to unknown territory."

Why is she looking around? Her body language? I think she's up to something.

"You didn't answer my question, Princess. Why are you in this area?"

"The Raziiair that you fought attacked a village of witches with no cause, so I meant to follow them and find out why."

"By yourself?"

"My Raziiair is of the Royal Crimson bloodline, and he will defeat them with me. How is it you have a Royal Crimson bloodline?"

What are you up to, Princess Retella? Time for a test.

"My Raziiair's mother is Tonique, my mother's best friend."

She didn't respond to Tonique's name. What is she...

Beth twists sideways, as the ice spear that Princess Retella lunges at her misses the soft flesh of her throat and cuts through the edge of her hoodie. Beth casts a shield over Taelene as she spins away from Princess Retella before casting a cluster of throwing knives. Princess Retella swats them away with a glowing hand and Beth shouts, "Sleazy trick using a wand when you're a Spirit Witch."

"As long as I kill you, who cares?"

Alabama accent. Little bitch.

The impostor spins, casting a sword at Beth's throat.

Beth flips backward, letting the sword skim past her cheek, then landing solidly on both feet, she casts a chain-mail net. Princess Retella throws both arms toward the net, burning it in the air, and Beth shoots an ice spear under the burning metal and hits her target.

The witch falls to the ground, and moments later, her identity spell fades, revealing the dead, gray eyes of a Blood Witch. Her Raziiair falls to its side, unconscious.

Beth waves her glowing hand at Taelene, dropping the shield.

"How did you know?" Taelene says, finishing her transformation.

"When I flew with your mother, she told me many things, and one was how well she's known in the African tribes. When I said her name, the impostor didn't react, and I knew she was lying." Beth pauses. "What I don't understand is why did a Natural Witch let Sorcha turn her?"

Taelene shakes her head. "No idea. Is she dead?"

"Unfortunately, yes. She was fighting to kill me. I think she wanted you."

"Beth, what's happening? Is it a coincidence that we meet the other Raziiair?"

"No. It was as if they were waiting for us. Someone knew we were coming. But how?"

"Maybe that one knows," Taelene says, pointing at the changed Raziiair.

Beth waves her hand. "*Vakne.*" (Wake)

The slim, muscular black man rolls to his side. "Where am I?"

Taelene recognizes his African accent from her home territory. "Southeast coast of England."

"Why have you brought me here?" The man looks up. "Pardon me. You are not the evil witch. May I ask who you are?"

"I'm Taelene, daughter of Tonique."

The young black man scrambles to his knees and puts his forehead to the ground.

"Forgive me for not recognizing you."

303

"You're forgiven because I didn't expect you to recognize me. Please stand."

The young man scrambles to his feet and loses balance, so Taelene moves to his side to steady him and feels a tingle through her body as she grabs his arm.

"Easy. Are you okay?"

"You are very kind, Taelene. Do you know why I am here? How did you break the spell?"

"That happens when you kill the witch that cast the spell," Beth says, pointing at the body.

The young man looks over at the body. "The witch who cursed me was black."

"She used an identity spell. Why did she want you?" Taelene says.

"I hear them talk about Tonique. They say she has returned, and the Raziiair will follow. If you are her daughter, then the talk is true."

He looks at Beth. "May I ask who you are?"

"A friend hitching a ride. You can call me Beth."

The young man smiles and makes a slight bow with his head.

"What's your name?" Taelene says.

"I am called Nadeh."

"You're Crimson. I thought I was the last of our line."

"My father, Hajiri, was the Royal Crimson for the king, and my mother was a Pearl Canary. When I was old enough to fly with a rider, they made me a gift to a Chinese prince, but the prince did not want a Pearl Canary and would not learn to fly with me. The king felt disgraced and was angry when I returned, so he gave my father to his youngest prince, and they both died in their first battle together because the prince would not train. The king executed my mother, and they sold me to the highest bidder who lived in Sierra Leone."

"So that was a big show when you attacked the others?" Beth says.

"Yes, they were her companions. I saw you when I took off from South Ireland, and we tracked you. We were originally going to America."

"Where did you come from?" Taelene says.

"Lake Malawi."

"How many days were you flying?"

"Over three."

"Where's Lake Malawi?" Beth asks.

"Southeast Africa," Nadeh says.

"Were all the Raziiair we saw today from there?" Beth says.

"Yes, over thirty have been born around Malawi."

"We only saw ten," Taelene says.

"The rest flew to America."

"How do you feel, Nadeh?"

"I am weak and hungry. They captured me in Sierra Leone over four days ago, and we fly to Lake Malawi and then here."

"Where's your wand?" Taelene says.

Nadeh points to the fallen witch. "She took it."

"Sit over here, and I will give you food," Taelene says.

Nadeh sits on the log, and with a twist of her hand, he has food and drink.

Taelene walks over to Beth. "What do you think?"

"I'm going to need a map of Africa to figure out if he's telling the truth," Beth replies.

"He is. I know where he's from, and the timing is right with a few stops."

"Then he's captured with a control spell and headed for the United States."

Taelene looks at Beth, saying, "Sounds a little historical, don't you think?"

"Taelene, I've met Sorcha and Rebekah, and I don't put it past them, but the part that's bugging me is the number of Raziiair. How is it your mother didn't know of the rookery and the thirty Raziiair? She told me the rookery under the castle was the last one."

"Good question. Time to contact Mamma."

Taelene circles her hand in front of her. "*Mayi, akumva ine.*"

"Taelene, what language do you use?"

"Chewa, mostly, but sometimes I slip our native Raziiair language in there. Mama wants to keep the old language alive, and it's fun to use. Reading is another story," Taelene snickers.

"What was your spell?"

"Mother, hear me."

"Same as me, but I use Norwegian because of Freya. Guess I'll have to learn Irish now that I know where I'm from.

"You've never known you were born in Ireland?"

"Nope. Or that my actual mother and father weren't the mother and father I knew."

"Holy crap, Beth."

"Ya, well. I hope I get to use that spell someday," Beth says.

Taelene winks. "I know you will."

The circling mist changes to a solid mass as Tonique's face comes into focus.

"Taelene, are you and LysaBeth alright?"

"Yes, Mamma. Mamma, how is it you didn't know about the rookery around Lake Malawi?"

"Taelene, I know of it, but Blood Witches destroyed it over twenty-five years ago. Why do you ask?"

"We have a Pearl Canary Crimson here that says Blood Witches captured thirty Raziiair at Lake Malawi to be taken to the United States."

"Taelene. There must be a mistake. Who is the Crimson?"

"He says his name is Nadeh."

Tonique catches her breath.

"Taelene, who is his father?"

"I think he said Hajiri."

"Mamma, are you okay? What's wrong?"

"Hajiri was your father's best friend. They both died in the same battle because of a vengeful king. The king had sold Nadeh into shameful slavery as a trophy for a warlord in Sierra Leone two days before the battle, and the king heard rumors that your father was going to help Hajiri retrieve his son. Another rumor was, the king suspected, his youngest son of not being his, but from the Queen's lover and put him on Hajiri's back for the battle. The king told the oldest prince, who always flew on your father, to kill the bastard son once he tethered to Hajiri. When your father realized what was happening, he tried to make it so the older prince couldn't kill his younger brother, and both your father and the older prince died because he lost sight of the battle. Hajiri saw your father die, and he too lost sight of the battle and died only moments after with the youngest prince."

Taelene feels a tear roll down her cheek.

"Mamma, why haven't you ever told me this?"

"It was too difficult, Taelene."

"I'm so sorry, Taelene," Beth says.

"I'm not," Taelene snaps back. "My father died with honor, trying to save his best friend instead of dying for killing, and I couldn't be prouder." Taelene looks back at her mother.

"Thank you for telling me, Mamma. I am very proud to say that I am the daughter of Tefari and Tonique."

Beth squeezes Taelene's hand and turns to Tonique.

"What of the rookery?"

"I was never told that the crystal was producing eggs again."

"Holy Hannah. Does everything happen because of a crystal? What crystal?"

"Do you remember the egg on top of the crystal column in the rookery under your castle, LysaBeth?"

"Yes."

"Now that you have brought life back to the castle, that Crystal Egg will fill the honeycomb wall with new Raziiair eggs. In two years, the egg develops, and you will have a new Raziiair child to train."

"Yeah, motherhood. Obviously, you were talking to Taelene."

Taelene bumps Beth with her elbow. "Hey. I want to make my own."

"What do we do here, Tonique?"

"I will find out about the rookery. Taelene, you must not lose sight of Nadeh until I find out how this happened."

Taelene looks over at Nadeh. "Yeah, I'm good with that."

"Bird-man?" Beth snickers.

"Mama. We'll take him to France with us."

Beth giggles. "Uh-huh?"

Without another word, Tonique disappears.

Taelene contemplates Nadeh's mannerism and clean, muscular outline as she saunters toward him.

Are you my bird-man? I felt that tingle, Nadeh. Did you?

Beth walks over to the fallen witch to recover Nadeh's wand, and a spy spider runs out from under the witch toward Nadeh.

"*Fryse*," Beth says as she points her glowing palm at the spider.

The spider explodes into smoke.

"What was that?" Taelene says.

"A spider. It was running toward Nadeh."

"We should have captured it."

"I tried to freeze it, but it exploded instead of stopping."

Taelene walks to Nadeh.

"Nadeh."

"Yes, Taelene."

"Come with us to France."

"Why? I would like to go home."

"Nadeh, you and I are the last of the Royal Crimson. Your father and mine were best friends, and they died in the same battle, so we need to stay together. I talked to my mother, and she's going to see what's left of your rookery.

Please, Nadeh. If you go back, they could capture you again or even kill you."

"Thank you for your concern and my freedom, Taelene, but I will go home."

Beth marches up from behind Taelene.

"Nadeh, I am LysaBeth, daughter of LysaSearin, and daughter of the Lysa Mother, and you are going with us."

Nadeh drops his food and kneels with his head bowed. "As the Lysa commands."

Beth turns to walk away and winks at Taelene, but Taelene shows no emotion.

Crap, I shouldn't have interfered.

Taelene looks back at Nadeh and catches her breath as he picks his food from the ground and puts it back on his plate.

"What are you doing?"

"Sorry."

"What are you doing with that food?"

"I dropped my food, and I am still hungry."

"You can't eat that."

"Why? Most days I eat like this or leftover scraps my owner has thrown away. I am but a dog to him."

"And you want to go back to that?"

"No, he is dead. The witch killed him. I want to go to Lake Malawi."

Taelene waves her hand around Nadeh's plate, giving him fresh fruit and cooked fish on a clean plate.

"No way you will ever eat dirty food while I'm around. How dare someone treat you like that?"

"Royalty has never treated me so well."

Taelene points to Beth. "She's the princess. I'm the woman who cares how you're treated."

Nadeh sets his new plate on the fallen tree, walks to Taelene, and takes her hand.

"I will go to France with you, or anywhere else you ask."

Taelene places her hand along Nadeh's face.

"Thank you. Now finish eating so we can go."

Nadeh nods and lets her hand go.

Taelene turns back to Beth, who places her hands in the surrender position.

"My bad."

"Yep. My bird-man."

They both smile.

FALLEN PRINCESS

Wednesday, September 3rd — 1300
Eastern Time — Boston

Beth. The French coastline.

"Where's the Château?"

Southeast corner of the Alps along the waterfront.

"We have to fly across France. Taelene, can you and Nadeh touch wings without us crashing?"

No problem. What are you thinking?

"If you get Nadeh close enough that your wings are touching, I can make both of you invisible."

Why not cast the spell?

"I don't know if it will affect your flight like a shield does. I don't think you want your bird-man crashing into the ocean."

Okay, good point.

Taelene lets out two quick squawks, and Nadeh slips to Taelene's right side until they're gliding, wingtips touching. Beth focuses her power of invisibility through her glowing hands and into the gripping bones on Taelene's shoulders. It flows over Taelene in waves, and

Beth watches as it moves across Taelene's wing toward Nadeh, then along his wing until he's cloaked.

"Done. Tell Nadeh to stay close, but safe."

You got it.

Taelene squawks again. Nadeh slips sideways to break contact and positions himself above and to Taelene's right.

They fly in silence until Taelene thinks. *Beth, there's the Château.*

"There are also lots of houses, hotels, and people."

Holiday hot spot, maybe?

"Nothing's easy, is it? Taelene, fly over the Château so I can get the layout and then land in the wooded area above the village."

Beth. What's going on?

"I'm gun shy at the moment. With everything that's happened and the extra baggage of Nadeh, I don't want to expose you or him."

Okay.

Taelene banks right and drops lower so Beth can see the Château and the boat docks attached to the back of the building before sweeping up the side of the sharp hill to the woods.

Beth, look. There's an opening in the trees just beyond that park.

"Perfect. Land there."

Taelene flares, landing on the grass, and Nadeh follows her lead.

Beth releases the invisibility cloak, and, climbing off, she waits for Taelene and Nadeh to transform.

Beth turns to Taelene. "You're sure that's the Château?"

313

"Yes. The white building with flags and the boat docks behind it."

"You two hide in the trees while I meet with the Guardians. We'll take it from there."

"Got it."

Beth swings her arm in a circle and says, "See ya," as she jumps through the portal.

Taelene takes Nadeh's hand. "I saw a path over here. Let's go this way."

Beth walks out of her portal in a wooden boathouse behind the Château La Grouse restaurant and hotel. She looks out a window, recognizes a young witch from Boston, so she steps out of the boathouse door, waits until the young witch sees her, and steps back into the boathouse. Moments later, a blue mist forms above the deck of a boat in the boathouse, and three young people step out of the swirling mist with their hands in front of their bodies like they're surrendering.

"That's an interesting way of exiting a portal," Beth says.

"Princess. I am Roxanne, and this is Jeremy and Richard."

"Why are there three of you?"

"This town is dangerous so, Lady Lauranna sent three of us because we look your age, and we can walk around looking like couples."

Beth thinks for a moment. "Okay, relax. Where is the wizard, 'Naise'?"

The threesome let their hands down, and Roxanne says, "He's in prison."

"What's he doing in prison?"

"He's a prisoner, and we have to get him out."

"WHAT?"

"I'm sorry, Princess. I thought you knew."

Beth makes a small mirror portal in front of her face. "*Vis Lady Lauranna*." (Show Lady Lauranna).

After half a minute, with no change in the portal, Beth puts her hand up by her shoulder and closes her fist to collapse the mirror portal.

"No one's answering the phone. Why is this man a prisoner?"

"The short version? His children overthrew him. Encased him in glass and took control of the prison."

"Where is he?"

"The lowest and most protected level of the prison, Princess."

"Any Natural Witches?"

"No, but many experienced guards who are Glazier."

Freya's warning, 'Don't fight the Glazier alone,' flashes.

"Princess, we were told you could make us invisible, and we could walk into the prison and get him. Is that true?"

"We can't just walk into the prison and get him. Roxanne."

Beth's words echo in her own head, and she realizes that only a few days ago, before her scars and escaping a near-death experience, she could have done it without hesitation. Now, she wants information and a plan. She smirks.

"We need a guard who knows the prison, so I can make him talk," she says.

Beth stares at Roxanne. "Alright. You're a blond-haired, blue-eyed beauty. Can you flirt?"

"No troubles in that department."

"Okay, now we need to find where the guards hang out."

Roxanne points her finger over her shoulder toward the Château.

"There are several of them in the hotel."

"Anybody up for a glass of wine?"

The threesome smiles at her and turns for the door with Beth hot on their heels.

Beth waits a couple of minutes after the threesome enters the restaurant, then walks in and joins them as the latecomer.

Wow! Is this nineteen-fifties Royal French decor? Velvet, wood and brass. Interesting.

"Any potential targets?" Beth says, sitting down and still soaking in the decor.

"I have a fish on the line," Roxanne says in a bragging tone.

Jeremy catches Beth's eye and, with a quick lift of his brow, shakes his head before looking at Richard.

"Are you saying he's smiling at Richard and *not* me?" Roxanne says.

Richard looks at Jeremy. "No way. He's not even good-looking, and he'll most likely smell like a prison, which means 'not good'. You go."

"Wrong gender for me, and he'll know in a second," Jeremy says, feigning sympathy. "Take one for the team?"

"You take one for the team, and I'll have a bottle of red," Richard snaps.

"Gentlemen. Do we have an agreement?" Beth asks.

"Unwillingly, Princess. Evidently, I'm the only one skilled in French and captivating enough to pull this off. Besides, the unshaven trucker types adore exquisite creatures like me," Richard says airily.

"Maybe you can introduce him to the finer points of life," Beth suggests.

Richard looks at the guard, who smiles at him.

"Princess, that suggests your mission is ten years long. Now, I will go buy a bottle of red wine with your money."

"Oh, please do."

Before Beth pulls her hand from her hoodie pocket, there's a slight glow, and she tosses five-hundred Franc on the table.

Richard palms the money, and as he moves past Jeremy, he lets his wand peek out of his sleeve, draws a circle on the table with the tip, and slips it back into hiding.

"Enjoy the performance."

As soon as Richard reaches the end of the bar to order the bottle of wine, the guard introduces himself and invites Richard to join him.

Forty-five minutes later, Beth looks at Roxanne and Jeremy.

"I've got the information I need to retrieve, Naise. You two watch out for Richard and bail him out if he needs you."

"Princess, you can't do this alone. They gave me orders to go with you," Roxanne says.

"Who?"

"Freya."

Beth thinks about Roxanne's answer and again listens.

"Stay close. I don't want to fight our way out. Understood?"

"Yes, Princess."

"Okay, let's go."

Beth and Roxanne, both invisible, stand on an outcrop of the mountain behind the prison. Beth examines the north-facing sheer wall of the prison mountain.

"It's overhanging from top to bottom and looks like the polished surface of a counter-top," Beth says. "I can see why the prison is so easy to defend."

Standing behind Beth's shoulder, Roxanne doesn't see Beth's eyes change to night vision.

Strange, no outside protection magic. Cocky much?

Beth changes her eyes back before Roxanne points to a cliff ledge near the bottom.

"Is that the lower entrance to the prison?"

"Good eye," Beth says. "That looks like the ledge the guard was describing. Ready?"

Roxanne nods, and with the spin of a skyward pointed finger, Beth drops a portal down on them.

Beth and Roxanne exit the portal onto a ledge eighteen inches wide and peer into the dark tunnel.

"Gives new meaning to 'Light at the end of the Tunnel,' doesn't it?" Roxanne says.

Beth places her hand against the tunnel wall. *"Aslore fare."* (Reveal danger).

Nothing happens, so Beth signals Roxanne, placing her finger across her lips, and enters the tunnel. The guard told Richard about a gate, and when they reach it,

Beth changes her eyes to night vision and sees no signs of magic. Beth clears her eyes and looks back at Roxanne, whispering, "Something's not right."

"What do you mean?"

"Magic leaves waves of pulsing light when it's used for sensing magical people, but there's no sign of protection magic outside, and I can't sense any magic on the bars of the gate."

"Maybe it's as the guard said, and someone forgot to put the protection back up after going through," Roxanne says. "Think about it. Why would you break into this place? It's not as if you're going to grab someone and run out of here."

"I don't like it. This is a prison. How do you forget to lock the gate?"

"Princess, do you think we should go?"

Beth contemplates the question and then reaches out and grabs one of the gate bars. Nothing happens.

"Wow, you are one gutsy princess. That could have gone very wrong."

Beth opens the gate and steps out of the tunnel into a passageway carved through the stone mountain. Floating balls of light shine on rippling gates of magic that hold prisoners in the cells lining the damp musky corridor. Beth hears someone walking toward them, so she pushes the iron gate back to Roxanne, crossing her finger over her lips, and dashes across the passage into an open cell.

Beth waits as the person walks by, and the footsteps fade to nothing, to step out of the cell.

"Where did she go?"

Beth walks back to the iron gate to look closer.

"Aah!"

Beth slams face first into the steel bars from the Glazier curse, hitting the small of her back. A searing burn rips through her nervous system, and the paralyzing magic stings as it rushes through her body to stop all muscle movement. She feels the icy grip of the glass wrapping itself around her legs and chest and her scream sounds like a moan.

She hears an evil laugh and sees Roxanne in her peripheral vision.

"Well, well, Princess. I should have said gullible instead of gutsy. It was easy to pump your royal ego. I guess you're going to miss the grand finale in Boston, but I will give your best to Queen Sorcha. I understand she has big plans for you after she kills the Royals." She laughs out loud. "Ta, Ta."

Beth's vision blurs as the glass covers her eyes, and then everything goes quiet.

A guard runs out from a cell. "*Ah Bon*, Monsieur Robert. Where do you want her?"

"Put her in the lowest dungeon with my father and siblings. I want guards at this gate twenty-four seven. They might attack to free the princess. Any mistakes, and I will execute every one of you."

Beth knows she's moving because shadows are changing on the glass, but she feels nothing in her body.

Voices are muffled sounds that clear into a male voice with a French accent.

"Papa, I have brought you the American sent to set you free, so you could strike back at Francois and me. Soon after her victory, Queen Sorcha will come for both of you. Then you can thank the American. But, until the queen arrives, you will have time to think how close you came to being free again."

"Now, Princess. I'm sure you can hear me, so allow me to introduce myself. I am Robert, the youngest of the family men, and I control this prison."

Beth can see the faded outline of Robert walking across her vision as he circles her glassed figure.

"I have learned many things since my father taught me his glass curse, and I find giving someone a small window in front of their eyes to be very useful for many reasons. I can torture the prisoner's mind by letting them see the things they crave the most, which, of course, is most effective on the deviant criminal, or I can give them happiness by letting them see a loved one."

Beth can see the outline of a person's head in front of her, and she hears a tap that rings as if someone tapped a spoon against a crystal glass. The outline of Robert's face becomes clear.

"*Bonjour*, Princess. Welcome to hell," he breathes.

His laugh is cruel as he steps away from her, exposing five other figures. Then Robert appears straight across the room beside a glassed figure.

"I'm sure you're surprised that the glass curse works on a Spirit Witch. Oh yes, I know who you are, but let me assure you, my father is a genius with magic, but not so much with his children."

Robert pauses, surveying his prisoners like they are trophies.

"Princess, let me introduce you to your temporary cellmates."

He casually throws an arm over the shoulder of the glass figure.

"Most important, of course, is Papa. Without him, there could be nothing. Also, there would be no joy, no love, no mother with him. Ahh, family drama."

Walking to Beth's left, Robert places his hand on the shoulder of another figure and stands very erect.

"This is the firstborn. My brother, the great Esian. The heir to the throne. The right hand of God, and commander of the Lagrandeur army of prison lords."

Beth recognizes hate, but Robert is pouring buckets of it out on his brother, Esian.

Robert pauses, slaps the figure's face, and continues walking.

"Ahh, more family drama."

Robert walks behind another figure on the left and places his hands on the shoulders.

"You might have noticed, by her figure, this is my beautiful sister Maria. I miss her the most because she is so beautiful. She is also powerful and dangerous, and since I have confessed to her, I used to enjoy peeking into her bedroom to watch her change and bath. I fear I can never release her because she might be upset with me, even though I wonder if she knew I was watching. Ahh, more family drama."

He kisses her cheek before walking across the room to face the two glass figures on the right.

"These are my other brothers. Evan," he says, holding his right hand out, "and Noah," holding his left hand out. "The quiet ones. And two of the most lethal fighters in our world. They are guilty of nothing. They are the victims of the family drama. Their only crime is 'trying' to make the other siblings get along, but they love Papa. It's strange how parents do things for select children and not others. Yes, no? Oh well, more family drama."

Robert turns back to Beth and walks so his face is only inches from hers.

"So, Princess, you can see what power and greed can do to a family. I'm sure we could have an exciting conversation about this, but I do not think you will be alive after Queen Sorcha takes you."

Robert laughs again. "Enjoy your time with my family."

Robert leaves the cell, barking orders in French.

"And as for you, Princess," says a woman's voice, "Queen Sorcha has something special in mind, but I don't want to ruin the surprise."

That's not Roxanne.

"Maybe we can feed you to the sharks, too. I don't think your guardian friend, Roxanne, enjoyed the experience. She screamed every time the shark took a piece of her. It was so dramatic. Ta, Ta."

She laughs, and Beth hears her walk away.

She must have used an identity spell. But how, or where, did she capture Roxanne?

Beth feels panic creeping through her.

I should have called Lauranna as soon as that envelope hit the floor, because they somehow knew about Roxanne meeting me in France. What about Jeremy and Richard? Are they part of this, or are they dead too? Was the restaurant a ruse? Is Taelene safe, or is Nadeh a setup?

323

BAD NEWS

Wednesday, September 3rd — 1400
Eastern Time — Boston

With wands in hand, the Guardians charge toward the swirling white smoke portal forming in the middle of the building.

"Invaders! Invaders!"

Beside it, another portal of fiery smoke forms, and the Guardians surround both.

Michael steps out of the white smoke with several other Irish on his heels.

"Drop your wands," says the Scottish Guardian captain.

Michael turns toward him and takes a few steps forward.

"Piss off, little girl, before I get your lovely blue dress dirty."

The captain walks closer to Michael. "Aye, brave talk from someone wearing a pumpkin skirt. Is that your boyfriend there, little flower?"

"You're still the ugliest Scot I've ever seen."

ROYAL SOULS

"You've no had a looking glass in your hut, have you, ya, Irish mutt? Or a bath by the smell of you."

Gale Anderson and Michael Birrell slam into each other, laughing and throwing their arms around in bear hug fashion.

"How are you keeping, Cousin?" Michael says.

The two burly men pull apart.

"I long for the shores of Scotland and the waves under my boat, cousin. And you?" Gale says.

"Aye, I miss the shores of Ireland as well. I hope to survive this, so I can go home where I belong."

"Aye, it's been a long road, and I hope you bring good news."

Michael stares at Gale, who says, "That look gives me no comfort, cousin."

"Nay, cousin, it doesn't look good."

Gale looks past Michael to see the glass statue between the four Pyre Wolf. "What's that?"

Michael looks over his shoulder and then back at Gale. "The carrier of the prince. He jumped in front of a glassing curse to save that one," Michael says, pointing at Aaghnya as she and Colleen step out of their portal.

"Pretty as she is. Why?" Gale says.

"Love."

"Fool. Didn't he understand his importance?"

"We told him, and all he could think of is the woman."

"Now, what do we do?"

"Colleen is working on a plan to kidnap a Glazier, and I've volunteered for the mission."

Gale steps next to Michael.

"It's a fool's mission, cousin. You no want to spend eternity caged in glass if you get caught."

"A fool's mission, cousin, and I volunteered you to join me."

Gale doesn't respond to his smiling cousin for a few moments, then they break into a full laugh, and Gale slaps Michael on the shoulder as the pair turn to walk to Angus and the Pyre Wolf.

With over four hundred Irish and Scots gathered in the warehouse, space is at a premium, and the pyre wolves have taken position around the statue in the center of the building. Their burning bodies heat the air and concrete floor, keeping everyone back an extra thirty feet, absorbing more of the precious space. As they lie down, facing the four directions, their bodies turn into smoldering gray forms with glowing red eyes.

A young witch, oblivious to the crowd, stands at the front of the Pyre Wolf gathering, awed by the enormous beasts, and a young Guardian approaches her.

"Are you alright, lass?"

She looks at him. "What are they?"

"Those are the first four pyre wolves. The biggest and the strongest."

The young witch looks back at the Wolves. "How did they get like that?"

"Well, when they announced the prince and princess were to wed, King Aed of Ireland gave King Aodh of Scotland two pairs of breeding Irish wolfhounds for hunting. After the wedding battle, King Aed's body went back to Ireland, and they put King Aodh into a royal pyre built on the shores of the Lake of Peace. The pyre sat near the waterfall that feeds the lake, waiting to burn for nine days and nights. After it's set afire, the lead Irish hound, Pyreus, started howling and snapping his teeth together and everyone at the funeral thought he was going mad. Then, the other three started doing the same, before the four of them ran and jumped into the fire."

"No one ever expected to see them again, but come morning, the guard change found the night guards unconscious, and the pyre, still burning, sat on the highest ledge overlooking the lake. The blue water lake had turned to a lake of red liquid that flowed like honey from the waterfall. The foliage around the lake died from the heat or burned from being touched by the red liquid. Then, standing on a rock ledge by the waterfall and overlooking the lake, are the four wolfhounds, near doubled in size and glowing from being wrapped in fire. Stairs leading up to the pyre have formed in the rock face overnight, but nothing can get to them except the pyre wolves. King Aodh's pyre still burns today, and the hounds guard it as if it's one of their cubs."

The young witch looks at him. "So, there's more?"

"Oh, aye. The Pyre Wolves have had a few litters since the year Nine-Sixty-Three."

She looks back at the wolves. "They have been around for more than a thousand years?"

"Aye, lass. They've been with Angus trying to find their prince, and now they won't leave his side until he's released to join with the princess again."

She looks back at him. "So, the prince is in the glass statue?"

"Aye, lass."

"So, release him and let them reunite before someone kills him."

"It's not that simple, lass. In the glass, they can't kill him because no magic can break the glass except the Glazier."

"What if someone steals him?"

The wizard smiles at her. "They'll never get past the wolves."

"What if they kill the wolves and then take him?"

"Wand magic, can't kill the Pyre Wolf. That's why they're so formidable."

The two stand silent until the young wizard turns to her.

"I'm Gareth."

"Hi, Gareth. I'm Lillian."

"How are they going to get the prince out of the glass?"

Gareth looks around before he leans closer to her.

"They're going to kidnap a Glazier and force him to remove the glass."

Lillian looks at him with a furrowed brow.

"How do you kidnap a Glazier?"

"Don't know. The Captains are working on a plan."

Lillian looks back at the statue.

"So, you get the prince out of the glass and then reunite him with the princess."

"That's not the prince you see in the glass. It's the carrier of the prince's soul. They get him out of the glass, and then Angus uses his Staff of Souls to draw the prince's soul out of the carrier."

"How does the princess get released?"

ROYAL SOULS

"Promise to have lunch with me, and I'll tell you."

Lillian looks at Gareth. "I would have taken lunch with you even without you telling me."

"Grand, but remember, it's a secret."

"I swear. But how do I know you're telling the truth?"

"My father, Captain of the Irish Guard, taught me so I could take his place if anything should happen."

"I will take your word then."

Gareth nods and continues.

"First, they have to get the prince out, and then they have to get the princess out of her Orb."

"The princess is here?"

"Aye, didn't you know? You're guarding the princess."

"My mother never told me why we're here."

"Well, now you know."

"So, when the two of them are free, they can reunite?"

"No. The souls of the prince and princess have to be inside a magic bubble that brings them back to the night of the wedding, and that magic takes many people."

Lillian looks at him, furrowing her brow again. "What do you mean?"

Gareth explains the Circle of Nine Witches to Lillian.

"That's it? Circle of Nine Witches and they reunite?"

"Well, yes. Except Lady Lauranna at the end."

"Lady Lauranna?"

"Aye, lass. Lady Lauranna is the great Raziiair Siren and must cast the white light of the Raziiair, so both souls can float into the bubble of white magic that she creates. As soon as they kiss, they cast the seed out to be born, and the magic of the world will be in balance again." Gareth

329

pauses. "I hope Queen Sorcha dies writhing in pain for all the good people she killed."

Michael calls Gareth to him, so Gareth doesn't see the angry scowl on Lillian's face.

"I'll come back," he says without looking at her.

Lillian gives Gareth an evil sideways look as he walks away.

"Next time you see me, it will be your last breath," she whispers.

Lillian turns and disappears into the crowd.

The Scots and Irish leaders gather near the pyre wolves with Angus and Colleen. When Lauranna, Breena, and Karse break through the crowd, Karse shows his shock at seeing his father in solid form instead of the earlier apparition.

"Father, what has she done to you?"

Karse walks to only a few feet from Angus MacShannachan.

"Steady yourself, young Chief," Angus says.

Karse regains his composer. "How did Sorcha do this to you?"

"She captured me during one of my hunts for her lair, then tried to change me into a Blood Witch, so she could use the Staff of Souls. My loyalty to the prince is so strong that she tried four times to change me with her blood, and failing, she threw me in her dungeon and left me for dead. Pyreus found me and freed me at a high cost to himself because Sorcha had her great cats guarding the dungeon. I dragged myself out of her castle, and when I broke through her shield, I fell over the cliff at Kilt Rock. A wand builder hid in a cave near where I went in the water, so he called a water horse to drag me to the surface. The wand builder recognized me, then moved me to a hidden cave inside the Faerie Pools and tried using the waters to cleanse away the blood of that evil witch. The water has lost most of its power, so my body is the best it can be because of how much poison she put into it."

"She will pay for this, Father."

Angus looks at Lauranna. "The gray skin and rotting flesh look are not as painful as never being able to hold your mother in my arms again, fearing I poison her."

Karse looks back at his mother to see the tears welling in her eyes, and he thinks about how he feels when he has LysaBeth in his arms.

"I understand, Father."

"So, your left arm shows you have taken a powerful witch for a wife."

Karse smiles. "The princess, LysaBeth, Father."

"Is she the one from earlier?"

"Aye, Father."

"I will speak with her later."

"Don't be sad, Father. All is well."

Angus gives a small smile and a quick nod of his head. "Still, my fiery head got the best of me."

"Yes, Father. I paid the price for that, but I welcome you to do it again."

Angus furrows his brow. "What was the price?"

"A long kiss."

Angus smiles and looks at Lauranna, and everyone can see they remember the days before Sorcha destroyed their ability to be together.

"Good. A Chief needs the love of a good wife to help him keep his head."

Angus turns to the crowd of Guardians.

"From this day on," Angus shouts, "Karse MacShannachan is now the clan Chief, and they shall know his wife as Lady LysaBeth."

The room bursts into applause and cheering as Karse drops to one knee and bows his head.

"Stand, Karse MacShannachan, as the clan Chief."

Karse stands, and on his left pectoralis muscle, a glow ring forms as the clan emblem burns itself into his skin, and he makes no sound.

"Now I have passed our survival to you, my son."

"I will honor our ways, Father."

Angus nods his head, signifying the end of his era.

"We have matters to attend to," Karse says.

The leaders of both groups of Guardians gather, and Aaghnya throws her hands over her head, making a giant arc, casting a shield, so no one hears the discussion.

Colleen opens with, "We have traitors in the ranks."

"How do you know this?" Angus says.

"Before Aaghnya and I stepped into the portal to leave the warehouse, I noticed the shadow of someone hiding behind a pillar, so she closed the portal, and we hid behind barrels. The young witch showed herself, not knowing we were still there, and she talked to Sorcha, saying we didn't know of the other spy. Someone here is a traitor."

Lauranna says, "We too had a spy, but LysaBeth killed her before she could kill us and take her Crystal back to Sorcha."

"What do you mean back to her?" Karse says.

"We thought someone had stolen the Crystal, but the Witch guarding it had switched to Sorcha's side and delivered it to her at the expense of six good Guardians."

Karse looks at Angus, who frowns.

"Father, Lochran MacIlraight tested his mortality by stealing the Crystal and Prince Stone back from Sorcha."

Angus laughs.

Karse looks around the group. "Nothing we have discussed here leaves your lips. Tell no one of the prince or princess or anyone else involved."

Michael sees Gareth looking back at where Lillian was. "Gareth, what's wrong?"

Gareth looks around the group before lowering his head and shaking it. "The young lass I was talking to when you called me. I told her how the prince and princess get reunited because she told me she didn't know why her mother brought her here."

"Irish or Scots?" Karse says.

"Scottish."

"What's her name?" Lauranna says.

"Lillian."

Lauranna furrows her brow, and after a few moments, she looks at Breena.

"I don't know of anyone with that name in our Guardians."

Breena shakes her head and shrugs her shoulders, agreeing with her mother. The two of them look at Karse.

Karse looks at Gareth. "Take someone with you and find the lass. Be cautious."

Karse's head snaps to his mother. "You and Breena return to the healing room and shield it. Start making preparation. LysaBeth will succeed."

Karse turns to Gale. "I want guards around the healing room at all times."

"Aye, Chief," Gale says.

"Colleen, do you have someone who can find a cloaking or identity spell?"

"No one that powerful in our group."

Karse stands silent for a few heartbeats. "I will take counsel from my father and Colleen."

Colleen nods slightly as Aaghnya drops the shield surrounding the group, and Angus leans closer to Karse, whispering to him.

Karse looks at Aaghnya. "Aaghnya, would you join us?"

Aaghnya nods as she turns back toward Karse, and again, throwing her arms in a large arc, she reforms a smaller shield.

Gale, Michael, and Gareth escort Lauranna and Breena back to the healing room, where a mix of Scots and Irish guard position themselves to protect the two ladies.

Gareth and Michael start their search for Lillian, and it's not long before Gareth calls.

"Michael, over here."

Michael steps up to Gareth's shoulder, and both men are looking at the corpse of the beautiful young witch Gareth knew as Lillian.

"Get Breena and be alert," Michael says.

Gareth returns with Breena, and she wails and falls to her knees as soon as she sees the corpse.

"Quick, get her back to the healing room," Michael says.

Karse runs out of a portal and pushes his way through the crowd of Guardians to get to Breena's side.

Kneeling, he pulls her into his arms, putting his lips to her ear and whispering, "Calm yourself, Sister. Don't show who you are."

Breena pushes her face into Karse's neck as he scoops her up and spins to rush her back to the healing room.

Lauranna hears Breena's cry, and a few moments after, she walks toward the door but Karse bursts through the shield with Breena in his arm.

Karse can see the fearful look on Lauranna's face. "What happened?"

"The fools. They showed Breena the corpse of a young witch."

He sets her on a cot gently.

Hearing Karse, Breena's sobbing escalates, so Lauranna sweeps her hand along the side of her head, and Breena collapses into sleep. Lauranna bends, putting her lips to Breena's ear.

"Weep in silence, Breena."

Lauranna looks at Karse.

"That will let her come to terms with what she saw without triggering her power."

"She is to have no contact with anyone but us, Mother."

Lauranna nods. "Who is the dead witch?"

"I don't know her."

"I'll send Gabrielle."

Casting a small portal in front of her, Lauranna instructs Gabrielle, her most trusted friend, to collect the witch's body.

Karse stands after a few moments of looking at his sister, and a small message portal forms in front of Lauranna.

"It's Sheena," Gabrielle says.

Lauranna turns to Breena. "Love lost to war is never good."

"Was it a close friend?" Karse says.

"No, Karse," Lauranna says, standing, and she pauses. "Breena and Sheena loved each other."

Karse furrows his brow and stares into his mother's sad eyes until her words make sense.

"Oh. Aye. Does Father know?"

Lauranna scoffs. "No. That old war dog would think he could change things by marrying her to the son of a Clan Chief."

Karse snickers. "Best kept to ourselves until after we reunite the prince and princess."

"Agreed. It will not need to be said then."

Karse kneels and takes her hand. "Hear me, Breena. We are sorry about Sheena, but know we are your family, and we love you."

Karse kisses Breena's forehead, then stands.

"How are you doing with preparations?"

"A few more hours, and the island will be ready."

"Island?"

"We have the princess hidden on Rainsford Island. I'm going there when it's dark to draw the circles and place the markers."

"How many people know about the island?"

"Freya, Egret, Breena, myself, and now you."

"The fewer, the better."

"Karse, do you think LysaBeth will succeed?"

"I have to believe in her."

Lochran walks in from the back room where he and Abigail had been resting.

"Karse, has there been any news from the LysaBeth?" Lochran says.

"Nay."

Abigail lets out a low growl as she rounds the corner from the back room.

"You're not well enough to go after her, so get it out of your head," Lochran says.

Abigail walks by Lochran, flicking her thick black tail, and it slaps hard against his back.

"Eh. What was that?"

Karse and Lauranna laugh.

"I too worry, Abigail," Karse says.

TRUE LYSA

Thursday, September 4th — 1900 Eastern Time — Boston

Backstabbing little tart. Whoever she is, she's going to pay for killing Roxanne and setting me up.

Beth sees herself twisting, pulling, jerking, and trying to bounce the glass off the stone floor to break it, but changes nothing, and she realizes the power of the Glassing curse.

None of my magic is working. How's that possible for a Spirit Witch? What's happening? I'm… I'm losing focus, and my vision is blurring.

Beth tries to close her eyes, but the bright lights around her don't fade.

Karse, I'm so sorry I left you.

Mom, I should have kept your crystal, because I need your strength now.

Freya, can you hear me?

Egret, can you hear me?

I can't believe we'll lose this war because of me? Some leader I turned out to be!

It's a sick person who invents a curse to freeze the body and leave the eyes and mind functioning?

Beth pauses.

I don't want to die here. Please, Karse. Save me.

Beth loses time as mental blackness takes over until her mind wanders to a day in the training arena, before Lochran entered her life. Exhausted, she enters a near delusional state.

I'm back in the training arena. I remember beating these six witches at Witch Ball by hitting all of them in under three minutes.

The memory changes and a trainer witch casts a curse that Beth can't block. It strikes her head and pain floods her brain. She screams in silence.

A flash of light and the memory fades anew. She's racing through high pylons on her witch board, and she remembers the day when she was eighteen and trying to break her own speed record for the one-hundred-mile pylon obstacle track race. The pylon she's leaning into, as she carves a tight one-hundred and eighty-degree turn, sprouts sharp edge spikes. Beth screams in silence again as her flesh burns from the cuts and her vision ripples like water.

It's her fourteenth birthday, and she's practicing jumping through portals to her witch board and dodging water balloons cast by her trainers. She's laughing until one balloon strikes her in the face, exploding with liquid. The liquid burns, and she screams, but no one hears her because the training witches keep laughing and casting more balloons.

Vertigo strikes, her vision blurs, and she feels as if she's falling, then her mind's eye clears.

This kitchen, it's my home in Boston before the fire. There's my mom and dad.

"Mom, Dad. Mom, can you hear me?... Dad, I'm here!" she shouts in silence.

Then her mom shouts, 'LysaBeth, dinner,' and six-year-old Beth runs into the room and sits at the table.

This is my birthday dinner. This is my sixth birthday.

Her mom and dad join her as she reaches for the bowl of sweet potatoes. The bowl jerks and slides toward her, moving faster as it gets closer until it hits her in the chest and falls to her lap. Her mom and dad laugh, then the sweet potatoes burst into flames, but her parents, laughing harder, do nothing to help her, and she screams, unheard.

Everything is black. Did I die? Was it Sorcha? How long have I been here? Is the war finished? Did we lose? I've heard nothing.

What's that? A small white dot... It's getting closer? It's getting bigger or moving closer to me?

The swirling circle stops, and Beth sees herself floating in front of it.

LysaBeth, the Universe is your power. Take from it.

The voice of the Lysa Mother echoes in her mind. Beth watches her floating figure reaching toward the pool of white, now taller than her, and she remembers a lesson about drawing life energy into her body. She sees her figure dipping her fingers into the white pool and Beth feels the warmth on her fingertips. She watches the white energy flow over her figure's hand, absorbing through her skin, and Beth feels it building in the pit of her stomach. Moments later, she feels the flow slowing, as though she has drawn as much as her body can take. Her figure and

ROYAL SOULS

the white circle fade as she focuses on the warmth of the energy rushing through her body. She falls to the ground, landing hard on her side, and draws a long deep breath. She lays quiet.

I'm out? Yes, I'm out. I did it. My body's tingling. It must be the blood circulation. I can hear distant laughter and smell the musky dank of damp stone.

Beth opens her eyes.

Alright. It took a while, but I can see the five figures. I have to get up. Okay, hands and knees. The stone is cold. Ouch, bloody rock is sharp. Take it slow, Beth. So far, so good. Time to stand. My legs… they're good. Easy. Still tipsy. Deep breaths. Stretch it out. Wow, my legs are doing great. That's it, walk it off. Come on, girl, get it together. How's the night vision? Good. How's the invisibility power? Snap. That was fast. Okay, we got this. What was that sound? Ugh, the rock scale from the ground is stuck to my hands and clothes.

Beth brushes her hands over her pants and hoodie, chasing the rock scale from her clothes and palms, then closes her eyes, calming herself, and the words flow easily.

"Thank you, Lysa Mother, for your guidance and strength," she whispers.

Beth opens her eyes and reaches her hand out to cast a shield spell on the cell gate.

What's this? My street clothes have changed to robes. Check it out. I have the family symbols on the edges. What are the extra ones on my chest? Hey, the robes move by themselves. What just hit my forehead? She lifts her hand to her forehead. *It's a crystal, like Mom's.*

Beth quiets for a few moments.

341

Taelene and I have more in common than I thought. I don't think I believed it until now. I didn't want to get involved, but here I am, doing what I was born to do. Now, I'm like my mother. A true Lysa.

Beth holds the crystal, and again the words feel natural, "Thank you, Lysa Mother, for your gifts."

Beth casts a shield on the cell gate, spins, and marches toward Naise.

She looks into his eyes through the sight box Robert created.

"I am LysaBeth, daughter of LysaSearin, daughter of the Lysa Mother, and I am here to free you. Any more treachery against my family from yours, and I will end your line."

Beth holds her hard stare into the eyes of the glassed figure. After a few moments, she places both hands on his shoulders, closes her eyes, and focuses on pure white energy pushing through the glass and into his body. Beth's hands glow, building light inside the glass shell until Naise's body falls to the cold stone and the remaining glass dissolves into smoke. Naise Lagrandeur, Grand-Witch of France, touches the hard rock and draws air for the first time in years.

A full minute of deep breaths, and he looks up at Beth.

"Mademoiselle, I would never have allowed my family to attack a Lysa. My sons Robert and Francois are criminals for what they have done, and I will have vengeance on them for getting my wife killed."

Naise uses his hands on Esian's glass figure to help him stand, and he looks over his shoulder.

ROYAL SOULS

"Please, free my sons. Leave Maria, as she started this trouble."

Beth gives him a stern look, saying, "Fine, and then we're going to talk."

"Yes, yes, yes. Whatever you need, Lysa, but please tell me. How is it you can remove my curse?"

"You don't tell me how you do it, and I won't tell you how I undo it."

"Yes. Please hurry before Robert or one of his guard's returns."

Beth puts her palm against the middle of Esian's chest and focuses on pushing pure energy into him until he drops to the ground. She does the same for Noah and Evan.

I'm not feeling any drain on myself, even though I'm using more magic than ever. Throttle back, girl. Save it for later. Don't... get... cocky.

"Naise," she says. "I need you to prevent Sorcha from resurrecting thousands of Blood Witches from the two prisons. Can you do this?"

"Yes. I built this prison, and like your White House, it has secret passages. My son Esian did the same when he built the Canadian prison."

"Okay, can you call your wands?"

"Yes. Robert was gloating one day and told me he has them here, as trophies, in his office. He is arrogant, and I will use that against him. Once you leave, we will get them."

"Why do I have to leave?"

343

"My sons have shamed us by attacking a Lysa. From this day forward, I will allow none of them to have a wand in hand when they face a Lysa again."

"We don't have time. Get your wands. You have a fight ahead of you, and I have to go back to Boston."

"Lysa, you must free the Nation leaders from the other cell."

"What nation leaders?"

"Sorcha ordered Robert and Francois to capture the nine Nation leaders to stop a ritual, but she only has eight, and they are in the cell next to us."

"The Circle of Nine Witches," Beth breathes.

"You know this ritual?"

"Yes. You free the leaders first and then go after Robert."

"Yes. As you wish."

Naise spins to the wall behind him, and telling his sons, *"Appelez vos baguettes."* (Call your wands).

The four men walk to a wall and place their palms against it while whispering in French and a chute pops open on each wall, releasing a wand. The four men point their wands at themselves, transforming into clean, well-dressed, healthy-looking men again.

"Very nice," Beth says.

"Noah, Evan. You free the Nation leaders. There are eight of them."

"Oui, Papa," Noah says.

"Esian, go to your prison and prepare to take it back."

"With pleasure, Papa."

"I will make Robert pay for his treachery."

"I know you are the Grand Witch of France and the most powerful of your region, and not that I doubt you.... but you realize they outnumber you?"

"No, Lysa. This is not true. I have trained Esian to be more powerful than me and Noah and Evan.... ha, ha. They fight like the ninja. When they were only four-years, I had them training with the master of Savate and then they took their skills beyond by themselves. They created a style where they cast magic while they spin, kick, jump, and run so fast that enemies drop like leaves in the fall. Esian and me have both tried to knock them down with no success. They are formidable."

"So, I take it that everything is under control?" Beth asks, looking at Noah and Evan, who have cold eyes and flexing jaw muscles.

"Yes, Lysa," Naise says, with confidence. "I promise. The trouble ends today."

"Okay," Beth says, turning away, then turns back. "Oh, ya. One more thing you should know. There's a spell that rebounds your glassing curse if you use it on anyone in your family."

"What do you mean, Lysa?"

"Francois invented a spell that rebounds the glassing curse if it's used against him or Robert. That's how he captured you."

Naise ponders the information for a few moments.

"Francois is brilliant, but Esian is even more so. Thank you for telling us this, LysaBeth, but we don't intend on using the glass curse."

Beth looks at the four emotionless faces.

"Ah, family drama. Time to go," she says.

As Beth turns to drop the shield on the cell gate, her robes wrap around her and change into her flight suit.

"*Magnifique*," Esian slips out, and Beth looks over her shoulder.

"My husband thinks so, too."

She looks at the red face of Naise, saying, "As soon as I touch that gate, it will alert everyone."

Naise smiles and waves his wand as if he's casting a fly-fishing rod. "I think not."

"I'm good to go then," she says.

Beth places her hand on the gate and waits to hear running feet or an audible alarm.

"Nothing," she whispers.

The five that were once cellmates part company as comrades, and from the small rocky ledge at the base of the prison, Beth portals back to the forest where they first landed. Taelene and Nadeh are nowhere to be seen, so Beth drops to her knee and places her palm on the ground, "*Finne Taelene*" (Find Taelene), and a glowing line that only Beth can see leads into the trees.

Yes. She's still here.

In the dusk of day, it's easy for Beth to follow, so she breaks into a run, and in less than a minute she finds Taelene and Nadeh sitting on a lake dock, holding hands and laughing.

"Hey, guys. We have to go."

Taelene scampers to her feet. "Where have you been?"

"Prison."

"Are you okay?"

"Never better."

"Where are we going?"

"Boston."

"I'm flying you to Boston tonight? Are you serious?"

"No. I'm flying you and Nadeh because we needed to be there ten minutes ago."

"That doesn't sound good."

"Yep. Tell you everything on the way."

Beth looks around to see no spectators and opens a portal to the dock suspended under the drop door that she and Tonique went out of when they left Boston.

ABIGAIL DYING

Thursday, September 4th — 2100 Eastern Time — Boston

The portal disappears, and the smell of the Boston harbor saltwater and rotting flora rush their nostrils.

"Ew. I wasn't ready for that," moans Taelene.

Taelene looks around at the dilapidated dock hanging from steel cables connected to large concrete piles that support the building, stretching out over the ocean. The dock swings with the added body weight, and waves bump against the concrete columns, misting the air.

"Beth," Taelene says.

"Yes."

"How much wine did you have in France?"

"Hush."

Both women snicker.

Beth points to a trapdoor above Taelene, whispering, "We're under the Guardian's warehouse. That big door dropped open so your mother and I could fly out of the healing room. I want to know if the traitors might be in there before we drop in."

"Got it."

Beth places a glowing palm against the floor above her, saying, "*Vis meg.*" (Show me).

The trio under the floor can see Lauranna and Karse talking. Breena is resting on a cot, and Abigail lies on the floor near Lochran.

"It's safe."

"Hey, who's the big handsome guy with black hair and glowing blue eyes?"

Beth looks at Taelene with a sultry smile. "That's my man."

"Oh ya. Good score, Princess."

"Yep. And he's a clan Chief's son."

"Package deal."

Beth swings her arm in a circle, forming a portal. "Yep. Let's go before I chew my way through the floor to get to him."

Taelene, with Nadeh in tow, laughs as she follows Beth through the portal, and Lochran looks up from his chair.

"Good timing, Princess. I think these two were going to swim to Ireland," Lochran says, pointing at Karse and Abigail.

Beth doesn't break stride until she leaps into Karse's arms to kiss him.

The passionate kiss lasts until she slips her face along his, and her lips are beside his ear. "I want you so bad."

Karse puts his face deep into her thick black hair until his lips touch her ear. "I would let the world burn to be with you."

Beth pulls her head back until she is looking Karse in the eye. "I thought we were trying to prevent that?"

She gives him a quick peck, and, releasing her grip, she slides down his body, landing on her feet.

"Hey, what's with the new tattoo?" she asks, sliding her hand over his pectoral.

"I am now Clan Chief."

"What happened to Angus? Is that why everyone looks so... depressed?"

"My father lives. He passed the title to me, and you are now Lady LysaBeth."

"Impressive. I go away for two days, Vay-kay, save my mother, learn to break the Glazier spell, commit felony jailbreak, become a Lysa, and everything changes around here."

It stunned Beth that no one laughed or asked questions.

"Beth. Who are these people?" Lauranna demands.

Beth turns inside Karse's arms, keeping her body against his.

"This is Tonique's daughter, Taelene, and Nadeh, the son of Hajiri. Guys, meet Lady Lauranna."

"The great Raziiair Siren," Nadeh says as he bows his head. "It is a great honor to meet you."

Lauranna gives a quick smile and a slight bow with her head.

"Thank you, Nadeh. I knew your father and mother. Your father was a great Raziiair, mercilessly sacrificed, and your mother, murdered by someone who never deserved her. It was a terrible loss to everyone."

"Thank you, Lady Lauranna."

Lauranna looks at Taelene and gives a gentle smile. "Little Miss Fiery Temper. I haven't seen you since you were six, but I have heard about your adventures. I see you finally accepted your calling?"

"Yes, Lady Lauranna." Taelene looks at Beth. "LysaBeth can be… motivating."

"Yes, she can. LysaBeth, what of your mother?"

"She lives, and Tonique is caring for her as we speak."

Karse squeezes Beth. "Good news, lass." And Beth pushes back into him.

"Will she be here?" Lauranna asks.

"No, she's too weak. There was little magic left in the castle when we arrived."

"Well, it's good she's found."

"What's happened? Why is everyone so… down?" Beth says.

"Where is Naise?" Lauranna asks.

"He's reclaiming his glass prison from his son Robert."

"Beth, we need him here!"

"Mother, calm yourself. Hear what LysaBeth has to say."

Beth looks over her shoulder at Karse and then back at Lauranna.

"Alright… Someone needs to tell me what's happening. NOW!"

"Our fight has taken a severe setback," Lauranna says. "The Irish Guardians have brought the carrier of the prince's soul to us, but he's frozen in glass, and without Naise, we may never reunite the Royal souls."

"Lauranna, I said, I learned how to break the glass."

Lauranna's reaction is like all the football stadium lights turning on at once. Her voice is musical when she asks, "You can free the carrier of the prince's soul?"

351

"Hell, yeah."

"How, lass?" Karse says.

"Robert attacked me in the France prison and used the Glassing curse on me. After feeling sorry for myself, the Lysa Mother came to me and told me to take power from the Universe. A pool of pure white energy appeared, and I saw my hand dipping into it. My body absorbed the energy, forcing the glass curse out of me, and I used the same energy to free Naise and his three trapped sons."

Beth looks around, and everyone is staring at her, bewildered.

"I can do this." Beth pushes out of Karse's arms and, closing her eyes, she changes to her Lysa robes. "I became a true Lysa, like my mother, when I defeated the Glassing curse in France. The Lysa Mother gave me these robes and my crystal."

Beth searches the beaming faces in the room and stops as her eyes meet Karse's.

"You're an amazing woman, LysaBeth."

Beth smiles, and Breena pops up from the cot, saying, "Everyone will be so excited. I can't wait to tell them."

Beth turns to Breena and snaps, "You will tell no one."

"Oh," Breena says, shocked.

"What do you know, lass?"

Beth looks at Lauranna and then back at Breena.

"Who did you tell about Roxanne going to France to meet me?"

"Only two other healers. Why?"

"Roxanne is dead, and I assume the one that killed her is the same witch Sorcha is using to push her power through to kill me. Who's the other one? I want to talk to her."

"A spy killed her, lass. She and Breena were very close."

"Sorry to hear that, Breena, but I can promise you, I'm going to find the traitors."

"LysaBeth, we don't have enough time to go through eight-hundred Guardians."

Beth turns and puts her hand against Karse's chest. "I have a gift which works when I'm invisible. It allows me to see an identity spell cloaking someone or the light of magic used to guard things. I'll find them."

Beth stops, looks around the room, and sees Abigail lying by a cot. She walks over, changing her robes to street clothes in stride, and kneels beside her.

"Abigail, I'm so sorry I haven't talked to you yet. My mind was on someone else." She looks over her shoulder at Karse.

Beth looks back at Abigail.

"Hey. What's with the festering sore in the corner of your mouth? And your wounds. Why aren't your wounds healed?"

Lochran clears his throat. "Look in her mouth. It's full of sores, and her gums are festering as well. Not to mention her eyes are going dull."

"The snow-cats must have had an acid spell on their claws and mouth. I've had the healers trying everything since you left," Lauranna says.

"No, Lauranna, it's not a spell. It's the black energy Sorcha was feeding the two lions, and now it's trying to eat Abigail."

Beth slides her hand along Abigail's neck, dragging it over her side until she feels her heart beating and places her other hand. She winks at Abigail before closing her eyes, and after a few seconds, her hands glow. The room is silent until a small cloud of black smoke forms above Abigail's head, and Lochran jumps from his chair.

"Princess, you're doing it. You're driving it out of Abigail."

Beth holds her focus until she feels the pure energy moving through Abigail like water through a strainer, and she opens her eyes to see the cloud of black energy hovering over Abigail's head. She puts a hand on each side, surrounding the cloud with a white glow, then slams her hands together, turning it into gray smoke.

Beth's hands stop glowing, and Abigail is slow to raise herself to her feet while Beth turns to Lochran. "She'll heal now."

Beth turns her head back to Abigail in time for a heavy pink tongue to drag its way from chin to hairline.

"ABIGAIL. You *biatch*. That was like a wet dishcloth dragged up my face. No kitty kisses."

Everyone laughs as Beth wipes her sleeve on her face a few times to dry the tongue swipe. Then, Beth launches forward to throw her arms around Abigail's neck, but Abigail sees the move and twists. Beth bounces off Abigail's shoulder, lands on her back, and Abigail pins her to the ground with her body weight. Abigail licks at Beth's face as she kicks and laughs and swings her head back and forth, trying to dodge the enormous pink tongue. The room fills with laughter.

When Beth comes back from washing the kitty slobber from her face, Abigail is lying at Lochran's feet while he strokes her neck, and Beth can see the wounds are healing.

Beth shakes her finger at Abigail as she walks past.

"You. You're in big trouble. Assault, with a wet weapon, against a Lysa and a princess."

"And the Clan Lady," Karse adds.

"Ya, the Clan Lady, too. And messing my hair. Abigail, you're a criminal."

Abigail flicks her tail around, then shoots her tongue out of her mouth and up the side of her face, holds, then slowly drags it back in.

"Bad kitty!"

Even Beth can't keep from joining in the laughter.

LITTLE SISTER

Friday, September 5th — 1000 Eastern Time — Boston

Queen Sorcha slumps on her throne in murderous contemplation.

The theater sized room carved into the core of the mountain, circled in empty wooden bleachers, used to be the challenge theater where prisoners fought conjured beasts to earn relaxation of their punishment, or visitation privileges, if they survived.

A red smoke portal appears, and Queen Sorcha, sitting up with both glowing palms aimed at the portal, watches the female figure, clad in red robes with runes around the edges, walk out of the smoke.

"Oh. You've got nerve."

"Oh, Sorcha. You can't still be mad."

Sorcha lifts herself from her throne, like a lioness rising to charge nearby prey.

"Yes. Having your mother steal and kill your lover causes me deep hate. I'm funny that way."

"So true. You always had a flair for the drama."

"Drama. Oh, really?"

"Sorcha, I didn't come here to fight with you. I came to help you."

"You mean you came to stick another knife in my back? Would you like the first one back, so you can use it again, or did you bring a spare?"

Lillian places her hand on her hip and cocks her eyebrow.

"No. You keep it to use on someone else. Consider it a gift of learning."

Sorcha yells and casts a rocket-fast, fiery ball at her mother, but it disintegrates a few inches away from her mother's smirking face.

"Are you done with the tantrum, or do you need a timeout?"

"Ahh!"

"Yelling doesn't help, Sorcha."

"I hate you. You're lucky we can't kill our bloodline."

"Okay, now that's over with, let's get to the reason for my visit."

"Please do, so you can leave and never come back."

"You might change your mind when I tell you what I have discovered."

"Get on with it!"

"Please, stop yelling." The room goes silent. "Oh, you're done?" She pauses as Sorcha glares at her. "I know how you can stop the prince and princess from reuniting and how you can capture LysaBeth without the Crystals or Stones or massive battles."

Sorcha sinks back into her throne, staring at her mother like an old cop trying to read a witness swearing a statement. She sits, contemplating, for a few moments.

"Bold statement, Mother."

"Not really, Sorcha. Considering, I've infiltrated the Guardians and gathered the information while only killing one witch."

Sorcha catches her breath. "You know where the royal souls are, don't you?"

"Yes, dear. Relax... They're in Boston. See, I'm here to help. Besides, I want to turn to dust about as much as you do."

A small portal appears with Rebekah's face in it, and Sorcha says, "Rebekah, I'm busy, darling."

"The prince and princess are in Boston, My Queen."

Sorcha looks at her mother, who flips both her hands outward and lifts her eyebrows, then back at Rebekah, smiling.

"Very well done, my pet. Now get everyone and everything to Boston and find where it will happen."

"Yes, My Queen."

The small portal disappears.

"See, Mother. Loyalty has its rewards."

"Are you sure about that?"

"Don't play games, Mother."

"Well, a little bird told me that Rebekah paid a visit to Obadiah."

"Why would she do that?"

"Maybe you should ask her, darling."

Sorcha contemplates before circling her hand, and a small window with Rebekah's face opens.

"Rebekah, darling. Are you sure about this information?"

"Yes, My Queen. I visited Obadiah, and he knew about an encounter in Boston involving Lochran. I sent a spy there, who saw a group of Irish and Scottish witches near the harbor. He knew two of them from his village."

"Why did you visit Obadiah?"

"He has over two-thousand witches under his protection, and I thought I might persuade him to join the cause, but to my surprise, someone had already tried."

Queen Sorcha doesn't respond right away.

"How are the preparations going?"

"I have sent messages to every coven leader. You will have at least six thousand witches fighting for you, my Queen. More if all goes well."

Sorcha leans close to the mirror portal.

"This will be a glorious victory for *us*, Rebekah. Carry on."

"My Queen."

Sorcha waves her hand, dissolving the mirror, saying, "She told the truth, Mother. Anything else?"

"We'll see, Sorcha. We'll see."

"How did *you* find out they were in Boston?"

"You make it sound as if I'm helpless. I have my resources."

"You're trying my patience, Mother."

"Fine. Do you think you can keep your mental state reasonable long enough to hear me out?"

"Careful, Mother."

"Oh, Sorcha, threatening me is about as useful as putting a sharp stick in your own eye, so stop it."

Sorcha sits back hard into her throne, hissing, "Whatever."

"You know how it is with men. You play with their minds through certain emotional moments, and they will tell you anything."

"So, you're sleeping with a Guardian? Why am I not surprised to hear that from the family trollop?"

"Mind... your... tongue. One more slash like that, and I will leave you out in the cold. Do you understand me?"

Sorcha celebrates her cut to the quick with a snarling smile.

"I'm happy your sister isn't such an unappreciative little bitch," Lillian seethes.

"Mother, tell me what you know or... Wait, what?" Sorcha snaps upright. "My... my what? My... sister? Is this some kind of sick joke?"

"Oh, no. Did I forget to mention that? Well, you know how it is when you forget to call or write to your mother. Anyway, now you know I managed to trollop out another you with a lot less... How do you say it? Oh yes, I remember, a lot less 'It's all about me.'"

Lillian casts a portal, and a young witch in flowing red robes, matching Lillian's, steps out.

Sorcha, wide eyed, catches her breath.

She has the family runes on her robes. Only blood kin can survive those symbols.

"Sorcha, this is Caitlin of the Scottish Guardians and your sister. Well, half-sister."

"So, this is your source?"

"Yes. Caitlin used an identity spell and got close to a young Irish Guardian who gave us all the information we need to stop the prince and princess from reuniting."

Still angered at the discovery of having a sister, Sorcha looks at Caitlin.

She's confident, striking with those full lips, sharp features, blue eyes, strawberry-blonde flowing hair. Hmm. Ulterior motive? Does Mother want my little sister on the throne?

Caitlin gives a slight nod. "Sister."

Sorcha's skin crawls with anger as the single word echoes in her mind, and the urge to attack climbs her spine and floods her brain.

"That's Queen… Sorcha."

"Sorcha or sister. Your call," Caitlin says.

Sorcha looks at her mother and then back at Caitlin. "Know… your… place."

Caitlin holds her composure through the stare-down.

"Oh, I very much know my place. Sister."

Sorcha climbs out of her throne and crosses the floor, stopping two feet from Caitlin.

"You will call me Queen Sorcha, or I will suck your soul out like sucking the pulp out of a grape."

"Whoops. Family curse. No can do," Caitlin says, winking at Sorcha.

Sorcha glares at Caitlin and is about to snap when Lillian interrupts.

"Not the introduction I had hoped for," she says. "Don't worry, Caitlin. Sorcha never played well with others unless they played her way."

Sorcha spins back to her throne.

"Why are you still here, Mother?"

"We need to work together and stop the reunion, Sorcha."

Sorcha eases herself into her throne chair, saying, "If you know so much, then you and Little Cubby go do it."

Sorcha stares at her mother, and after a few moments, she looks at Caitlin, and an evil grin of realization grows on Sorcha's face.

"Aw, is little sister only a Wand Witch? Did you get the blood but not the power?" Sorcha laughs. She can tell by the anger in Caitlin's eyes she's right. "Well, well, Mother. I guess she's not perfect after all?"

Sorcha looks back at Caitlin.

"I guess that will be *Queen*... Sorcha, Little Sister."

"Whatever," Caitlin says.

"Tell me what you know, Mother, and then I will decide if we play together."

"Are you going to play nice, or are we going to fight again?"

"Again, that depends on the value of the information."

"I found out that the Crystals and the Stones are not the only keys to the ritual," Caitlin says. "Lady Lauranna is the last key. She is the Raziiair Siren who must cast the pure white light around the circle of witches, so the two souls can reunite in the pure light."

Sorcha, silent, contemplates the scenarios for stopping the reunion.

"They still can't get the prince out of the glass," she says.

"They're going to kidnap a Glazier," Caitlin says.

A gunshot-like noise echoes, then the trio hears the cracks of magic casting, and they look toward Francois' private entrance.

ROYAL SOULS

"Again, your information is correct, Mother. I think the effort to capture a Glazier is underway," Sorcha says.

Sorcha makes a quick circle with her hand, and Rebekah's face appears in a mirror portal.

"Rebekah, the prison is under attack. Set a beacon. I'm sending all the Blood Witches to you, now."

"Yes, My Queen."

Sorcha stands up and waves her glowing hands in a wide arc over her head, sending the Blood Witches to Rebekah. She looks at Lillian.

"Success favors the prepared. I had Francois thaw all the Blood Witches over the last few days. Time to go."

Sorcha casts a portal. "You can follow me or stay here and fight," she says. "Your choice." Sorcha steps through the portal, followed by Lillian and Caitlin.

***

Rebekah casts her wand like she's cracking a whip, and a blinking red beacon floats to the middle of an empty baseball field. She watches as two-thousand witches appear, like water through a spout, under cover of her shield spell.

Rebekah's eyes search the incoming flow of witches. "Where are you, Francois?"

Panic roots in her stomach and, looking around, she sees a wizard who guarded the prison's foyer the last time she was there.

"Have you seen Francois?"

"No, Madam Rebekah. He was fighting the attackers and sent us away."

"Who was attacking, and why would he send you away?"

"We do not know, Madam, but they entered the prison without being detected, and that should not have been possible."

"What do you mean? How don't you know?"

Rebekah, eyes cold, jaw muscles tight and flexing, holds her stare and the guard's eyes widen as he goes pale. She turns away, casts a portal to the small man-door that she and Midas entered during their last visit to the prison.

Rebekah ignores the cutting cold and blowing snow and casts a light globe toward the rock face.

Why is that door open?

Rebekah points her wand toward the door as she advances.

Careful to check both sides, she steps through the door and waits.

She points her wand at her feet, changing from high heels to a soft shoe. Slow and deliberate with each step, she makes her way to the double doors of the throne room. Rebekah stops, listens for sounds outside the wind blowing through the open man-door, then steps in.

Boom…. pop… pop… crack.

Those are casting explosions. There's a magic fight happening behind Francois' door.

Rebekah, cautious, walks toward the closed door until…

BOOM!

The door on Francois' private entrance explodes into pieces, and he backs out of the dungeon passageway, defending himself. Then Francois lets out a pained shout, flailing backward. Without hesitation, Rebekah moves with the instinct of a combat veteran, retrieving a man down, and reaches Francois before his attackers.

Francois regains consciousness.

Where am I? A comfortable bed. I smell food cooking.

He sits up and looks around the semi-dark room. Rebekah is sitting in an armchair in the corner.

Francois stares at her for a few moments.

"Where are we, *Cherie*?"

"My little hideaway that no one knows about."

"Did you save me, *Cherie*?"

"Yes."

"*Cherie*, you risk so much. Why?" Francois stands up. Rebekah stands and steps toward Francois. "I'm playing a hunch."

Francois walks until he is only a foot from Rebekah.

"*Rebekah.* I will never forget this. You saved my life."

Rebekah feels Francois' hand against her waist, and she lets him step against her.

"Francois, who attacked you?"

"It was my brother, Esian."

"That doesn't sound good for Robert."

"No, *Cherie*. I think it is bad for Robert. If Esian is free, then Papa is also free."

Francois' face is only inches from Rebekah's.

"Francois, remember what I promised you if you tear my heart out," she says.

Neither Francois nor Rebekah have felt the sensations of a passionate kiss in years, so when their lips make crushing contact, they both break into a gyrating frenzy of passion, driving their bodies against each other.

"I have to get back to Queen Sorcha," Rebekah says. "I've been away too long."

"What will you say?"

"That I went back to the prison to check if she had escaped and had to hide to avoid capture."

"Will she believe you?"

"When I tell her who attacked you, she'll believe me."

"Where will I be?"

"On your way to France."

"But I will stay here. No?"

"Yes. No one knows of this place. Don't use any magic outside this room and don't…. leave this condo."

He kisses Rebekah, slow and passionate, and says, "Thank you, *Cherie*."

She searches his eyes. "I'll see you when it's finished."

"Yes. Then we can go somewhere warm together, forever."

Rebekah gives him a gentle smile. "I'm going to hold you to that."

She stands up and turns away from Francois. "*Cherie*, wait."

Rebekah turns back, letting her arms fall to her sides. She doesn't move.

"*Cherie*, you are exquisite."

She picks her wand up from the night table, and, with a simple wave, she dresses in a black three-quarter dress, split halfway up her thigh, and high heels.

"Stay here. Wine and food are in the kitchen. See you soon."

"As you wish."

She steps through her portal, disappearing with a slight sound like air being sucked into a hole.

***

Rebekah walks through the locker room corridor of the old baseball stadium to see leaders of covens from around the world gathered in small groups. They acknowledge her as she enters each room to check who has arrived.

As she exits the corridor into the dugout, she hears, "Rebekah."

Rebekah turns, making a slight bow.

"My Queen. I'm happy to see you escaped the prison in time," and she climbs the stairs from the dugout to the weed-infested playing field.

"What do you mean, Rebekah?"

"When I reached the prison, I found the front door open and Francois defending the throne room by keeping the attackers in the dungeon passageway. The attackers made their way through, and I had to hide to avoid capture."

"Well done, Rebekah. Do you know who attacked?"

"Yes, My Queen. It was Francois' brother, who escaped from the prison in France."

"I can only assume that none of the three-thousand Blood Witches hidden there will arrive?"

"We know nothing yet, my Queen."

"Where is Francois?"

"He said he was going to France to check on his brother Robert."

Sorcha moves closer to Rebekah and then spins to Lillian and Caitlin.

"Rebekah, darling. My mother and 'new' little sister were just explaining how we defeat the Guardians and capture LysaBeth without a battle."

"Is this a joke? New little sister? Did you buy her from someone, My Queen? I don't understand."

Sorcha laughs.

"No, Rebekah. I didn't buy her, but my mother felt it prudent to have a second child and not tell me until now."

Rebekah knows of the tension between Sorcha and her mother and asks, "Is this a ruse?"

Sorcha laughs. "Rebekah knows you too well, Mother."

Lillian bites back, "I never concern myself with opinions from the hired help."

Rebekah knows Lillian is a Spirit Witch, and she can't defeat her, but she still returns the volley. "No. But you sleep with them and make bastard children."

Lillian brings her glowing hand forward. "Why, you dirty little farm trash!"

Sorcha steps forward with both hands glowing.

"You dare protect her against your own?" Lillian barks.

Sorcha smiles. "I told you, Mother. Loyalty has its privileges."

Lillian snarls at Rebekah, then drops her hand, and Sorcha retreats in victory.

"How do you know she's your sister?" Rebekah says, locking eyes with Caitlin.

"Mother had her dressed in robes with the family runes on them when she first introduced her."

Rebekah still doesn't break eye contact with Caitlin.

"My Queen, how does this plan work?" Rebekah says.

Caitlin steps forward enough that Rebekah's hand goes behind her back.

"Careful, Little Sister. When people get too close to me, Rebekah's 'kill first' reaction is legendary."

"I'm only getting close enough to avoid prying ears, so shorten the leash."

Rebekah responds with an open-mouth, full teeth-bared snarl that should have put a pit bull on the run, and Sorcha steps between the two.

"Oh, Little Sister. You have much to learn. Rebekah is off-leash and has walked at my side since the beginning."

"Sorcha, it's near time," Lillian says. "We need to focus on the bigger picture."

Queen Sorcha turns to Rebekah and winks, so Rebekah gives a slight nod. "My Queen."

"What's the plan, Mother?"

"Well, Big Sister. We don't know where they have hidden the Princess yet, but we know they are guarding the prince in a warehouse on the waterfront."

"She must be close," Sorcha says.

"Still. No one can get near the prince because of the pyre wolves and eight-hundred Guardians," Caitlin says.

"We will have six thousand witches here to take him by force," Rebekah snaps.

"Oh? How do you propose to get past the pyre wolves?" Caitlin says.

"Get on with it, little sister."

"We need them to expose where the princess is, and then we capture both and destroy them, which ends the war forever."

"And if the plan fails, they complete the reunion, and we don't know who will survive when the dust settles, literally," Sorcha says.

"Not if we kill the last key," Caitlin says.

"What do you mean, 'last key'?" Rebekah says.

"Lady Lauranna," Caitlin says. "She is the last key, and the last living Raziiair Siren. She must cast the Raziiair shield of pure white light for the souls to rise into and reunite. Kill her, and it's over. We can capture both souls, kill them, and the magical world is ours for the taking."

"It's mine already, Little Sister."

"Not yet, *Big* Sister. You've been trying to end the prophecy for more than a thousand years, and I did the footwork for this information in less than five years. I'm getting something out of this without being treated like the weak step-sister of the wicked witch. So, deal with it."

"Yes... and for a thousand years, I have shaped a dynasty by winning battles and surviving treachery. I have spent day and night gathering an army of dedicated witches and warlocks and survived a curse that should have killed me ten times over," Sorcha's eyes blacken and her robes float outward, shadowing her as spiked wings, "And because of this I am the most powerful Spirit witch alive. You'll do as I say, my little wand witch sister, or I'll put you in a cage under Rebekah's care. Understood?"

Queen Sorcha holds her dark pose for a few moments and Lillian breaks the stare-down.

"Let's squabble later. The sun is setting."

ROYAL SOULS

Sorcha recovers, her eyes returning to their natural gray, saying, "I take it you have a plan for killing Lauranna?"

"All worked out... My Queen."

Queen Sorcha shows no emotion, telling Caitlin she accepts her surrender.

"Is that the same as saying that you're still working out the details?" Rebekah asks.

"The details are for family only. Shouldn't you be rounding up the sheeple?"

Lillian discreetly looks at Sorcha and sees a quick smirk on her face from Caitlin's comment. She can tell that Sorcha likes Caitlin.

"Tell... *us*," Sorcha snaps.

"I have a sacrificial patsy under my control who will kill Lauranna before she enters the ritual," Caitlin says. "The two souls will be within our grasp, and all you have to do is send the sheeple in to die, and we kill the prince and princess."

Caitlin looks around at the other three with a mischievous grin. "Game over, for good."

"Know this, Little Sister," Sorcha sneers. "You're born of the modern-day, so if you fail and the dust flies, and I somehow survive, I will make it my life's mission to find you and make you suffer. And if Rebekah survives, I promise her she can be your warden. Do you understand?"

Caitlin dismisses Sorcha's threat by shrugging her shoulders and saying, "Ooh, scary."

Caitlin and Lillian step into a portal and disappear, leaving Sorcha and Rebekah to contemplate the plan.

Sorcha turns to Rebekah.

"Make sure we have a full battle plan in place and, if the opportunity should arise, kill them both. Mother and little sister are playing at something. I'm sure they have a plan to kill us."

"With pleasure, My Queen."

"Rebekah. Being a bitch is part of the role I must play. When you and I are alone, as we were the day in your office, Sorcha will do, and I was wrong to scold you like I did. We need each other to survive this, and you have been there for me from the beginning and… I know I would have died on the battlefield if it hadn't been for you."

What the… An apology?

"Thank you, Sorcha. My loyalty has never waned."

Sorcha turns away from Rebekah as she tightens her jaw in response.

Oh, hasn't it?

"Sorcha, are you at full strength?"

"I have what I need hidden away. Make sure everything is ready. I'll be back."

Sorcha casts a portal to take her to the next victims of her soul-sucking survival.

Rebekah stares into the dusky night.

If we survive this, Sorcha, I'm not spending whatever mortal life I get, being your pet.

PREPARATIONS

Friday, September 5th — 2100 Eastern Time — Boston

"LysaBeth, how are you going to find the spies?" Karse asks.

"Lochran, come here," Beth says.

"Aye, Princess."

"I'm going to be invisible and up in the rafters," she tells Karse. "You and Lochran are going to be on the ground, and I'll tell you where the spies are standing."

"Princess. If you're shouting at us from the rafters, why be invisible?"

"Lochran…" Beth snaps, making a fist at him, before touching his ear, then Karse's, and walks twenty feet, with her back to them.

"Can you hear me, Lochran?"

"Oh, aye, Princess. Now I understand."

Karse laughs and slaps him on the shoulder.

"Jeez, Lochran," Beth says.

Beth turns invisible as she floats toward the rafters, and Karse and Lochran make their way through the barrier at the healing room door.

"Hold it, guys. We need a new plan."

373

"Why do you say that, lass?"

"I can see five people using identity spells."

"That's impossible."

"Return to the healing room. Plan B."

Lochran looks into the rafters, "What's plan 'B'?"

"Lochran, go."

"Aye, Princess."

Karse laughs and gives Lochran a quick shove.

"Stop asking questions, soldier."

"Oh, aye. Especially with that one. You'll be doing the breaststroke with the sharks."

"Keep talking, Lochran," Beth says.

Lochran goes silent, and Karse laughs again.

Beth touches the ground, becoming visible again, and Lauranna approaches her.

"LysaBeth, it's getting dark out, and we need to prepare. We cannot start until we know there are no spies."

"I understand, Lauranna."

Beth looks at Karse. "I guess it's time to go big."

"What's the plan, lass?"

"Time to let everyone know the Lysa fight for the prince and princess. And while I'm doing that, I'll capture the five witches that are using cloaking spells."

"Grand plan, Princess," Lochran says. "Can you succeed?"

"That does it," Beth growls, and she snaps her fingers.

Lochran disappears, and Abigail growls.

"Relax, Abigail. I dropped him off the pier," Beth says.

Abigail growls and slaps her paw on the floor.

ROYAL SOULS

"I think she's trying to tell you that Lochran can no swim, lass," muses Karse.

Beth snaps her fingers again, and Lochran hits the healing room floor in a splash of Atlantic water, flailing like a drowning man.

"Whoopsie," Beth says, and Karse laughs as Beth raises her arms out to her sides.

Karse gets a lustful look and says, "Do you know, lass? Those robes and crystal make you quite fetching."

"Good thing we're married." Karse smiles as Beth says, "I'm going to portal into the rafters above the Pyre Wolf."

Beth looks at Lauranna. "It's time for the big game."

Beth swings her arm, and swirling white mist forms beside her and in the rafters, and she hears the Guardians shouting.

Beth floats out of the portal to see hundreds of wands aimed at her.

A Guardian shouts. "Hold! That's not the evil queen. Hold!"

"I am LysaBeth," she announces, "daughter of LysaSearin, daughter of the Lysa Mother, and I fight for the prince and princess. Six hours from now, we will be victorious."

The Guardians cheer, and the five people using identity spells make their way closer to the pyre wolves.

"LysaBeth, how will you get the prince out of the glass?" Colleen says. "We went to capture a Glazier, but they've disappeared."

Beth sees this as the best opportunity to capture the spies because they're only a few feet apart. She floats sideways until the glassed figure of Rhynan is between her and the spies, aiming her palms out toward Rhynan and the unsuspecting targets.

"*Frys spionene.*" (Freeze the spies).

A flash of light from her hands and the five spies, and three accidental targets, drop like sheets from a clothesline.

"She's attacking!" someone from the crowd yells.

"Hold!" Karse shouts. "Five of the fallen are spies. Step aside."

Beth lands near Pyreus and points at the fallen witches. "Those three and those two are the spies. The other three will recover soon."

"Wait!" Colleen says, stepping out of the crowd. "Those three aren't spies." She points to three men.

"Why are they using an identity spell?" Beth says.

"They're trying to find the spies that we learned of earlier, which, I assume, are these two?"

"How do you know this?"

"Because they belong to the Irish Guardians, and I assigned the mission."

Karse steps forward. "Why was I not told of this plan?"

"We didn't tell anyone for security reasons."

"When it's over, we are going to have this conversation again," Karse says.

"Ha. When it's over, one way or the other, none of us will be around for the conversation," Colleen says, turning and walking away.

Beth gives Karse a confused look. "What did she mean by that?"

ROYAL SOULS

"The Day of Dust. The Last Rest. Call it what you will, but it still means dead, again," says an Irish Guardian.

"Day of Dust? What's that?" Beth asks, looking at Karse.

"When the Prince and Princess reunite, it will sow the royal seed to a woman in the princess' bloodline. The magic that holds us here ends, and we turn to dust," answers the Irish Guardian.

Beth looks at him, blank, then back to Karse and pauses before she turns to disappear into a portal.

"LysaBeth, wait..."

Karse stares at the space left by Beth disappearing, and his heart sinks. He turns to Lochran, standing in a puddle of water from his dripping kilt, points, and with a broken voice says, "Take those five to the hold, but separate those two from the rest."

Karse walks into the healing room with a sullen look on his face.

"Karse, where's LysaBeth?" Lauranna asks.

"Gone, Mother."

"Gone where, Karse?"

"I don't know, Mother."

"What happened?"

"She learned of The Day of Dust."

"Only now? Why?"

"I didn't want to tell her I might die even if we win."

"But you won't."

"What are you saying, Mother?"

"The blue light that formed around you and Beth when you married removed you from the Staff of Souls. You will only die if it's in battle or by old age."

377

Karse pauses, surprised and oblivious to everything around him, until Lauranna leans sideways to look past him.

He turns to see Beth, tearful but smiling.

"I'm sorry, LysaBeth, but I knew I had a chance of surviving The Day of Dust, so I said nothing, and I know now it was foolish to keep it from you. Please, forgive me."

Beth melts into his arms. "I heard Lauranna, and you're going to spend the next five-hundred years making it up to me. Never do that to me again."

"I promise. Never again, my love."

Beth pushes back from Karse and turns toward Lochran and Abigail. Abigail is in her human form, healed, with both her arms around Lochran and her head buried in his neck.

"Abigail. Why didn't you tell me?"

Abigail turns to Beth. "We hoped to end in victory and always be a wonderful memory."

"Abigail, that's not fair."

"When I first met you, I cared because of Princess Mehla. Then, I cared enough for you to fight the snow lions to the death. Today, you saved me and strengthened me with the white energy, so now I am ready for battle, and I can die with honor."

"Abigail. I don't want you or Lochran to die."

"Lauranna told us that Taelene was to be your protector from childhood. Now you have your real protector."

Taelene steps forward. "Abigail, no. You will always be Beth's first protector."

"And you will always be her true protector."

"I can't believe this. Abigail, Lochran, Lauranna, Breena. In what, five hours? You're going to…." Beth chokes on the words. "Turn to dust, and you're fighting to make sure it happens?"

"The Universe gave us a second chance to right a grievous wrong," Lauranna says. "The child born after the reunion will save magic because without magic, there will be no life."

"I understand, Lauranna, but there must be a way for you to survive this."

"There is none," a voice booms with the words of finality. "Time has ended for our bodies and when we return to the Staff, we will stay in the next life."

Karse turns his body to the deep voice. "Father."

"Karse, gather the forces and send the signal," Angus says. "Your mother needs protection while she builds the circle. LysaBeth, I am sorry for my earlier conduct."

"I understood why you assumed," Beth says, putting her hand in Karse's. "I'm sure this handsome rogue has collected many hearts."

"Still, no excuse."

"Angus… Dad. What's a family without a little drama?" Beth says.

"Karse has chosen well," he replies with a gentle smile that Lauranna hasn't seen in many years.

Beth snickers. "I'm not convinced I gave him much choice."

"The time is here. Where is the Glazier?"

"We don't need one, Father," Karse says. "LysaBeth can break the glass."

"Is this true?"

"Yes. I've done it."

Everyone waits in silence for Angus to respond, and it surprises Lauranna.

"Lauranna and I would have enjoyed our grandchildren," he says.

"LysaLauranna Macha O'Corry and Angus Killian MacShannachan will know their grandparents through the stories," Beth says. "They will know everyone's sacrifice."

Karse looks at Beth. "You've already worked all this out, lass?"

"Do you disagree?"

"You do Clan MacShannachan a great honor, lass."

Beth feels a hand sliding around her shoulder and looks right to see Lauranna's beaming face.

"See, Angus and I live through The Day of Dust," Lauranna says.

Angus nods at Karse. "The time is near to call the prince and princess."

"Lochran, time to gather," Karse says.

"Karse, we found the Captain of the Guard dead a few days ago," Angus says.

"A significant loss, Father. Sorcha's trying to remove leadership."

"A good strategy," Angus says.

Karse pulls his wand from his waistline, waves it at Lochran, and changes him to wearing a full-dress kilt and a broach of Clan MacShannachan. "Gather your men, Captain."

Lochran takes a stoic stance. "As you command, Chief."

Lochran gives Abigail a longing look, and they kiss.

"Karse, it's dark out," Lauranna says. "Time to go."

"We need to gather your protectors first, Mother."

"Everything's ready, Karse. Your job is to protect Breena."

"Lady Lauranna," Beth says.

"Lady LysaBeth. Look after my son and have many grandchildren for us."

"I'm not sure which one of those requests will be the easiest."

"Lady Lauranna." Taelene stands near Nadeh, who has not left her side since they met.

"Taelene, I'm glad you and LysaBeth are together, and I hope you have found what you were looking for," Lauranna says.

"It was an honor meeting the great Raziiair Siren."

"Nadeh, take care of Taelene."

"Lauranna."

"Abigail, Lochran. See you soon."

"Lauranna, my love."

"I'm looking forward to a very long hug on the other side, Husband."

"I have missed you very much, Lauranna, and wish only to hug you until the next life for us."

"Lady Lauranna," Gabrielle says. "It is time."

The blue smoke of Lady Lauranna's portal fades away, and everyone looks back to Karse.

"Once she starts the circle, we are at war," Karse says.

"How long, Karse?" Beth says.

"An hour at most. Why?"

"I have to do something for Jack. I promised."

"Aye, lass. He, too, has earned his happiness."

"Back soon."

Beth gives Karse a quick cheek peck and slips through a portal.

JACK'S REPRIEVE

Friday, September 5th — 2200 Eastern Time — Boston

"Jack, wake up."

He rouses, shifts in his half-waking state.

"Jack! Wake up!"

His eyes fly open to see Beth looming over him, and he bolts straight up, looking around to orient himself.

"What? How did you find me?"

"DUH. The homing spell on your side. Come on, Dick Tracy, we have to go."

"Where?"

"To get you your life back."

"Are you serious?"

"Yep. By the way, I like the new condo. I presume it came furnished?"

"Yes, and thanks to you, I can take a shower." Jack stands up from the armchair where he'd nodded off.

"A step in the right direction. Have you got something better to wear?"

"I haven't had time to shop yet. It's been a long time since I've had money, you know."

Beth snaps her fingers, and Jack wears a suit and polished leather shoes.

"Now you look good. The Chief will approve."

"The Chief? Where is he?"

"His office."

"This late?"

"Yes, I've checked. Are you ready for your second flying lesson?"

"Don't let me fall over this time."

"I've got you."

A small circle of white smoke appears head high and six feet back from the front edge of Chief of Police Patrick O'Reilly's desk. He stares at it from his chair, unsure if he can believe what he sees as the circle of smoke grows. His hand slips to the drawer handle to his right, and he slides it open for quick access to his gun. Beth steps out of the full-sized portal, and the Chief slips his hand into the drawer, palming the gun, until Jack steps out.

"Sir. Sorry for the intrusion."

"Jack? Jack Sebastian?"

"Yes, sir."

"That's a neat trick. Care to explain what's going on here?"

"Sir. This is Beth O'Corry."

"So?"

"The little girl who disappeared from the hospital in the incident for which the other Chief fired me."

The portal of smoke disappears, and the Chief moves his gun to his lap as he sits back in his chair.

ROYAL SOULS

"Sorry, Chief," Beth says, "but I'm on a tight schedule, so put the gun back in the drawer and tell me what you need to give Jack his job back."

"How did you do the smoke circle thing?"

"It's a portal, and I'm a witch. I made myself invisible at the hospital and walked out. That's why you don't see me on video."

The Chief laughs. "The Boston witch stories, hey? Yep, never heard that."

"Come on, Patrick. You know I wasn't derelict. The department used me as the sacrificial lamb because nobody could explain it. All I wanted to be was a good cop. Jeez, you even vouched for me to get on the force."

"I know, Jack. I know. But what do I do? Tell everyone she's a witch and made herself invisible? And get fired? Besides, there's no such thing."

"Yo, Chief. Pick something," Beth interrupts.

"What?"

"Pick something you want right now."

"Okay," the Chief says, thinking. "You don't produce, and I arrest both of you."

"Ya, sure you will," Beth laughs. "Tell me what you want."

"I'm starved. I haven't eaten since lunch. How about… let's see… Irish lamb stew and soda bread? Oh, maybe throw in a pint of Guinness," he snickers.

"Since you have so many important papers on your desk, how about over there?" Beth points, and her hand glows for a flash.

Chief O'Reilly stands up from his desk, holsters his gun, and walks to his six-chair meeting table. A place-mat

385

with a bowl of Irish stew, a plate of soda bread, and a pint of Guinness sits on the polished wood surface. The Chief picks up the pint and takes a sip.

"It's real. How? That's not possible. This has got to be a trick."

"Okay. One more time and you pick the spot."

"A twenty-five-year Scotch and a Cuban Cohiba on the coffee table, now," he points.

Beth tosses her hand toward the coffee table with another quick flash of light from her hand.

"I thought you were going for something hard," she says.

"Patrick," Jack pleads. "I know it's hard to believe, but it's true. She's the real thing."

"Well, the bottle of Scotch and the box of Cubans prove that, don't they? How do I explain you getting reinstated and her disappearance?"

"Easy," Beth says. "There was a large vent grill, held on with one screw, leading into the next room around the corner, so I climbed through and slipped out of the hospital through the basement. I'll give you my fingerprints, which should clear you, Jack. You guys work out the details, but look at it this way. Jack comes to you because he knows he can trust you and avoids the lawyers, saving the City millions. Now, you're a hero to the City. Jack's name gets cleared, and he gets his job back. Everyone's happy."

"No arguing the lawsuit will be a monster the City can't afford, considering how much unexplained money the City is losing," the Chief says as he walks back to his desk, slides into his chair, and contemplates.

"There's actually a grill big enough for you to go through in that room?"

"Yes, there was when I was nine."

"We took your fingerprints when you were in the hospital, right?"

"Yep." Beth walks up to the corner of the Chief's desk and puts her hand on the polished wood. "I'm sure you have someone who knows how to lift those prints?"

"Absolutely and, Jack, I'm sorry this happened to you, and I hope you only partially blame us." He looks at Beth.

"Sir. If I get my career back with opportunities to get back on track, then I'm happy."

"I can arrange that, Jack."

"Sounds to me like you boys are going to play nice."

"Thanks, Beth."

"Hey, no problem, but let me know if the City tries to pull anything. You know how to call me." Beth points to his ribs.

"Will do. Thanks."

"Oh, Chief. Do you know anyone on harbor patrol?" she asks.

"Sure. It's one of my departments. Why?"

"Can you call and tell them to stay away from the fog bank in the harbor later?"

"Do I even want to know why?"

"Witch… magic… stuff. Not for the non-magic folk. Get it?"

"Got it."

"See ya."

"Hey, where did she go?"

"She does that, Sir."

387

WITCHING HOUR

Saturday–September 6–0000

Beth reappears in the healing room only a few feet from Karse.

"Nice to have you back so quick, lass."

"A promise kept and a wrong undone."

Beth looks around at the sullen faces of Abigail, Lochran, Taelene, and Nadeh before she sees Freya and Egret standing against the wall.

"Freya, Egret. Why are you here?"

"LysaBeth, we have many reasons to be here," Freya says. "First, to return the amulet. Remember, only release Princess Mehla after the Orb rises, or she will rampage." Freya holds the amulet out to Beth.

"Okay. That doesn't sound good," Beth says, taking it.

"Child, Freya, and I have been working on discovering Sorcha's plan. We think she has been testing you."

"Testing. How, Egret?"

"Testing your power and the strength of your force," Karse says as he walks up to Beth. "Sound battle strategy. Know your enemy's strength and weaknesses and prepare for both."

"Karse is right, LysaBeth," Freya says. "That's why they never finished the attack at the warehouse. But Sorcha has made a great mistake in her assessment."

"What mistake?"

"Her efforts, so far, were to break your will. Make you appear weaker than her. She gave brief hints of what she was planning, but not truly what she intends."

"Distraction," Karse says in a contemplative tone.

"Yes, young Chief," Freya says. "But the effort to distract was before LysaBeth joined with the Lysa Mother and drank from the pool of pure energy."

"How did you know?"

"We felt the shimmer," Egret says.

"LysaBeth," Freya says. "Now, you can do things we could never have taught you, but you haven't had time to learn how to use the Lysa power from the Universe. Sorcha draws evil, black energy, which is weaker than white energy. You can crush it."

"So, it's up to me again?"

"No, lass," Karse interjects. "You're a leader. You must show strength and courage. Fight your battle and let the soldiers fight theirs. If you win, we all win."

"And go, poof. Thanks."

"It's the battle that ends the war, lass."

Beth looks around at everyone in the room.

"Okay, we need to outmaneuver that life-sucking bitch and end this."

"The last minutes of this day near," Angus says. "Lauranna and I could not have hoped for a better couple to rule in our stead. Karse, remember your lessons and keep your emotions under control."

"I will, Father."

"LysaBeth. I am very proud to call you my daughter by law. This will be your greatest battle and victory."

"Thank you, Angus... Dad. Our world will remember the sacrifices of the MacShannachan Clan."

Angus thumps the end of the Staff of Souls on the ground to cast a fiery portal behind him and, spinning, he walks into the smokey fire to prepare for his last battle.

Karse is silent as the last wisps of smoke disappear, and Beth takes his hand.

"He didn't know how to say it, but he's proud of you, and he loves you."

"Aye, same here, lass."

The clock tower at the fish market chimes at midnight.

"Witching hour, big boy. We've got work to do."

"Aye, I need to check on Lochran. It's his first command."

"Go. I need to talk to Abigail."

***

Rebekah surveys the dilapidated sports stadium and the three thousand plus witches that have crammed into it. A young goth girl with heavy metal pouring out of her earbuds walks past, spinning a ball of fire at the end of her wand. She carries a handmade broom that looks more like a studded dog harness for a Pyre Wolf. Rebekah turns to walk away and bumps into a witch wearing a floppy hat and a sack dress.

"Oh, dear me. May the queen bless you," the young girl, floating butterflies at the end of her wand, says.

Rebekah watches the witch as she dances away and mumbles, "Yes. May the queen suck your soul out, you airhead."

Rebekah shakes her head. "The tenth-century meets the twenty-first. Portal jumpers, broom, and board riders unite. This plan reeks of failure."

Rebekah stops to watch a new age witch jump out of a portal to another witch's broom, cast a fireball at a makeshift target on the forgotten ball diamond, and then jump into another portal.

"Hit and run tactics. Old school meets new. Hope is still alive," Rebekah says.

Rebekah looks to an old soccer field to see many board riders on every board size, from a skateboard to a surfboard. A young wizard dressed in baggy three-quarter pants, a tie-dyed t-shirt, and sandals, with a Rastafarian braid and hat, carves his board through the field of other board riders. He swings a hurling stick at a floating ball, and another board witch spins backward, knocking the ball out of the way with the tail of his board. A teammate shoots at the lacrosse-dressed goaltender, who snaps his arm and goalie lacrosse stick upward, missing the ball, and the opponents' team roars a cheer for the score. Rebekah stops a young man with a fat lip and a taped gash over his eyebrow, carrying a hurling stick.

"What do you call that game?"

Rebekah has to work to understand the heavy cockney accent. "BOG. It's a street game that mixes hurling, hockey, and lacrosse. Boarders Only Game. I got knocked out," he says, pointing to his bruised face and smiling. "Can't talk, gotta see if I can get back in the game."

He bounces away, shouting because his team has scored.

"Impressive, are they not, Madam Rebekah?"

Rebekah looks at the guard from Francois' prison.

"We'll see when they're under fire."

"*Oui*, Madam, always the test."

"Blood Witches hear me."

Rebekah spins to see Queen Sorcha standing on the roof of the announcer's box. The crowd freezes at the sound of her voice, and the chatter dies. Several Blood Witches gather nearer the box, approaching their queen with apparent apprehension. Sorcha waits for complete silence.

"Tonight, we fight for the survival of our way of life!" Her voice is shrill and clean. "More than a thousand years ago, I had a plan to kill the prince and princess, so this night could never arrive." She pauses, looking out over the masses. "But someone ignored me, and here we are."

Queen Sorcha snaps her arm out to her side, and moments after, Midas Pohl floats into view, arms waving and legs kicking as he screams, "Mercy, My Queen! I beg you!"

Rebekah is on the verge of laughter. "Finally. She's going to suck his soul out in front of everyone," she breathes.

"This Cassubian cur started the attack on the Royals before I gave the command, and I have spent over a thousand years searching for the souls of the prince and princess. Tonight, both souls will be within our grasp."

Queen Sorcha jerks her arm, snapping her fist shut, and Midas Pohl implodes into charcoal dust.

The crowd gasps, and several people cheer.

"That's a new one," Rebekah mutters, and Francois's warning, 'be cautious,' echoes in her mind.

"Blood Witches, do not fail me."

Queen Sorcha disappears, and Rebekah turns to walk away but hears. "Rebekah, darling. What did you think?"

Rebekah reaches out and grabs the young butterfly witch by the arm, and spins her toward Queen Sorcha.

"My Queen. This young witch and I bumped into each other, and she excused herself with 'May the Queen bless you.' I think… she… should be a full Blood Witch."

New age witches nearby hear Rebekah's offer and gather closer.

"Oh, wonderful. What's your name, my dear?"

The young witch looks at Rebekah, and then the Queen, confused. "Your Majesty. I'm called Morning Star."

"Well, Morning Star. Why don't you stick out your tongue and close your eyes?"

Queen Sorcha pricks her finger with the needle fitted into her thumb ring and holds it over Morning Star's protruding tongue until a single drop lets loose the end. It contacts the pink flesh, and Morning Star throws her arms out to her sides as her head snaps back.

"I know the power of the Queen," Morning Star hisses as she falls to her knees, sits back on her haunches, and her eyes open. "I will kill the Royals."

"What lovely gray eyes you have, my dear."

"Thank you, My Queen."

Rebekah looks around and spots the goth girl staring at Morning Star with eyes wide.

"What do you think, sweetie? Care for a high?"

"Oh yeah. Please. Do me next."

"Step this way, young witch, and if anyone else wants a rush, line up behind me."

"Well done, Rebekah."

"My Queen," Rebekah smiles, thinking, *More sheeple for her army.*

SECRET MISSIONS

Saturday, September 6th — 0200

Abigail and Beth release their hands and hug each other. "I love you, Abigail. I'll never forget you." And they separate, so they're looking at each other.

"Stay focused on your duty and let the rest do theirs," Abigail says. "You win, and we all win."

Beth nods. "I know, but I still can't believe it. Now, I need to talk with Taelene."

Before she walks away, Lochran bursts through the healing room door. "We found the enemy."

Karse comes in behind him. "Calm yourself, Captain."

"Chief, the enemy is in an old sports stadium near the outskirts of the city."

"How did we get this information?" Karse demands.

"A young lass from the Scottish guard, while patrolling, saw a witch disappear through a shield over a stadium on the outskirts of the city," Lochran answers.

"Why are we patrolling so far out?"

"Angus was sending a patrol out to the edge of the city every few hours for a look-see, and it worked."

"Lochran, bring the witch to me."

"Aye, Chief."

Lochran walks to the doorway and sticks his hand out.

"Wait," Beth says.

Lochran pulls his empty hand back.

"What is it, LysaBeth?"

"Karse, it feels wrong. It's like a gift timed right."

"Who's the witch?" Breena says.

"Caitlin," Lochran says.

"I've known her since she was little," Breena says.

"Karse, it feels too opportune. Inviting her through the barrier makes another weak spot," Beth says.

"Let's talk to her outside the healing room," Karse says, winking at Beth.

Lochran and Karse leave the healing room and return minutes later.

"I'm going to send a small patrol with Caitlin to see if her story is true," Karse says.

"How long will that take?"

"Only a few minutes."

Five minutes later, when the patrol returns, Karse and Lochran meet them outside the healing room. After a brief discussion, both men return to the healing room where Beth awaits.

"It's true then," Lochran says as they walk back into the healing room. "Their hiding under a shield spell at the abandoned sports field."

"Aye, so it seems. But we cannot find how many are there without exposing that we know," Karse says, looking at Beth. "LysaBeth might be right. It's too opportune. Maybe they're trying to draw us into a smaller fight. A distraction." Karse winks at Beth again.

"We can put a lookout near it," Lochran says.

"Aye, but make sure they're above it and can see all sides. Send four Guardians."

"Aye, Chief."

"Wait." Beth turns and nods to Taelene. "Taelene and I will go."

"Why?" Lochran asks.

"We can see the shield, and maybe I can see through it."

Taelene and Nadeh walk up to Beth's side.

"I will go with them without a rider," Nadeh says.

"LysaBeth," Karse protests. "We need you here."

"We can fly high over the stadium, see if there's any sign, and come right back," she insists. "If they're right, then Nadeh can fly back, and you send the troops."

Karse nods, so Beth, Taelene, and Nadeh turn to the back of the healing room, where the trap door opens to the underside of the building. Taelene and Nadeh enter the supplies room first, but Beth stops a few feet back from the threshold, where the concrete floor changes to wood. Changing her eyes to check for boats under the building, Beth, in a deliberately louder voice, says, "Okay, let's get these supplies to the front."

Taelene and Nadeh look back at Beth in confusion until Beth presses her finger across her lips, holding her other hand in the stop position. Taelene and Nadeh freeze. Beth points to the floor then walks her fingers on her palm, signaling someone is under the floor.

"Take those two boxes there."

Taelene and Nadeh each grab a box, walk back toward Beth, and the trio retreats to the healing room.

As they walk around the curtain, Karse, preparing to say something, sees Beth put her finger across her lips, and his hand slips behind his back to draw his wand from its holster.

Beth presses into his arms, whispering, "The enemy is underneath us."

Beth slides out of his arms and turns to Abigail and whispers the same in her ear.

"The lookouts are on the way," Lochran says.

"Good. Get the rest of the Guardians ready to attack the field as soon as they see the witches are there."

"But…" Karse, his finger across his lips, signals Lochran to walk to him, but Abigail gets to him first.

Abigail takes her face away from Lochran's ear.

Karse pulls Lochran to him. "We need to let everyone know without alerting the enemy. Do you know what I mean?"

"Aye, I understand."

"Go."

"Let's get the rest of the rations for tonight," Beth says.

Beth signals Karse to come with her as she forms a looking glass and leans into him.

"Wand Witches can't see through heavy concrete, but I can."

Karse looks, seeing hundreds of witches on witch boards and brooms under the concrete floor and hundreds more hovering under the wooden floor that reaches out over the water.

"The volume of the other room is still the same, so Lochran is succeeding," Karse whispers.

"What time is it?" Beth says.

"A little more than an hour to go," Karse says as he swings his body into Beth's and puts his lips to her ear.

"LysaBeth. We must protect Breena."

"Okay, Karse. What aren't you telling me? Again."

"Breena is a Raziiair Siren. She will live past our victory. She has to live and have children, or we lose the Siren forever."

"Holy crap, Karse. Why didn't you tell me sooner?"

"I am responsible, not you."

Beth's hand slides up the side of his head, then he feels her powerful grip twisting his head to look her in the eyes. He lets out a slight whimper.

"Mister. I'm tired of you not telling me things. I'm your wife and the princess, and you need to get a new attitude. Do you hear me?"

"Aye, sorry, love."

Beth lets Karse go as she lets out a low grunt of frustration.

"I can put her in an armor shield that nothing can break."

Karse rubs the side of his head.

"Good idea, lass. I think I'm bleeding."

Beth jabs her fist into his ribs, making him groan.

"Do that again, and I promise you will definitely be bleeding."

Karse looks around the room at the blank faces staring back at him.

"Aye, newlyweds. Learning each other."

No one changes their looks, so he turns away and walks toward Breena, still rubbing his head. Beth looks at Taelene and Abigail and winks.

Lochran walks into the room and nods his success at Karse as he continues toward Beth.

"The brown girl wants to take her boyfriend out of the glass," he says. "Forty-five minutes to go."

"Game time," Beth says.

Beth walks to Karse. "Time to break the glass," she says and continues out the door where the pyre wolves stand, with one facing in each direction.

Pyreus lowers his head and starts growling at Beth as she approaches, and Beth stops only inches from his nose.

"I'm in the right mood to beat your ass with a fire extinguisher," she says, and breathes a stream of ice-cold air into his nostrils. Pyreus shakes his head and sneezes as he moves out of her way.

"I thought as much," Beth says.

Aaghnya makes a graceful bow toward Beth and holds it until she gets beside Rhynan.

"We've never met. I'm LysaBeth."

Standing straight, Aaghnya says, "It is a great honor to meet a Lysa."

"I hear you're a powerful witch."

"The mother has blessed me with many gifts."

"I hope you're ready to use them because we're in a fight and heavily outnumbered."

Aaghnya nods, throws her arms out in a big arc, casting a shield over the three of them.

Beth changes to her robes, then placing her glowing palm against Rhynan's chest, a white light flashes, blinding Aaghnya and filling the shield. As the light fades, Rhynan drops to the floor, drawing full breaths, and

Aaghnya dashes to his side, lifting his head and pulling him to her chest.

"Rhynan. My Rhynan Doon. You have come back to me."

Aaghnya looks at Beth. "Thank you, Princess."

"No problem. Keep him alive for another forty minutes because we need what's inside him."

"Yes, Princess. I will keep Rhynan until we are old."

"Wonderful. Invite us to the wedding."

Aaghnya, so focused on Rhynan, doesn't respond to Beth's comment.

WARRIORS UNITE

Saturday, September 6th — Less than an hour to go

A blue smoke portal forms in the back supply room, and Gabrielle staggers out.

"They are attacking the island," she says, panting.

Karse shakes his head at Gabrielle and points to the floor as he crosses his lips with a finger, but he's too late. They hear a witch under the wooden floor scream, "ATTACK!" and Karse spins to everyone behind him shouting, "TO BATTLE!" and waving his wand, drops the protection shield guarding the healing room.

An explosion rips the wooden section of the building away from the concrete floor and drives the debris toward the warehouse. Karse looks over his shoulder as Gabrielle reaches the concrete archway between the exploding wooden healing room and the warehouse. She gives him a soft smile, throws herself in the air, and spins back toward the exploding section of the building. Debris rockets toward Gabrielle, suspended in the air with her arms out to her sides, and she casts a shield to protect the others from the explosion. The shock wave rolls past Gabrielle and through the warehouse, tumbling near everyone, but the flying debris stops as though suspended in time. Then Gabrielle's shield shoots the debris back at the attacking force, all but annihilating it with the shrapnel of wood and metal, and Karse witnesses Gabrielle's life explode into smoke.

"Retreat!" yells a Blood Witch.

"Nadeh, we fly!" shouts Taelene.

Beth's heart sinks as the healing room explodes, and she stands, near shock, until she hears Taelene's Raziiair call as she slips across the horizon from behind a remaining sidewall of the warehouse. Beth breaks into a run, casting a ball of light through an open forklift door of the remaining dockside of the warehouse.

"Move!" Beth yells as she touches her ear.

"Karse, do you hear me?"

"LysaBeth, they have started their attack on the island."

"Stay alive, husband."

"And you, my love."

Beth touches her ear again.

A path opens between Beth and the forklift door, and as she crosses the threshold, she's surrounded by red smoke and when she clears the smoke, dressed in her flight suit, she locks eyes with Karse. He covers his heart with his hand and he remembers the first time he saw her at the warehouse. As he watched her step from her portal, cloaked in a glow like an angel, Karse thought her a rare, muscular beauty with facial features chiseled, as though the gods themselves performed the work. He heard no sound, felt no wind, and had no sense of smell or taste. His heart pounded as hard as a hammer striking the anvil.

He remembers sitting on his Rostovie Wolf-Horse and asking himself. "Is this the Angel of Death? Has this beautiful lass stopped time and taken my life away with me, no feeling or knowing the last moments I existed? Am I waiting for my heart to stop?" And it happens again, as if minutes are flying by. No sound, he feels no wind nor smells or tastes the ocean air. His heart pounds and as Beth nods at him and launches herself through the air as though diving into the harbor waters, his senses return and his stomach knots with fear.

"Lysa Mother, protect you, my love," he whispers.

Taelene sweeps up from below the dock surface, catching Beth as she falls through the open shield feathers and landing in the saddle.

Need a ride, Princess?

"Nice catch, tough girl."

Where are we going?

"The island is under attack."

Which island, Beth?

"We should be able to see the shield."

How did they find out?

"There must still be a snake in the grass."

Must be.

"Let's take it to them," Beth says.

Agreed.

Beth changes her eyes to night vision and looks up to see Nadeh circling.

"Nadeh is high," she says. "And I assume you two have worked out your signals?"

Ahh, ya. About that.

I to hear you, Princess, comes Nadeh's voice.

"What the what? Taelene. How did that happen?"

Beth. It's not what you think. Nadeh and I might have… forever… agreed to make baby crimsons after this over.

"Oh, I'm pissed."

What? Why can you marry, and I can't?

"No. It's not that. I'm pissed because I didn't get to use my maid of honor status."

Okay then, it's official. A double wedding.

"Done."

They both laugh.

Taelene, behind you! Nadeh says.

Beth pokes through the shield feathers and looks back to see a flock of Raziiair moving in fast.

"Wow, that's an enormous flock of Raziiair."

Beth. I don't want to kill Raziiair.

"I agree. The Raziiair are victims of a spell, but the riders volunteered to let that psycho queen drop blood into their mouths, so they get zero compassion from me. How do we defeat them?"

We target the riders only.

"Tall order. Let's try it."

Thanks, Beth.

As Beth tucks in again, she connects her eyes with Taelene and notices a faint wave of magic in the distance.

"Taelene. This is going to seem weird."

Wow. What did you do?

"I'm sharing 'my' night vision because it can show me things, like that wave."

Where's that coming from?

"That's shield magic."

Is that the shield over the island?

"Yes. But I don't see anyone attacking it. Nadeh, can you see the shield?"

Not the shield, but I will see the magic being used to attack it.

"Nadeh, do you see anything?"

No. No fighting.

"They don't know which island. It's a trick for us to show the island. Quick, turn back and dive toward that small one."

That will put the enemy high, and they will have the advantage, Taelene.

I might need you to change their focus, Nadeh, Taelene replies.

I can do that.

"No. We need Nadeh as our lookout. Nadeh. Don't expose yourself," Beth orders. "Avoid the fight for now and keep us informed of what you see. You are our eyes up high. Do you understand?"

As you wish. I will widen my circle.

"Taelene, land at the edge of that island, and I'll make us invisible. They'll think we went under a shield."

I won't be Raziiair anymore.

"Don't worry. I have a plan. Which island is that?"

Hangman.

Taelene flares, but Beth makes them invisible in the air, and they crash to the rocky sand of Hangman Island. Beth rolls over her shoulder twice, stopping on one knee, and presses her hand deep into the sand. "Panserskjold" (Armour Shield).

"Ow. A little lower could have been nice," Taelene says.

"Sorry, Taelene, but I had to make it look real."

The first enemy, Raziiair, turns toward them only seconds after the shield covers the island.

"Wow. They took the bait."

She touches her ear. "Karse."

"Aye, love."

"What's happening there?"

"Nothing. Father is back and ready to take the prince to the island, but we don't want to jump him into a battle."

"There isn't one."

"What are you saying?"

"Whoever told you the island is under attack was lying. It was a trick to get us to show which island."

"I don't understand why Gabrielle lied and then sacrificed herself."

"Karse, let's deal with that later. I'm going to the island to talk to Lauranna. Which one?"

"Rainsford."

"Okay. I've got the enemy busy setting up to attack Hangman Island."

"How did you do that?"

"Let's keep that for the pillow talk."

Beth can hear the subdued laughter in Karse's voice. "My pleasure, Princess."

"Later." She touches her ear.

Beth turns back to Taelene, who is still lying on her side.

"Ready to go?"

"Beth, I'm hurt."

Beth walks around Taelene to see blood soaked sand. She kneels to find a gash in her top six inches long and a chunk of metal sticking out of her skin.

"You picked up a rusty piece of metal on the landing."

"You mean crash landing, right?"

Beth looks closer at the wound. "Taelene, it's serious. There's a smack of dirt in that wound. We need to remove the metal and get it cleaned out before I can heal you."

"Is there a healer on the island?"

Beth points her finger skyward and casts a portal above them.

"There better be," she says, snapping her fingers, and the portal drops.

A ring of fog builds out from Hangman Island's shores. Flowing over the water surface, the fog rises to block the City's view of the harbor, then creeps toward the Atlantic ocean.

"My Queen. We followed a Raziiair to Hangman Island and watched her fly through a shield. They are using fog as a cover. Should we start the attack?" asks a leading Blood Witch.

"Excellent. Do not attack. Do you understand me?"

"Yes, My Queen. We wait."

Sorcha waves her hand to close one mirror portal and open another.

"Rebekah, attack Hangman Island with everything."

"Yes, My Queen."

The Civil War-era plantation manor, looking dilapidated with rot, sits surrounded by signs warning the condemned property and no trespass. It's part of the masking spell covering the pristine mansion with gardens full of vegetables and orchards with trees filled with fruit. What looks to be a dangerous, moss laden swamp on the outside is fields of cotton and berries that often have machinery moving through them. But it's quiet at two-forty in the morning.

Inside the mansion, Queen Sorcha sits on the throne chair she took from King Aodh's castle, and above her head, perched on the seat-back, sits a raven, three feet tall. The raven's head follows Sorcha as she stands and walks around the back of the chair, and brushes her hand on the raven's back, asking, "Do you remember that night, my pet? The night that guard persuaded unsuspecting twelve-year-old Rebekah to join him for a drink of wine, laced with a sleeping potion? When I discovered the guard's plan, I sent you to find Rebekah before he could finish his foul deed, and you, my pet, drove your beak through that filthy pig's head. Do you remember how Rebekah swore allegiance to me for the rest of her life?" Sorcha slaps a vase from a table, smashing it against a wall. "After learning of the guard's plan and her narrow escape?"

A person, hearing Sorcha's screaming and the smashing vase, half steps from behind a wall but lingers in the shadows.

"Rebekah, darling. You... have lied to me. Francois lays in your bed, at your not-so-secret hideaway, awaiting my victory, but I'm afraid your plans, whatever they may be together, are going to be delayed."

Sorcha turns to the figure in the shadows.

"Are you ready to stretch your wings and get revenge on the Royals, my dear?"

A gray-eyed black man steps out of the shadows.

"Yes, My Queen."

He bows, and his blanket slips to the floor, revealing deep, cut scars on his back.

"Then it's time for Tefari, the mightiest Crimson Raziiair, to fly into battle one more time and get revenge for the senseless killing of his wife and daughter."

"I ask only for my revenge on the Royals."

Sorcha waves her hand in front of herself and changes into black, flowing robes with Princess Sadreen's crown sitting on her head.

"Finally... the end. And we'll both get revenge."

Tefari changes to his Raziiair form, and Sorcha mounts the disfigured saddle.

"Time to repay a few people," she hisses.

***

Guardians on Rainsford Island, surrounding the treed Drumlin, watch with wands pointed as the portal lifts skyward, leaving Beth and Taelene on the rock and sand mixed shore, in the same position as they were on Hangman Island.

"Princess. We didn't expect you yet," says Lauranna, looking down from the top of the Drumlin.

"Taelene's wounded. She needs a healer."

An elderly woman floats from the grassy top down to Beth.

"I am Erin. I have taken Tonique's place until she returns." Her quiet but confident English tone relaxes Beth.

She feels the calm flow over her in waves and says, "You're a Whisperer?"

"Yes, Princess. You are well-trained."

"My name is LysaBeth."

"Yes, LysaBeth. It is an honor to meet a Lysa."

Beth had been told of Whisperers during her training. How they can take the pain away, calm an angry beast, and even stop a blood-thirsty ruler from killing by whispering calm thoughts. They taught her that dark Whisperers are rare, but they can use their power to destroy kingdoms if they turn dark.

Erin reaches for Taelene, and Beth grabs her hand.

"*Vis Meg.*" (Show me).

A white glow flows from Beth's hand and around Erin. Beth releases her hand.

"Had to make sure Taelene is safe."

"Yes, LysaBeth."

Erin leans to Taelene's ear, whispering, and Taelene's head falls to her arm as she fades into sleep.

"We can move her now."

Two healing witches that joined Erin wave their wands over Taelene, levitating her and themselves from the ground to the grassy knoll of the Drumlin, thirty feet above them. Erin looks at the wound as Taelene floats by and then back at Beth.

"She is Raziiair?"

"Yes."

"She will not fight this battle. The metal is in the muscle, and it will not heal today."

"If you can clean it, I can heal it with pure white energy."

"If you heal her fast, it will forever harm her flying. White energy does not weave the flesh back to its original state like our magic, and remember, white energy does not solve everything, LysaBeth."

"I need Taelene. I need to fly and fight at the same time."

"Taelene will not be ready."

Erin floats away, following the witches who carry Taelene, and Beth levitates to catch up, asking, "What about Faerie Water or pure Faerie Pool water?"

Erin turns back. "Yes, pure Faerie Pool water will speed the healing, if we had any. The pools have lost their magic long ago."

Rebekah hovers her witch board, as over three thousand board, broom, and portal mounted witches surround Hangman Island, and she shouts, "Now!"

They bombard the shield with destructive magic for a full minute, with no effect, and Rebekah shouts, "Cease fire. Cease fire."

The exploding curses have cleared the fog from the top of the shield, so Rebekah glides her board close to the surface of the shield and kneels. Cautious of a hidden curse, she touches her wand on the shield. "Nothing," she says and places her hand on the cold, wet surface of the armor shield. After a few moments, she shouts to the Blood Witches, "They've tricked us."

Rebekah's board shoots straight up as she stands and spins toward the open ocean as she shouts, "Spread out. Search the islands for another shield."

Rebekah casts a mirror portal, and Sorcha's face emerges.

"My Queen. They have tricked us. The shield on Hangman Island is an armor shield, and there's no life on the island."

Sorcha's eyes turn black with rage.

"I've started a search for another shield, My Queen."

"We have fifteen minutes to find it. Do not fail me, Rebekah."

The mirror turns to gray smoke, and Rebekah contemplates the call.

That's the first time, ever, that her eyes have turned black against me. There's more to this.

Rebekah makes a tail turn with her board, like a surfer cutting into a wave, in time to see a witch's energy ball bounce off Rainsford Island.

"There you are. Surround that island!" Rebekah shouts as she casts a mirror portal.

"Sorcha, we found it."

"Ten seconds, and I'll be there."

"We'll wait for you."

"Please do, darling."

The mirror turns to smoke and after a few seconds, Rebekah holds the tip of her wand near her bottom lip and whispers. She casts a spin ball that carries the message to Francois, before she changes from her dress and heels to magical armor.

"Fashion will have to wait. No sense taking chances."

"LysaBeth."

Beth, looking out over the eastern water, breaks from her thought trance.

"Lauranna."

"We need your barrel of water."

"My what?"

"The barrel of water Egret gave you. We need it."

Beth looks confused for a few more seconds. "Oh no. I forgot about it. Be right back."

"What barrel?" Erin says.

Beth fades away like water evaporating and returns the same way, with the wooden barrel in her arms.

Lauranna takes the barrel from Beth and pauses while looking into her eyes.

"LysaBeth. You have great power. Be careful that it doesn't consume you."

"I will, Lauranna, but I didn't know I could do that. Why do you need the barrel?"

"Follow me."

Lauranna, a single wave of her hand as if wiping moisture from a ten-foot glass sheet, drops the veil of natural vegetation protecting the Circle of Nine Witches, centered on the North-East end of the island. A kilometer wide ring of ground in the center of the Drumlin levels and smooths with sand and grass. Marker stones, laid out by Lauranna, rise inches above the ground, forming the Circle of Nine Witches. Lauranna leads Beth and Erin into the center of the Circle, saying, "Egret told you it has the pure water of the Faerie Pools, but..." Lauranna sets the barrel at the edge of an indentation in the ground nine feet long, six feet across, and three feet deep. Lauranna stands as she pushes her palm against the side of the barrel, and it falls into the hole, cracking open like an egg. "It has what makes the pure water in the Faerie Pools."

The barrel of water splashes to the bottom of the indentation, and small, winged Sylphs and Undines play in the water as it gets deeper. Hundreds of glass vials tinkle as they roll over each other to settle at the bottom of the pool. Lauranna waves her hand, and the vials float out of the filling pool to the side.

An angelic female spirit rises from the pool's center, and Lady Lauranna gives a slight bow with her head, saying, "Water Spirit."

The Water Spirit looks at Beth and gives her a slow, deliberate nod of respect, saying, "I see the glow of white energy. You must be a Lysa."

Beth returns the nod. "I am LysaBeth, daughter of LysaSearin, and daughter of the Lysa Mother."

Still, in her flight suit, Beth changes to her robes of gentle green.

"We need your strength because we have been asleep for too long," the Water Spirit tells her.

"How can I help you?"

"Feed us white energy, so we can feed the princess. Be warned, though. The shield will drop, and the ceremony must begin for you to feed us."

"Lauranna. I hurt Taelene when we distracted the enemy to Hangman Island, and with the shield gone, we're exposed."

"The shield must come down so the Universe can hear my Siren call, and the Raziiair know they're needed."

"What time is it?"

415

"We have ten minutes."

Beth waves her hand in a circle and a vial of Faerie Water, from the stack on the ground, drops into her other palm. Beth hands it to Erin, saying, "Only one drop."

"She will not be drinking the water. I will mix it in a potion to pour in the wound and with the Mother's blessing, you will have your Raziiair, LysaBeth."

"Thank you."

A flaming portal opens in the middle of a field and, led by Angus and the Pyre Wolf, Aaghnya and Rhynan float out of the fire in a protective bubble.

"It's time. Take the prince to the building," Angus says as he points the Staff, and a small shack appears to the side of the Circle.

Angus points the Staff at the east side of the Drumlin and opens a portal ringed in shifting colors.

The first through, the African warriors, dressed in wraps decorated with runes and paint on their bodies, carry shields that flow with the same shifting colors as the ring, and spears, also their wands, glow at the tips. They chant as they form a circle around the ceremony, a hundred feet from the center, and then quiet. A giant man of the warrior tribe, wearing a headdress, takes a position in the warrior circle and at the edge of the Circle of Nine Witches. He starts a low, resonating tone and, as it gets stronger, Beth feels it vibrating in her chest. The rest of the warriors stomp their feet in rhythm, tapping the butt ends of their spears on the ground, as the big man chants in his language while doing a slow dance. He shouts to the sky, slams his hands together, over his head, with a loud gunshot clap, and a warrior clone steps out of each African warrior in the circle. The new warriors rise and slip back as if they're on the next level of bleachers in a football stadium. The big man repeats his chant and dances until five rings of African warriors stand near thirty feet high around the ceremony.

Beth turns back to the portal as multi-colored dragons appear in the ring and a Chinese woman dances out of the smoke. Dressed in silk robes, with her hair floating around her head and shoulders, she spins and flips in moves Beth recognizes as martial arts. She's followed by a small army of female and male warriors, each of whom takes a place between the African warriors on the upper two layers.

The ring colors change to multiple images of a rising sun as the leader of the Samurai Wizards rides out of the portal on a two-headed horse. Barking an order, Samurai wizards flood out of the portal and surround the African warriors ahead of their bottom row. The horse-mounted leader shouts a command, and the Samurai draws their swords of glistening white energy, taking a stance and shouting, 'Hai'.

The portal ring changes to rolling red and blue colors and Beth catches her breath as a slender Asian woman with dark hazel eyes, a rounder face with high cheekbones, dressed only in vines and leaves, slips out of the blue smoke.

She stops in front of Beth. "Are you the Lysa?"

"I am."

"We are the Earth Witches of forty-five from Korea, and we come to serve the princess who saved us from certain death over a thousand years ago. I foresaw that today is the day that most of us will return to the Earth, but that is our willing sacrifice."

"How can I help you?" Beth says.

"Once we build ourselves over the ceremony, you can feed us your white energy to strengthen our bond and keep us alive longer."

"I will."

She bows to Beth, and the Earth Witches form a circle between the battlefield and the Nine Witches, holding the Crystals.

The ring of the portal changes to purple and white, and flashing images of idols from India. The mystical Indian warriors, dressed in white satin with royal purple turbans and sashes, flood out, taking positions between the African Warriors on the lower three levels. They draw swords with vapor-like blades, rippling with color as light passes through.

Beth turns to watch the Earth Witches shape-shift into trees and shrubs. Their roots sink deep into the ground, and their branches twist together, weaving a framework similar to the crafted gold cage around the amulet jewel that holds Mehla.

Beth looks back to the portal as images of mountains fill the portal ring and the Yamabushi wizards, who live solitary lives in the mountains of Japan, flood through the portal and climb the branches of the Earth Witches. Beth watches as they stop along the way to deposit magic protection in the pockets between the branches, where a curse might slip in. The branches reach the highest point, making an open ring for the Raziiair Sirens light, that the Yamabushi must protect. Beth kneels, placing her hand against the trunk of the lead Earth Witch and her other hand on the ground. She closes her eyes.

"Mother Lysa, please give them the strength to endure."

Beth feels a rush as her body glows, and the white energy flows through her, into the tree base and the earth. She opens her eyes, surprised to see small flowers and bright green leaves growing on the tree branches, and Beth looks up to see the Yamabushi wizards meditating.

"Now that's discipline," she says.

The crack of the collapsing portal surprises Beth, and she jumps to her feet. Then Lauranna slips her hand around Beth's arm, startling her.

"Calm, LysaBeth. Now, we must drop the shield."

"So begins the battle."

"It has already," and Lauranna looks skyward.

"I wish I had Taelene."

Princess, what happened to Taelene? demands Nadeh.

"Nadeh? Where have you been?"

I followed three Raziiair to New Orleans, where I saw a Crimson Raziiair break out of a masking spell.

"Wow. Points for tenacity."

What happened to Taelene?

"She's hurt because my plan to trick the enemy away from this island didn't go well, and she can't fly yet. Nadeh, I thought you and Taelene were the only Crimson Raziiair left."

We thought that was true, but it's here now.

"Can you see the rider?"

Yes. The rider is wearing black robes and a tiara.

"Oh no. Nadeh, that's Sorcha. You must stay away from her. She's an evil Spirit Witch and will kill you in a blink."

Princess. The Crimson is not as quick as it should be. I think something has injured it, and I am faster and more maneuverable, but I need a rider.

Beth doesn't respond for a few seconds.

"Do you know how pissed Taelene will be when she finds out I rode you into battle?"

Not as pissed as she is going to be if you don't get on me and finish this. Taelene's thoughts surprise them both.

"Taelene, you're awake," Beth says, as Taelene's wing shadow flows across the ground.

Hell yeah. Get your silver spoon ass in the saddle, and let's finish this thing, girl. Or do I have to take you for another round?

"Happy to have you back, tough girl."

The fog has flooded the Boston Harbor, covering the boats anchored and stopping the ones still trying to outrun the thick white mist. Above Rainsford Island, bursts of bright light silhouette flying witches as they twist and turn, avoiding or casting curses at their enemy. The occasional scream ends with the sound of a large object splashing into the harbor, but sometimes it's silent before the splash.

"Watch your flank, Lochran," Karse warns as he turns his Rostovie Wolf-Horse, and dodges a curse. Lochran turns his witch board, casting a curse, hitting his target, then spinning away from the flailing witch.

"They're jumping out of portals and on to brooms and boards," Lochran replies. "How do you fight that?"

"Do the same."

"Oh, aye. Good idea."

Karse laughs, then sees the ripple of the shield over the island dropping.

"Lochran, the shield is dropping."

"Aye, we're at war."

Karse turns his steed and casts a curse that knocks a portal jumper back through the portal. A broom flying witch makes the mistake of getting close to Karse as he avoids a curse, and Karse wheels his horse, grabs the shaft of the witch's broom and separates it from the rider.

"Lochran, have you tried one of these?" Karse asks, holding the broom over his head.

"No. Have you?"

"What? And give up my horse. Are you daft?"

"Aye, give it over. I'm going to die either way, so I might as well try something new."

Lochran jumps from his board and grabs the broom.

"I'm sure I'll get an ill-placed splinter from it." But Lochran gets a pleasant surprise as he straddles the broom, landing on a seat that fits him, and sling stirrups catch his heels.

He tucks his kilt under his rear, saying, "Aye, I could get used to this."

He rolls and casts a curse that takes another broom rider out of the fight.

Karse looks around at the Guardians fighting against odds of five to one, and he feels the desperation. A sharp scream and a Blood Witch turns to glass in midair and falls to the island's rocks below, shattering into pieces.

Another Blood Witch shouts, "The Glazier are helping the Royals!"

Naise Lagrandeur leads over three-hundred Glazier into the fray from the East, and the Blood Witches scatter.

"The shield has dropped! Attack the island!" Queen Sorcha screeches as she puts her Raziiair into a dive.

Sorcha sees Rebekah at the other end of the island, with a full shield in front of her, leading two-thousand witches on brooms, and boards, on a frontal assault that takes them into the largest gathering of Royal supporters.

"I see you're wearing your armor, Rebekah," Sorcha mumbles. "Clever girl, but that won't save you."

Rebekah focuses on the small building to the side of the pool of Faerie Water, where she knows Aaghnya will have Rhynan. She snaps her wand downward, changing it to a semi-transparent blue-light sword she uses to cut through the front line of warriors. Rebekah's shield takes a curse from the African Warrior leader, almost knocking her from her board. She recovers and breaks off from her frontal attack, turning toward the small shack as two more glass figures crash into the rocks. Rebekah glances up in time to see a Glazier cast a curse at her, and she carves a turn like a professional snowboarder, dodging it. She swings underneath the Glazier, turns her body backward, and casts a curse, petrifying the Glazier. The petrified Glazier falls hard on the sharp rocks along the beach edge, and Rebekah laughs as she cuts another turn to rally her troops.

ROYAL SOULS

"I see Rebekah's in top form," Beth says as Taelene takes flight.

Do you want to go kick her butt first? Taelene says, laughing.

Taelene, do not mistake Rebekah's power. Tonique's voice rings in, and Beth hears it through her connection with Taelene.

Taelene flips her head left and then right to see wings on the eastern horizon.

Mamma? Is that you flying in from the East?

Yes, Taelene. Now focus on the fight.

Tonique? How can we hear you from so far away? What are you doing here? Where's my mother?

LysaBeth. Raziiair has the ability of telepathy, as do the Lysa. Now calm yourself.

Beth catches her breath as her mother's voice echoes through her connection with Taelene.

Mom? Is that you?

Yes, LysaBeth. Now calm yourself and be the witch you are. We only have minutes until we must release the prince and princess.

Mom, it's dangerous for you to be here.

I'm fine, sweetheart. I have touched the pool of white energy. Now, you must focus. LysaBeth, listen to my voice. Let the calm flow through you, and think of healing the magical world, and the Universe will share its power. No one person matters. Calm yourself.

LysaBeth closes her eyes and gathers her rampaging emotions. She imagines the white energy flowing into her and her body tingles.

Beth, I feel that, and we're not even tethered, Taelene thinks.

Beth opens her eyes, and the battle takes shape in slow motion.

A giant flash of light and Taelene turns her body, so her breastplate shields Beth.

She levels her flight. *Beth, are you okay?*

"Yeah. What happened?"

Look at the circle. The top of the circle shield's gone. Something destroyed half of the Yamabushi wizards, and the rest are running on the branches of the Earth Witches, casting magic.

Taelene turns to circle the shield.

"Look, Taelene. A dark rot is taking over a line of branches. Oh, no! That line leads to the head Earth Witch. The leaves and flowers in the line are wilting."

As the rot touches the ground, the branches crumble, and a wisp of smoke rises.

"Another witch lost. I'll bet Sorcha did that," Beth says.

"Tonique, do you see that?" LysaSearin says.

That's... That's impossible. It can't be.

"Tonique. Is that Tefari?" LysaSearin says.

What? My father's here?

Taelene, stay where you are. Focus on the fight.

Mama, that's my father?

Yes, and if he is under Sorcha's control, he is the enemy.

Mama... you don't mean that. Taelene chokes on the thought.

Stay where you are, Child. Listen to me for once. LysaSearin, I need to go.

"I understand, Tonique," and LysaSearin pops into the air like a pilot ejecting from a jet fighter as Tonique turns away to chase the Crimson.

LysaSearin casts a four-foot Witch Board to land on as she changes from her flight suit to robes and surveys the battle.

Half the enemy has pulled back, forming a circle of Blood Witches high over the island. The circle begins a slow descent, with every witch casting curses at the top of the Guardian force. The barrage of curses threatens to push the Guardians to the ground, until a portal opens and over two-thousand witches, loyal to Obadiah, pour out.

Bolts of lightning strike Blood Witches by the hundreds.

"K.... Killian?" LysaSearin stutters, and she spins her board toward the lightning source.

"Say what!" Beth shouts, and she turns Taelene toward her mother.

"LysaBeth, it's your father."

"How do you know?"

"He is the only one that I know of capable of controlling lightning."

"LysaBeth, look at the Circle," Nadeh thinks.

"Got it, Nadeh. Mom, it's time."

A spout of swirling water, shaped like a trumpet lily, hangs above the burned top of the circle.

Taelene, I need to stand.

What? What are you saying?

Taelene!

Taelene breaks left, then goes vertical in a spin. Beth takes a curse to the body that's absorbed by her flight suit, and she turns Taelene into her attacker.

"Galen. You slithering little sniper," Beth shouts.

Raising his wand above his head, Galen spurs his Rostovie Wolf-Horse forward and shouts, "Time for you too—!"

Galen disappears from his steed, dropping his wand into the harbor waters.

"Ya, whatever, Loser," Beth says.

That was too close. Thanks, Beth. Where did you send him?

"Shark fishing in Australia. He's the bait."

Taelene laughs.

"You and me, girl. Now let's focus," Beth says.

Yeah, sorry.

"We need to power the Faerie Pool water. Circle the water spout. I need to stand."

Taelene opens her shield feathers, and Beth stands on the saddle as air sacs fill, locking her feet like a snowboard binding. She circles her hand over her head, casting a whip of white energy as Taelene turns to fly a circle around the water spout. Beth flicks the whip, so its tip falls into the flute, and it pulses as the white energy flows into the water.

Angus, Staff in hand, stands lost in thought while Rhynan and Aaghnya, holding hands, stand silent near a bed with a carved headboard. Angus draws a heavy breath and looks out the small window of the shack to see the wave of the dropping shield.

"They're dropping the shield. It's time," Angus says, and he casts a hard look at Aaghnya.

Letting Rhynan's hand go, Aaghnya turns to him. She puts her hand on his chest and says, "Rhynan, the Circle Ritual has started."

Aaghnya unbuttons his shirt until Rhynan's hand presses hers flat against his chest and he says, "Aaghnya... No."

"Rhynan, what is wrong? Do you not want me?"

"More than anything, Aaghnya. You are the greatest thing that has ever happened to me, but what I don't want is to make Rebekah right."

"I don't understand, Rhynan."

"Back at the coffee shop, Rebekah asked you if I knew it was only duty and not love."

"Yes. But I told you that my duty has changed to love. You sacrificed your life for me by taking that curse."

"And… if I didn't have the prince inside me, it should have killed me. Aaghnya, I'm on borrowed time. I heard them talking while I was in the glass, and I know there's a risk for you if we do this. I know there's a chance that the power of the prince could kill you as he passes out of me, and I won't let you sacrifice yourself so I can live. You deserve a good life with a guy who knows magic and what your life should be."

Tears streaming down her face, Aaghnya says, "Rhynan Doon. You will listen to me. I need you to be with me forever."

"I'm going to be with you forever, Aaghnya, no matter what happens, because I have loved no one until you."

Rhynan slips his hand around Aaghnya's waist and pulls her body tight to him to kiss her. Aaghnya lingers on the kiss and then pulls back.

"That is better, Rhynan. Now...."

The side of the building explodes inward, and Aaghnya spins Rhynan away from the concussion and flying debris. They fall to the ground, separated. Angus hurls backward, crashing through the slat wall of the building, landing on old foundation stones. Aaghnya tries to lift herself, but a piece of re-bar through her side pins her to the ground, so she places her hand on Rhynan's foot and shields them both.

A broom rider explodes through the standing side of the building, and seeing the Staff of Souls laying on the ground, he grabs it without stopping, and aims for an opening.

Pyreus barks and jumps to the remaining roof of the shack. Teine runs full speed, launching herself from a bird observation dock to Pyreus's back and into the air. The broom riding wizard catches fire as Teine's flaming jaws lock onto his midsection, and he screams as she tears him from his broom that catches fire from her front paw.

Angus runs to catch the falling Staff, and Rebekah casts a death curse at him, laughing in anticipation until a broom riding witch slips between Angus and the curse. The broom rider flails and spins as Angus catches the Staff, and Rebekah pivots her board in time to dodge Angus' retaliation. Rebekah turns again and, exiting across the rubble of the shack, she catches her breath as she passes over the broom rider who blocked her curse.

Lochran MacIlraight.

ROYAL SOULS

Rebekah feels an emptiness deep inside her, and she screams at him.

"Damn you! Why?"

Rebekah shoots skyward to the side of a low cloud, and looking back at Lochran, her mind flashes her memory of his face when she first met him, and her heart pounds. She knew him as a rogue, and her father threatened to kill him if he ever caught him near her, but that didn't stop him. Lochran professed his instant love for Rebekah at their first meeting, and for the next two months, he tracked Rebekah, making hit-and-run appearances, until one day they met away from her father, Paulrig Kheel. Rebekah was so taken by Lochran's efforts that she kissed him when she told him she had to get home. Their rendezvous became more frequent and more passionate until one day, in the forest's silence, Rebekah stood up from their grassy bed and untied her dress. She remembers Lochran's calloused hands scratching against her skin and the nervous look in his eyes as they swam in the pool of adolescent love. For the next four months, they risked everything to swim the waters of adulthood until one night, after dinner, Rebekah developed stomach cramps. During the next two days, the cramps worsened until Paulrig saw the loss of a grandchild. He burst from his hut in a rage, grabbed his wood axe, and went hunting.

Rebekah thought Lochran was dead, but to pacify Paulrig, the king sent Lochran to protect his reign of the Orkney Islands. When she saw him again, they both had grown to different people, but she still felt the want for him.

"That feeling has never gone away," she admits.

Rebekah snaps back and sees Angus running toward Rhynan as the Princess's Orb rises from the pool of water.

"Sorry, lass, but there's no time for a courtship," Angus says, looking at Aaghnya, "and I told him what needed to be done if your plan fails."

Angus puts the Staff near Rhynan, and his hand shoots up, grabbing the middle of it. Aaghnya screams at Rhynan's sacrifice.

Angus lifts, and the prince's soul, holding tight to the Staff, lifts out of Rhynan's body.

"Angus, old friend."

"O'Manus, old friend."

"Aaghnya," Prince O'Manus says. "You have sacrificed much, so the princess and I might reunite. We will not forget your loyalty."

Aaghnya jumps from the ground, screaming as the re-bar rips through her flesh, and she casts a shield over them as the remaining roof of the shack drops.

The three look skyward to see Rebekah floating on her board.

"Well, well, well. Prince O'Manus. Oh my, and a dead Rhynan. Sorry for your luck, sweetie. I suggest ice cream and a chick flick."

Rebekah laughs as she flies away and stops behind the cover of a cloud again before casting a mirror with Sorcha's face on it.

"My Queen. The prince is out, and the ceremony has started."

"Two minutes to kill at least one of them," Sorcha says.

"Sorcha. Have you seen your mother or little sister?"

ROYAL SOULS

"Neither…. but look up."

The blackness takes over as Rebekah plunges into the water.

"Lady Lauranna."

Lauranna turns to the voice.

"Yes, Sarah?"

Sarah flicks her wand upward from beside her leg. A dagger punctures Lady Lauranna's solar plexus, continuing upward until it cuts the inferior vena cava open at the bottom of the heart.

Beth makes the last circle around the water spout and she sees Lauranna drop to her knees.

"Lauranna?"

Beth touches her ear. "Karse, your mother."

She launches herself from Taelene's back and lands near Lauranna. Beth looks at Sarah's blank stare as Caitlin charges forward, shouting, "I'm going to kill you for that."

Beth puts her hand out, stopping her.

"Wait. She's in a trance. She's being manipulated."

Beth snaps her fingers, and Sarah disappears while Caitlin runs away.

Beth leans over Lauranna, saying, "Lauranna, can you hear me?"

Breena comes around from outside the Circle, and seeing her mother on the ground, she runs, then drops to her knees beside her.

"Mother. Do you hear me?"

Karse looks at the circle and sees his mother lying on the ground, so he drives his steed toward her. Karse, reckless about reaching his mother and sister, forgets about the surrounding battle, and a bolt of gray light strikes his horse, knocking his wand from his hand and unseating him.

As he falls, he shouts. "LysaBeth!"

Beth looks skyward at the man she loves falling and shakes her head. She snaps her fingers, and Karse rolls across the ground to only a few feet from her.

"Thanks, lass. Lost my wand."

"What, again? Time to put a string around your neck."

Karse scrambles to his mother's side.

"Mother... Mother." Karse gets no response. He looks at Breena.

"Come, Sister. Time to let loose. You must do it now."

Karse carries Breena, sobbing, to the stone pad carved with runes near the glowing water pool and places her on her knees.

"Think of Mother and your sweet lass, Sheena. Let it come out and call the Raziiair."

He kisses her on the cheek, then clears the circle as the nine witches stand and start chanting.

Breena sobs, and a gentle glow forms around her body and the chanting of the witches increases.

"Karse, stay on the ground. I need to be in the air," Beth says.

"Aye, lass. Oh, can you send my wand if you see it?"

Beth shakes her head and snaps her fingers.

Karse's wand drops to the ground only feet from him, and, picking it up, he looks at Beth with a big smile and says, "Found it."

432

"Love can be painful," she sighs and runs as Taelene skims across the ground at the side of the Drumlin. She throws herself in the air, as if she's diving over a barrier into a pool, and lands on Taelene's back, sliding into the saddle, and Taelene climbs.

Damn, you're getting good at that, Beth.

"Thanks. Where's Tonique?"

Chasing my dad. Open water, east.

Beth looks to see Tonique chasing the Crimson in a long turn.

"Where's my mother?"

West, over the city. She chased a couple hundred witches off, and she's coming back.

"My father?"

Follow the lightning behind us.

Beth turns in time to see a half dozen witches fall at his hand.

"Okay, Sorcha. What's your game?"

The flock of ravens drops on Beth and Taelene, like black tar, pecking and clawing as they drive Beth under the shield feathers. Taelene rolls her body and folds her wings into a power dive. The attack stops as fast as it started, so she loops, opening the shield feathers for Beth to attack.

"The ravens, they're gone. Taelene, are you okay?"

Yeah, what the hell? Are you okay?

"I'm good."

Sorcha has Tefari in a wide turn over open water when Tonique catches up with him and lets out a shrill call. Tefari slows, and Tonique, touching his wingtip, swoops underneath him so Sorcha can't harm her. The gentle brush of their wings reunites them and their lifelong telepathic connection.

"Tefari. Tefari, it's me, Tonique."

"Tonique? How? I thought the Royals murdered you and Taelene."

"Lies, Tefari. You were told lies. By whom?"

"Well, me, of course," Sorcha says. "I couldn't have two of the greatest Raziiair in history fighting against me and stealing *my* Raziiair away, now could I?"

Sorcha shoots up from her saddle, casting curses from each hand that strike both Tefari and Tonique. The two great War-birds shrill in unison before they fold their wings around their bodies and plunge into the ocean.

"Tonique.…" LysaSearin cries out.

Mama, can you hear me? Taelene chokes back a sob.

"I felt her die, LysaBeth," LysaSearin whispers.

Mama. Oh, Mama…

"I felt your pain, Taelene. I really felt it."

LysaBeth, the Orb.

Beth glances toward the ritual circle to see the top of the Orb protruding from the pool in the middle.

"Got it, Nadeh. Taelene, I'm sorry, but we gotta get in this fight."

I understand, Beth. We all have our jobs to do.

Beth turns Taelene toward LysaSearin as a figure with a hooded cloak and eyes of glowing green slits floats to her side.

"Mom. Lookout."

"Hello, LysaBeth." The male voice is gentle with an Irish accent.

Beth draws a sharp breath.

"Dad?"

"Yes. It's wonderful to meet you because I have watched you grow, and you have become a powerful witch. I could hear you across the battlefield."

"How…. how could you hear me that far away?"

"The Lysa's telepathy connection intensified, for me, when your mother connected with you."

"I have so much new stuff to learn now that I am a Lysa."

"In time, LysaBeth," Killian says.

A flash of light wraps around Killian and LysaSearin, and Taelene twists right, rolling and looping over as she forces her shield feathers to hold Beth in the saddle.

"What was that? Hey, where are my parents?"

Beth looks behind her to see Lillian standing on a platform extension, like a diving board sticking out from her portal, laughing and shouting, "Enjoy the time spell, little niece!"

"Bring them back."

"Ta, Ta." Lillian steps backward into her portal and disappears.

Taelene dives, twisting away from the cords of a blue Raziiair shooting over them. Beth reconnects with Taelene to see four more Raziiair above, positioning themselves for an attack.

Beth shoots darts from glowing hands, hitting two riders, scrambling the rest.

"Thanks, Taelene. You saved me."

Beth, we have got to stop saving each other and win this fight.

"I hear that."

Beth, the Orb.

Beth looks through the feathers as Taelene banks left to see the witches in the circle, all pointing wands, crystals, or artifacts at the Orb.

"This is it, Taelene," Beth says, glancing to the battle. "Oh no, Abigail".

"Taelene. Sorcha has a new Raziiair, and she's cast two snow-cats, same as the last ones, into the battle outside the Circle of Nine."

"Now it's time," Queen Sorcha laughs, as she channels dark energy to the Snow Lions.

Abigail, protecting the Circle of Nine Witches, slashes back as she battles the two snow lions.

"Abigail's against two snow-cats," Beth says.

Beth changes her eyes to night vision and sees the black tethers floating through the sky from Sorcha to the Snow Lions.

"Sorcha's feeding them dark energy. We have to save Abigail."

Let's do it.

"I'm going to tether myself. Open your shield feathers."

Trial by fire, huh?

"Sorry, no choice."

Beth hooks her life tether to Taelene's 'T' bone, stands in the saddle and the air sacs lock her feet in place.

"I'm going to share my sight with you, Taelene, so you can see the dark magic. Full speed loop, Captain."

Taelene's wings pull hard through the air, picking up speed and climbing. Beth feels Taelene's body throwing everything into her wings, and she pumps her legs in rhythm as the red glow starts.

"You go, girl!"

Taelene snaps her wings back as she dives, and her glow lights up the entire island.

Beth, I see the black streams.

Beth circles her arms above her head, casting two whips, and the faster she weaves her arms, the longer the whips get.

Taelene circles the Orb and aims toward the two cats.

"Taelene."

Yeah?

"When I say to, flip, so I'm closest to the ground."

You got it.

Taelene aims for Abigail, and a powerful energy flows from Beth as she calmly says, "Wait... Wait... Now."

Taelene rolls as Beth pulls her arm back over her head and the tip of the whip misses Taelene as it snaps to follow Beth's arm. The tip of the second whip nicks a rouge feather along the side of Taelene's throat, and it turns pure white.

Beth casts the first whip, cutting halfway through the snow-cat before it breaks Sorcha's tether, and the cat disintegrates into charcoal dust. The second whip cuts into the remaining snow-cat's rear quarter, and it releases its bite on Abigail's hip as it roars in pain. Abigail twists her body as the snow-cat rolls over, and she lunges onto its back, delivering the final blow, then falls to her side.

Beth closes her eyes and whispers, "Abigail. We need you."

Abigail's head falls to the side, and her tongue falls out of her mouth.

"Abigail. No!" Beth cries out.

Taelene flips Beth upright, and Beth unleashes a flurry of lashes on the enemy as Taelene circles around the Orb.

"I have to go to Abigail."

Beth, we have our jobs to do.

"I know, but the one I gave Abigail is crucial for our victory. We need to do it for her."

Beth, look. Abigail.

Beth looks back to Abigail. "She's gone."

Beth looks to the other side of Taelene to see Abigail dragging the back half of her body across the ground, making her way into the circle.

Beth closes her eyes again and whispers, "You can do it, Abigail."

"Aw. Did your little kitty get hurt?" Sorcha laughs. "Too bad you won't have Princess Mehla to help you either, cousin."

Beth's light whips disintegrate as she hears the taunt.

Taelene arcs her body back toward Sorcha's voice as Beth puts her hand where her amulet should be.

"Ravens. They love shiny objects," Sorcha snickers as she jumps off a Raziiair to a black and gray witch board and holds the amulet at the tips of her fingers with an evil laugh.

Taelene, go help win the fight. I got this. Beth thinks, reaching down and holding the rings of her tether, so the 'T' bone lets go before jumping from the saddle and snapping her fingers to cast a witch board.

ROYAL SOULS

"Where are my parents?"

"Relax, Cuz. They're alive." Sorcha laughs.

"Oh, look, the princess. Futile without the Raziiair Siren, isn't it?" Caitlin says as she floats up to Beth's back right side.

Beth recognizes Caitlin's voice from France and without looking at her, she says, "Guess I know who was controlling Sarah."

"Isn't it wonderful? My daughters playing nice." LysaLillian says as she reappears at Beth's back-left, to complete the triangle.

Beth casts a shield over herself, saying, "Sorcha. Where's your number one? Not having Rebekah join the party?"

"She lied to me, so she paid the penalty."

"Wow. Now you don't have any friends. You should have kept your crazy in the bag."

"Enough games," Sorcha says. "Shall we, Ladies?"

Sorcha, LysaLillian, and Caitlin circle their hands as if they're rubbing an invisible globe while whispering a chant. Two glowing magic lines flow left and right from their chest to the other two, linking their powers.

"Now, Cuz. Let's see how you do against three Spirit Witches."

Sorcha's eyes turn black, and Beth can see the anger that drives Sorcha in the taut jaw muscles.

Beth smiles, saying, "So, this is the evil triangle?"

Breena's glow increases with the rapid chanting from the circle, and her Raziiair Siren call starts as a scream of terror and continues rising in pitch until it's silent. The

Raziiair white light shoots through the top of the Earth Witch structure and the Raziiair Sorcha captured begin bucking, spinning, and twisting, like wild ponies refusing their riders. Blood Witches, some losing their wands as they're thrown from the saddle, plunge to earth, and the Raziiair rise to join a circle led by Nadeh.

9 – 6 – 3

0300

The intensity of the white light cast by Breena penetrates the fog and the streetlight sensors along the shore turn off the streetlights.

Beth glances down at Abigail, saying, "Now, Abigail."

Abigail lifts her blood-soaked head from the round flat-stone next to Breena, heaving and coughing like a cat clearing a hairball, and the gold neck chain, still attached to the amulet, falls from Abigail's mouth. The amulet rolls against her front teeth and, using her tongue, she slips it under her large fang and bites down, driving her fang tooth through the gold and magic glass, and it explodes open, releasing green light. Abigail's head drops hard to the flat-stone, and the amulet falls out of her mouth, breaking apart, and green smoke shoots skyward. Princess Mehla's image stops in front of Abigail's eyes, and Mehla smiles softly, saying, "Abigail, we will win this war because of your suffering and sacrifice. We love you, Abigail."

Abigail's chest heaves one more time and her cat-eye color fades to blank as her tongue falls to the flat-stone.

A long, slow release of her final breath is the last sound Abigail makes.

"How's that for tricky, Cuz? You get a fake amulet, and we have a backup Raziiair Siren."

Beth laughs, releases her shield and witch board, crosses her arms across her chest, and drops toward the Princess' Orb, into the explosion of green light and smoke. Moments later, strings of green and white light shoot out of the green cloud, lassoing both ankles of LysaLillian, Sorcha, and Caitlin, as Princess Mehla and LysaBeth rise to the middle of the evil triangle. Their glowing palms face each other, and threads of magic float back and forth at their fingertips as a circle of soft green light surrounds them.

LysaLillian catches her breath seeing LysaBeth in robes and an emerald rune stone hanging from her full head of hair and mumbles, "She looks like LysaSearin."

Regaining her composer LysaLillian shouts, "Sorcha, you fool. Why didn't you tell us she's a full Lysa?" LysaLillian says.

"Because she wasn't when we last met... Mother. Oh, ya. Didn't you forget to tell me little sister is a Spirit Witch?" Sorcha says.

Beth and Mehla hang their arms out to their sides as the emerald rune hanging on their foreheads pulses in rhythm.

"How about this, ladies?" Beth says. "First, Mehla and I share our power with the witches fighting for the Royals." Thousands of strings of green and white light shoot outward from their fingertips as the green light surrounding them explodes outward like a shock wave,

ROYAL SOULS

enhancing the powers of the Guardians and supporting witches.

Beth's eyes glowing white, and Mehla's green, Beth says, "Now Mehla and I throw you little tarts a well-deserved beat down before we entomb you for all eternity?"

"Enough!" LysaLillian shouts. "It's time for both of you to disappear forever, Little Niece."

LysaLillian's side sweeps her hands toward Princess Mehla, but before she can cast, Princess Mehla snaps her arm out, with her hand shaped as if grabbing a water glass, and LysaLillian's body jerks into a crucifixion position.

"Sorcha?" Princess Mehla says. "You favor the practice of stealing souls for your survival, do you not? In fact, you've stolen so many souls that it's turned you into a rabid, blood-thirsty animal. Do you wish to know how it feels to lose someone that way?" Mehla's eyes lock with Sorcha's. "Shall I?"

"No!" Caitlin shouts. "My mother doesn't deserve to die that way!"

"Caitlin's right. Our Mother doesn't deserve t—" Sorcha goes silent, drawing a sharp breath as LysaLillian's eerie scream pierces the night, and the feeling as if her heart is being torn from her chest grips Sorcha. Caitlin screams as her mother's soul separates from her body, and both turn to dust, falling to the waters of Boston harbor.

"I'll kill you!" Caitlin screams and casts a barrage of curses at Beth and Mehla that explode a foot short of contact.

"See what happens to young witches who play with evil old witches?" Beth says as she wraps Caitlin in a glowing white rope, pinning her arms to her body.

443

"I'm going to murder you for killing my mother!" Caitlin shouts.

"I'll be waiting for you on the other side, Little Witch," Princess Mehla says. "But think of this before you attack. The prince and princess will reunite. Were your mother and sister going to survive the Day of Dust?"

"You know what, Little Cousin?" Beth says. "I'm going to do you a favor. I'm going to ask the Lysa Mother to take you back and give you another chance. But first, we're going to ask her to see the person you truly are."

"My mother told me she doesn't exist. She said it's a bedtime story for good little witches to wish magic upon themselves."

"I was told the same," says Sorcha.

Beth grins and casts a string of white light around Caitlin's wrist, and on the other end, a ball of white light floats high above Caitlin.

Caitlin doesn't shift her murderous glare from Princess Mehla, and Beth lifts her head and hands to the stars.

"Lysa Mother, see your daughter."

Moments later, Sorcha laughs as the white light attached to Caitlin fades until it goes black as the night, then Caitlin screams as a stream of white light shoots down from a star, and she disappears in a mist.

A soft voice fills their ears.

"LysaBeth. One from the Lysa bloodline who is that evil must not live."

"We trust your wisdom, Lysa Mother."

"I heard her," Sorcha says. "The Lysa Mother. She's real? She exists?"

"How about that? You missed your chance," Beth says.

"The time is here," Mehla says. "Thank you, LysaBeth. I wish you and your new husband good fortune and many children."

"Thanks, Mehla. I hope I get to see you again."

Mehla passes the green tether still holding Sorcha, before she drops a hundred feet to the Circle below, and the links between her and LysaBeth fade into nothing.

"Wow. When that woman sets her mind to doing something, she gets it done. Doesn't she?"

"How did she kill my mother?"

"We figured out how you were sharing power through your little spy and knew you were trying to use her to kill me. Then, when you linked with your sister and mother, Mehla used your soul-sucking power against your mother by linking to her. Sorcha, linking, is for a group of wand witches to control a natural witch breaking the laws of the Universe and disobeying the Lysa Mother, not for sharing power. The three of you broke the laws again, and Mehla used that against you. So, technically, it was you who pulled your mother's soul out."

"Yes, well. My little spy didn't survive the full release of my power, either. I thought I could help her build the strength, but evidently not."

"Yeah, the Universe is funny that way. The laws against possession are absolute."

"Then why did it work with Princess Mehla?"

"Simple. She's dead."

Sorcha is silent, then says, "I'm the only one left who knows the year of your parents' time spell."

"Sure, if your mother didn't lie to you."

"Okay. I'll give you that one."

"My mother is a full Lysa, so she'll figure out a way to get back to me."

Beth casts an armor bubble around the two of them and looks around to see Blood Witches disappearing like raindrops in a lake.

"Sorcha. There's something the Lysa Mother asked me to show you before the end."

Beth casts a rope of white light that wraps itself around Sorcha's waist, and, yelling with pain, Sorcha drops to her knees. The rope disappears after a few moments, and Sorcha draws a full breath.

"What did you do to me?"

"The Mother cured you."

"What?"

"Yeah. Your curse. It's cured."

"That's impossible."

"Oh, really? Look at your wound you, idiot."

Sorcha separates her robes at her waist.

"The wound... it's gone. How?"

"That's the power of the Mother."

"My mother told me it was a lie," Sorcha growls. "She told me she tried to connect to the Mother and got nothing."

"LysaLillian wanted the power to kill her mother, the first LysaSearin. Of course, Lysa Mother didn't talk to her. Look at you. You tried to use a love potion and your body to become a Queen. How did that work out?"

"I... I didn't want to be common," Sorcha mumbles.

"If you had put half the effort into becoming a true Lysa instead of evil, you could never have been common."

Sorcha stands, fist clenched. "Easy for you to say, Princess. You have everything!"

"Oh really? You mean fifteen years of thinking I killed my parents because of you. Oh, and don't forget the intense training and loneliness during those fifteen years. Wow, you are so self-centered."

"What do you mean?"

"Do you remember ordering your Blood Witches to attack a house in Boston fifteen years ago?"

Sorcha thinks. "Yes, I do. The two Guardians living there had information of a key to the last victory."

Beth throws her arms out to her sides, saying, "Ta Dah!"

"You?"

"Yep, little ole me. That was my house."

Sorcha laughs. "Wow, talk about missed opportunities. Obviously, the Universe was on your side from the start."

"Look around, Sorcha. The Mother wants peace, and I was born for that purpose. So yes, the Universe is on my side."

Sorcha looks around and then at the Orb to see both the prince and princess. "Well then. I guess it's time."

"It is, and I don't think it's going to end well for you."

"It's good to see you again, old friend," Prince O'Manus says.

"And you, My Prince," Angus says with a slight bow of his head.

"I see Sorcha drew a heavy price from you."

"I no matter, O'Manus, but my heart is heaviest as I look at the body of my wife laying on the battlefield."

"I'm sure she waits for you, Angus."

"As does your princess. Take the Staff and go to her. Free us from tyranny."

"Another time, my friend."

"Another time, my friend."

O'Manus glances back at Aaghnya, saying, "Indian Princess, all is not lost." Aaghnya makes a graceful bow and her head swims as she collapses on top of Rhynan's body.

Prince O'Manus floats across the circle's center as Princess Sadreen floats out of the Orb. Princess Mehla slips through the top of the white light and hovers eye level with her sister.

"Mehla, thank you."

"You would have done the same for me, Sadreen."

"Yes, Mehla, and I'm sorry you didn't get to marry after us. He was a great warrior and the son of a Chief."

"It's okay. I know he's happy with his new bride. She is a powerful woman who will lead well."

"Mehla. How do you know this?"

"I met his wife, LysaBeth, during the hunt for you two."

"It's time, My Princess."

"Mehla..."

"Another time, Sadreen. Go to O'Manus. Free the magic world from this ugliness."

"I love you, Mehla."

"And I love you, Sister."

ROYAL SOULS

Princess Sadreen turns and floats across to Prince O'Manus, placing her hand on top of his.

"I have missed you, My Prince."

"I have missed you, My Princess. I failed to protect you. Will you ever forgive me?" Prince O'Manus says.

"I was foolish and didn't listen to you. Will you ever forgive me?"

Prince O'Manus smiles. "No matter how it goes, you will never let me be at fault?"

"No matter how it goes, My Prince."

"I don't deserve such love and devotion."

"That's what marriage is, my Prince. No-fault. Only love and devotion."

"Our children would have been magnificent because of you."

"Look at how many of our children we lost in this foolish war. When will we learn?"

"Our child will have your passion for peace, My Love."

"And yours for justice, My Husband."

Their lips touch and a small, green light glows in Princess Sadreen's womb. As their bodies fade together, the ball of light grows to the size of a cantaloupe and shoots skyward.

Princess Mehla smiles and fades into the white light.

"The reason I have both of us in this bubble is because of the two potential outcomes," Beth says. "On the one hand, if you turn to dust, I want your remains in a jar, locked in a place so inaccessible that you can never rise from the dead. If you survive, I want to beat your sorry ass and take Princess Sadreen's tiara. Then I'll put you

449

in glass and place you somewhere so inaccessible that the world will never hear your name again."

"Holding a grudge, are we?"

"Well, as Robert would say, 'Ahh, family drama.'"

Beth shifts her eyes for a moment to see a small white ball shoot past them.

Princess Sadreen's crown drops to the floor of the bubble, loud as a whisper.

"What the what? Where is she? No dust?"

Beth touches the side of the bubble. *"Vis meg."* (Show me).

"Sorcha's gone. There's no way she could've escaped," Beth says.

Beth looks around, and everything has disappeared.

"Not a single sign of a battle. Even the shack is standing," Beth mutters.

She picks up the crown and feels strange, then everything goes black.

Fabric softener. I smell fabric softener. Oh, nice. Soft flannel cotton. Feels so good rubbing against my face.

Beth opens her eyes.

"You had me worried. Welcome back."

"Jack? Where am I?"

"My apartment."

Beth turns to sit up, but the pain in her side slows her.

"What happened?"

"You guys sure know how to make the news. Freak light storm over Rainsford Island. Biblical Angel battle in the skies. Someone nailed it, saying it was the witches of old scraping it out to free the magical world."

Beth puts her arm across her forehead. "Less sunlight in the eyes, please?"

"Oh yeah. Sure. I'm enjoying the new life, and the sunshine feels good." Jack draws the curtains.

"What's happening? Where's Karse?"

"Don't know where anybody is."

Jack brings a cup of tea around to Beth.

"Everyone's gone," he says.

Beth shakes her head at the cup of tea.

"Take it, Beth."

Beth looks up to take the cup, and Jack sees the tears rolling over her cheeks.

"I think the rest of the world could take a lesson from you witches regarding cleaning up a mess," Jack says.

Beth scoffs. "Yeah. It works every time. Wipe everything out and start again. We can call it the Dinosaur Spell."

Jack sips his tea as he watches Beth's shoulders shake. He doesn't have to see her to understand the pain she's feeling.

A couple of minutes go by, and Jack takes a deep breath to break the silence.

"Beth, do you want something to eat?"

"No. Thanks, Jack. I should go home."

"Maybe it's not good to be alone right now."

"Sadly, I'm used to it."

Beth turns to Jack. "How did you find me?"

"Oh yeah. Wow, what a ride. It was spectacular. I never want to drive a car again."

"What?"

"Yeah. That distress signal thing you put on me woke me." Jack points to his ribs. "My palm was glowing, so I put it against my side, and one of those smoky ring things you guys jump through appeared right there." Jack points to the middle of his kitchen.

"And?"

"I stepped into it because I thought you sent it. Beth, that was the coolest ride ever. I was flying in a glass tube and saw everything around me. And fast! Holy crap, I couldn't believe I went from my apartment to Rainsford in three, maybe four seconds. That's a forty-five-minute drive on a good day."

"Where was I?"

"Lying in between the rocks. I guess that's where you got the bruised ribs."

"Yeah. Thanks, Dick Tracy."

"That's Lieutenant Detective Tracy, if you don't mind."

Beth smiles, "Nice. Congrats."

"Thanks for my life back, Beth."

"Glad it worked out."

"Anyhow, I scooped you up and stepped back into the smoky thing, and we came here."

"Did you see anything? Any signs of the fight?"

"Nothing, Beth. When the witch's clean house, you do it good." The room is silent until Jack reaches into his pocket and says, "Oh, I found this lying beside you."

Jack walks over to Beth, and she sets her tea on the coffee table as she stands. Tears start flowing again as Jack places the bracelet in her open hand.

"Abigail."

ROYAL SOULS

"Glad I found something important to you."

"Thank you, Jack."

Beth pushes the bracelet against her chest.

"I miss you, Abigail."

"What do you say we see what's happening in the non-magic world?"

Jack grabs the remote control and turns on the television.

"Nobody knows where the black jaguar came from," the news reporter says. "We're told it's at least twice the size or more of a normal jaguar, with fight scars on both sides of its body. Doctor Lorimer, a zoologist, says they're going to capture the big cat to see if they can find its origin. Good luck with that, Doctor. Now to the weather."

"Aah. Sorcha, you trash bucket. Nice try."

Beth reaches her hands to the sky and fine threads of white, blue, and green light, twisting together like a DNA helix, pierce the ceiling of Jack's condo and wrap around Beth's wrists. She's jerked from the floor and spirals upward toward a swirling ring of multicolored light. Beth shoots through the swirling light that explodes like glass hit by a bullet.

"Really, Sorcha?"

"It was worth a try. Almost worked."

"Memory shaping? Running out of card tricks, are we?"

"Hey, a girl's gotta do."

"Sorcha, I am so done with you."

The green ball cast from Princess Sadreen's womb pauses beside Beth, and Sorcha throws her glowing palms forward to cast a killing curse, but nothing happens.

453

"Ya, nice try, Sorcha. Like it would be that easy?"

"How? That's… that's impossible?"

"Not with a binding spell."

"What? How?"

"The tethers. Mehla showed me how and we spelled the tethers that wrapped around your ankles. It only stops you from doing harm, unlike a binding ritual that would seal your magic, like a Coven of Nine can do. It will only last for a short time, but it's going to be long enough to stop you."

Beth becomes lightheaded as a vision takes shape, and she puts her hand on the armor bubble to steady herself.

"Having problems? Maybe you need to take a break and get something to eat. We can come back in… a few thousand years and do this then."

Beth looks at the Royal seed, saying, "I understand."

Beth looks at Sorcha with a calm smile. "The baby will be born."

Sorcha drops her hands and scoffs at Beth. "You mean we're done with this world?"

"No, Sorcha. Only you."

The blue light from three in the morning on August twenty-ninth appears, swimming from the west towards the floating bubble. Penetrating the shield, it wraps around Sorcha, and she screams as the light tightens around her body and fades from bright blue to dull gray.

Princess Sadreen's crown lands on the pile of dust. Beth looks around at the disappearing witches and sees Lochran's body lying by the remains of the shack. The sky over the battlefield turns gray as it rains dust, and Lochran disappears. Beth looks past her feet to see Abigail's cat form disappearing, and the dust cloud gets thicker.

"I love you, Abigail."

A flash of blue and green light wraps around the remaining light from the Raziiair Siren, collapsing the Circle of Nine Witches, and the Staff of Souls catapults out, and Karse catches it.

Breena stands from the Faerie Pool water and turns to see Karse with his hand over his heart and kneeling on one knee. She looks in the direction Karse is bowing to see her father, fully healed, holding her mother in his arms. Angus kisses his wife's cheek, and they fade into the falling dust. Breena turns back to Karse as he stands, raises her hand, waving before she returns to her hidden body with a flash of blue light. She's followed by a cascade of light bursts as the leaders of the Nations disappear.

A twisting wind builds around Karse, drawing the dust of the Guardians into a swirling funnel. Lifting from the ground, then stopping high above Karse, as he lifts the Staff over his head and the tip of the funnel reaches for the gem. Silence follows the funnel, disappearing into the gem.

"Thousands of lives return home. Sleep in peace," Karse says.

The nine Crystals and the artifacts used in the ceremony lay scattered, so Karse taps the end of the Staff on the ground, and the Crystals and artifacts fade into tiny puffs of smoke that join to form King Aodh's face.

"Young warrior. What is your name?"

"I am Karse MacShannachan, son of Angus and Lauranna."

"I knew your father and mother well. How is it you live past the victory?"

"I married a Lysa before the battle ended."

"Was she drawn to you like a moth drawn to flame?"

"Yes, and I to her."

"Your marriage is of the prophecy, and you will rule Scotland. The Staff will lead you through the tunnels and to the castle. Stand on the King Stone in the throne room, tap the end on the floor, then sit on the throne. It will restore Scotland and Brae's Garden. Rule wise, be fair, and avoid war at every opportunity."

"It will be as you command, King Aodh."

The ghostly face fades and slips into the gem. Karse makes a slight bow of his head.

"Sleep well, Great King."

The remaining warriors raise their weapons and shields in a victory cheer. The surviving clones of the African warriors return to their host or disappear with the loss, and the giant warrior, helped by two others, casts a portal to their home.

Beth surveys the battlefield as the survivors gather the wounded and dead of the New Age Witches. The trees and plants over the circle collapse, and nine Earth Witches help each other to a swirling ring of soil that drops and they disappear. The remaining Samurai carry their leader, victim of Rebekah's blade, to a portal near his fallen horse. Few Yamabushi survived the most heavily attacked area, and they gather in a meditation ring, chanting, and a portal forms overhead, drops, leaving none. The Chinese gather around their lost leader, and a portal drops.

"Thousands of magical people from around the world lost to one person's vengeance over a thousand years. What a disgrace and waste of magic," Beth says.

Beth casts a jar into her palm and circles her finger above Sorcha's dust. The dust floats into the jar and the lid snaps shut. Beth spins her finger around the top of the jar, whispering, and a band forms around the lid, sealing it forever.

"Never to be found again, Sorcha," Beth says before the jar disappears with a flash of light from her palm.

Beth circles her hand over Princess Sadreen's tiara, and as it rises, a thin beam of green light reaches into the eastern night sky.

"A beacon."

The tiara slips through the armor shield and shoots toward the light.

"Back to Ireland, Sadreen. The new baby will be close," Beth says.

Beth waves her hand, collapsing her armor bubble as Taelene slips beneath her, and she drops into the saddle. She sits quiet, feeling the wind against her face, as Taelene starts her spiral toward Rainsford Island.

"Not yet, Taelene. Can you fly around for a while?"

What's up, Beth?

"Our parents, the people lost in this stupid war. The cost is unbelievable. Look around, Taelene. It's sad, and it's because of one person. LysaLillian."

I thought it was Sorcha?

"No. Sorcha is as much a victim of her mother's hatred as everyone else. So is Caitlin. The three of them died because LysaLillian was told, by her father, that LysaSearin abandoned her when really, he kept her only to get back at her mother for leaving."

Who told you that?

"It's in LysaSearin's diary. Every try she made to get LysaLillian from her father without breaking the laws of using magic against mortals."

Beth, that's crazy.

"Think about it, Taelene. That's what started this whole thing. Two adults fighting like children over a child."

Pathetic.

"I know."

They soar in silence through the dark sky as the city streetlights turn on again, and then Beth looks down, saying, "Karse is waving at us, Taelene. Look, his horse is swimming to the beach."

Down we go.

As they descend, movement catches Beth's eye.

"Taelene. Nine o'clock low on the beach. What the heck is that?"

Beth changes her eyes to night vision. "Of course, she survived. What the hell?"

That's impossible!

Beth taps her ear to include Karse.

"Nope. It's Rebekah."

"What? I don't believe it, lass," says Karse.

Beth, is this a sick joke?

"Sorry, Taelene. She's flopping around on the beach like a fish out of water. I'm going to have a chat with psycho number two. Karse, she's directly to your left."

Taelene silently crosses over Rebekah as Beth jumps from the saddle and floats to the ground without Rebekah hearing her. Beth watches Rebekah pat the ground, searching for something, and Beth can see her wand against a rock, only a few feet behind her.

"Have I got a dungeon offer for you?" Beth says.

Startled by Beth's voice, Rebekah jumps and then lays back and props herself on her elbows.

"I see victory has brought out your sense of humor."

"Minus the evil laugh that you and the bitch queen enjoyed so much."

"Yes, well. Those days have disappeared, haven't they?"

"Oh yes, they're gone, and so is she. What happened to you?"

"Sorcha."

"So, that's what she meant. What was the lie you told?"

"I saved Francois from his brother, then kept him at my secret hideaway and told Sorcha he was going to France."

"Maybe not so secret?"

"So it seems. Now what?"

"Fear not, *Cherie*. I have come for you."

"Francois?"

Francois walks out from behind a large rock with his wand pointed at Beth.

"Consider yourself lucky, *mademoiselle*. The only reason you are not in glass is that you do not have your wand pointed at my Rebekah."

"Okay, sure," Beth says.

"Francois."

"*Oui, Cherie?*"

"This is Lysa... Beth."

"*Cherie*, I am told the Lysa is dead."

Beth, still in her flight suit, changes to her robes.

"*Merde*," Francois says. Shaking his head, he puts away his wand.

"May I help Rebekah stand, Lysa?"

"Sure, why not? Leave her wand."

Rebekah stands with Francois' help and keeps hold of his hand.

Wow. Rebekah's really hanging on to him. What's that about?

"Rebekah, why did you save Francois?"

"Really? Now?"

"Yep."

After a brief pause, Rebekah says, "When I met Francois at the glass prison, a feeling from my teen years resurfaced, and I knew I could love him. I also realized we trapped him in a business relationship with Sorcha, and it was going to cost him his life. I heard his prison was under attack, and I could only think of saving him. Afterwards, we made love." She turns her head toward Francois. "The kind of love that makes choices easy, at any cost."

Karse walks into Beth's sight at that moment and Beth says, "I haven't had the experience yet."

Rebekah catches her breath, "Oh.... You are full of surprises. I assumed a field of broken hearts."

"Nope. None."

"*Mademoiselle.* We only want to live in peace, away from the fighting."

Royal Souls

"Yeah, well. Sorcha's dust, so the fighting is over, but your family is out to kill you. I'm sure Rebekah has a few enemies still lurking in the shadows, so here's my deal. House arrest or a place so inaccessible I'll need to pump air at you."

"What? That's idiotic. Sit in a house and wait to be killed? Get it over with and do it now," Rebekah says.

"You're the only one being an idiot, Rebekah. Here's how it works. I put a locator on you both, and you two do the world, but a single crime against anyone and the locator turns you to dust. That's my offer."

"Why let us go?"

"No more killing. It's senseless. Time for it to stop, Rebekah. Do you understand that?"

"I accept your offer, LysaBeth." Francois turns to Rebekah. "*Cherie*, please?"

"Francois, I'm blind. Take the offer and..."

Beth steps forward, and Rebekah takes a slap to the side of her head.

"Ouch. What the hell was that for you, little... Oh. My eyes. They're clearing."

"I was really hoping to kick-start your eyes, but I guess a slap will do."

Karse laughs, and Rebekah looks over her shoulder.

Turning back to Beth, she says, "A slap-start works. Deal."

"Put your hands out, palm down."

Rebekah and Francois hold their hand out, and Beth pushes her glowing finger into the backs, leaving a tiny luminous dot.

"You're done. Now go."

461

Rebekah picks up her wand, slides it in her sleeve, and takes Francois' hand.

Rebekah looks at Beth. "I was a young girl the last time anyone did something decent for me. Thank you."

"If you have children, teach them right. Oh yeah, I forgot one thing. Any indications that the Blood Witches are up to something, hold your finger on that dot. Remember what happens if you're trying to set me up."

Rebekah looks at the glowing dot. "Why do I have two dots?"

"What? Show me your hand," Beth says.

Beth takes Rebekah's hand. "Give me your other hand."

Beth closes her eyes, and after a few seconds, she opens them and smiles at Rebekah.

"Did you ever wonder why you survived The Day of Dust?" Beth asks.

"Yes, and I still don't understand, but I'll take it."

"Invite us to the Christening."

"Really?"

"Really."

Suddenly, amplified by a megaphone, a voice rings out of the darkness. "This is the Boston Harbor Police. You are trespassing on protected property. Stay where you are. You are under arrest."

Beth snaps her fingers over her shoulder, flipping the boat.

"Whatever, Chief," she says.

"Doing the right thing, are we?" Rebekah says.

"Hey. The dungeon offer is still open for you two." Beth raises her eyebrow.

Rebekah looks at Francois and then back to Beth with a sultry smile. "Mine, too."

Francois opens a portal, and they disappear as Beth shakes her head.

"Time to go, Taelene. Where are you?"

"Look up."

Nadeh flies over them, and Taelene waves from the saddle.

"See you in a couple of weeks, Beth."

"Where are you going?"

"Lake Malawi."

"You go, girl."

The remaining Raziiair from Lake Malawi takes formation behind Nadeh as he flies toward Africa and Beth walks up to Karse, puts her arms around his neck, saying, "You're not afraid of heights, are you?"

"Why?"

Beth snaps her fingers, and they disappear.

"I don't get it," one officer says. "Calm waters. What flipped the boat?"

The other officer looks around as he moves onto the beach, saying, "I don't know, but they're gone. The people have disappeared and so has the fog."

"Maybe we should have listened to the Chief."

"You don't tell, I won't."

"Deal."

SHADOW WITCH

Saturday, September 6th — 0430

Aaghnya, dressed in all white robes with no shoes or jewelry, kneels beside Rhynan's body, which floats inches off the ground over a prayer mat. She waves her hands over him, slowly, as if pushing smoke back and forth, saying a prayer in Tamil, and Petia kneels by her side.

"We have lost much, Sister, but there is peace now."

"Yes, Petia, we have lost much. I will not search for another Rhynan."

"Aaghnya, you must. Rhynan would want you to have a life with children. You are in pain, so don't make a terrible decision."

Through the tears, Aaghnya says, "He was a kind man and would have been a good father. Like ours."

"Those words fill my heart with happiness."

Aaghnya and Petia split apart with a side roll, coming up on one knee, pushing their glowing hands toward the female figure standing near the back wall of the room.

"Who are you?" Aaghnya demands.

"I am Rhynan's mother, Melissa, and I'm here to give Rhynan the happy life he deserves with you."

ROYAL SOULS

"I don't understand how this is possible?"

"You understand that I'm a witch like you. Right?"

"Yes."

"Good. Let me explain how all this came to be."

"We will listen."

Aaghnya and Petia stand as their hands return to normal and fall to their sides.

"My parents had no magic, so I didn't know about my magic until I was twenty and met Prince O'Manus."

"Prince O'Manus? How?"

"He had been watching me since I first met my husband, James, and during the aftermath of one of his drunken rages, we conceived Rhynan. Prince O'Manus came to me while I hid in a closet, telling me of my magic and the princess, so we made a deal to ensure Rhynan's survival. The terms were simple. I had to name him Rhynan, and I couldn't tell him about magic or use any magic to protect him. The hardest part was having to leave him with his father when he turned nine."

As her hands tighten into fists, Aaghnya says, "You are a terrible mother."

"Let me finish before you crucify me."

"Fine, but do not tell me a story of lies to make you look a better person."

"Prince O'Manus felt Princess Sadreen's pulse somewhere in North America, but he couldn't find the exact location, and after three-hundred years of trying, he formed a strategy."

"Rhynan's father was a wonderful man when I first met him but, after we married, something changed. He took to drinking, became pals with guys from a shady

465

crowd, and eventually lost his job as a welder. Then, he became muscle for hire for a man named Midas Pohl."

"The Blood Witch?"

"Yes, Aaghnya, and through that relationship, the prince discovered how to follow Sorcha and Rebekah without being noticed. Not long after, Rhynan's father became mean as a junkyard dog, even toward me, and the prince knew Midas was using control magic on him."

"That would poison his mind if Midas used too much magic and let him continue with drinking," Aaghnya says.

"It did poison him. But having Rhynan grow up in those horrible conditions with the prince controlling him from inside made Rhynan timid and unassuming, ensuring the prince could go undetected. The prince worked with me, teaching me magic, through Rhynan's gestation, and I practiced daily until Rhynan turned nine."

"You sentenced Rhynan to death before he was born?"

"No, Aaghnya, I didn't. To protect Rhynan, I sentenced myself to become a Shadow Witch for eternity, and I sentenced him to life with a beautiful witch."

Rhynan's mother pulls, from under her robes, a dark glass jar containing a pulsing light.

Aaghnya walks closer to the light. "Is that Rhynan's soul?"

"Yes, Aaghnya. Like the prince said, 'All was not lost, Indian Princess.'"

Aaghnya smiles through free-flowing tears.

"When Rhynan was born, his father was in a pub with his pals, so I cast the spell Prince O'Manus taught me to switch him with Rhynan's soul. This also started the clock ticking to change me from a normal witch to a Shadow Witch forever. Three days later, his father saw him for the first time and told me I should have flushed him down the toilet because he looked like one of his turds."

"He was a terrible man," Aaghnya whispers.

"Yes, Aaghnya, he was. But I'm uncertain he deserved the painful death of alcohol that took him. I try to believe the good man was still in there, and Midas used him until the alcohol consumed him from the inside."

"I can have my Rhynan back now?"

"Please remember, this Rhynan has magic, and it will be out of control until you teach him how to use it. He will be like an infant, but with power."

"Yes, I will do this."

Rhynan's mother lightly places the glass jar in Aaghnya's hands.

"Please take care of him, and I hope he will forgive me."

"I will tell him of your sacrifice, and my Rhynan will forgive you. You will visit your grandchildren."

The woman's smile blurs as she melts away, and Aaghnya spins toward Rhynan's floating body. She kneels, places the jar under him, and pulls the lid off so the pulsing light can penetrate his body.

Aaghnya pulls the empty jar back, and his body falls to the floor.

"Ow. That hurt."

He rubs the back of his head as he opens his eyes.

"Aaghnya, I dreamed I died. I met the prince, and he told me where to find a chest of gold. In Scotland. I didn't know I was Scottish."

"Rhynan Doon. You are a Scottish man, and you are mine."

"Sounds good to me, but I think we're going to need the gold while I find a new job. I'm pretty sure I'm fired."

"Rhynan, you are safe, and we will be okay."

Aaghnya helps Rhynan stand, then slips her arms around his neck, pulling his face to hers. The smell of jasmine perfume, the soft touch of her lips, and her warmth against his body rush to his senses. The kiss, slow and passionate, lingers until Rhynan's body relaxes into hers, and she releases her arms enough to slide her face along his to whisper, "I love you, Rhynan Doon."

Rhynan squeezes her body tight to his, saying, "Aaghnya. I remember dying. It didn't scare me because I was dying to save you. I love you that much."

Aaghnya pushes back from Rhynan with a quick peck to his cheek. "This will never happen again, Rhynan Doon. Sorcha and Rebekah are both gone and all their evil with them. You are safe with me."

"Aaghnya, that's great. I'm so excited I could burst," he says, stepping back.

"Rhynan, you must calm down."

"Aaghnya, I really want to go to Scotland and find that chest of gold."

With a slight 'pop' sound, Rhynan disappears, and Aaghnya casts a white light string into the rippling air circle left by him.

Aaghnya shakes her head and looks at Petia.

"Scotland is nice this time of year," Petia says.

"This will be harder than I was thinking. I must go find my man child," Aaghnya says and dives into the rippling air.

Petia giggles.

***

Dumghill and Egret stand on the highest point across the land where they can see the lifeless Faerie Glen.

Egret reaches for Dumghill's hand. "Finally, Dumghill. We are home."

"So much time away, Egret. Much work to be done."

Egret waves her hand across her body with her palm pointed at the Faerie Glen.

"All of Sorcha's dark magic has gone with her. Now we can bring the glen alive again."

Both Dumghill and Egret lift their arms out front of them with their palms pointed at the glen and together say, "*Thig dhachaigh uile.*" (Come home all)

They hold their glowing hands until the light fades, then drop their hands to their sides, and the castle, which lay in ruin, takes shape as the stones lift back to their original places. A puff of smoke rises from the chimney as the last stone slips into place, and a shock wave signal explodes outward, calling everyone back to the glen. The mounds around the castle, sunk from loss of the housing support underground, pop to their old heights as the structures, hidden from the ordinary world, rebuild underneath. The trees, gardens, and farmland, destroyed by the Blood Witches, reshape into the fertile lands they were before the war. A giant puff of smoke rises from the wand maker's chimney that stands behind the castle mound, and Dumghill smiles, knowing the fires have lit.

"Egret, you know how to make a house a home."

"And that's where we should be, but first, we need a drink." Egret takes Dumghill's hand, snapping her fingers, and they fade into smoke with the slightest 'poof' sound.

"Do you remember the feel of the mist, Egret?"

"Yes. It was like being wrapped in a soft, warm blanket."

"Aye, that's me, as well."

"Dumghill, do you feel it? The life is almost gone from the pools."

"Look, Egret."

A soft, blue light glows behind the waterfall, and as Egret and Dumghill walk closer, steps appear down the side of the rock wall. Reaching the bottom of the waterfall, they slide behind the curtain of falling water to the cave where they last saw their parents.

As they enter, the cave lights cast a warm glow, and the male voice says, "Welcome, my Children. I am Prince Brae. You have had a hard, successful journey, but it is not over yet."

"Prince Brae? As in Brae's Garden?

"Yes, Egret."

"I don't understand," Egret says. "The child will be born."

"And when she is, the second journey begins for those with magic."

Dumghill and Egret look at each other, then Dumghill shrugs his shoulders, saying, "I thought it might be too good to be true."

They both laugh, and the voice says, "Drink and rejuvenate your magic."

Dumghill and Egret step to a table that has four glasses on it. Two glasses glow blue, and the other two are of silver light, with tiny sparkles swirling above the rim.

"Why are they different?" Egret asks.

"The blue liquid woke your magic and sustained your lives during the first journey. Drink it now, and you will have a longer life and be stronger because the magic has seeped deep into your souls."

Egret and Dumghill each take a glass and drink the blue liquid. The cave comes to life like it did with their parents, and the voice says, "Eat and drink. We have much to talk about."

After several hours of discussion, Egret says, "This will be fun."

"I can't wait to get the wand-making shop in full production," Dumghill laughs and clasps his hands together with a smack.

After their laughter settles, Egret says, "You haven't told us about the other drink."

"You were born disfigured and cast out," Prince Brae says. "If you wish, you can drink the silver drink, and you will look like your children."

Egret and Dumghill stand and walk to the table. Each places a hand around the stem of a glass, then hesitates. Looking at each other, they join their empty hands.

After a long silence, Dumghill says, "Egret. I have always known I'm not meant for the human world I was born into. The day you and I became partners, I realized you are a gift. A gift I will cherish forever and never ask for any changes. I will love you in any form you wish to take."

"The days you spent away, hunting for disfigured children and mystical creatures, were the hardest days I ever faced because I couldn't see yours," Egret says. She draws her hand away from the glass. "I have no vanity, only love for you and our children."

"I think we are going to stay as we are, and everyone else will have to deal with their jealousy," Dumghill says.

Both laugh and throw their arms around each other. When they step apart, the glasses disappear, and the blue light at the entrance fades.

"Looks like it's time for us to go home, but first…."

Egret waves her hand and a barrel, like the one she gave Beth, appears at the edge of the waterfall.

"Freya gave me two barrels the first time I met her. She told me one was for the last battle and the other for the pools after our victory. Care to do the honors, Handsome?"

Dumghill smiles, struts over to the barrel, and gives it a light kick. It splits open like an egg, falls into the pool, and Sylphs and Undines flit about in a dance fit for a celebration as the waters glow again with magic.

"Now we go home, Husband."

"I can't wait to sleep in our bed."

Egret looks at him with a raised eyebrow. "Sleep? I don't think so."

Dumghill laughs.

THE NEW ROYALS

Saturday, September 6ᵗʰ — 0500

A sliver of light pierces the night over the high ledge that Tonique landed on when Beth first visited her home. She looks around, recognizing the protruding rock Taelene slammed into the first time they flew from the ledge. Beth has memories, but now she has to face the castle without the hope of her mother waking. Beth looks at Karse as he stands near the edge of the cliff, and she watches as the gentle breeze swings his hair across his face.

"Care to see my castle, Karse?"

He looks at Beth and says, "Aye, lass. Then I can show you mine… once I find it."

She lifts her hand to the crevasse edge and the other toward Karse, and they pass through the swirling green smoke and out the other side, where Karse can see the magnificent gardens in front of the castle.

"LysaBeth, It's spectacular."

Beth hooks her arm inside Karse's and says, "The interior is amazing."

They walk toward the castle, and Beth says, "I had another vision."

"When, lass?"

"When the seed was cast from Princess Sadreen, it hovered beside Sorcha and me, and it showed our daughter playing with another child."

"Whose child?"

Beth stops. "The seed child. The most powerful witch to be born to royalty?"

"Oh, aye. Where were we?"

"The seed is here, in Ireland. The woman will have to be from the bloodline of Princess Sadreen's family."

"That could be difficult to find."

"The seed kept flashing the numbers nine six dash nine three six."

"What do you think it meant?"

"It could be a time. Today. Maybe nine-thirty-six."

"That could be morning or night?"

"I don't know, but it gives us a starting point for a locator spell."

"You can do that?"

"I need to talk with the Lysa Mother."

"Aye, lass."

"Yep. Then I need to have a nice long talk with you."

Karse walks the rest of the way to the castle with a full grin.

Beth changes to her robes and kneels on the leather pad in front of the emerald rune stone.

"Lysa Mother, hear your daughter LysaBeth. I seek the birth of the seed child."

Beth leans forward, placing her head against the emerald rune stone, and waits for the ring of her crystal, but hears nothing.

"Strange. The Mother isn't answering," Beth says as she straightens.

Karse laughs. "When my mother no answers, it was so I will solve the problem myself."

"Never thought of that."

Beth sits back on her haunches, calming herself, and focuses on the seed.

"Ah!" Beth cries out.

Karse bolts to her side.

"LysaBeth, are you alright, lass?"

Beth opens her eyes and looks at Karse.

"Karse, what happened?"

"Another vision, but this time I saw part of it."

"What did you see?"

"A wolf ran across the room, and a farmhouse appeared."

"You called out for Claire. Who is she?"

"I know where the seed is. Help me stand."

"Aye, lass. There you go. How do you know where?"

"Because we're still part of the prophecy."

"How do you know, lass?"

"The vision showed me our daughter playing with Aynet."

"Who is she?"

"Aynet, Little Fire, is the seed baby. LysaLauranna is important to the future."

"Why the wolf?"

Beth ponders the vision, then says, "Of course. It makes sense now. The first names of the kings both mean fire."

"Aye, King Aodh and King Aed."

"The family names in the vision are Coinin and Faolan. They both mean wolf."

"That can't be, lass."

"That's not all. The fire wolf is the Pyre Wolf. All of their names, in some language, mean fire, so Pyreus and Gaisras are the two kings. Pyreus is King Aodh, and Gaisras is King Aed. I'll bet that when the queens died, they became Teine and Lasair."

"Wait, lass. This can't be. King Aodh and Queen Isabelle only had Prince O'Manus. How could the bloodline continue?"

Beth turns to him and grabs the front of his shirt. "It seems you Scots are quick to lift your skirts."

"LysaBeth, my Love. You can no call it a skirt. It's a kilt. You wound my pride."

"Oh, yeah. I find anyone up that skirt, but me, and I'll wound more than your pride."

"Why do you think I could betray our love?"

"Karse, I'm sorry. You didn't deserve that. It's that way too often, when I walked around people, I could hear the conversation about someone cheating on someone."

"Aye, lass. The modern world has lost its way with standing by your chosen mate. They learn too early to throw things away and get another. I understand, but fear not, the magic assures you are the only woman for me."

"Built-in chastity belt. I like it."

They both laugh.

"Karse, I'm sorry I said that."

Karse hugs Beth. "So, you're saying King Aodh had a bastard son?"

Beth releases her hug, and they step apart. "Not a bastard. A known estranged son."

"What's the difference?"

"Shortly before Prince Aodh met Queen Isabelle, he met a young woman who was the only remaining survivor of a village attacked by the Norse. She was the Chief's daughter and escaped by using her magic to hide in the trees. Young Prince Aodh found her when he was hunting and started visiting her and, as teenagers do, they fell in love. Then Prince Aodh met Isabelle and two years later, the king announces their marriage, but Kaelyn was with child. Prince Aodh went to his father with his dilemma, and they secreted Kaelyn off to Ireland because they couldn't cancel the arranged marriage without starting a war. Kaelyn understood, and she had everything they needed for her and the baby. She married an Irish Chief but left Prince Aodh's baby boy with the last name of Coinin. He grew to become a Chief back in Scotland and continued the magical bloodline."

"Still don't understand, lass."

"Not done yet."

"Aye, sorry."

"King Aed and Queen Draya had a baby boy who didn't attend the wedding. On the day of the massacre, the baby boy turned one, and they secreted him away until he was old enough to be king. He had many children, and they used the family name of Faolan. The seed is in the unborn child that Draya Faolan carries, and guess who the father is?"

"A Coinin?"

"Yep. Aidan Coinin, Son of Sithech Coinin."

"I know that name. He is the Coinin clan Chief."

"Good. You can make the introductions."

"What do you mean, lass?"

"I have to talk to Draya and Aidan. Put your formal dress on."

"LysaBeth, please."

"What?"

"I asked you not to call it that."

"Seriously? Formal dress, as in your best clothes."

"Oh. Aye."

"Little girl," Beth breathes.

"Oh, aye. You're going to pay for that."

Beth spins her arm, casting a portal, then turns back to Karse with a sultry smile and says, "I hope so."

"Ah, LysaBeth. You no can do that. We married three days ago, and I've no even touched you. When you look at me like that, it breaks my mind, lass."

Beth grabs his hand and, walking to the portal, says, "One more thing to do and then…."

"Where are we, lass?"

"The hidden farm of the Coinin family. We're in County Clare, Ireland, outside the City of Ennis."

"In your vision, Clare wasn't a name, but a place."

Three men exit the house with wands at the ready because a portal in the front yard at five-thirty in the morning is unexpected. As they get closer, slowing to a walk, the older man orders the others to lower their wands.

"I am Sithech Coinin, Clan Chief. We're honored with a visit from Clan MacShannachan. Where's Angus?"

"I am Karse MacShannachan. My father, Angus, and mother, Lady Lauranna, gave their lives to the victory of reuniting the prince and princess."

"It's done?"

"Aye."

Sithech falls to one knee and his sons, Aidan and Seamus, step to his side, placing a hand on their father's shoulder.

"Sorcha killed our mother and recruited our sister," Aidan says.

A few moments of silence go by, and Sithech stands.

"Thank you for bringing the good news, Karse."

"We lost many good people," Karse says.

"Aye, that bitch deserves to be in hell," Sithech says.

Sithech looks at Beth. "My apologies, my lady. The runes on your clothes look familiar."

"Chief Coinin. May I present my wife, Lady LysaBeth?"

The three Coinin men wave their wands in front of their bodies, changing into formal clan attire before making a traditional bow.

"Lady LysaBeth, we're honored."

"As am I, Chief Coinin," Beth says with a slight bow of her head.

"We heard the Lysa had risen against Sorcha but didn't believe it," Sithech says.

"Sorcha is dead. I bottled her ashes and placed them where no one can reach."

"Thank you, Lysa. We will honor your family for as long as a Coinin heart is beating."

"Thank you for your loyalty, Chief Coinin."

"Why do you visit our home, Lady LysaBeth?"

The front door opens, and Draya Faolan steps out of the rustic log house.

"I'm here to speak with Draya and Aidan."

Draya walks to Aidan's side. "You're the one from my dreams."

"I am LysaBeth, daughter of LysaSearin, and daughter of the Lysa Mother."

"I am Draya Macha Faolan and my husband, Aidan O'Manus Coinin."

"How close are you to delivery?"

"It feels as if today could be the day."

"I need to speak with both of you. In private."

"We keep no secrets in this family," Aidan says.

"It wasn't a request."

"As you wish, Lysa," Sithech says, and nods his head at Aidan.

Beth walks closer to Draya and Aidan and casts a shield over them.

"Everything I'm about to tell you is not to be told to anyone else."

Draya and Aidan nod their heads in silence.

"Aidan, you are the bloodline of Prince O'Manus," Beth says, and tells about the unknown son of King Aodh.

"Draya, you are in the bloodline of Princess Sadreen." and tells of the baby brother who became a king on his first birthday.

"The seed cast from the reunion of Prince O'Manus and Princess Sadreen is in your baby."

Draya catches her breath, and she lays both hands over her unborn child.

"She will grow into the most powerful witch we will know, and no one must know where she is until the Universe says so. Do you understand?"

Both nod and answer, "Yes."

"How will we know?" Draya says.

"My magic started by me reaching for a bowl of sweet potato and having it drop on my lap. I was six," Beth says.

"So, when she's six, then?" Aidan says.

"Could be sooner, could be later. What I'm saying is the Universe will let you know through an event such as that, but when her magic shows, you must conceal it from everyone. She must look like an ordinary witch until the Universe says it is time for her to be known."

"Oh, of course. We understand," Aidan says.

"Remember, tell no one of the seed. Understood?"

"Yes, Lysa," they both say in unison.

"One more thing. My daughter is essential to your daughter, Aynet."

"Aynet. Is that to be her name?" Draya says.

"Yes."

"That name means Little Fire. She'll be like her mother," Aidan says, snickering.

"Aynet, it will be then," Draya says, giving Aidan a playful poke.

In her mind, Beth hears, *Share the Universe.*

"The Mother has spoken to me. Will you both take my hand?"

Beth holds her hands out to the couple, and they slowly raise their free hand to Beth's as they clasp their hands together.

A slow glow of gentle white light fills the shield bubble for a few moments and then disappears.

Beth hears in her mind, *They never asked. They believe.*

"You didn't ask why."

"Because we believe in a greater power that gives us our magic and tries to keep balance," Draya says. "I know you are that balance because you defeated Sorcha."

"I wish it had only been me against Sorcha. We all lost because of the people we lost. War is senseless and costly."

"Are you saying Little Fire will be the end of all Witch war?" Aidan says.

"I hope so," Beth says.

"We will honor the old beliefs, LysaBeth," Draya says.

"That means you'll teach Aynet the truth."

"Nothing but," Aidan says.

"Draya, your aura ripples with many colors. Are you a healer?"

"Yes, a doctor."

"Good, you will deliver my baby," Beth says, and she waves her hand to drop the shield.

"You honor me, LysaBeth."

Beth walks back to Karse, and as she casts a portal a short distance behind him, she turns to Aidan and Draya.

"I look forward to our daughters playing together."

Beth and Karse turn to walk to the portal when Karse stops.

"When do we have this daughter?"

Without breaking stride or even looking at Karse, Beth says, "Nine months from today."

She smiles to herself.

NEW PLAN

Monday, September 11th — 0800 — Delta, BC, Canada

"Good morning, everyone. I am Director Montague MacLeish. I will be here until we find suitable replacements for Rebekah Kheel and Rhynan Doon, along with a few upper and middle management personnel that did not fit with the restructured TDF Logistics. Thank you."

Montague MacLeish holds a stoic pose as the staff shuffles around each other to return to their cubicles.

"What a handsome man," Charlotte says.

As they arrive at their shared cubicle, Cindy says, "Handsome? That's a God. Those gray eyes are to die for."

THE END

CPSIA information can be obtained
at www.ICGtesting.com
Printed in the USA
LVHW101229141022
730612LV00025B/97